32

God Is Red

God Is Red

Vine Deloria, Jr.

GROSSET & DUNLAP
A National General Company

Publishers   New York

Contents

1. The Indian Movement. 3
2. America Loves Indians . . . and All That. 23
3. Indians of America. 39
4. The Religious Question. 57
5. Thinking in Time and Space. 75
6. The Problem of Creation. 91
7. The Concept of History. 111
8. The Spatial Problem of History. 129
9. Origin of Religion. 151
10. Death and Religion. 169
11. Human Personality. 189
12. The Group. 209
13. Christianity and
     Contemporary American Culture. 225
14. Tribal Religions and
     Contemporary American Culture. 247
15. The Aboriginal World
     and Christian History. 273
16. Religion Today. 289
     Notes and Commentary. 303
     Appendices. 317
     Index. 367

God Is Red

Chapter 1

The Indian Movement

"WE ARE AT war with the United States," Vernon Bellecourt cried. "To your stations!" In 1972 as Indian protesters rushed into the Bureau of Indian Affairs headquarters building in the nation's capital, Washington policemen prepared for a siege, and the first dramatic confrontation between American Indians and the federal government in more than a century began.

During the fall of 1972 there were continual complaints by American Indians about a number of shootings in Indian country in which Indians had been murdered without reason. Local officials did their best to cover up the incidents, and when the Indians appealed to the federal government for redress, they met with studied delays and deaf ears. So in early October, a caravan known as the Trail of Broken Treaties had been formed.

Coming initially from Seattle and Los Angeles, automobile caravans filled with Indian protesters, winding their way toward the nation's capital, visited the different reservations along the route and picked up more protesters at each stop. Rallies were held on the larger reservations, where the grievances of a century were recited by the reservation residents. Tribal officials, fearful that their favored status as Interior Department mascots would be jeopardized, hastily began to downgrade the importance of the protest, implying that it was primarily a movement by urban Indians who had no relationship with the tribal community. Yet a considerable number of reservation people joined the caravan, so that by the time it reached Washington, D.C., more than 80 percent of the participants were reservation residents.

The trouble began when the protesters discovered that no food and lodging provisions had been made for the stay in Washington. The advance men, who were supposed to have made room and board arrangements, actually spent their time making pronouncements and speaking to groups, instead of doing the tedious and unromantic jobs of locating churches, hotels, and dormitories for the caravan participants. The Interior officials were astounded to learn that there was no lodging available to the protesters, since the advance men had assured them that everything had been taken care of.

During a conference in the Bureau of Indian Affairs building, the government officials offered to find a lodging place for the protesters as a ploy for getting them to leave the building's immediate vicinity. Participants began to gather in the auditorium of the Bureau of Indian Affairs to wait for final word on their disposition for the night, and when some government building guards began to push some of the younger protesters around, fear of violence spread through the building. People were reluctant to leave, thinking that they would immediately be arrested or worse by the police waiting outside. When word came to the people quietly waiting in the auditorium that police guards had clashed with some of the protestors near one of the doors, the tension broke: the Indians sealed off the Bureau building, taking control of every door and window that could possibly be used by the police to enter.

The building was taken over by the Trail of Broken Treaties protesters on Friday night, November 3, 1972, the weekend before the Presidential elections. Government negotiations began almost immediately and continued through the weekend; Indian leaders promised to vacate the building, but continuous threats of violence from the police surrounding the building held the invaders in a virtual state of panic. The building suffered tremendous damage each time a potential invasion by the police seemed imminent. Desks and files were randomly piled against outside doors and windows in an effort to defend the building.

During the weekend some of the Indians attempted to go to Arlington Cemetery to hold religious services for fallen Indian war dead, particularly Ira Hayes, hero of Iwo Jima, and Sgt. Ernest Rice, a Winnebago hero of the Korean War, who was buried in Arlington when the good people of Iowa refused to allow his burial in a white cemetery in Sioux City. The caravan people went to federal court hoping to have reversed the U.S. Army order that banned the protesters from the national cemetery on the basis that they constituted a partisan political group. But the tensions between the Indians and the government were so high by the time the court ruled in their favor on Monday that few caravan members bothered to go to the service. Most of them remained within the building, hoping to protect the caravan's elderly and children.

On November 9, nearly a full week after occupying the Bureau of Indian Affairs headquarters, the Trail of Broken Treaties Indians left Washington. During that time, the protesters removed numerous government records and files as "hostage" material to ensure a peaceful departure. Capital police eschewed the brutality practiced on other occasions rather than risk a retaliatory burning and destruction of government files. The protesters scattered and returned to their reservations, leaving the nation shocked and dismayed. According to stories in the *Washington Post*,[1] the damage to the building was $2.3 million, a figure that the newspaper said was exceeded only by the 1906 San Francisco earthquake and fire and the burning of Washington by the British during the War of 1812. In the history of destruction of federal property, the Trail of Broken Treaties protest was given a respectable third place. Later testimony before the House Subcommittee on Indian Affairs placed the actual damage at something more than a couple of thousand dollars, and the figure continued to decline as more specific knowledge was gained about what had actually been destroyed.

In the wake of the destruction, even moderate and sympathetic Indians were dismayed by the activists' actions. The Bureau of Indian Affairs headquarters had contained priceless objects of Indian art, including paintings by Indians of notable stature (now deceased). The activists hardly gave a thought to preserving Indian cultural treasures. Their fear of violence was so intense that they simply chose whatever was at hand to use in the barricades. From Acee Blue Eagle's irreplaceable paintings to the urinals in the men's room, the Bureau of Indian Affairs was destroyed.

Elected tribal officials were brought to Washington, where Robert Robertson, director of the Vice-President's National Council of Indian Opportunity, orchestrated their protests and demands for the prosecution of the protest leaders. The fact that the tribal chairmen were little more than puppets in Robertson's hand negated much of their impact in Indian country. But the rage and concern of Indians across the nation was evident. At best the lofty moral stance of the American Indian community lay in ruins. Indians were no longer the silent peaceful individuals who refused to take dramatic steps to symbolize their grievances. They had become simply another protest group.

The capture of the headquarters of the Bureau of Indian Affairs by the Indians of the Trail of Broken Treaties Caravan was the climatic event of a movement that had remained, for the most part, on the back pages of the nation's newspapers. For nearly a decade, the Indian people's frustration and rage had been rising, but in most cases in which the movement was reported, it was considered a pleasant respite from the fury, confusion, and threats of the blacks and Chicanos. The message of the American Indian, a recital of broken promises and loss of sacred lands, never reached the public in a form making it possible to capitalize on the outpouring of good will that the American public held for American Indians.

This public had heard Indian complaints about broken treaties and confiscation of sacred mountains for years. But what did it matter? The public was confused at almost every turn. What could be done about a broken treaty now? Most Americans thought that the respective tribes' problems were facts of American history, not problems of the present. There was no outpouring of assistance for Indians comparable to the frenzy that gripped the North at the height of the Civil Rights movement.

Throughout the last decade, Indian activists chose, sometimes cleverly and sometimes stupidly, symbols that they believed would convey the importance of their lands and religions to the rest of America. In a nation where few people had ever questioned the superiority of Anglo-Saxon and Christian values, the Indians' emphasis on land and religion seemed an anachronistic fantasy of the American frontier. Many people applauded the Indian activists, but it is doubtful if very many understood them. Even the greatest success of the last century, the restoration of the sacred Blue Lake area to the people of Taos Pueblo in New Mexico, failed to achieve any significance in the general populace's worldview. In the Blue Lake controversy, the whole distinction between Indians and non-Indians could have been seen—if anyone had been interested.

Theodore Roosevelt, on a great conservation trip in 1906,

decided that the timberlands in northern New Mexico should be placed in a national forest for their protection. Carson National Forest was created by Executive Order, and when the government surveyors had finished laying out the boundaries, the sacred Blue Lake, central to the practice of the Pueblo religion, was safely within the forest. The people of the Pueblo immediately petitioned the government for the lake's restoration. They explained that it was their major religious shrine and that the Pueblo would die without its sanctuary for the perpetuation of its religion. The Interior Department sided with the Pueblo in 1912, supporting a return of the lake to them.

The Department of Agriculture, however, had other ideas. It considered the forest the personal property of the Secretary of Agriculture and refused to allow the lands to be restored. The valuable timber that grew on the slopes of Blue Lake was an incentive to the officials in the Department of Agriculture to keep the area. They saw their task as keeping the area safely away from the rest of American society until the timber companies were ready to use it. In that way they could assure themselves of a powerful outside constituency at appropriations times, thus guaranteeing their continuance as a government agency.

The struggle continued for a period of sixty-four years without the Agriculture Department budging the slightest inch in its position. After the Second World War, it appeared as though the battle had been won by Agriculture. Clinton P. Anderson, conservative Democrat from New Mexico, served first as Secretary of Agriculture (1945-48) and then as U.S. Senator from New Mexico, on the Senate's Interior Committee (1949-70). In due time Anderson, who had come to Washington in the 1930s as a youngster and friend of Lyndon B. Johnson and the New Deal power structure, achieved a prominent place on the Interior Committee and substantial influence in Congress. Since any Indian legislation to return Blue Lake had to go through the Interior Committee, the fight was regarded as over.

In 1965 the Indian Claims Commission heard the claims of the Taos Indians against the United States. The commissioners admitted that the United States had illegally taken the Blue Lake area and offered a substantial sum as compensation. The commissioners were astounded when the Indians refused the money. They wanted the Blue Lake area returned to them. If the commission would not do that, the Indians did not want it said that they had sold their sacred shrine. They told the commission that they would refuse the compensation.

It seemed that for someone in America to turn down a dollar was unusual. When it was a little group of Indians living on the edge of starvation, it presented a more profound and difficult moral question than is usually raised in government circles. The Indian Claims Commission agreed to settle the remainder of the case without making any decision on Blue Lake, while the Pueblo went to Congress to see if they could get the lands restored.

Led by Paul Bernal, a spokesman for the Taos Indians, the movement to restore Blue Lake to the Pueblo began in 1965. Paul traveled across the nation many times, speaking to groups and urging them to contact their senators and congressmen to demand support for the bill to restore the lake to the Indians. A groundswell gradually built; one by one, the senators on the Interior Committee began to break their united front. Other congressmen began to take interest in the restoration as the persistent Taos spokesmen refused to accept the series of compromises offered by Clinton Anderson in an effort to still the movement.

In November of 1970 President Nixon took a hand in the matter, and the White House began to apply pressure on its friends in Congress to get Blue Lake returned to the Taos people. The extent of the national support Bernal had

generated can be understood by the entrance of Richard
Nixon into the controversy. If the movement was so politically strong as to entice President Nixon to take sides, it had to
be a winning hand. [2]

The Senate Interior Committee still had major anti-Indian
personalities on it, however, in the Democratic lineup of
Chairman Henry Jackson, Clinton Anderson, Lee Metcalf,
and Alan Bible. Anderson steered his compromise bill to give
what basically amounted to a continued-use permit to the
Pueblo, dependent on the goodwill of the Forest Service. The
Senate Interior Committee amended the House of Representatives' bill, which allowed the Pueblo to take the land in
trust.

When the compromise bill hit the Senate floor, Senators
Fred Harris and Robert Griffin offered a bipartisan amendment to the Anderson compromise. The surprises in voting
underscored the effectiveness of the Indian lobbyists. The
voting also showed that many of the senators had been hiding
under liberal and conservative labels and were forced to come
out into the open on the vote. Frank Church, until then
regarded as an Indian enemy, voted with the Indians. Barry
Goldwater, [3] generally chastised for his dogged conservatism,
also supported Taos. Lee Metcalf and Henry Jackson,
regarded as liberals, bitterly opposed the Indians, Metcalf
going so far as to deride the Indian religion on the Senate
floor, trying to stop the amendment.

In December 1970 President Nixon signed into law the bill
that restored 44,000 acres surrounding the sacred Blue Lake
to the people of the Taos Pueblo. The significance of the law
could not be underestimated. It was the first clear sign, as
Senator Charles Percy noted in his speech on the bill, that the
Indian religious practices would be given equal respect along
with Christian ceremonies.

Remembering the Blue Lake fight, let us examine the
approximate chronology of the recent Indian activist inci-

dents and review the issues raised in each demonstration. Present in all of them, we shall find something of the same integrating force, the same desire for communal integrity exemplified in the Blue Lake struggle.

A great many small and sporadic events were crowded into the last decade of the Indian movement, but the year 1969 probably marks the beginning of the massive and sustained drive by American Indians to bring their message to the American public. Leading into 1969 was the famous confrontation between the Mohawks of Canada and the Canadian officials at the Cornwall (Ontario) Bridge, linking Canada and the United States.

In 1968 the Canadian officials began to demand that the Mohawks pay tolls to use the bridge and customs on the goods brought back from the United States. This move by Canada violated a series of treaties and agreements with the Indians of North America originally made by Great Britain, the oldest and most specific of which was Jay's Treaty (1794) between the United States and Great Britain. On December 18, 1968, the Mohawks, featuring Kahn-Tineta Horn, former actress and model and confidant of Dick Cavett, blockaded Cornwall Bridge as a means of forcing the issues of tolls and customs payments.

Canadian police rushed onto the bridge and arrested the Indians. When the case came to trial in late March 1969, the travesty of Canadian justice became clear. Kahn-Tineta Horn was charged with obstructing ten police officers. It was patently obvious that one little Indian girl could not have obstructed so many large policemen, so that the people in the courtroom began to laugh. As their laughter reached a crescendo, the prosecutor admitted that he had not read the charges before coming into the courtroom. He had to ask for a recess to see with what the Indians were to be charged.

Upon returning, the prosecutor promptly announced that Miss Horn was being charged with having an offensive weapon that she had intended to use against the police. It turned out that the alleged offensive weapon used by Miss Horn was a small knife more on the order of a fingernail file than a scimitar. The charges against her were dropped.

The issue of the treaty was not so easily disposed of, since the evidence introduced at the trial indicated that not only was the 1794 treaty still valid, but that in 1933 the Cornwall-Northern New York Bridge Company had paid the Mohawks 798 dollars for the land upon which the bridge was built. The agreement included the right to pass freely over the bridge under essentially the same terms as originally described in Jay's Treaty. The question of an illegal demonstration was quickly foreclosed by the Canadian court for fear that the liability of the Canadian government for other offenses would be shown. For example, the Indians, and probably the Canadian officials, knew that the Iroquois had valid title to about 85 percent of the lands of Ontario. [4]

With this partially successful effort to get Canada to abide by the 1794 treaty and the 1933 agreement, the modern Indian movement can be said to have gotten off to an energetic, if somewhat humorous, start. The Mohawk's objection, voiced then and since, is that the Jay treaty means that the international boundary does not apply to the Mohawk settlements, which are partially in Canada and partially in the United States. If the border is recognized by law, then the Mohawks become citizens of both Canada and the United States. If the border is not recognized, the Mohawks are a nation with international status.

Pressure began to build in Indian country following the Cornwall Bridge incident. One of the major eruptions occurred later that summer at the Gallup (New Mexico) Ceremonial. A number of young Navajos passed out a mimeographed statement denouncing the festivities as basically dominated by Chamber of Commerce whites and derided their "interest" in Indians.

Gallup, New Mexico is a study in contrasts. It proudly

brags that it is the Indian capital of the world. Yet nowhere in the world are Indians more systematically brutalized than in Gallup. It is estimated that from 50 to 72 percent of the business done by white businessmen derives from the Indians. As a commercial center, the town is almost totally dependent on its Indian trade. The town power structure, however, does virtually nothing for the Indians who come to Gallup, except take their money. The town's sole accomplishment to date is nearly destroying the Gallup Indian Center by firing Herb Blatchford, the Navajo who laboriously built the center after it had been bankrupted by white directors in the early 1960s.

On August 16, 1969, at the height of the annual Chamber of Commerce festivities known as the Gallup Ceremonial, Michael Benson, June Tracy, and Linda Hubbard, all teenaged Navajos, passed out their leaflets at the entrance of the ceremonial grounds. Their mimeod sheet was entitled "When Our Grandfathers Had Guns." It presented a fairly accurate picture of the treatment Indians received in Gallup. It refuted the publicity releases, issued by the white businessmen who controlled the Ceremonial, that presented the Indians seen by tourists in Gallup during the ceremonial as "a happy people." The town fathers were livid. The three young people were denied permission to pass out the leaflets and escorted from the ceremonial grounds.

The reaction of the Gallup businessmen supported the contentions of the young Navajos better than any other evidence they could have mustered. Not only were the young people systematically harassed by townspeople, but the incident was made part of an ongoing campaign to destroy the Gallup Indian Center by economic and political pressures. The point of the leaflet, the reduction of Navajo and Zuni Indians to a state of perpetual drunkenness by harassment and discrimination by the white businessmen of Gallup, was never mentioned.[5]

In the Pacific Northwest things were going no better. The

Quinaults of the western part of Washington had repeatedly pleaded with the non-Indians using their beaches to refrain from littering the shorelands. The tribe owns twenty-nine miles of beach on the Pacific coast, and it has been kept relatively primitive for most of the century. It may be the last long stretch of clean beach left on the West Coast.

But the whites continued to litter the beach. They stole or destroyed Indian fishing nets hung out to dry; removed large quantities of driftwood, which in many instances had solidified the coastline from erosion; and defaced some of the prominent and famous landmarks along the beach by painting school numerals and so forth.

Hoping to correct the most blatant practices, the tribal council invoked its zoning powers against the intruders and closed the beaches to everyone except tribal members. The outcry of the whites in Washington was incredible. They completely lost sight of the issues of littering, property destruction, and landmark defacement, accusing the tribe of being selfish for wanting to close the beaches. Although the beaches were tribal property, they seemed to feel that they had a right to use them for their own purposes. Appeals were made to the governor of the state to institute legal proceedings against the tribe to force them to reopen the beaches or to seek federal aid in taking away the tribe's power to control access to its own beaches.

The Quinaults held their ground, puzzled that people who talked boldly about conservation and ecology would want to ensure deliberate destruction of the state's last remaining stretch of good beach. Attorney General Slade Gorton of Washington, in defiance of existing federal law precluding tribal affairs from state laws, said he did not think that the tribe had the "unchallenged right to exclusive control of the beaches." The state officials were so shortsighted as to believe that no conservation issues were involved and that the Quinaults were merely trying to make trouble.

The state finally backed off. It would have been ridiculous

to have gone into the federal courts in an effort to force the tribe to allow whites to litter the beaches in the face of overwhelming evidence of perpetrated damages. The beaches remained closed.[6]

The beach closure struck directly at the heart of the Indian-white relationship in the same way that the Taos Blue Lake controversy had done. The Quinaults viewed their beach as an intimate part of their communal existence. They were determined not to tolerate its senseless destruction. While not as specifically a religious shrine like Blue Lake, the beaches of the Quinault nonetheless conveyed a tremendous spiritual quality to the people. During the Blue Lake struggle the Pueblo people were often violently opposed by the conservation groups, which charged that the Indians would pollute the lake area if it was restored to them. But these groups were strangely silent with respect to the Quinault beaches. Strangely quiet.

The major event of 1969, of course, was the occupation of Alcatraz Island in November. Shortly after the island was closed as a prison in 1964, a number of Sioux Indians then living in the San Francisco Bay Area landed on the island and claimed it under the 1868 Fort Laramie Treaty with their tribe. In 1964 there were few people around in the Indian community willing to risk a prison sentence to demonstrate a legal technicality, so the invasion sputtered and died. For the record, the first Indian invasion of Alcatraz was led by Allen Cottier, Dick MacKenzie, and Adam Nordwall.

The years passed, and the people always kept a wary eye on the island. Adam Nordwall, in particular, figured that given sufficient manpower and favorable press, a successful invasion could be pulled off. As early as the winter of 1969, plans had been made secretly in the Bay Area to land on the island and reverse the doctrine of Discovery in favor of the Indians. But still lacking was that certain spark to bind the different Bay Area groups together as a feasible force.

As October ended a large convention of Indian groups met

in San Francisco to form a national organization for Indians living in urban areas throughout the country. The night after the convention dispersed, the Indian Center caught fire and burned completely. It was a singularly tragic event for San Francisco's Indian population, which had laboriously built its center over two decades. The center formed the focus of community life for Indians living in the area. Suddenly they were without a meeting place, lacked the social services that their programs had provided, and had practically no way to begin again.

The stage was set for the invasion. On November 9, a little more than a week after the San Francisco Indian Center had burned, a small contingent of Indians landed on the island and spent several exciting hours being chased by the watchmen, who had been hired to keep people away from the abandoned prison island. Not the least discouraged when they were taken ashore the next morning, the Indian invaders, mostly college students from Berkeley and San Francisco State College, reorganized and ten days later landed some two hundred Indian people on the rocks, securing it for a period of eighteen months.

The story of Alcatraz deserves a book in itself. The numerous details of life on the rock and the parade of personalities involved with the Alcatraz occupation are not as important as the original intent of the Indians who occupied the rock. Upon laying claim to the island, these people issued a proclamation explaining why they had come.[7] They visualized Alcatraz as a spiritual center where people of various tribes could come to learn the traditions and religions of the different tribes from resident spiritual leaders.

The intent of the Alcatraz Indians was to set up a total community on the former prison island that would redeem it from its tragic past. An ecological center to replace the barren and rusted prison cellblock was conceived; the sacred plants of all tribes could be grown there and used in healing ceremonies. An Indian university was also advocated. It would be a place where history would not be interpreted so as to justify a program of systematically extinguishing the country's original inhabitants, but rather a place where a true history of the inner relationships of various cultures would be created. A job training center and one for Indian artists and craftsmen was planned; the latter would help pay the overhead for the operations of the whole community. This was the broad scope of the dreaming young college students who landed on Alcatraz.

The Alcatraz invasion was hardly a quarrel over land titles or a clever stroke of publicity. It became, of course, a shuttlecock batted about among government agencies—all of which vied for the inside track, in case the Administration should decide to give the island to the Indians. Rather it was an effort, albeit premature, to establish a totally Indian community for emphasizing the inherent strengths of the respective tribal communities across the nation. As the government failed to understand it and as the population became more migrant and fluctuated greatly, the original goals of the movement were abandoned and the vision died.

The media caught the spirit of the Alcatraz invasion, promptly making it an international cause. Movie stars flocked to the rock to be seen with Indian college students. Motion picture makers drooled at the opportunity to do a contemporary Indian picture featuring the rock. Almost every Indian who had touched the rock was offered a chance to write a book describing the capture of America's most famous and infamous prison. The media unfortunately tended to emphasize the physical exploits of the invaders and failed to investigate the Indians' ultimate intentions of setting up a spiritual center.

By the time that things had settled down and constructive proposals had been advanced for the use of the island, every politician had exploited the issue for his own use, and the activists were landing on other surplus government lands hoping for the same media attention. The media, however, was already shifting to Women's Lib. When the media no longer glamorized the Alcatraz Indians, no one cared any more, and the government swooped in and took the survivors off the rock with no incident.

Alcatraz was regarded as the symbolic quest of American Indians for a permanent homeland and freedom. Many stories humorously pointed out the similarity of the island to existing reservations—no water, no jobs, no houses, no educational facilities, and so forth. In the minds of many Indians, the island came to symbolize the need of American Indians to regain the continent, if not in fact at least in spirit. It still remains as a singularly beautiful experience for those people who managed to get there.

Alcatraz set the pattern for many of the subsequent incidents in the Indian movement. But the corresponding drive to identify a central issue seemed to lapse. In the months that followed the Alcatraz invasion, the Pitt River Indians attempted to reclaim their ancestral lands in northern California. Through a series of rather shady transfers their lands had come into the possession of some of California's large corporations. The Pitt River tribe had asked to be specifically exempted from the California claims case so as to pursue its own just claims and legislation against the corporations and government agencies that were denying them lands not yet legally taken from them by the government. Its case is still pending.[8]

The Indians in the Seattle area looked askance at the proposed closing of part of Fort Lawton, an army post in the northwestern area of the city. Under an old statute, abandoned army posts were supposed to be used for Indian education, and so the city's urban Indians, in need of a center and training programs, asked for the surplus acreage at Fort Lawton for their use. The city promptly asked for the land for another park (Seattle already had so many parks it was running a deficit every year), and the battle was on.

Jane Fonda had come to Seattle to work against the Vietnam War and found a place for herself in the invasion of Fort Lawton. She received a great deal of criticism for her activities, but one thing is fairly certain: Jane was able to focus the attention of the press on the event, and the television stations came out in force, thus dampening the intentions of the soldiers and city police to use extreme measures against the Indians.[9]

Invasions now appeared to come from every direction. Iroquois protesters landed on Stanley Island, which formed part of the St. Regis Mohawk reserve. The island extended a short distance into the St. Lawrence River and had been leased by the government in 1900 to an American citizen for the magnificent sum of six dollars a year. Lots on the island were worth upwards of twenty thousand dollars for use as summer cottages, make the annual rental of six dollars look like an excellent investment for the Yankee realtor.

Part of the controversy revolved around the interpretation of the Iroquois status in their relationships with the United States, Great Britain, and Canada. The Iroquois had signed a treaty with Great Britain before the invasion of French Canada during the French and Indian Wars, which ended in 1763 with the removal of French military power from the North American continent. The Iroquois thus maintain that they were joint conquerors of Canada and deserve to be regarded as coowners. The Iroquois legal position is probably correct, but the separation of Canada from Great Britain by the North America Act of 1867 has so tangled the legal relationships that the United States and Canada have been able to take the position that the Iroquois have no international status, without any foreign nation objecting to this interpretation of the facts.

Almost inextricably intertwined with this legal problem

was the fact that certain scholars had arranged in 1909 for the confiscation of the Iroquois wampum belts from the Onondagas as part of a drive to build up the collections in the museum at Albany. The wampums recorded the sacred and political history of the League of the Iroquois, thus giving silent testimony to the status of the Iroquois as originally defined in the relationships with Great Britain.

The wampum belts were kept in Albany in a vault, although the anthropologists at the state museum painted vivid pictures of little school children filing by the display cases by the millions every day learning about the history of New York State. The belts, however, were keenly missed by the Iroquois in dealing with Canadian officials and trying to recount their struggle with the French and English centuries earlier. The Iroquois were fighting not only for their lands and treaty rights but for their religious belts, which would complete the reintegration of their League on its traditional basis. It became impossible to separate the different struggles in the East so as to solve any of them. After a two-year fight the State of New York passed a law allowing the Iroquois to reclaim five of the minor belts, not those that both the Iroquois and scholars considered important. [10]

And thus it went, rocketing from coast to coast. The Indian movement covered a variety of topics in obscure and nameless places during 1970. For example, in June the big explosion was the attempt of the Pitt River Indians to reclaim their lands once again from the Pacific Gas and Electric Company. Led by Mickey Gemmill and Richard Oakes, who had commanded the Alcatraz occupation through its first crucial months, a task force of Indians occupied the lands near Big Bend, California.

Again the issue was twofold. The lands had been illegally taken from the Indians without any due process guaranteed them by the federal Constitution. The Indians had been excluded from the California claims case on the grounds that they had separate and identifiable claims to particular lands. And the religious community question was every present. The Pitt River Indians wanted lands to reconstitute their tribal life, including reestablishment of their tribal religion, which depended on that particular location near Mount Shasta. The Indians were arrested and tried for trespass but, like the original Mohawk controversy at the bridge, were acquitted.

The summer of 1970 saw the movement overflow its channel and expand into almost every state where any significant number of Indians lived. In almost every case an immediate and identifiable injustice with respect to confiscation of Indian lands was the issue. The Indians of Chicago established an Indian village as a protest against housing discrimination in the city, pointing out that they had been forced into the cities because their lands had been taken by the government.

The American Indian Movement occupied the dormitories of Augustana College in Sioux Falls, South Dakota, as a protest against the lethargy of the churches in assisting Indians. AIM had earlier been to a meeting of the National Council of Churches with no visible effect. As AIM chapters became active, the movement spread to cities with federal surplus property. A lighthouse was seized at Sault Sainte Marie, Michigan. Federal property in Milwaukee was invaded to bring about the establishment of a school. USAF property in Minneapolis was seized by the home chapter of the American Indian Movement.[11]

As the final hearings on the passage of the Blue Lake restoration bill were being heard in the nation's capital, in Wisconsin the DRUMS organization, fiercely anti-terminationist Menominees seeking repeal of their termination law of almost a decade ago, began a series of demonstrations to save their lake lands. The Tuscaroras, Western members of the Iroquois League, drove a group of whites from their reservation, where they had been living in a trailer park. The summer ended in spectacular fashion with the demonstration at Sheep Mountain in the Badlands of South Dakota and a capture of Mount Rushmore in the Black Hills. The protest involved restoration of Indian lands taken from the Oglala Sioux during the Second World War for target practice and never returned.[12]

The first phase of the Indian movement spent itself as the tendency of activists to make claims on federal lands ebbed. It was apparent that the American public would not support a general policy of restoration of tribal lands. At the national political conventions in 1972, the Indian delegates pushed through amendments to both platforms advocating return of federal surplus lands to tribes, but the amendments were hardly understood by the delegates. They received approval primarily because, as David Brinkley was heard to remark, "They do love Indians."

Chapter 2

America Loves Indians... and All That

IT IS RATHER difficult to describe just how America began to embrace Indians in recent years. Perhaps the first response of white America upon learning that Indians still existed in some remote canyons of the West was shock. Few people had realized that any Indians still survived in the backwaters of American life. Their discoveries too often took the form of learning that Indians had enjoyed for nearly a century treaty rights that seemed to give Indians superior rights to those that they and their white neighbors enjoyed. As early as the opening years of the 1960s, state game wardens, state tax authorities, and local police did their best to force Indians into the mainstream of white society by moving against the legal rights of local Indians. Needless to say, local officials did not demand that blacks and Chicanos be given the same rights as whites; only that rights Indians enjoyed be taken away from them.

The California Indians, for example, had been systematically neglected by generations of state and federal bureaucrats. In the 1850s the federal government had signed a series of treaties with the bands and tribes of Indians of that state.

These treaties gave the Indians clearly defined reservations in certain areas of the state, primarily in places not wanted by whites or inaccessible to them. But as the gold fever grew in intensity, arriving settlers began to prowl the length and breadth of the state looking for gold, and the objections to federal preservation of Indian ancestral lands were loud and violent. The miners embarked on a program of systematic genocide against the Indians of California, and whole tribes were massacred to prevent them from holding their lands intact and out of reach of the gold-crazed miners. Political pressure was intense in Washington, D.C., and the California Indian treaties were never ratified by the U.S. Senate. Instead, they were conveniently buried in the Senate archives, where they remained as classified documents for half a century. The whites of California did not even want the description of the Indian reservations known.[1]

During the Great Depression the Bureau of Indian Affairs was given orders to find lands for the many homeless Indians of California. The survivors of the massacres of the century before had gathered in small pockets of poverty in the extreme southern and northern mountain and desert regions of the state. But agriculture was having a hard time in California in the 1930s, so the program was used to assist the wealthy white ranchers and farmers rather than the Indians. Lands that were classified by the Department of Agriculture as "submarginal"—that is to say, as lands that could not produce sufficient crops or income to support a family—were purchased from the whites to prevent their bankruptcy and given to the Indians as lands upon which to live. The California Indians were told to go to the new pieces of federal property, which had been lands that could not support the whites, and they would be organized as new federally recognized Indian tribes. Then they were forgotten by the federal government and remembered only when their desert lands became valuable and California began to need addi-

in that state, ostensibly for fishing, resulted in no convictions on any charges whatsoever. Convictions were generally overturned on appeal, and so the record of the state grew worse and worse. A pattern of discrimination was evident, yet vehemently denied by Governor Dan Evans and his administration. Yet the majority of the arrests for fishing violations turned mysteriously into charges of resisting arrest, disorderly conduct, inciting to riot, loitering, and other obviously spurious indictments, indicating that the intent of Washington State was systematic harassment to prevent Indians from fishing.[5]

The Indians faced daily surveillance by army helicopters that conveniently flew overhead from nearby Fort Lewis, a military installation across the river from Frank's Landing, center of the Indian fishing struggles. Non-Indians giving assistance to the Indian fishermen were also soon placed under surveillance as "domestic subversives." Dick Gregory, who had come to Washington to help publicize the fishing rights struggle, was closely investigated by army agents. In the paranoiac worldview of the state and army officials, Indian fishing was just short of being a Communist takeover of the Northwest. In reality less than one hundred Indians from three small tribes not together numbering 1,200 people were the subject of the dispute.[6]

Outside of deliberate efforts to harass Indians, however, most backlash was not intentionally evil. It came as a result of whites attempting to relate to Indians. Unfortunately the only Indians they wanted to relate to were those of Dee Brown and the historians. As 1971 opened, events took on an eerie aspect that has not yet calmed.[7]

Whites who had never before taken an interest in Indian affairs now began to develop one. In early June 1971 an Indian skeleton was uncovered on the Cemetery Road near Lowville, New York. It was promptly taken in tow by the Lewis County Historical Society as an artifact. Sakokwenonk, a Mohawk chief, asked for the skeleton back. "Many times people of the sciences do not respect the dead," Sakokwenonk wrote to Arthur Einhorn, curator of the Lewis County Historical Society, "and instead of making matters right, cause further difficulties by taking the bones into their own houses and places of work storing them there, or bothering them further."

Einhorn, one of the few intelligent anthropologists in the nation involved in Indian matters, used his influence to get the skeleton returned. The Mohawks took the bones to their reservation and conducted proper burial ceremonies. Almost as if this incident was a trigger on an unsuspecting weapon, whites took to the fields in an effort to dig up Indian burial sites. Believers in a collective unconscious could not have had a better indication of a supraindividual mind than the apparently spontaneous movement across the nation by whites to desecrate Indian gravesites. Yet the Mohawk case received virtually no publicity so that one cannot say that people followed the Lewis County incident deliberately.

In mid-June 1971, forty-five students from the Minneapolis area, sponsored by the Twin Cities Institute for Talented Youth, went to Welch, Minnesota, to begin a six-week project in excavating the site of an Indian village. The motivation for the students' fieldwork was puzzling. Apparently with the best of intentions, they believed that if they dug up the Indian village remains they would be paying the highest respect to Indian culture. The students dug for about five weeks, carefully collecting materials, almost all categorized as "artifacts."

The Indians of Minnesota were outraged at the excavations. They believe, like the Mohawks, that the dead should be left alone. The American Indian Movement, led by Clyde Bellecourt, invaded the site one evening about suppertime. They took shovels away from the students, filled in the trenches, burned the excavation notes, and offered to compensate the students for property losses. They did not, however, want any further digging. They advised the students and newspaper reporters that they did not believe their ancestors had buried their dead for the express purpose of having another culture dig them up and display their bones.

The archaeologists directing the dig apparently could not understand the viewpoint of the AIM members. Les Peterson, a Minnesota Historical Society member who had headed the dig, said "five weeks of work down the drain," indicating that the moral question of disturbing the dead had somehow eluded him. The students also failed to comprehend the problem. One student who has been planning a career in archaeology said that the incident made her lose respect for Indians. Another student was in tears as she tried to explain how carefully the students had been with the materials they had uncovered. "We were trying to preserve their culture, not destroy it," a third student remarked.

None of the whites could understand that they were not helping living Indians by digging up the remains of a village that had apparently existed in the 1500s. Daniel Dalton, assistant AIM program director, said that if the situation were reversed and it were the Indians digging up the site of a white village all hell would have broken loose. The general attitude of the whites, however, was that they were true spiritual descendants of the Indians and that the contemporary AIM Indians were foreigners who had no right to complain about their activities.

The whole state of Minnesota was aroused by the incident. People chose sides and filled the newspapers with comments supporting one side or the other. Few of the non-Indians understood the Indian objections to disturbing the dead. In view of the fact that the state of Minnesota was at that time pursuing a single-minded course of levying an additional tax on the Indians of the state, thus driving them further into poverty, the controversy indicated a deep-seated belief by

Minnesota whites that the only real Indians are dead ones.

Minnesota was a hotbed of compassion, however, in comparison to its neighbor to the south, Iowa. In early June 1971, the state highway department began a new road project about two and a half miles from Glenwood, Iowa. Work progressed until one day a bulldozer blade uncovered an unmarked cemetery. It was quite old, and the bodies were only about six inches beneath the topsoil. A white man, Ernest Barker, who lived in nearby Pacific Junction, estimated that the cemetery was at least a century old, since he believed that his grandmother and three of her children had been buried there in 1867.

As the roadwork continued, bits of tombstones and the bodies of twenty-seven people were uncovered. One of the bodies had next to it several hundred glass beads, some brass finger rings, and metal earrings. From the absence of such remains next to the bodies of the other tombstones, this body was tentatively identified as the remains of an Indian girl. The remains of the twenty-six other bodies were reverently taken to the Glenwood Cemetery and reburied. The remains believed to be Indian had another destination, however, according to state officials.

State Archaeologist Marshall McKusick demanded that the bones be sent to him under the provisions of an Iowa law that entrusted him, as state archaeologist, with articles of historical significance. An Indian woman, Running Moccasins, demanded that the bones be given proper burial. She discovered that the bones had been taken to Iowa City, where they were destined for space in a museum.

Running Moccasins called Marshall McKusick's office several times, but he refused to answer her calls. When questioned about his stand on the matter, McKusick replied, "I don't want that woman to think in any way that if she raises a fuss, I'll give her a couple of boxes of bones." She then called on Governor Robert Ray of Iowa, who was too busy to see her, allowing his aides to handle the problem.

McKusick remained firmly committed to his stand, claiming, "I just can't go giving remains to private individuals. It sounds nice to say just give them back to the Indians so that the girl can be reburied, but I have to follow the Code of Iowa." Later McKusick said that it would take a court order for him to release the remains to the tribe to which the girl belonged. Apparently he was unable to discover the tribes to which twenty-six white bodies had belonged and rather than place all the bones down at Iowa City, he took only the Indian remains to his museum, allowing the white bones, which under the Code of Iowa, were of no "historical significance," to be reburied at the Glenwood Cemetery.

By early fall of 1971, Indians were on the defensive all over the country, trying to prevent the looting of their burial grounds. Whites were just as determined to preserve Indian culture in their terms, if they had to dig up every Indian skeleton in the nation. Near Pedricktown, New York, the Abnaki Archaeological Society continued its exploitation of an old Abnaki village site, uncovering its ninth body in less than a year. The *Philadelphia Inquirer,* in a story about Abnaki in early September, optimistically related that the digs would reveal a cross-section of Indian life and not just burial patterns.

In neighboring Pennsylvania, the looting of Indian graves became a community function. The Archaeology Section of the William Penn Memorial Museum in Harrisburg uncovered three Susquehannock villages. Four graves were exposed, containing two infants and two adults. The expedition, led by Ira F. Smith III, was termed an "overwhelming success." "The West Branch Project was not only a great success from the scientific standpoint," he related to the *Paxton Herald,* "but, perhaps more important, from the human interest it generated. We received a tremendous amount of genuine interest, enthusiasm, and even volunteer participation from local residents. All too often, people fail to comprehend what we are trying to do in these field explorations, and seem to resent our presence in their locality."

So Pennsylvania, once founded by the Quakers on terms of good faith with the Indians, had resorted to community grave-robbing as a summer project. The "bonus" of the summer's work was the discovery of a Susquehannock cemetery on the edge of the selected site.

In Illinois the Field Museum of Natural History was not to be left behind in the race to uncover Indian skeletons. Anthropology students, digging under museum auspices, unearthed the remains of nine Indians buried under a motorcycle path in a forest preserve. The museum made its find public, with glowing reports that the bodies were those of Miami Indians of the late seventeenth century. Since the Miamis used to live in Indiana before they were forced to Oklahoma, the museum made plans to ship the remains to the University of Indiana for display.

The Indians of Chicago arrived at the museum to confront Dr. Donald Collier, museum curator and a man who helped the Albany scholars to postpone restoration of the Iroquois wampum belts. Matthew War Bonnet, leader of the Indian delegation, demanded that the bones be given to the group for ceremonial burial in a Winnebago burial ground in Wisconsin. The Indians of Chicago had been a particularly active group, and so to forestall a major incident, the museum agreed to return the bones for burial.

The Indians took the bones to Wisconsin Dells and held a burial ceremony. They built a hardwood coffin for the remains, and the museum, in a hasty effort to recoup some semblance of respectability, paid for the evening ceremonial fire, hired a medicine man to perform the ceremonies, and provided gifts to be given at the ceremonies. The museum wryly noted that, despite providing financial support for the Indian ceremonies, it did not want to be considered a "soft

tional tax revenues. By the late 1960s, the state began efforts to tax Indian lands.

The clientele for Alcatraz and other invasions was ready-made, created by the federal government through neglect. The forced relocation of reservation Indians to cities on the West Coast had added to the migrant and largely transient population of Indians in California. Last hired and first fired, they were pushed from city to city, town to town. With the exception of San Francisco and Los Angeles, few California cities had Indian centers.

In almost every other part of the country, Indians were treated with disgust and disdain by the whites in their region. South Dakota was littered with signs reading "No Dogs and No Indians Allowed." Oklahoma systematically oppressed Indians, although the Indians were so browbeaten that they simply accepted their lot and few recognized the inequality. They simply assumed that the Indians' lot was meant to be somewhat harder than that of whites, because they were stupid Indians. Washington State had systematically broken the six Indian treaties over fishing rights, and sportsmen's clubs with membership predominantly of redneck whites demanded and received curtailment of Indian fishing rights in violation of the federal laws.

It was in Washington, probably the state in the Union in which Indians are most discriminated against, that the first overt action of white backlash broke out. A number of young whites had been attracted to the fishing rights struggle by listening to the Indians from Washington describe their struggle on the rivers. So a few young whites, long-haired and concerned, made the trek back to the Pacific Northwest with the Indians who were returning home. They came to Frank's Landing and other Indian fishing grounds and spent several weeks living with the Nisquallies and Puyallups in their little communities.

Just after the Labor Day weekend in 1970, a fishing camp

was set up near Tacoma, Washington, and the Indians were busy fishing and making preparations to take the fish back to their homes. Some non-Indian youngsters were in the camp, but on the whole it was an Indian camp. Almost three hundred Tacoma city police, state game wardens, and state police silently surrounded the camp. They trained telescopic rifles on the adult males who could be seen easily from the bushes in which the military force was hidden.

Then the camp was raided. Tear gas was thrown into the camp. The better-known Indian fishermen and women were rushed and brutally beaten. As many as six burly policemen grabbed little Allison Bridges, a slip of a girl weighing some one hundred pounds and standing just a whisper above five feet. Indian teenagers with long hair, worn in traditional Indian fashion, were beaten with long clubs and flashlights. The people in the camp were arrested for disorderly conduct—the raid, after all, once begun was disorderly! The camp was leveled; the Indians' cars were impounded and taken to Tacoma, where they were virtually destroyed while in police custody.

It turned out after the arrests that the police did not have jurisdiction over the Indian fishing camp. The raid had been illegal. By this time pictures of police brutality had been shown on national television, and the nation had suddenly discovered that Indians were still fishing. Even though the police knew that the raid had been illegally undertaken, they sent a bulldozer into the camp and completely destroyed the remnants of the Indian tents and nets that had survived the initial raid.[2]

With all the attendant publicity, the federal government had a very embarrassing situation on its hands. It had been covertly cooperating with the state game department to stop the Indian fishing. The treaties read, and the public began to demand, that the federal government protect the Indian fishermen. U.S. Attorney Stan Piktin filed a suit against the

State of Washington as a means of covering over the controversy. What the government asked was basically to have the court transfer the decision in an earlier Oregon case to be effective in the State of Washington.

The case dragged on for more than two years before the court even decided which parties were supposed to be suing which. The case presented by the United States could hardly be called an advocacy of the Indian position, and some individual Indians petitioned the court to make the United States a defendant with the State of Washington, thereby clarifying the situation. The court ruled against them, denying them the right to enter the case at all. The case is still languishing.[3]

As the movement's action began to pick up, the new interest in Indians meant that the reservations were literally overrun with whites wanting to help Indians who became bitterly resentful when told that there was no spot for them. The Hopis, always a popular tribe with non-Indians because of the spectacular Hopi dance for rain that involves the handling of live reptiles, were flooded with young whites wanting to remain on the reservation and study the Hopi way of life.

State governments began a systematic search for ways to assert state jurisdiction over the reservations. In the past there had been no knowledge of Indians at the state government level—other than an acknowledgement that the Indians were the responsibility of the federal government —and states had left Indian tribes alone. Now with what appeared to be an increasing interest in Indians, state governments began to assert all manner of claims against tribal governments. Some states maintained that they had primary taxing authority over the reservations, in spite of longstanding Supreme Court decisions that forbade state taxation of Indian reservations.

Whites in Washington, Arizona, New Mexico, and

Minnesota had long refused to provide any services to Indians, because they felt that the tribes received funds and services from the federal government. Their attitude was that nontaxpaying Indians were no concern of theirs. With the new interest in Indians, however, state governments suddenly decided that they could tax Indians while refusing to provide them with services funded by the increased taxes.[4]

New Mexico forced a case against a Zuni man for state income tax, and his lawyer stipulated away all of the assertions that had traditionally protected the Indians from state taxation. Minnesota picked up the ball and asserted its right to tax Indians on the Red Lake Chippewa Indian Reservation even though a federal law, P.L. 280, specifically exempted the reservation from all operations of state law. No sooner had Minnesota been quashed in court than Arizona decided that it could tax the Navajos, despite the fact that the state legislature had made no move to assume any jurisdiction over the massive Navajo reservation. What is significant in all of these cases is that the lawsuits and tax attempts were all measures undertaken by individuals working in state governments, who had suddenly decided on their own initiative to move against the Indian tribes.

In no case of taxation or attempted taxation had the state legislatures made any move to assume jurisdiction over the Indian tribes concerned. By federal law the proper procedure would have been simply to pass a bill that conformed to federal requirements to have the state assume jurisdiction, civil and criminal, over the people of the respective reservations. No state that moved in against the Indians did this. Instead the various tax and game departments would simply order the state police, game wardens, or tax agents to move against the Indians. The whole movement spoke of a new type of intrusion and oppression of Indians.

Washington State, of course, led the list of states in which the Indians were persecuted. More than one hundred arrests in that state, ostensibly for fishing, resulted in no convictions on any charges whatsoever. Convictions were generally overturned on appeal, and so the record of the state grew worse and worse. A pattern of discrimination was evident, yet vehemently denied by Governor Dan Evans and his administration. Yet the majority of the arrests for fishing violations turned mysteriously into charges of resisting arrest, disorderly conduct, inciting to riot, loitering, and other obviously spurious indictments, indicating that the intent of Washington State was systematic harassment to prevent Indians from fishing.[5]

The Indians faced daily surveillance by army helicopters that conveniently flew overhead from nearby Fort Lewis, a military installation across the river from Frank's Landing, center of the Indian fishing struggles. Non-Indians giving assistance to the Indian fishermen were also soon placed under surveillance as "domestic subversives." Dick Gregory, who had come to Washington to help publicize the fishing rights struggle, was closely investigated by army agents. In the paranoiac worldview of the state and army officials, Indian fishing was just short of being a Communist takeover of the Northwest. In reality less than one hundred Indians from three small tribes not together numbering 1,200 people were the subject of the dispute.[6]

Outside of deliberate efforts to harass Indians, however, most backlash was not intentionally evil. It came as a result of whites attempting to relate to Indians. Unfortunately the only Indians they wanted to relate to were those of Dee Brown and the historians. As 1971 opened, events took on an eerie aspect that has not yet calmed.[7]

Whites who had never before taken an interest in Indian affairs now began to develop one. In early June 1971 an Indian skeleton was uncovered on the Cemetery Road near Lowville, New York. It was promptly taken in tow by the Lewis County Historical Society as an artifact. Sakokwenonk, a Mohawk chief, asked for the skeleton back. "Many times people of the sciences do not respect the dead," Sakokwenonk wrote to Arthur Einhorn, curator of the Lewis County Historical Society, "and instead of making matters right, cause further difficulties by taking the bones into their own houses and places of work storing them there, or bothering them further."

Einhorn, one of the few intelligent anthropologists in the nation involved in Indian matters, used his influence to get the skeleton returned. The Mohawks took the bones to their reservation and conducted proper burial ceremonies. Almost as if this incident was a trigger on an unsuspecting weapon, whites took to the fields in an effort to dig up Indian burial sites. Believers in a collective unconscious could not have had a better indication of a supraindividual mind than the apparently spontaneous movement across the nation by whites to desecrate Indian gravesites. Yet the Mohawk case received virtually no publicity so that one cannot say that people followed the Lewis County incident deliberately.

In mid-June 1971, forty-five students from the Minneapolis area, sponsored by the Twin Cities Institute for Talented Youth, went to Welch, Minnesota, to begin a six-week project in excavating the site of an Indian village. The motivation for the students' fieldwork was puzzling. Apparently with the best of intentions, they believed that if they dug up the Indian village remains they would be paying the highest respect to Indian culture. The students dug for about five weeks, carefully collecting materials, almost all categorized as "artifacts."

The Indians of Minnesota were outraged at the excavations. They believe, like the Mohawks, that the dead should be left alone. The American Indian Movement, led by Clyde Bellecourt, invaded the site one evening about suppertime. They took shovels away from the students, filled in the trenches, burned the excavation notes, and offered to compensate the students for property losses. They did not, however, want any further digging. They advised the students and newspaper reporters that they did not believe their ancestors had buried their dead for the express purpose of having another culture dig them up and display their bones.

The archaeologists directing the dig apparently could not understand the viewpoint of the AIM members. Les Peterson, a Minnesota Historical Society member who had headed the dig, said "five weeks of work down the drain," indicating that the moral question of disturbing the dead had somehow eluded him. The students also failed to comprehend the problem. One student who has been planning a career in archaeology said that the incident made her lose respect for Indians. Another student was in tears as she tried to explain how carefully the students had been with the materials they had uncovered. "We were trying to preserve their culture, not destroy it," a third student remarked.

None of the whites could understand that they were not helping living Indians by digging up the remains of a village that had apparently existed in the 1500s. Daniel Dalton, assistant AIM program director, said that if the situation were reversed and it were the Indians digging up the site of a white village all hell would have broken loose. The general attitude of the whites, however, was that they were true spiritual descendants of the Indians and that the contemporary AIM Indians were foreigners who had no right to complain about their activities.

The whole state of Minnesota was aroused by the incident. People chose sides and filled the newspapers with comments supporting one side or the other. Few of the non-Indians understood the Indian objections to disturbing the dead. In view of the fact that the state of Minnesota was at that time pursuing a single-minded course of levying an additional tax on the Indians of the state, thus driving them further into poverty, the controversy indicated a deep-seated belief by

Minnesota whites that the only real Indians are dead ones.

Minnesota was a hotbed of compassion, however, in comparison to its neighbor to the south, Iowa. In early June 1971, the state highway department began a new road project about two and a half miles from Glenwood, Iowa. Work progressed until one day a bulldozer blade uncovered an unmarked cemetery. It was quite old, and the bodies were only about six inches beneath the topsoil. A white man, Ernest Barker, who lived in nearby Pacific Junction, estimated that the cemetery was at least a century old, since he believed that his grandmother and three of her children had been buried there in 1867.

As the roadwork continued, bits of tombstones and the bodies of twenty-seven people were uncovered. One of the bodies had next to it several hundred glass beads, some brass finger rings, and metal earrings. From the absence of such remains next to the bodies of the other tombstones, this body was tentatively identified as the remains of an Indian girl. The remains of the twenty-six other bodies were reverently taken to the Glenwood Cemetery and reburied. The remains believed to be Indian had another destination, however, according to state officials.

State Archaeologist Marshall McKusick demanded that the bones be sent to him under the provisions of an Iowa law that entrusted him, as state archaeologist, with articles of historical significance. An Indian woman, Running Moccasins, demanded that the bones be given proper burial. She discovered that the bones had been taken to Iowa City, where they were destined for space in a museum.

Running Moccasins called Marshall McKusick's office several times, but he refused to answer her calls. When questioned about his stand on the matter, McKusick replied, "I don't want that woman to think in any way that if she raises a fuss, I'll give her a couple of boxes of bones." She then called on Governor Robert Ray of Iowa, who was too

touch," thus indicating that its overture was more of a "bribe" than a gift.

The final, bizarre, and perhaps fitting touch to this summer of looting was the invasion of a century-old Nez Percé burial ground near Clarkston, Washington. Thieves invaded the sacred grounds and drove rods into the ground to locate the coffins of the Indians. Then they dug up the graves to take any jewelry that might have been buried with the bodies. The Indian skulls were stolen, many of them severed from the rest of the skeletons, and sold in an underground market in California, where they brought as much as twenty dollars each.

A white dentist paid an exhorbitant price for the skull of Chief Joseph, the beloved leader of the Nez Percé whose thrilling dash for freedom formed an important chapter of Dee Brown's *Bury My Heart at Wounded Knee*. With Chief Joseph's skull safely in the dentist's living room being used as an ashtray, evening television viewers could watch Dick Cavett and John Niehardt discuss why the Indians would not survive the twentieth century and why the contemporary Indians were mere caricatures of their ancestors.

The final insult came in 1972, when five whites captured Raymond Yellow Thunder, a fifty-one-year-old Sioux from the Pine Ridge reservation in Gordon, Nebraska. They severely beat him and then stripped him of his clothes below the waist and pushed him into an American Legion hall while a dance was in progress, to the amusement of the aging whites, who had fought in the Second World War and Korea allegedly to protect human dignity. He died later from the beating.[8]

At the call of the American Indian Movement more than 2,000 Indians swarmed into Gordon to demand justice. But the case was hushed up, Yellow Thunder's body was quietly buried, and his relatives were denied permission to see the body. The State of Nebraska had set up an Indian commission that was supposed to deal with relations between Indians and whites, but it ducked the Gordon incident. The federal authorities, who had been called in during civil rights killings, decided that they had no jurisdiction, even though federal law requires that the Justice Department protect Indians.

After much confusion and stalling, the whites responsible for the killing were finally charged on lesser counts and tried in Alliance, Nebraska, a town almost as notoriously anti-Indian as Gordon. They received light sentences for what might have been the state's most shocking crime had Indians committed it against a white person.

Again it appeared as if the collective unconscious was working in a predetermined channel. In Arizona and California there were killings of Indians under extremely suspicious circumstances. In both states the killings were hushed up as quickly as possible, and local officials made statements indicating that they did not regard it a serious crime to kill an Indian. The old frontier mentality had returned to the West with a vengeance. In spite of protests by a broad spectrum of Indian groups and marches asking for justice, the state governments refused to respond with investigations of the killings.

Indian country was clearly alarmed but determined not to panic. Appeals were made to the Justice Department for assistance in seeing that some elementary form of justice prevailed. But the Justice Department refused to do anything to help the families of the slain Indians. It was strange behavior for an Administration pledged to preserve law and order in American society. Talk began in Indian country of marching on Washington to ask for a federal law making it a crime to kill an Indian. Russell Means, one of the most energetic activists, demanded that Indians be designated as an "endangered species," if nothing else.

Then on a lonely piece of land in California, Richard

Oakes, leader of the Alcatraz movement, was slain by a guard of a YMCA camp. The guard, Michael Morgan, claimed that Oakes had appeared from behind a clump of trees and, menacingly, come toward him. He alleged that he had fired at Oakes in self-defense. There were, however, no weapons on or near Oakes at the time of the shooting. According to Indian witnesses, Oakes had gone to the camp to inquire about a young Indian boy, who had had trouble with Morgan earlier in the week. Morgan was charged with "involuntary manslaughter" and set free on five thousand dollars bail. Indian country was livid. On September 25, 1972, five days after Oakes' death, the Trail of Broken Treaties began to pick up many enthusiastic volunteers. [9]

As Election Day neared, young Indians from all over the nation began to consider how they could bring their situation to the attention of the nation's political leaders. The original plan was to present both Presidential candidates with a platform of Twenty Points which, if carried out, would most certainly change the condition of American Indians. But as the movement took hold, goals began to blur, and the desire simply to confront the seats of power and demand redress began to assert itself.

On November 2 as the protesters were beginning to leave the Bureau of Indian Affairs, a scuffle broke out, and the first day of what had been planned as a peaceful week-long protest in the nation's capital by some one thousand Indians had turned into the capture of the Bureau headquarters and a week of destruction and confrontation. At first the press appeared sympathetic, and the initial stories about the confrontation appeared to favor the Indian activists. But as time wore on, it became apparent that the interior of the building was being damaged and the tone of the press began to change; by the time the building was abandoned on the following Thursday, the concentration of the news media was almost exclusively on the destruction of the building. The

Twenty Points were hardly mentioned. Richard Oakes was a figment of history, and the grave-robbing seemed almost unreal in retrospect.[10]

The peculiar tragedy of the Indian movement is that it has never been able to influence the intellectual concepts and values by which white Americans view the world. Indians remain an exotic and unknown quantity. The quality and pathos of their lives remain unexamined and beyond the concern of most Americans. Because of their inability to pierce the veil of insensitivity and ignorance which shielded them from the rest of America, Indians appeared to be simply another ethnic group in search of an identity in a society that was rapidly leaving its period of ethnic confrontation.

As the Presidential election returned Richard Nixon to power for another term, it was painfully apparent that the American public desired, for the greatest part, to relive the 1950s. It was, perhaps, no coincidence, that national news magazines featured the return of the 1950s as a period of national existence to be emulated as some 76 million people filed to the polls to re-elect President Nixon in one of the greatest landslides in American history.

Plainly the Indian activist movement had stalled on a plateau. Broken treaties and broken urinals marked its crest and its future was yet to be determined. It would be on the stark plains of Wounded Knee that all the diverse elements of Indian country would finally merge in a violent and incomprehensible protest that would produce a cry of agony from every American Indian.

Chapter 3

Indians of America

As THE CIVIL Rights movement began to be eclipsed by antiwar protests and the discovery by the communications media of other racial minorities, a demand arose for additional information about American Indians. This interest was tremendously increased by the Alcatraz experience, and it was further heightened by the continuing efforts of Indian activists across the nation. In an effort to respond to the increasing market for books about Indians and by Indians, a number of publishers eagerly sought out manuscripts on Indians by both Indian and non-Indian authors.

Until this development, Indian literature stereotyped the Indian condition, thus hampering rather than helping the intelligent examination of the state of contemporary Indian affairs. The field of literature on American Indians is totally unlike any comparable field of American study. It breaks down into a number of easily categorized viewpoints which when taken together reveal much more about the conception of America held by the reading public than about American Indians, past and present. A review of the types of literature available on American Indians indicates that insofar as the Indian activists believed (and still believe) that they could tap the wellspring of hidden white sympathy, the task was almost totally hopeless and futile.

With the exception of N. Scott Momaday's Pulitzer Prize-winning novel, *House Made of Dawn,* and Borland's *When the Legends Die* and *Stay Away, Joe,* there have been few successful novels of modern Indian life. *Little Big Man,* Thomas Berger's fantastically successful novel of the old West, covers Indian life and culture obliquely, and its time period could hardly be said to relate the nature of contemporary Indian life. A great many novels have not even had the success of *Little Big Man.* In attempting to present in fictional format Indian life as it was experienced in the last century, most novels have fallen into a "go-in-peace-my-son" style, with the credibility of the plot dependent on the lonely white trapper, gunfighter, or missionary who comes across the Indian princess. The parallel between the unexpected and fortunate event in the Horatio Alger stories that catapults the hard-working hero to fame and the fortunate "salvation" event that makes the Indian tribe accept the white hero in the Indian novel is no mistake. It is virtually impossible to change cultures or economic status without what would appear to be an almost supernatural intervention.

Where other fields of literature have so successfully enabled people to empathize with conditions and cultural variances, novels about Indians have been notably bereft of the ability to invoke sympathy. Rather they have been dependent on an escapist attitude for their popularity. As a consequence, both the Indian activist movement and the field of Indian literature have suffered tremendously from the inability to invoke an atmosphere of sympathetic reader response. There has been and is no emotional unconscious which can be tapped on behalf of the American Indian, insofar as he is a person like other people. His sufferings are historic and communal; this is the lesson which America has learned from its literature on Indians.

The communal nature of Indian personal existence is

further supported by the presence of a large body of literature on the histories of the respective tribes. For generations it has been traditional that all historical literature on Indians be a recital of tribal histories from the pre-Discovery culture through the first encounter with the white man to about the year 1890. At that point the tribe seems to fade gently into history, with its famous war chief riding down the canyon into the sunset. Individuals appear within this history only to the extent that they appear to personalize the fortunes of the tribe. A mythical Hiawatha, a saddened Chief Joseph, a scowling Sitting Bull, a sullen Geronimo; all symbolize not living people but the historic fate of a nation overwhelmed by the inevitability of history.

Some of the earliest Indian protests challenged this image of Indians and the numerous false stereotypes projected by this type of literature. Sincere but unknowing whites honestly asked us less than a decade ago if we still lived in tents, if we were allowed to leave the reservations, and other relevant questions, indicating that for a substantial number of Americans, Indians were still shooting at the Union Pacific on their days off. The result of this protest was that several writers of books on Indians added a final chapter in which a quick sketch of the contemporary condition of the tribe was reviewed.

As late as 1964 many publishers thought 1) Indians could not write books, and 2) any book written by an Indian would be "biased" in favor of Indians.[1] Whenever the subject of Indians writing their own books arose, even the friendliest of non-Indians stated that a great many Indians had written books, and that we should be content with what they had left. The trail of books written by Indians is significant if considered as the recorded feelings of a race once extant, but insignificant if it is meant to communicate modern social and legal problems that have created and intensified poverty conditions among a segment of the American population. Even today many people feel that the old books on Indians are sufficient to inform the modern American public about the nature of Indian life and to give him sufficient information about Indians for him to make an intelligent choice as to how best to support Indian goals and aspirations. One historian wrote that there are already a sufficient number of books by Indians, and that books chronicling contemporary outrages should not be published, because they stir up bad feelings between Indians and whites. He recommended *Sun Chief* (the autobiography of a Hopi, published in 1942), *The Son of Old Man Hat* (the autobiography of a Navajo, published in 1938), and Black Hawk's autobiography (published in 1833). Can these books correctly inform the reader on the struggle of the Navajo and Hopi against Peabody Coal Company at Black Mesa?[2]

This fundamental cleavage of information about Indians and information by Indians about particular and pressing problems has come to dominate Indian concerns, but it has not even begun to penetrate the non-Indian world. During the years when the National Indian Youth Council was coming into existence and young Indians were attempting to get sympathetic non-Indians to listen to their story, quite often the non-Indian would reply that he was very interested and had recently read *Ishi in Two Worlds* (a story about the last member of a California Indian tribe, who spent his final days as a mascot of a California museum in the first decade of this century).

The increasing awareness of younger Indians that something was dreadfully wrong was recorded in Stan Steiner's *The New Indians,* published in 1968. In this book Steiner reviewed the developments within Indian country since the Second World War. He pointed out the fact that the tremendous sums the federal government was spending for Indian education were beginning to produce results. Rather than a quiet group of civil servants, however, the younger Indians were becoming political theorists, activists, and cultural revivalists. Steiner warned of the impending land-slide of concern, which was bound to manifest itself in continuing protests against federal policies that had never taken into account the nature of Indian society or the deep feeling of betrayal the Indian community has held throughout the twentieth century.

Unfortunately for everyone, the reading public, the literary critics, and many of the people most directly concerned with the problems of modern Indians were attracted to two other books also published in 1968. Alvin Josephy published his famous *The Indian Heritage of America,* and Peter Farb published the famous book with the long title, *Man's Rise to Civilization As Shown by the Indians of North America from Primeval Times to the Coming of the Industrial State.* Both books were best sellers and popular book club selections. Josephy devoted all of twenty pages in a 365-page book to the period from 1890 to 1968, failing to cite any contemporary Indian political leader at all and mentioning the National Indian Youth Council once in passing.

Farb did a brilliant analysis of prehistoric Indian cultures, covered items which had not previously been on any anthropological agenda, and cleverly wove together almost all of the relevant information on Indian cultural deviations into a 332-page book. His work was considered by reviewers as a major step forward in understanding the American Indians. He did not, however, mention the Indian Reorganization Act of 1934, which has formed the basis for communal survival in the postwar world. He did not mention the Indian Claims Commission of 1946, which has attempted to redress the injustices of land confiscation through relitigation of land claims. Farb frankly stated that he would leave such a job to another. How he came to figure that he had taken Indians up to the modern industrial state, however, is another question, since his book appears chronologically to stop shortly after the Dawes Act of 1887.[3]

The incongruity of the impact of the three books becomes more apparent with the addition of other facts. Josephy and Farb were among the inner circle of consultants upon whom then-Secretary of the Interior Stewart Udall relied for his knowledge concerning the formation of policy on American Indians. Steiner was regarded as a itinerant relic of the Jack Kerouac school of wanderers, a person who could not conceivably possess any information on Indians that would be relevant to the formation of policy. In 1968 the inherent schizophrenia of the Indian image split and finally divided into modern Indians and the Indians of America—those ghostly figures that America loved and cherished.

In the next four years it seemed as if every book on modern Indians was promptly buried by a book on the "real" Indians of yesteryear. The public overwhelming turned to *Bury My Heart at Wounded Knee* and *The Memoirs of Chief Red Fox* to avoid the accusations made by modern Indians in *The Tortured Americans* and *Custer Died for Your Sins*. The Red Fox book alone sold more copies than the two modern books. Each takeover of government property only served to spur further sales of the Brown review of the wars of the 1860s. While the Indian reading public was in tune with *The New Indians, The Tortured Americans, The Unjust Society* by Harold Cardinal, a Canadian Indian, and other books written by contemporary Indians on modern problems, the reading non-Indian public began frantically searching for additional books on the Indians of the last century.

The result was the publication of a series of books that were little more than scissors and paste jobs—the anthologies. *Touch the Earth* by T. C. McLuhan and *I Have Spoken* by Virginia Armstrong consisted of a series of excerpts of the speeches of famous chiefs with a few short quotations from living Indians to give the book a timely flavor. T. C. McLuhan inserted a number of sentimental sepia pictures of old chiefs riding along the crest of the canyon to add further maudlin emotions to an already overemotional book. The public took T. C. to heart, and *Touch the Earth* also hit the book clubs. She is now happily living in England, her brief venture into Indian affairs apparently finished, her only accomplishment the perpetuation of traditional stereotypes of American Indians in the public's mind.

In addition to the sentimental anthologies, a number of books were rushed into print and hopefully to judgment; they were little more than editing jobs on reports to government agencies. Among them was *American Indians and Federal Aid* by Alan Sorkin, a study done by the Brookings Institution under a grant from the Donner Foundation. The book was complete with numerous tables demonstrating Indian poverty but void of any references to the forces then moving in Indian affairs. *Big Brother's Indian Programs * With Reservations,* by Sar Levitan and Barbara Hetrick, a study funded by the Ford Foundation, was published shortly after Sorkin's book. It is distinguishable from Sorkin's book chiefly through its use of photographs as if there really were Indians alive today.

In the fall of 1972 there were no less than 75 books on American Indians released. Most staggered into print, received few reviews, and collapsed. It was plain that the initial phase of interest in Indians was over. Then just before Election Day, the Trail of Broken Treaties arrived in the nation's capital, ready to do battle with the powers that be. In little over a week the Administration, the tribal leaders, and a great segment of the American public sat stunned as the Indian activists completed their destruction of the Bureau of Indian Affairs, collected some 66,000 dollars in travel money from the federal government, and set off to terrorize the headquarters of some tribes and field offices of the Bureau of Indian Affairs. Somehow American Indians had arrived in the twentieth century.

In order to understand why this particular event occurred, we must try to understand the reception that modern Indians have received as they have tried to communicate their immediate problems to an uncomprehending society. When a comparison is made between events of the Civil Rights movement and the activities of Indians over the last decade, one thing stands out in clear relief: Americans simply refuse to give up their longstanding conceptions of what an Indian is. It is this fact more than any other that today inhibits solution of the Indians' problems and projects the impossibility of their solution in the near future.

Let us pretend that the black community will receive the same conceptions and receptions in the Civil Rights struggle that the American Indian community has received in its struggle. It is 1954, and the Supreme Court has just handed down its famous case, *Brown vs. Topeka Board of Education;* the Civil Rights movement is beginning to get under way. Soon there is a crisis in Montgomery, Alabama, and Dr. Martin Luther King begins to emerge as a credible leader of the Civil Rights forces.

At a news conference King is asked about the days on the old plantation. He attempts to speak on the bus boycott, but the news media rejects his efforts. It wants to hear about Uncle Tom, the famous black of literature. The news conference ends with the newsmen thoroughly convinced that King is merely a troublemaker, that everything is fine down on the old plantation, and that everything will be all right if the blacks would simply continue to compose spirituals.

Two books are published recounting the blessed days of slavery on the one hand and the cultural achievements of the tribes of black Africa in the 1300s on the other. They are almost immediate successes on the best-seller lists, and the American public worries about the Muslims confronting the primitive tribes of the interior of the African continent and changing their culture. In a desperate effort to raise the issue of Civil Rights in American society, Martin Luther King writes *Stride Toward Freedom*. Outside of a few people who seem to intuit that things are not well down South, King's ideas are ignored. Two new black writers, James Baldwin and LeRoi Jones, publish books that have a sporadic, perfunctory reception, and they are ignored.

The movement continues to grow with television coverage and feature-length descriptions of the poverty conditions of the black community, prefaced by quotations from Booker T. Washington and George Washington Carver to the effect that blacks should remain separate until earning the right to participate in American society. The Freedom Rides begin, sparking a series of anthologies of Negro spirituals about traveling to the promised land. A "Negro Travel Book," showing the great migrations in Africa in the 1300s, becomes a best seller.

Finally the movement grows intense as plans are made for a march on Washington. People rush here and there, preparing for the march; the activists down in the Deep South are in trouble. Some have been killed for attempting to register voters. On the literary front, however, things are different. A new book, *Bury My Heart at Jamestown,* has rocketed to the top of the best-seller list. More than 20,000 copies a week are being purchased. People reading the book vow never again to buy and sell slaves. Sympathy for the slaves is running at a fever pitch, while Martin Luther King is downgraded because "he doesn't speak for all the Negroes."

As the march gets under way, television finds a new hero. Field Hand Boggs, an elderly black who claims to be 101 years old and a nephew of Nat Turner, is discovered almost simultaneously by *The New York Times* and the Dick Cavett Show. Field Hand Boggs has copied 13,000 words from *Uncle Tom's Cabin* by Harriet Beecher Stowe and is passing it off as his "notebooks" laboriously compiled over a century of struggle. Field Hand Boggs becomes the number one folk hero of America, and he recounts for thrilled television audiences his glimpse of Abraham Lincoln and General Grant sitting on the White House lawn the day that he gained his freedom. The march is conducted in virtual isolation.

As the Civil Rights movement proceeds, the literature shifts its emphasis; old government and foundation reports complete with charts and graphs are trotted out with fancy dust jackets that make them appear to be the latest battle communiques from Atlanta. Anthologies of spirituals become very popular, and those that are interspiced with faded photographs of slaves working in the cotton fields prove the most popular. Introductions to these anthologies sternly inform us that we must come to understand the great contributions made by slaves to our contemporary culture. "More than ever," one commentary reads, "the modern world needs the soothing strains of 'Sweet Chariot' to assure us that all is well."

And finally Watts. As the section of Los Angeles burns, people resolve to do better. Government officials ask for full prosecution of the rebels, all the while handing out hundred-dollar bills to the rioters and advising them to go back to Virginia and South Carolina and sin no more. A Task Force is created of officials of various government departments to study the federal relationship to Civil Rights problems and to report back its findings no later than six months after its authorization.

What seems ludicrous in the black situation as recounted here is precisely what has happened in the American Indian situation without anyone cracking a smile. At the height of the Civil Rights struggle, for example, would anyone have seriously entertained the idea that a 101-year-old man with a tenuous claim to black blood or heritage would truly represent the struggles of the black community? Certainly no intelligent critic would be taken in by such a hoax (fraud is rarely used when discussing minority groups).[4] Yet it not only happened to American Indians, but a substantial portion of the public yearned for it to happen.

What we therefore have been dealing with for the major portion of a decade is not American Indians, but the American conception of what Indians should be. While Dee Brown's *Bury My Heart at Wounded Knee* was selling nearly 20,000 copies a week, the three hundred state game wardens and Tacoma city police were vandalizing the Indian fishing camp and threatening the lives of Indian women and children at Frank's Landing on the Nisqually River. It is said that men read and write history to learn from the mistakes of the past, but this could certainly not apply to histories of the American Indian, if it applies to history at all.

As Raymond Yellow Thunder was being beaten to death, Americans were busy ordering *Touch the Earth* from their book clubs, attempting to indicate their sympathy for American Indians. And as the grave robbers were breaking into Chief Joseph's grave, the literary public was reading his famous surrender speech in a dozen or more anthologies of Indian speeches and bemoaning the fact that oratory such as Joseph's is not used anymore.

The tragedy of America's Indians—that is, the Indians that America loves and loves to read about—is that they no longer exist, except in the pages of books. Rather the modern Indians dress much the same as every other person, attend pretty much the same schools, work at many of the same jobs, and suffer discrimination in the same manner as do other racial minorities. One can assume that, for all practical purposes, American Indians are the same as the other oppressed groups in American society. The most militant literature and underground newspapers have indeed tried to corral the respective minority groups with women and gay people to present a common front, to be known as the Third

World, against the WASP Establishment. According to this mythology, all of the oppressed peoples share more in common as victims than they do as individual groups with the mainstream of American society.

This simplification overlooks the obvious historical facts that even historians such as Alvin Josephy keep well in front of their readers. The cultural and social worldview of American Indians derives from a completely different background than that of every other group in American society. Where other groups suffer deliberate discrimination and oppression, American Indians are the only group whose oppression comes primarily from an effort to help them change into replicas of the white man. Where blacks and Chicanos dare not enter, Indians are dragged by well-intentioned people who cannot leave them alone.

Thus it is that the cherished image of the noble redman is preserved by American society for its own purposes. If most literature on Indians and many of the recent books reflect nothing else, it is that there exists in the minds of non-Indian Americans a vision of what they would like Indians to be. They stubbornly refuse to allow Indians to be or to become anything else. Even if they have to resuscitate a 101-year-old figure claiming to be a Sioux chief, they will have their Indians of yesteryear.

Perhaps the sole breakthrough in the field of literature about Indians has been a number of books dealing with Indian religions. For some peculiar reason, several books about tribal religions have come through the whole merchandising process and survived the faddish interest in Indians to present a credible body of work.

Ruth Underhill's book, *Red Man's Religion*, presents a quick survey of the various religious beliefs of the tribes, and as a general survey it has merit. A recent book by Anthony F.C. Wallace, *The Death and Rebirth of the Senecas*, approaches the threshold of examination of the nature of Indian tribal religions, but the work is oriented toward a historical review of the reforms made by Handsome Lake in the traditional Iroquois religion, thus dealing only peripherally with contemporary Iroquois religious feelings. *Sweet Medicine* by Peter Powell is the first recent book attempting to explain a tribal religion in a serious vein. In this effort it closely follows *The Sacred Pipe* by Joseph Epes Brown and *Black Elk Speaks* by John Niehardt, which were transcriptions of conversations with Black Elk, the Sioux holy man, several winters before his death in the early 1950s.[5]

Nearly all of these books eschew the traditional approach of expositional development as though the authors were dealing with exotica. And the books have a tremendous impact on the Indian people who read them. More than one Indian political organization has based its approach to modern problems on *Black Elk Speaks*. Almost as if triggered by an unconscious reverence for Indian religions, these books reflect a refusal to bow to popular Indian stereotypes and simply reveal the basic beliefs and ceremonies in which tribal life had been expressed over the centuries. One concludes that, whereas other facets of Indian life and political history might be bent to accommodate non-Indian ideas, one cannot twist Indian religious ideas without destroying their underlying integrity; so unified was the outlook of the Indian tribal religions, it apparently was fairly simple to develop the major themes without inserting the value judgments, which were always editorially inserted in the histories and anthologies.

Coincidence or not, in the summer of 1972 as Indian country was tensing for the eventual showdown in the fall, two major books on Indian religion were published. One was *Lame Deer, Seeker of Visions* by John (Fire) Lame Deer and Richard Erdoes, an autobiography of a Sioux holy man. The book reveals a great deal about the general atmosphere of reservation life and the events in the life of John Fire, who is called Lame Deer by his people. Readers accustomed to the pious rigidity of Protestant tracts on the devotional life were shocked at Lame Deer's casual approach to such taboo subjects as death, sex, and religion, yet from the pages of the book shone a wisdom found in few religious books.

Even more controversial was *Seven Arrows* by Hyemeyohsts Storm. *Seven Arrows* is unique: an attempt to make a contemporary religious statement using traditional stories, mythologies, and symbols of the Cheyenne people. Purists who expected a recording of ancient Cheyenne rites and ceremonies in the manner of *Sweet Medicine* were rocked with the simplicity of Storm's approach, as well as the decided lack of obedience to the anticipated rigid form of exposition. Storm in great measure succeeded in stepping outside of a time-dominated interpretation of Indian tribal religion and created a series of parabolic teachings concerning the nature of religion. Few people have understood him—or forgiven him.

What is most noteworthy about these books is that they give a preliminary form to the most important statements that can be made in an Indian context to illustrate the difference between American Indians and the rest of American society. And they came at a crucial time in the development of the Indian movement and in the development of an integrated sense of there being a field of Indian literature. Young whites had already intuited the existence of some hidden factor in Indian life that made it qualitatively different from the world in which they had grown up.

Several years ago as the flower children movement was waning, the books about Don Juan, the Yaqui religious leader, began to become popular. A substantial number of young people took up the Carlos Castenada books as if they were the final word on Indian religion, and the message of the books began to permeate the counterculture minds. Few Indians recognized anything having to do with Indian religion in the books. Where were the sacred mountains, the healing ceremonies, the tales of creation and historical migrations? Yet for a substantial number of readers, Castenada played an important tune with his writings. *The Teachings of Don Juan* and *A Separate Reality* indeed spoke of a different drummer. It was only with Castanada's *Journey to Ixtlan* that the books began to take on a discernible Indian shape.[6]

As one reflects on the nature of books written by and about American Indians, however, and if one accepts the premise that a different and perhaps separate reality is contained in the Indian religious teachings, then suddenly the body of literature becomes coherent. The tribal histories speak of the integrity of the tribal communities in a way in which histories of other nations can never speak. The writers are able to deal with a steady and rather homogenous group for a distinct period of time. With the defeat and reduction of the tribe to suppliants for the nation's charity, a major change occurs so that if one speaks of the tribe at all it must thereafter be of a people who had been shattered by forces so powerful as virtually to wipe them from the face of the earth.

The novels make a valiant effort to invoke the feeling of former days of communal integrity and common fate. Yet the literary device cannot sustain itself on plot alone, for the era is so far removed from modern experience as to preclude itself from description. What is left is an effort through use of a clipped style of formal English to communicate the tremendous sense of being that existed in the tribes until quite late in their existence. Only the books attempting to survey conditions of all Indians in a general interpretive sweep can be said to fail in their effort to educate us about Indians. It is at this point that Josephy and Farb become farthest removed from the realities of Indian existence then and now.

And finally the anthologies. They blossom like weeds in an untended garden. They contain essentially the same selections. Hardly a collection does not have Red Jacket's reply to the missionaries, Chief Joseph's surrender speech, and Chief Seattle's famous remarks on the signing of the treaty surrendering his homeland. Indeed, if one were to take the anthologies seriously, one would visualize the Indians of old as a collection of poets who happened to be present while the army was fighting some nebulous group in the hinterlands. The anthologies present a sanitized version of the winning and losing of the trans-Ohio West. Few readers see a bloody, exhausted Chief Joseph in his last minute of freedom trying to save his tribe. They see a dignified chief, blanket draped respectably across his arm, giving a well-composed finale to the old frontier.

It is this very sanitized nature of the anthologies that indicates the impossibility of finding meaning in the field of Indian literature. For most of the century it has been necessary for people of the different tribes to keep reminding non-Indians that all tribes are different, that they have different histories, different languages, different cultural values, and different religions. So thoroughly entrenched has this idea become, even among Indians, that it has been virtually a gospel that no sense can be made of the general topic of Indians, but each and every peculiarity and distinction must be emphasized to interpret correctly tribal uniqueness.

The anthologies would indicate, however, that a different situation in fact occurs. The speeches contain a startling similarity from beginning to end. Speeches by Senecas in the 1790s have the same tenor and outlook as to speeches by Nez Percé and Yakimas given a century later. From one end of the country to the other, the selections appear as if they were one general feeling shared by Indians with respect to their tribes, to their lands, to the birds and animals, and to the intrusions of the white man into their lives. Where careful distinctions can be made in other areas, unless one is intimately familiar with a certain selection, one cannot identify which Indian chief said what. If there was ever a homogeneity, it is found in the anthologies of Indian Speeches, *I Have Spoken* and *Touch the Earth*.

When one considers the nature of the selections used in the anthologies, the analysis becomes even clearer. The one common thing that each tribe experienced was its invasion of its homeland by western European white men. The similarity in the speeches is not accidental, therefore, in an important aspect. Almost every speech was given on the occasion in which the tribe was confronted with the need to respond to a consistent opposing force that immediately threatened tribal existence. While we can affirm that all tribes have uniqueness with respect to their attitudes toward the federal government, missionaries, and white society in general, the same basic response was made. It is possible, in this sense, to identify an "Indianness" which is intimately shared by all American Indian people—the response made to white society.

When whites therefore find an apparent homogeneity in Indian response, they have every reason to feel that they are dealing with a unified social or racial group. Even more, the anthologized selections revolve around those topics which have traditionally distinguished Indian concerns from the concerns of white society—lands, communal existence, conceptions of freedom, Indian religious attitudes and beliefs, the conception of death, and the value of individual existence. It is the fact that many whites have discerned in the historical Indian response a quality of life distinctly different than what they have come to experience in their own society that makes them return to the Indians of yesteryear, instead of confronting the contemporary Indians.

Strangely enough American Indians also look to the hero war chief of the past for patterns of contemporary existence. Insofar as modern religious men incorporate the values of the old days, they are in demand today as teachers. The customs and traditions of a century ago are becoming more and more important to the Indians of today. Posters printed by the activists concentrate on the old war chiefs. Bumper stickers reflect former glories, defiance about lands, and an affirmation of the eventual triumph of the Indian cause. It may surprise Indian and non-Indian alike, but the young people who occupied the Bureau of Indian Affairs had a full complement of holy men and held ceremonies several times during the occupation.

The impasse seems to be constant. Indians are unable to get non-Indians to accept them as contemporary beings. Non-Indians either cannot or will not respond to the problems of contemporary Indians. They insist on remaining in the last century with old Chief Red Fox, whoever he may really be, reciting a past that is basically mythological, thrilling, and comforting.

Chapter 4

The Religious Question

INDIAN ACTIVISTS HOLDING religious ceremonies in the Bureau of Indian Affairs and concluding their stay by looting the building seems incongruous and ridiculous, unless we probe deeper into the nature of the relationship between red and white men. Indian activists accused of fomenting the destruction made a rather weak reply. What about the rape of the North American continent, the destruction of tribal cultures, the wasteful use of human beings, the deprivation of rights to a helpless minority? Do not these crimes make the destruction of a building pale to insignificance, they ask.

Do they?

In one sense the capture and destruction of the Bureau of Indian Affairs appears as an historical anachronism. Watts burned in 1965, the urban areas seethed and burned following the death of Martin Luther King in 1968. Is not the Indian occupation of a federal building in the nation's capital an event dreadfully out of time? Is it not the final spasm of the rugged 1960s, when any type of change was considered beneficial, and the institutions of society were considered not only obsolete but malignant? Only if we believe the Indian effort is raising the same issues as those raised in the early 1900s can we make that judgment.

There certainly was an aspect in which the Indian takeover of the Bureau of Indian Affairs was an event of the 1960s, although occurring in 1972. Since 1968 the major Christian denominations had been pouring funds into social movements of all kinds. They believed deeply in the militant version of black power as violent confrontations, and grants were made to organizations within the respective minority groups that they were sure would produce the desired confrontations. A group that snapped and snarled about their social problems stood a much better chance of receiving funds from the churches than did a group that calmly and carefully articulated a problem that they hoped to solve.

Church officials often gauged their relevancy in proportion to the violence of the groups they were funding. Any church not receiving its share of frothing-at-the-mouth demands for money felt isolated from the great events of the American social movement. Thus it was that when the American Indian Movement captured a dormitory at Augustana College in Sioux Falls and presented a set of demands carefully worked out by sympathetic Lutherans in secret sessions, the Lutheran churches eagerly embraced the Indian cause. While they had not been overly enthusiastic about helping the blacks during the Civil Rights movement, some church officials felt that they could get the same kind of action from the Indians without taking a position on a social movement that would antagonize their church members.

Many Lutherans were ecstatic when informed by Indians that they were guilty of America's sins against the Indians, and they embarked on a massive program of fund-raising to pay for their alleged sins. But they were not the only victims, since the Presbyterians, Episcopalians, and Congregationalists all gleefully responded to being told that they had been responsible for nearly all of the problems of American

Indians and that they could purchase indulgences for these sins by funding the Indian activists to do whatever they felt necessary to correct the situation. By early 1971 almost every major Christian church had set up crisis funds to buy off whichever Indian protesters they might arrange to have visit them. Confrontations escalated as each group sought to become more relevant than its competitors, and the path toward destruction was clearly visible to everyone. In a real sense Christian churches bought and paid for the Indian movement and its climactic destruction of the Bureau of Indian Affairs as surely as if they had written out specific orders to sack the Bureau headquarters on a contractual basis. The churches should be made to reimburse the American taxpayer for the destruction of federal property, if any argument must be made with respect to the importance of property when discussing the incidents of the Indian movement.

Not every Indian protest was inspired by the financial rewards to be gained from the churches by playing the protest game. Many of the incidents were valid protests by a people who had suffered too much for too long. Even more, younger Indians had seen in the Civil Rights movement that the institutions of this country respond only when there is a threat to their property, or when disorder in their lives forces them to confront problems that have not been solved for generations. Yet the Civil Rights issue was peripheral at best when understood in the Indian context. The different tribal groups suffered discrimination and prejudice on a peculiarly tribal basis, and the broken treaties meant immediate hardship for the different communities. Could young Indians enter a Civil Rights movement and press for removal of discriminatory hiring practices while enjoying preference under federal law for employment in tribal programs?

Few Indians ever accepted the premises of the Civil Rights movement, and if the tribal chairmen demanded the prosecution of the Indian militants following the departure from the destroyed Bureau of Indian Affairs building, it was a weak response compared to tribal reactions on being asked to join in the Civil Rights movement and marches half a decade earlier. That the basic goals of the Civil Rights movement could not attract more than a handful of Indians at any one time should give pause to everyone. What was it that turned Indians off other than the fear that they might be identified with blacks as a minority group?

If we glance backward into American history, we may find a partial answer—at the least, an indication sufficient to raise the questions that at some point must be asked. The Civil Rights movement was probably the last full-scale effort to realize the avowed goals of the Christian religion. For better than a century, the American political system had proclaimed the brotherhood of man as seen politically in the concepts of equality of opportunity and justice equally administered under the law. While the NAACP Legal Defense and Education Fund fought a series of brilliant court battles making a goal for the great Supreme Court decisions, in the background certainly lurked the great Christian message of the brotherhood of man.

When the struggle in the South reached the point of open boycott and nonviolent protest, it was the black Christian church leaders such as Martin Luther King, Ralph Abernathy, and Andrew Young who spearheaded the movement by translating Christian doctrines into political tools of resistance and eventually conquest. In large measure, the Civil Rights movement was a movement that found its ideology, strategy, and meaning in Christian religious doctrines. King's famous letter from jail in Birmingham was not addressed to the political leaders of the South or to liberals of the North, but to the Christian churchmen of the South, who were intent on reducing the Christian religion to a comforting and spineless recital of creeds.

There had to be a point in western history at which the whole ethos of the Christian religion was placed on the agenda to discover if the whole thing worked. The Civil Rights movement became the acid test in the field of domestic relations. Before the Civil Rights movement, however, one must look at the Nuremberg trials as the moment of history in which Western Christianity achieved its greatest influence. In those trials the victorious Allied nations presumed to speak for all of civilized mankind and judged the Nazi leaders not as losers, but rather as men who had violated the basic tenets of man's civilized and religious existence. In doing so, in setting themselves up as judges, the Western nations had first to overlook their Russian allies and second affirm before all of mankind that they assumed that they stood sinless before all men and before history and were fit to judge.

After the Nuremberg trials it became more or less inevitable that the Western nations would fall victim to the moral and intellectual weaknesses in their own societies. Could one really judge Nazi leaders when in one's own nation captured German prisoners of war received better treatment than the black citizens who had captured them? No, the Civil Rights movement once Nuremberg had taken place was inevitable. From a crest in historical meaning, the logic of national identity called for an effort to realize the reality of the Christian religion on a political basis. America really had no choice but to embark eventually on a quest for post-Nuremberg meaning. That the Civil Rights movement began under the benign Eisenhower was an indication of the terrible conflicts in which America and its religious sensitivity would engage. If nothing else, Eisenhower personified the good citizen, the American Christian gentleman, the man to whom all good accrues because of his faithful adherence to the American credo.

It was this terrible inconsistency that many Indians sensed as they approached the Civil Rights movement. In attempt-

ing to distinguish Indian concerns from the concerns felt by
the black community and understood by their white allies,
many Indians began to discover their own culture; they
began to trace out the reality of their own religious experiences and began to distinguish between the technological
superiority of the white man and his moral corruption and
the falsity of his religious facade. It was during the Eisenhower years that the religious ceremonies of many of the tribes
came out in the open after many decades of suppression.

Through the 1960s the Civil Rights movement gained
power and strength, calling millions of people to commitments that many had never considered making. One
cannot but review the many martyrs of the Civil Rights
movement, black and white, to understand the violence of the
time and many religious people's depth of commitment.
From the era came men such as Malcom Boyd and Harvey
Cox, who in retrospect appear as valiant pioneers discerning
a break in the ecclesiastical curtain, yet committed and
powerless to break out of the deteriorating situation.

Perhaps the Civil Rights movement held too much promise
of a better society. The fervor it inspired in people could not
be maintained in the face of exhausting sacrifices for a few
intangible accomplishments. Within it was the implicit
promise that a better society was but a short distance into
the future, and the reality of that society became a means of
sustaining the broken heads and broken spirits of the moment. For many young people not in the social movements, the goal of discovering a reality to existence took a different track. The middle 1960s also saw the rise of drugs as
an immediate release from the complexities of modern life,
and Timothy Leary's admonition to "drop out, turn on, and
tune in" spoke of the same stability of reality in the religious
field as did King's dream of a just society. As the two
movements began to intertwine, the formation of a "counterculture" was suggested as a means of explaining the apparent

alienation between the two general modes of American existence.

Martin Luther King spoke out against Vietnam. Suddenly a new international dimension impinged upon the consciousness of America. True to his Christian ideals and with insight rarely granted to a man, King saw the pervading nature of racism and oppression that led directly from the Christian idea of history. That we were in Southeast Asia at all derived directly from our conception of ourselves as guardians of history against all movements that would upset the balance we had achieved by military and economic power alone. King saw that there could be no solution to domestic problems without a solution to international problems. And solving international problems meant giving up the Western interpretation of history and the role of Western nations in history.

Stokely Carmichael burst on the scene with his cry of Black Power, and the question of community integrity dominated conceptions of measuring social change. No longer was it possible to pass Civil Rights laws. Now the hold over local communities had to be surrendered. The idea of forming a unified and homogenous nation vanished as blacks demanded the right to dissent culturally, and other groups, as if waiting for a signal, charged into the breach in the ideology of integration. Christianity had been built on individual response to external and often internal events. A universal brotherhood of responsible citizens had been visualized in which with every man acting responsibly, no rupture of the social fabric would occur. Now it was all gone. In its place stood the racial, and later ethnic communities, demanding the right to national existence in a melting-pot society where there was to be neither Jew nor Gentile.

Finally the ecologists arrived with predictions so chilling as to frighten the strongest heart. At the present rate of deterioration, they told us, mankind could expect only a generation before the species would be finally extinguished. How had this situation come about? Some ecologists told us that it was the old Christian idea of nature: the rejection of creation as a living ecosystem and the concept of nature as depraved and an object for exploitation, nothing more. Almost immediately young whites who were attracted by ecology were accused of copping out on the Civil Rights movement. A diversion, black activists cried, a means of taking the pressure off the corrupt governmental structures that refuse to give us our rights.

What happened in the last decade is that, in all probability, the logic of Western culture and the meaning of the Christian world view which supported the institutions of Western culture were outrun by the events of the time. Brotherhood of man may be a noble ideal, but can it be achieved in any society that is not homogenous? Probably not, we discovered. At a certain point in the struggle for realization, it became apparent that goals of the Civil Rights movement could not be achieved, because people did not subscribe to them and because the goals were, after all, abstract projections of an ideal world, not descriptions of a real world.

The collapse of the Civil Rights movement, the concern with Vietnam and the war, the escape to drugs, the rise of power movements, and the return to Mother Earth can all be understood as desperate efforts of groups of people to flee the abstract and find authenticity, wherever it could be found. It was at this point that Indians became popular, and the vast and rapid interest that was generated in Indians as seen in literature would seem to indicate that America was looking for more than another minority group with which to play. The stoic and heroic red man, who had somehow gotten along in an almost idyllic existence prior to the coming of the white man, seemed to hold the key to survival and any meaning that America would now find for itself.

If America was fooling itself, American Indians doubly fooled themselves. Every meeting, every convention, every gathering featured Indian spokesmen enthusiastically telling those assembled that the day of the American Indian was at hand. Ecological advertisements featured Indian actors paddling their canoes through polluted waters with tears running down their faces. Indians were ecstatic—and mistaken. People began inquiring about the basic values of Indian life, and the rhetoric began to flow. Optimism ran rampant; it appeared as if for the first time Indians would be allowed to speak freely.

Almost immediately Indians came into contact with the world outside their tribal experiences. The churches insisted on funding activist groups' demonstrations to the consternation of tribal officials. Indian activists became, in many instances, little more than puppets dancing for the liberal dollars. Many felt it more important to capture a mountain and the evening headlines than to fight against continuing confiscation of lands via termination. The Colville Reservation was nearly terminated for lack of people to oppose the policy, while a thousand miles south hundreds of young Indians milled around on Alcatraz looking for something to do.[2]

Tribal officials with a heady sense of power demanded and received lucrative government contracts under the new policy of self-determination, and by taking the federal funds forever surrendered their rights to criticize the policies of the Bureau of Indian Affairs. Every new idea proposed in Indian conferences resulted in the creation of a new national organization of Indians. The emotional conflicts of interest mounted, and political wars for control of large organizations with large budgets intensified to the point of near-violence. What America would not see and American Indians unfortunately could not see was that they both were attempting to relate to the Indians of yesteryear.

America attempted to find authenticity in American Indians, manifesting this effort in a number of diverse ways some of which bordered on the bizarre. Many years before William Carlos Williams wrote: "The land! Don't you feel it? Doesn't it make you want to go out and lift dead Indians tenderly from their graves, to steal from them—as if it must be clinging even to their corpses—some authenticity."[3]

In 1971, of course, many Americans did just that. Exhausted spiritually, they began seeking the reality of Indian life in the American Indians' bones and burial places. That Christian peoples or even quasi-Christian peoples could commit such an outrage is perhaps an indication of the extent of their desperation. And if these were not Christians committing these acts, why did not the "real" Christians raise their voices in protest? Especially in the Iowa incident recounted earlier, the voices of even the "true" Christians were notably stilled.

Among the Indian activists a tremendous interest in tribal religions manifested itself early in the movement. Attendance at tribal ceremonies became almost as necessary as attendance at protests. The American Indian Movement became so attached to the tribal religious ceremonies that more experienced Indians began referring to them as the Indian version of the "Jesus freaks." But few Indians realized the extent to which the world had changed since the days of Chief Joseph. It was no longer feasible to charge the wagon train, yet the tactics and emotions of the activists led directly to that state of mind. During the occupation of the Bureau of Indian Affairs headquarters, many observers noted that some of the people were ready and willing to die in combat rather than give an inch in the negotiations. It was almost as if the Ghost Dance had returned with its tragic vision of Wounded Knee.

What we have basically experienced in the recent Indian interest and the ensuing uprising in November of 1972 has been a tragic case of simultaneous arrival by all segments of

American society at a state of religious crisis of unsuspected proportions. Americans are searching for a different religious understanding of the world, and in spite of the apparently short-lived Jesus movement, many people are seeking answers in American Indian religions, which must involve some form of reconciliation with the American Indian and his lands.

While the American Indian belief in the religious nature of lands has been neglected by non-Indian peoples, it has also been buffeted about by Indians themselves in recent years. The desperate nature of the Indian activist movement in reclaiming lands could be expressed best in political confrontations, but the understanding of the spiritual nature of lands still remained as an experience shared more by traditional and older Indians than by activists. Outside of *Seven Arrows* by Storm and speeches by Thomas Banyaca and some of the Hopi leaders, there has been a sparsity of effort made by Indians to educate Americans on the complexities of living with a particular land.

The American white man is the victim of a process long predicted. Nietzsche and Kierkegaard both foresaw nearly a century ago a tragic breakdown in both the vision and values of Western man. For Kierkegaard the solution to the problem became the exercise of an incredible power of will, which would lead Western man back to the world's fundamental realities, as he knew it. Purity of heart, Kierkegaard thought, is to will one thing—the good, and having willed the good, it would eventually follow, although few people would realize the tremendous spiritual and psychological costs required.

Nietzsche announced the death of God and the creation of the superman, perhaps glorifying so much in the will to power that he could not see the moral flaw in the exercise of energy without a benign goal as a precondition. In the rise and fall of National Socialism, we found Nietzsche's superman coupled with an incomplete, distorted theory of genetic science and history. Both Kierkegaard and Nietzsche attempted to solve the problem of the decay of the Western vision of the world by using an Avis approach: Try harder. Yet their suggestions were so abstract as to prove demoniac in the practical area of daily life.

A more common sense approach to solving the problem of Western moral and intellectual inadequacies came in the earlier years of this century, when Walter Rauschenbusch (1861-1918) and others promulgated the social gospel. They visualized the fulfillment of the Christian kingdom on earth in the social reform movements of the American political arena. Labor organization and restrictive laws on child labor and pure foods became a realization for them of the Western peoples' potential for creating a heavenly society without divine intervention.

When the social gospel was brought into full confrontation with the American political system in the Civil Rights movement, it proved as ephemeral as any other doctrine. While advances were made in legislation, attitudes simply hardened around other things that politically could not be changed. Eventually the conservative backlash overwhelmed the social gospel, when the Richard Nixon/Spiro Agnew/ Billy Graham theology of unquestioning submission to political decisions and concentration on a "personal relationship" with God gained popularity. For a substantial number of Americans, there are no answers needed for there are no questions to be asked. Yet because the drama is continually played out in religious terminology, we must conclude that the basic unanswered question is that of religious breakdown.

Perhaps we have now come to realize that Western man cannot find his way in society either by demythologizing his condition as Kierkegaard, Nietzsche, and the social gospel people have attempted or remythologizing it as Billy Graham and the Fundamentalists have tried to do. Perhaps an entirely new analysis of the nature of society must be undertaken, perhaps a new understanding of the nature of religion must be found. Recent literature would appear to indicate that people are already venturing on new paths of social analysis, trying to describe for us the task that lies ahead. We must begin to take our intellectual pioneers seriously for the first time in our existence.

Gary Wills, for example, finds in two books, *Nixon Agonistes* and *Bare Ruined Choirs,* sufficient reason to believe that a political and religious turning point has occurred in the last decade. James Michener in *A Quality of Life* projects a sense of search for a new conception of our position in social history, finding a religious dimension about to be unveiled. The analysis of Harvey Cox in *The Secular City* remains valid for the segment of society that affects us most vitally—the affluent, educated urban man, who is found in embarrassing numbers in educational institutions and the communications media.

While Charles Reich bubbles with optimism in *The Greening of America,* and we find ourselves unable to justify it, his essay on "The New Property" easily qualifies as a crucial analysis of our contemporary problem in understanding the nature of wealth and income. Even more important, perhaps, Alvin Toffler's *Future Shock* and Vance Packard's *A Nation of Strangers* indicate the nature of change in which we are involved. Can we survive increasing speed and constant migration and hold the same religious convictions about the world that men held two centuries ago? Or that they held even a century ago? Or in the previous decade?

Almost everywhere we turn whether we be red, white, black, brown, or yellow, we are confronted with the necessity of renewing our vision of the totality of our existence, our understanding of the nature of the universe, and the paths by which we can move forward as diverse peoples upon the continent. At no point, however, have we dug sufficiently into the nature of the problems we face to tear ourselves away from traditional assumptions and find a place to stand from which we can view the breadth and depth of the task.

The basic divergence of viewpoints between American Indians and the rest of American society must be seen, as mentioned before, in the conception of land, and the choice appears to be between conceiving of land as either a subject or an object. This analysis agrees, strangely, with the view expressed by Albert Camus in *The Rebel,* an analysis of death and suicide. Camus finds that:

> The profound conflict in this century is perhaps not so much between the German ideologies of history and Christian political concepts, which in a certain way are accomplices, as between German dreams and Mediterranean traditions . . . in other words between history and nature.

> Christianity, no doubt, was only able to conquer its catholicity by assimilating as much as it could of Greek thought. But when the Church dissipated its Mediterranean heritage, it placed the emphasis on history to the detriment of nature, caused the Gothic to triumph over the romance, and, destroying a limit in itself, has made increasing claims to temporal power and historical dynamism. When nature ceases to be an object of contemplation and admiration, it can be nothing more than material for an action that aims at transforming it. These tendencies—and not the concepts of mediation, which would have comprised the real strength of Christianity—are triumphing, in modern times, to the detriment of Christianity itself, by an inevitable turn of events.[4]

If, as Camus would define it, the choice of this century is between history and nature, and the rise of temporal power as a Christian goal has overshadowed its ability to mediate, then it would appear as if the twentieth century will be a time when fundamental religious conceptions must be overhauled.

Perhaps nowhere in Western culture is Gothic Christianity as defined by Camus so apparently strong as in the United

States. Unhampered by the traditional tie between church and state, the American continent has seen a great proliferation of Christian sects that at least appear to exert a civilizing influence in American society. That this influence is often minimal cannot be doubted in view of the recent Vietnam experience and the domestic conflicts among the haves and havenots and the respective racial groups.

The domestic struggles, however, have not been a total political or religious disaster; in many senses the struggles of the last decade have given a much broader meaning to the nature of American citizenship than it ever enjoyed before. Much of the political polarization has been sparked by the various types of Christianity present and active on the American scene. From the major traditional Protestant denominations on what could be called the domestic left to the flag-waving Fundamentalists on the right, Christians of all persuasions have been involved in either the foreign or domestic affairs of the last decade.

Neither left-wing nor right-wing interpretations of Christianity has been able to impress its views on its polar opposite. While the Fundamentalist churches appear at present to be attracting a much greater following, the political causes they apparently espouse would certainly indicate an intellectual bankruptcy of the most profound degree. More established Protestant churches involved to a greater degree in Civil Rights and poverty-type programs likewise seem to depend on a sterile conception of social problems and social change, and while they are more in tune with actual social conditions than their brothers on the right, they are more concerned with their collective guilt as WASPs than with providing any significant leadership in solving social problems.

In the area of ecology more than any other field, the Christian churches appear to be helpless. It is precisely this field that forms the cutting practical edge of which Albert

Camus speaks. In the conception of man's religious understanding neither left-wing or right-wing Christianity appears
to understand the nature of the ecological disaster facing us.
Rather they both seem to vest their faith in the miraculous
ability of science to solve the problem of the dissipation of
limited resources.

The contemporary Christian mythos has been developed
over a period of two centuries in which the exploitation of
human and natural resources became increasingly sophisticated. With the singular concern for historical reality seen
in its propensity to missionize, Christianity has avoided any
rigorous consideration of ecological factors in favor of
continuous efforts to realize the Kingdom of God on earth. As
the twentieth century of Christian existence closes with social
and political chaos perhaps symbolized best by Lieutenant
Calley and extreme racial tensions in the Western countries,
we can conclude that the effort to build the nations of
Western civilization as prototypes of the Kingdom of God has
been largely for naught.

The very diversity of the American people as revealed in
the recent racial and ethnic power movements has probably
given American Christianity a handicap that the domestic
churches of no other nation have had to face. By the same
token the presence of such diversity enables the United States
more than any other nation to undertake specific experiments
in solving social and ecological problems. The present
orientation of American intellectuals is not promising. Analysis appears to be centered on the possible minor adjustments
to the social theories that came to dominate the 1960s rather
than to a fundamental revision of our conception of the
nature of our existence.

As against the various suggested analyses of misconceived
social theories of the last decade, we have seen an increasing
reliance on the development of citizens groups, chief of which
is John Gardner's Common Cause, which primarily seeks
increased activity and fails to demand examination of the

basic assumptions about the nature of man and society. The deterioration of American community life as recorded in Vance Packard's *A Nation of Strangers* would seem to indicate that rootlessness has become the major feature of American existence. Precisely how responsibly exercised citizenship can flourish in this situation, which is being increasingly aggravated by the faster pace of existence described in Toffler's *Future Shock,* is apparently no consideration of the new citizenship movement.

Nearly half a century ago Chief Luther Standing Bear of the Sioux tribe commented on this strange inability of the white man to come to grips with the reality of American existence:

> The white man does not understand America. He is too far removed from its formative processes. The roots of the tree of his life have not yet grasped the rock and soil. The white man is still troubled by primitive fears; he still has in his consciousness the perils of this frontier continent, some of its fastnesses not yet having yielded to his questing footsteps and inquiring eyes. He shudders still with the memory of the loss of his forefathers upon its scorching deserts and forbidding mountaintops. The man from Europe is still a foreigner and an alien. And he still hates the man who questioned his path across the continent.

> But in the Indian the spirit of the land is still vested; it will be until other men are able to divine and meet its rhythm. Men must be born and reborn to belong. Their bodies must be formed of the dust of their forefathers' bones. [5]

It may not be sufficient, therefore, to advocate a higher ethical content to political, religious, and business activities or to seek in education an answer to what must presumably be a philosophical attitude toward existence rather than a specific belief or set of beliefs about existence. Attempting to shift the American/Western/Christian outlook from a preoccupation with a particular history and the great concern with time to an examination of spaces, places, and lands requires more than the relatively simple admission of guilt before ecological gurus. Rather a total reorientation as to the impact of viewing life in different categories must be established. Robert Ardrey's famous study, *The Territorial Imperative,* indicates the strong influence of "living space" on living species. As such it forms a basic reference point from which new considerations can be understood.

Both the Mediterranean heritage of Western Christianity and the American heritage of the American Indian tribes do not require a redefinition of spaces and places in terms of temporal concepts, but rather a relinquishment of temporal attitudes altogether and an acknowledgment of the reality of places, the essential need of life systems for spaces, and the reformation of social and political ideas around communal rather than individual considerations.

When social problems of domestic America are viewed in this light, it becomes quickly apparent that ideologically the domestic world is characterized by the dichotomy of American Indian and immigrant theories of social existence: Those who have been formed of the dust of their forefathers' bones, and those who were never able to release their spirits to the realities of the continent. One could not conceive, for example, of an American Indian feeling "lost" or alienated on the North American lands—only in the cities and other artificial constructs of the continent.

D. H. Lawrence once remarked that while the American Indian would never again control the continent, he would forever haunt it. Perhaps the ultimate meaning of control is the ability to haunt. We come, then, to both a necessity to change and a possibility to do so. In attempting to contrast the worldviews of the American Indian with the imported assumptions of the immigrants who have been unable to find roots in this land, we can do no worse than to identify alternative paths to choose. The choice, of course, is another matter.

Chapter 5
Thinking
in Time and Space

THE DIVISION OF domestic ideologies may appear to be quite artificial to many people. Traditionally we have been taught to define differences neither by ancestral backgrounds nor cultural attitudes but by political persuasions. Conservative and liberal, terms initially that described political philosophies, have thus taken on the aspect of being able to stand for cultural attitudes of fairly distinct content. Liberals appear to have more sympathy for humanity, while conservatives worship corporate freedom and self-help doctrines underscoring individual responsibility. The basic philosophical differences between liberals and conservatives are not fundamental, however, since both find in the idea of history a thesis by which they can validate their ideas.

When the domestic ideology is divided according to American Indian and Western European immigrant, however, the fundamental difference is one of great philosophical importance. American Indians hold their lands—places—as having the highest possible meaning, and all their statements are made with this reference point in mind. Immigrants review the movement of their ancestors across the continent as a steady progression of basically good events and experiences, thereby placing history—time—in the best possible light. When one group is concerned with the philosophical problem of space and the other with the philosophical problem of time, then the statements of either group do not make much sense when transferred from one context to the other without the proper consideration of what is happening.

Western European peoples have never learned to consider the nature of the world discerned from a spatial point of view. And a singular difficulty faces peoples of Western European heritage in making a transition from thinking in terms of time to thinking in terms of space. The very essence of Western European identity involves the assumption that time proceeds in a linear fashion; further it assumes that at a particular point in the unraveling of this sequence, the peoples of Western Europe became the guardians of mankind. The same ideology that sparked the Crusades, the Age of Exploration, the Age of Imperialism, and the recent crusade against Communism all involve the affirmation that time is peculiarly related to the destiny of the people of Western Europe. And later, of course, the United States.

The postwar generation of which we are a part has refused to accept any alteration of this fundamental premise. It is particularly revealing that the first major doctrine enunciated as an anti-Communist foreign policy was that of containment. In containment it was believed the spread of Communism would be restricted to certain geographical areas from which no further intrusions of Communist ideologies could emanate. The anachronistic nature of this theory should be apparent. Western political ideas came to depend on spacial restrictions of what were essentially non-spatial ideas. The inherent contradiction of opposing dissimilar definitions within a single theory proved fruitless to the colonial powers in Southeast Asia, Africa, and India.

Without venturing further into the field of foreign affairs, it may be well to note in passing that the determination of two American Presidents not to be the "first to lose a war," when winning that war in any final sense would have meant total destruction of a land and a people, would seem to indicate the extent to which Western peoples—and particularly Americans—have taken the dimension of time as an absolute value. Our withdrawal from Southeast Asia would seem to show that in some collisions, history is clearly negated by geography. We have seen this phenomenon before in the two classic, unsuccessful attempts by Napoleon and Hitler to conquer Russia, in which the country's vast interior subdued military forces that appeared to be riding the crest of historical change.

The disclaimer of colonialism in recent years has presented Western peoples with a major dilemma. Deprived of their traditional source of wealth from the undeveloped and former colonial nations, they now have little choice but to seek ways of rechanneling their present wealth through the various forms of social organization already present domestically. A certain stasis has been achieved, perhaps unwittingly, which means a major shift in political thinking among Western peoples. The creation of wealth today is more dependent on new technology than on the exploitation of untapped resources. That is not to say that exploitation of mineral and other resources will not continue. As undeveloped nations continue their own growth, severe modifications of exploitation must occur as well as more sophisticated forms of colonialism, if Western countries are not to suffer economic collapse.

It is doubtful if very many Americans understand the fundamental nature of this shift from the colonialist attitude. At best it means a humanization of peoples who for centuries were considered merely producers of raw materials and consumers of those products they were allowed to share. At worst the end of one form of colonialism means the beginning of a movement to feudalize political systems around the globe so as to stabilize the economic conditions of the more affluent nations. Either approach means that the ecological problem is not dealt with, the problem of technological dehumanization is not reduced, and the breakdown of individual and community identity is not reversed.

There can be little doubt that a major part of the Western world is now suffering from an increasingly complicated task of revitalizing institutions to prevent collapse. Revitalization has been primarily one of attempting to force outmoded institutions to respond to novel situations for which they were not created. If we take Alvin Toffler's *Future Shock* seriously (and there does not seem to be sufficient reason to consider it a trivial analysis), or if we recognize the logical conclusion of both Buckminster Fuller and Marshall McLuhan, we reach neither a planet Earth of a spaceship nature nor an instantaneous universe of communications, but the disappearance of time itself as a limiting factor of our experience. In a world in which communications are nearly instantaneous and simultaneous experiences are possible, it must be space that in a fundamental way distinguishes us from one another, not time.

The world, therefore, is not a global village so much as a series of non-homogeneous pockets of identity that must be thrust into eventual conflict, because they represent different arrangements of emotional energy. What these pockets of energy will produce, how they will understand themselves, and what mini-movements will emerge from them are among the unanswered questions of our time. If we believe that religion has a presence in human societies in any fundamental sense, then we can no longer speak of universal religions in the customary manner. Rather we must be prepared to confront religion and religious activities in new and novel ways. The absence of a homogeneous sense of time, a universal history, must certainly make its appearance if it has not already done so.

Beneath the mini-movements on the local level, we will most certainly find the emergence of religious movements that appear out of time, movements that have been somehow triggered either by the influences of the places in which they have originated or movements of restoration that seek to invoke some type of authentic religious experience to validate the identity of the emotional pocket. Already we are finding a fascination with the satanic in southern California, long a hotbed of Fundamental Christianity, coupled with a determined drive to return to the comforting and reasonably debilitating religion of yesteryear.

What may prove to be particularly unnerving will be the apparent contradiction in social issues as triggered by the various currents of emotion moving in particular locations. In the last election the presence of a marijuana proposition and a rigid smut proposition on the California ballot may have indicated that the redefinition of religious principles has already begun to manifest itself. The unfortunate factor in both propositions was that both depended for their validity on traditional assumptions of social reality. Neither attempted to effect a fundamental change in conceptions of reality, only to move backward or forward along the traditional time scale of values.

The needed basic change depends on a realization of the revolutionary reorientation of definitions that must occur when time is negated and space becomes more dominant. Religion has often been seen as an evolutionary process in which mankind evolves a monotheistic conception of divinity by a gradual reduction of a pantheon to a single deity. The reality of religion thus becomes its ability to explain the universe, not to experience it. Creeds and beliefs replace immediate apprehension of whatever relationship may exist with higher powers. As time becomes less important in understanding religion, the whole monotheistic thesis is threatened. Yet our supernatural experiences do not necessarily lead to a monotheistic conclusion.

So too with one of the related concepts of monotheism, that of revelation. In traditional terms a revelation occurs at a point in time, and succeeding generations are more dependent on their understanding of the original revelation than upon their immediate experience of deity. Almost all of the world religions are partially dependent on a revelation at some point in history. Contemporary people are more dependent on the validity of the original revelation of their religion in an educational sense than they are on their own immediate experience in a qualitative sense. For many religions this dependence means that belief replaces experience, and proofs of a logical nature are more relevant than additional revelations.

Revelations must somehow be phrased in the cultural beliefs, languages, and worldviews of the time in which they occurred. As times change and cultures become more sophisticated, sciences come to present a broader view of the universe, and languages become infused with foreign words and concepts, and the original revelation also takes on a different aspect. Revelation has generally been considered as a specific body of truth related to a particular individual at a specific time. This glimpse into the eternal, as it were, is too often taken as universally valid for all times and places. If the universal nature of religions has not been the subject of debate, it should be our immediate concern.

In shifting from temporal concepts to spatial terms, we find that a revelation is not so much the period of time in which it occurs as the place it may occur. Revelation becomes a particular experience at a particular place, no universal truth emerging but an awareness arising that certain places have a qualitative holiness over and above other places. The universality of truth then becomes the relevance of the experience for a community of people, not its continual adjustment to evolving scientific and philosophical conceptions of the universe.

Holy places are well known in what have been classified as primitive religions. The vast majority of Indian tribal religions have a center at a particular place, be it river, mountain, plateau, valley, or other natural feature. Many of the smaller nonuniversal religions also depend on a number of holy places for the practice of their religious activities. In part the affirmation of the existence of holy places confirms tribal peoples' rootedness, which Western man is peculiarly without. The development of shrines in the religious life of the practioners of world religions would seem to indicate that this spatial dimension cannot be avoided as men seek religious experiences. Why then must theological reality be defined solely in temporal terms as in Christianity?

One of the features of Western religious practice has been the dependence on teaching and preaching techniques. The Christian religion has been singularly involved with proclamations of its "good news," primarily through missionary activity and exhortations to its believers of the efficacy of its ethical system. It places a major reliance on the possibility of individual personality change in seeking followers. It has, however, been notoriously inept at invoking within its adherents a high standard of conduct.

Changing the conception of religious reality from temporal to spatial terms involves severely downgrading the teaching/preaching aspect of religious activity. Rearrangement of individual behavioral patterns is incidental to communal involvement in ceremonies and the continual renewing of community relationships with the holy places of revelation. Ethics flow from the ongoing life of the community and are virtually indistinguishable from tribal or communal customs. There is little dependence, either on an individual or community basis, on the concept of progress. Value judgments involve present community reality and not reliance on past or future golden ages toward which the community is allegedly moving or from which the community has veered.

In conjunction with this notion, the severence of religious reality from the other aspects of community experience is not as distinct. A religion defined according to temporal considerations is placed continually on the defensive in maintaining its control over historical events. If, like the Hebrews of the Old Testament, political, economic, and cultural events can be interpreted as religious events, the religious time and the secular time can be made to appear to coincide. If, however, the separation becomes more or less permanent, as in Christianity and Western concepts of history, then religion becomes a function of political interpretations as in the Manifest Destiny theories of American history, or it becomes secularized as an economic determinism as in Communist theories of history. Either way the religion soon becomes helpless to intervene in the events of real life, except in a peripheral and oblique manner.

The variety of mankind's religious forms has often been understood as involving various stages of community existence. In a theological interpretation that sees time as predominant, the only relationship that can occur between religions is one of judging according to preconditioned cultural values. From this type of attitude, stretching along a historical time scale, religious reality is judged according to the cultural technology produced by the society. The ultimate nature of religious activity becomes secondary to the material productions demonstrable by the particular group.

Eliminating temporal considerations from an examination of religious activities, we are left with the question of the function of religion in societies. Do religions differ because they involve different relationships between a community and the lands on which it lives? One would be led to consider this relatively simple question for the first time in a new sense by observing the different religions in relation to the lands on which they live and not to their supposed position along an evolutionary scale. The rain dance of the Southwestern

Indians, for example, is probably almost totally dependent upon the nature of the lands on which those Indians live. For example, one cannot imagine the Indians of the Pacific Northwest needing or having a rain dance. Instead, therefore, of attempting to find categories to explain the development of each religion over a period of time, we are led more to an examination of the nature of the lands upon which the community must exist. Religion thus becomes a present examination of community needs and values, not a progression of conceptual advances.

Time has an unusual limitation. It must begin and end at some real points, or it must be conceived as cyclical in nature, endlessly allowing the repetitions of patterns of possibilities. Judgment inevitably intrudes into the conception of religious reality whenever a temporal definition is used. Almost always the temporal consideration revolves around the problem of good and evil, and the inconsistencies that arise as this basic relationship is defined almost always turn religious beliefs into ineffectual systems of ethics.

Space has limitations that are primarily geographical, and any sense of time arising within the religious experience becomes secondary to present geographical existence. The danger that appears to be lurking in spatial conceptions of religion is the effect of missionary activity on a religion. Can it leave the land of its nativity and embark on a program of world or continental conquest without losing its religious essence in favor of purely political or economic considerations? Are ceremonies restricted to particular places, and do they become useless in a foreign land? These questions have never been raised in a fundamental manner within Western religious circles, because of the preemption of temporal considerations by Christian theology.

The problem of religious imagery is also confounded when we shift from temporal patterns of explanation. The procedure by which religious imagery arises is still the subject of great debate among theologians. It is such a serious problem it has jumped the boundaries of religious thought and has also become the subject of psychoanalytical investigation. How do men conceive of the symbols, doctrines, insights, and sequences in which we find religious ideas expressed? How do we come to conceive deity in certain forms and not others? Theological explanations that depend on temporal world-views would appear to be relatively helpless in examining this question. Perhaps the best that can be said is that temporal theologians place great reliance upon the poetic imagination as the source of religious symbolism. The best and most lofty considerations of a society or culture over a period of time eventually distill themselves into a poetic mythology that comes to express the community's experienced realities. That is about as close as we can come when using temporal conceptions of religious reality—eventual distillation of concepts and symbols.

If the spatial dimension of religion is considered, the answer would appear to be fairly clear. *Something* is observed or experienced by a community, and the symbols and sequences of the mythology are given together in an event that appears so much out of the ordinary experiential sequence as to impress itself upon the collective memories of the community for a sufficiently long duration of time. The basic myth may be refined to some extent, but it is not subject to very much editing, since it is the common property of the community, not the exclusive property of the community's poets or religious leaders.

When considering the multitude of flood stories, for example, we can suggest the possibility of a planetwide flood at some specific time, because of the appearance of the story in many diverse religious traditions. But only if we can accept spatial dimensions to religion can we reach this conclusion, because the flood, experienced in a number of places, gave rise to the legends that recorded memories of the flood.

Remaining committed to temporal concepts, we can only conclude that at a certain stage in evolution it became necessary for societies—extremely diverse and with little in common—to have evolved a myth about a flood. Often this is
precisely the contention, and the universal need for baptism
is advanced as sufficient reason for the creation of the story.
Yet all religious traditions have not depended on baptism.

We are virtually helpless to understand the very symbols,
stories, doctrines, and ideals that religions have traditionally
espoused if we are content to define religion according to
temporal terms of explanation. Once we leave time behind
and consider the nature of geographical events of extraordi-
nary nature, we can begin to project the possibilities for
understanding the nature of religious language and the
efficacy of religious doctrines as an explanation of man's
religious experiences. It is, if we will consider it, a very
different thing to create a religion out of the best of ideas,
symbols, and explanations.

There appears to be a peculiar relationship between
thinking in temporal and spatial terms. We are inevitably
involved, whether we like it or not, with time, but when
attempting to explain the nature of our experiences, we are
often not necessarily involved with spatial considerations
once we have taken time seriously. The whole nature of the
subject of ethics appears to validate this peculiarity. Ethical
systems are notorious for having the ability to relate concepts
and doctrines to every consideration, except the practical
situations with which we become involved. Ideology un-
leashed without being limited to the real world proves
demoniac at best. One could project, therefore, that space
must in a certain sense precede time as a consideration for
thought. If time becomes our primary consideration, we
never seem to arrive at the reality of our existence in places
but instead are always directed to experiential interpretations
rather than to the experiences themselves.

A great segment of the American public has been rudely pushed beyond the traditional temporal doctrines of Western man by the influence of the modern communications media. This is the true nature of the problem of postwar American society. The meaninglessness and alienation discernible in our generation results partially from our allowing time to consume space. The shift in thinking from temporal considerations to spatial considerations may be seen in a number of mini-movements by which we are struggling to define American society. Ecology, the new left politics, self-determination of goals by local communities, and citizenship participation all seem to be efforts to recapture a sense of place and a rejection of the traditional American dependence on progress—a temporal concept—as the measure of American identity.

A great many other considerations could be made in attempting to define how our consciousness is gradually shifting away from Western cultural and religious patterns. Development schemes of the federal government began as early as the Great Depression, when the Tennessee Valley Authority marked the first departure in programming from traditional patterns—railroads, settlement, and industrial development—to considerations of the regional nature of growth. Since that time the Missouri Valley Authority, the Appalachian Development Authority, the Four Corners Development Authority, and the river compacts of states have evolved, so that geographic considerations are playing a much more important role in how we conceive social, economic, and political problems.

The field of religion has been peculiarly isolated from this development in American thought. Rather, theological considerations have fluctuated from Fundamentalism to social gospel and back. If we consider the social gospel and activist church involvement in social problems such as Civil Rights as an indication of concern with the problems of this world and land, we can find even in the theological movements of the past generation a movement away from temporal considerations.

It is doubtful if American society can move very far or very significantly without a major revolution in theological concepts. In a very real sense religious doctrines define the brooding sense of identity without which societies appear helpless to function. The present theological vacuum is being filled to a great degree by efforts to establish exotic religions in America. The great appeal of oriental religions that appear to provide a meaning to contemporary answers, the demonism and fascination with satanic cults, and the rejection of traditional mainline denominations for the simplicity of Fundamentalism all seem to indicate that a comprehensive effort to derive a new religious conception of the world is badly needed.

Before we can have a new theological understanding of our situation, however, the tools of analysis of religious ideas must be changed. This will require a tremendous reversal of ideas that have been held by Western peoples, particularly Christians, for many centuries. Perhaps religions can answer only a few questions concerning our existence; Christian doctrines have attempted in the past to answer everything. Perhaps we will find that the present situation makes it impossible for religion to function at all; perhaps we are stuck with psychodrama and other scientific techniques.

Many of mankind's religions have been held in deepest contempt because they do not in some manner measure up to the definitions of religion as promulgated by Western/Christian ideas of the nature of religion. They were held invalid, not because they did not provide an understanding of the universe with which that particular society was confronted, but because they did not coincide with ideas held by Western society that is heavily dependent on its technology and nearly independent of its religious ideology.

In almost every instance in which other religions were considered as invalid, it was because the categories of explanation were those derived primarily from temporal considerations of how the world ought to be. If the categories are turned around and the Christian religion is judged by nontemporal categories, the story becomes somewhat different. In most instances Christianity has either no answer or an extremely inadequate answer to the problems that arise. The difference is notable. While Christianity can project the reality of the afterlife—time and eternity—it appears to be incapable of providing any reality to the life in which we are here and now presently engaged—space and the planet Earth.

American Indian tribal religions are among those so downgraded, because they did not fall into the easily constructed categories of religion as defined with temporal concepts and doctrines. Yet in a variety of ways the American public, searching for a sense of authenticity that it cannot find in its own tradition, is turning to the American Indian as it wishes to visualize him. It is not simply the nobility of the novelists or the tragic vision of the historians that America is seeking. In a very real sense, the quest is for the religious insight of the American Indian.

In seeking the religious reality behind the American Indian tribal existence, Americans are in fact attempting to come to grips with the land that produced the Indian tribal cultures and their vision of community. Even if they avoid American Indians completely, those Americans seeking a more comprehensive and meaningful life are retracing the steps taken centuries before by Indian tribes as they attempted to come to grips with this land. Recently Congress discussed compensation as a principle of criminal law. The days of the oriental potentate and justice as vengeance may be closing. If so, would not the religion that sees deity as the stern judge of mankind also be fading?

In the pages to come we will deliberately place several concepts of general religious interest under examination. We shall attempt to define in Western terms that nature of Indian tribal religions as they differ in their method of framing questions from a predominantly spatial conception of reality. And we shall discuss traditional Christian solutions to these questions, comparing the two types of answers to learn if any distinct differences do in fact exist.

We cannot, of course, pretend to give an exhaustive answer to any particular question or to present a final definition of either Indian tribal religions or traditional Christian ideas. What is important is that alternative methods of asking questions or of viewing the world may arise. By learning where differences can or do occur at least one thing may become clear. Before any final solution to American history can occur, a reconciliation must be effected between the spiritual owner of the land—the American Indian—and the political owner of the land—the American white man. Guilt and accusations cannot continue to revolve in a vacuum without some effort at solution.

In suggesting a process of reconciliation, we may perhaps find a new avenue for social movements by which the rest of our society can come to understand new approaches through which it can find itself. In view of the present confusion and divergence of energies, even to suggest a method of reconciliation would appear to be fruitful.

Chapter 6

The Problem of Creation

INDIAN TRIBAL RELIGIONS and Christianity differ considerably on numerous theological points, but a very major distinction that can be made between the two types of thinking concerns the idea of creation. Christianity has traditionally appeared to place its major emphasis on creation as a specific event while the Indian tribal religions could be said to consider creation as an ecosystem present in a definable place. In this distinction we have again the fundamental problem of whether we consider the reality of our experience as capable of being described in terms of space or time—as what happened "here," or what happened "then."

Both religions can be said to agree on the role and activity of a creator. Outside of that specific thing, there would appear to be little that the two views share. Tribal religions appear to be thereafter confronted with the question of the interrelationship of all things. Christians see creation as the beginning event of a linear time sequence in which a divine plan is worked out, the conclusion of the sequence being an act of destruction bringing the world to an end. The beginning and end of time are of no apparent concern for many tribal religions.

But the act of creation is a singularly important event for the Christian. It describes the sequence in which the tangible features of man's existence are brought into being, and although some sermons have made much of the element of light that appears in the creation account of Genesis and the prologue of the Gospel according to St. John, the similarity of the two books and their use of light do not appear to be of crucial importance in the doctrine of creation. For the Christian it would appear that the importance of the creation event is that it sets the scene for an understanding of the entrance of sin into the world.

Intimately tied with the actual creation event in the Christian theological scheme is the appearance of the first people—Adam and Eve. They are made after the image of God. It is important that this point be recognized, as it has affected popular conceptions held by Christians and seems to have some relevance to central theological doctrines. As the Genesis story relates that the first people were made after God's image, Christians, although not necessarily their Hebrew predecessors and Jewish contemporaries, have popularly conceived God as having a form similar to man. That is to say, God looks like a man. Paintings represent Him generally as an old man, deriving perhaps from the old Hebrew conception of the "Ancient of Days."

The first distinction between Indian tribal religions and Christianity would appear to be in the manner in which deity is popularly conceived. The overwhelming majority of American Indian tribal religions refused to represent deity anthropomorphically.[1] To be sure, many tribes used the term "grandfather" when praying to God, but there was no effort to use that concept as the basis for a theological doctrine by which a series of complex relationships and related doctrines could be developed. While there was an acknowledgment that the Great Spirit has some resemblance to the role of a grandfather in the tribal society, there was no great demand to have a "personal relationship" with the Great Spirit in the same manner as popular Christianity has emphasized personal relationships with God. [2]

The difference between conceiving God as an anthropomorphic being and as an undefinable presence carries over into the distinction in the views of creation. Closely following the creation of the world in Christian theology comes the disobedience of man, Adam, in eating the forbidden fruit growing on a tree in the Garden of Eden. In this act as recorded in Genesis, mankind "fell" from God's grace and was driven out of the garden by the angry God. The major thesis of the Christian religion is thus contained in its creation story, since it is for the redemption of man that the atonement of Jesus of Nazareth is considered to make sense.

With the fall of Adam the rest of nature also falls out of grace with God, Adam being a surrogate from the whole of creation in a very real sense. This particular point has been a very difficult problem for Christian theologians. While it adequately explains the entrance of evil into the world, just how it could occur in a universe conceived as perfect has been difficult for theologians to answer. St. Augustine preferred to think that God himself had taken the form of the snake that, in the story, talked Eve into eating the forbidden fruit. [3] St. Augustine's solution has not generally been accepted, even though it appears to explain the logical sequence.

Perhaps of more importance are two aspects of the Christian doctrine of creation bearing directly on us today. One aspect is that the natural world is thereafter considered as corrupted, and it becomes theoretically beyond redemption. Many Christian theologians have attempted to avoid this conclusion, but it appears to have been a central doctrine of the Christian religion during most of the Christian era. No less a thinker than Paul Tillich attempted to reconstruct the doctrine into more satisfying terms that would be acceptable to the modern world. In a rather complex analysis in his *Systematic Theology,* Tillich wrestled with the problem:

> Christianity must reject the idealistic separation of an innocent nature from guilty man. Such a rejection has become comparatively easy in our period because of the insights gained about the growth of man and his relation to nature within and outside himself. First, it can be shown that in the development of man there is no absolute discontinuity between animal bondage and human freedom. There are leaps between different stages, but there is also a slow and continuous transformation. It is impossible to say at which point in the process of natural evolution animal nature is replaced by the nature which, in our present experience we know as human, a nature which is qualitatively different from animal nature.
>
> And, as there are analogies to human freedom in nature, so there are also analogies to human good and evil in all parts of the universe. It is worthy of note that Isaiah prophesied peace in nature for the new eon, thereby showing that he would not call nature "innocent." Nor would the writer who, in Genesis, chapter 3, tells about the curse over the land declare nature innocent. Nor would Paul do so in Romans, chapter 8, when he speaks about the bondage to futility which is the fate of nature. Certainly, all these expressions are poetic-mythical. They could not be otherwise, since only poetic empathy opens the inner life of nature. Nevertheless, they are realistic in substance and certainly more realistic than the moral utopianism which confronts immoral man with innocent nature. Just as, within man, nature participates in the good and evil he does, so nature, outside man, shows analogies to man's good and evil doing. Man reaches into nature, as nature reaches into man. They participate in each other and cannot be separated from each other. This makes it possible and necessary to use the term "fallen world" and to apply the concept of existence (in contrast to essence) to the universe as well as man.[4]

Like many other Christian thinkers, Tillich cannot break

the relationship between man and the natural world in which both share a corrupt nature. Even his dependence on evolution appears to be but a temporary nod to the reflections of science, since he stands ready to label the nature of man corrupt at whatever point in the evolutionary process a human being comparable in psychological processes to ourselves emerges.

Indian tribal religions also held a fundamental relationship between human beings and the rest of nature, but the conception was radically different. For many Indian tribal religions the whole of creation was good, and since the creation event did not include a "fall," the meaning of creation was that all parts of it functioned together to sustain it. Young Chief, a Cayuse, refused to sign the Treaty of Walla Walla because, he felt, the rest of the creation was not represented in the transaction:

> I wonder if the ground has anything to say? I wonder if the ground is listening to what is said? I wonder if the ground would come alive and what is on it? Though I hear what the ground says. The ground says, It is the Great Spirit that placed me here. The Great Spirit tells me to take care of the Indians, to feed them aright. The Great Spirit appointed the roots to feed the Indians on. The water says the same thing. The Great Spirit directs me, Feed the Indians well. The grass says the same thing, Feed the Indians well. The ground, water and grass say, the Great Spirit has given us our names. We have these names and hold these names. The ground says, The Great Spirit placed me here to produce all that grows on me, trees and fruit. The same way the ground says, It was from me man was made. The Great Spirit, in placing men on earth, desired them to take good care of the ground and to do each other no harm. [5]

The similarity between Young Chief's conception of creation and the Genesis story is striking, but when one understands that the Genesis story is merely the starting place for theological doctrines of a rather abstract nature while Young Chief's beliefs are his practical articulations of his understanding of the relationship between the various entities of the creation, the difference becomes apparent. In the Indian tribal religions, man and the rest of creation are cooperative and respectful of the task set for them by the Great Spirit. In the Christian religion both are doomed from shortly after the creation event until the end of the world.

The second aspect of the Christian doctrine of creation that concerns us vitally today is the idea that man receives domination over the rest of creation. Harvey Cox, a popular Protestant theologian, articulates rather precisely the attitude derived from this idea of Genesis: "Just after his creation man is given the crucial responsibility of naming the animals. He is their master and commander. It is his task to subdue the earth."[6] It is this attitude that has been adopted wholeheartedly by Western peoples in their economic exploitation of the earth. The creation becomes a mere object when this view is carried to its logical conclusion—a directly opposite result from that of the Indian religions.

Whether or not Christians wanted to carry their doctrine of man's dominance as far as it has been carried, the fact remains that the modern world is just now beginning to identify the Christian religion's failure to show adequate concern for the planet as a major factor in our present ecological crisis. Among the earliest scholars to recognize the Christian responsibility for our present situation of ecological chaos was Lynn White, Jr., who gave a presentation entitled "The Historical Roots of Our Ecological Crisis" in 1967 before the American Association for the Advancement of Science.[7] White presented the same previously discussed criticism of Christian theology, emphasizing the tendency of the Christian religion to downgrade the natural world and its life forms in favor of the supernatural world of the Christian postjudgment world of eternal life. But he was extremely kind for a man who had his intellectual arguments honed so fine that he could have gone for the jugular vein, had he wanted. White proposed that St. Francis be made the ecological saint.

A number of Christians appear to be taking up White's thesis, and one frequently hears arguments that St. Francis represents the true Christian tradition. The Franciscan tradition is not a major theme of either Christian or Western thought, however, and it would appear as if advocating St. Francis as a patron of the Christian attitude toward creation is not only historically late but uncertain. White's thesis proved unbearable to Dr René Dubos, of New York City's Rockefeller University, who gave a presentation in 1969 at the Smithsonian Institution in Washington, D.C. on "A Theology of the Earth."[8] In it Dubos disclaimed White's charge against Christianity. Dubos contended that other societies had also created ecological disasters. He felt that Christianity was therefore not to be held accountable for the shortcomings of Western man. He buttressed his thesis by references to St. Francis and, more particularly, to St. Benedict, founder of the Benedictine Order. Dubos found that the Benedictine work rules, which at that time included draining swamps and filling in lowlands, were more suitable for modern man than St. Francis' ideas of nature worship.

Dubos' valiant defense of Christian thought lacks a number of substantial considerations. While other societies did create ecological disasters, Dubos would be hard put to find in the theologies of many other religions either a command to subdue the earth or the doctrine that the creation had "fallen" and shared responsibility for a man's direct violation of divine commands.

Further indications of Dubos' miscalculation of Christian sincerity, and evidence, perhaps, that Christians have not yet understood the complexity of the ecological crisis are evidenced by the recent liturgy of the earth created by the National Cathedral in Washington, D.C. The confession used in this liturgy exemplifies the extent to which even aware Christians have misunderstood the seriousness of the ecological problem.

> Lord God, we say here in Your presence and before each other that we, both individually and collectively, have not been good stewards of Your earth. We have fouled the air, spoiled the water, poisoned the land, and by these acts have gravely hurt each other. We know now that this has and will cost us, and for these and all other sins we are truly sorry. Give us, we pray, the strength and guidance to undo what we have done and grant us inspiration for a new style of living. [9]

Even in this attempt to bring religious sensitivity to the problem of ecological destruction, one can see the shallow understanding of the basis of the religious attitude that has been largely responsibile for the crisis. No effort is made to begin a new theory of the meaning of creation. Indeed, the popular attitude of "stewardship" is invoked, as if it had no relationship to the cause of the ecological crisis whatsoever. Perhaps the best summary of the attitude inherent in the liturgy is, "Please, God, help us cut the cost, and we'll try to find a new life-style that won't be quite as destructive." The response is inadequate, because it has not reached any fundamental problems; it is only a patch and paste job over a serious theological problem.

There is another, more serious problem involved in the Christian doctrine of creation. For most of the history of the Christian religion, people have been taught that the description of the event of creation as recorded in Genesis is historical fact. Although many Christian theologians have recognized that at best the Genesis account is mythological, it would be fair to conclude on the basis of what is known of the Christian religion that many Christian theologians and a substantial portion of the populace take the Genesis account as historical fact.

This issue has been a particularly difficult problem in the

last century in America. The Scopes trial in Tennessee (1925) is perhaps the most publicized of the incidents marking the conflict between literal believers of Genesis and those who regard it symbolically, either as an analogy or as a mythological representation of a greater spiritual reality. The fact that people in a number of states, most prominently California, are presently petitioning their state legislatures to require the Genesis account of creation in school indicates that the desire of many Chiristians is to believe in spite of the evidence, not because of it.[10]

Indian tribal religions have not had this problem. The fact that tribes are confronted with a particular land with its life forms has been sufficient. The task which the tribal religions have seen is that of relating the community of men to each and every facet of creation as they have experienced it. Dr. Charles Eastman, the famous Sioux physician, relates a story in which the Indian viewpoint of the historicity of creation legends is illustrated:

> A missionary once undertook to instruct a group of Indians in the truths of his holy religion. He told them of the creation of the earth in six days, and of the fall of our first parents by eating an apple.
>
> The courteous savages listened attentively, and, after thanking him, one related in his turn a very ancient tradition concerning the origin of maize. But the missionary plainly showed his disgust and disbelief, indignantly saying:
>
> "What I delivered to you were sacred truths, but this that you tell me is mere fable and falsehood!"
>
> "My Brother," gravely replied the offended Indian, "it seems that you have not been well grounded in the rules of civility. You saw that we, who practice these rules, believed your stories; why, then, do you refuse to credit ours?"[11]

The difference in approach goes back to the basic consideration discussed earlier. If a religion is tied to a sense of time, then everything forming a part of it must have some validity in a temporal sense. Christians are thus rather stuck with asserting that the account of Genesis is an actual historical recording of the proceedings whether or not some of the theologians consent to such an interpretation.

More important, perhaps, is the fact that the major theologian, Paul, made the historicity of the Genesis account the most important aspect of his theory of redemption. Paul's theory has formed a major part of the Christian teachings, and while some of the Christian sects would not agree with everything Paul wrote, he is not an insignificant figure in Christian history. Paul writes in Romans:

> Sin, you see, was in the world long before the Law, though I suppose, technically speaking, it was not 'sin' where there was no law to define it. Nevertheless death, the complement of sin, held sway over mankind from Adam to Moses, even over those whose sin was quite unlike Adam's.

> Adam, the first man, corresponds in some degree to the Man who was to come. But the gift of God through Christ is a very different matter from the 'account rendered' through the sin of Adam. For while as a result of one man's sin death by natural consequence became the common lot of men, it was by the generosity of God, the freegiving of the grace of the One Man Jesus Christ, that the love of God overflowed for the benefit of all men.

> We see, then, that as one act of sin exposed the whole race of men to God's judgment and condemnation, so one Act of Perfect Righteousness presents all men freely acquitted in the sight of God. One man's disobedience placed all men under the threat of condemnation, but one Man's obedience has the power to present all men righteous before God.[12]

It would appear that if the Genesis account of Adam's disobedience is not a historical event (that is, an event that can be located at some specific time and place on the planet), subsequent explanations of the meaning of the death of Jesus of Nazareth are without validity. We have no need to question the historical existence of Jesus of Nazareth, although that particular conflict has also consumed considerable energy in the past. But we cannot project from the historical reality of Jesus as a man existing in Palestine during the time of Augustus and his successors to the historical existence of a man called Adam in a garden someplace in Asia Minor. Yet without the historical fact of the existence of Adam, we are powerless to explain the death of Jesus as a religious event of cosmic significance.

At best we can conclude that the Christian doctrine of creation has serious shortcomings. It is too often considered not simply as a historical event but as the event that determined all other facts of our existence. It is bad enough to consider Genesis as a historical account in view of what we know today of the nature of our world. But when we consider that the Genesis account places nature and nonhuman life systems in a polarity with us, tinged with evil and without hope of redemption except at the last judgment, the whole idea appears intolerable.

There are, to be sure, numerous accounts from the various tribal religious traditions relating how an animal, bird, or reptile participated in a creation event. We have already seen how some Indian people regarded such stories and the lack of belief in the historical nature of the event. Within the tribal accounts is contained, perhaps, an even greater problem, the problem of origins of peoples and religions, which we shall take up in a later chapter. At no point, however, does any tribal religion insist that its particular version of the creation is an absolute historical recording of the creation event or that the story necessarily leads to conclusions about mankind's good or evil nature.

The relationships serving to form a unity of nature are of vastly more importance to most tribal religions. It is crucial to remember that when we turn from discussing the Christian concepts of the creation to those of the Indian tribal religions, we pass from using concepts in a temporal sense to the technique of using them in a spatial or given sense, to what we can observe with a limited geographical and individual horizon. The Indian is confronted with a bountiful earth in which all things experienced have a role to fill. The task of the tribal religion, if such a religion can be said to have a task, is to determine the proper relationship that the people of the tribe must have with other living things.

Primarily in the world with which he is confronted is the presence of power, the manifestation of life energies, the whole life-flow of a creation. Recognition that the human being holds an important place in such a creation is tempered by the thought that he is dependent on everything in creation for his existence. There is not, therefore, that determined cause which Harvey Cox projects to subdue the earth and its living things. Instead the awareness of the meaning of life comes from observing how the various living things appear to mesh to provide a whole tapestry.

Each form of life has its own purposes, and there is no form of life that does not have a unique quality to its existence. Shooter, a Sioux Indian, explained the view held by many tribal religions in terms of individuality:

Animals and plants are taught by Wakan Tanka what they are to do. Wakan Tanka teaches the birds to make nests, yet the nests of all birds are not alike. Wakan Tanka gives them merely the outline. Some make better nests than others.

In the same way some animals are satisfied with very rough dwellings, while others make attractive places in which to live. Some animals also take better care of their young than others. The forest is the home of many birds and other animals, and the water is the home of fish and reptiles. All birds, even those of the same species, are not alike, and it is the same with animals, or human beings. The reason Wakan Tanka does not make two birds, or animals, or human beings exactly alike is because each is placed here by Wakan Tanka to be an independent individuality and to rely upon itself. [13]

To have differences, even among the species of life, does not require then that forces be created to gain a sense of unity or homogeneity. To exist in a creation means that living is more than tolerance for other life forms, it is recognition that in differences there is the strength of creation and that this strength is a deliberate desire of the creator.

Tribal religions find a great affinity among species of living creatures, and it is at this point that the brotherhood of life is a strong part of the Indian way. The Hopi, for example, revere not only the lands on which they live but the animals with which they have a particular relationship. The dance for rain, which involves the use of reptiles in its ceremonies, holds a great fascination for whites, primarily because they have traditionally considered reptiles—particularly snakes—as their mortal enemy. In this attitude and its ensuing fascination, we may illustrate, perhaps, the alienation between the various life forms which Christian peoples read into the story in Genesis. This alienation is not present in tribal religions.

Behind the apparent kinship between animals, reptiles, birds, and human beings in the Indian way stands a great conception shared by a great majority of the tribes. Other living things are not regarded as insensitive species. Rather they are "peoples" in the same manner as the various tribes of men are peoples. The reason why the Hopi use live reptiles in their ceremony goes back to one of their folk heros who lived with the snake people for a while and learned from them the secret of making rain for the crops.[14] It was a ceremony freely given by the snake people to the Hopi. In the same manner the Plains Indians considered the buffalo as a distinct people, the Northwest Coast Indians regarded the salmon as a people. Equality is thus not simply a human attribute but a recognition of the creatureness of all creation.

Very important in some of the tribal religions is the idea that men can change into animals and birds and that other species can change into men. In this way species can communicate and learn from each other. Some of these tribal ideas have been classified as "witchcraft" by anthropologists, primarily because such phenomena occurring within the Western tradition would naturally be interpreted as evil and satanic. What Western man misses is the rather logical implication of the unity of life. If all living things share a creator and a creation, is it not logical to suppose that all have the ability to relate to every part of the creation? How Western man can believe in evolution and not see the logical consequences of this doctrine in the religious life of people is incomprehensible for many Indians. Recent studies with the dolphin and other animals may indicate that Western man is beginning to shed his superstitions and consider the possibility of having communication with other life forms.

But many tribal religions go even farther. The manifestation of power is simply not limited to mobile life forms. For some tribes the idea extends to plants, rocks, and natural features which Western men consider inanimate. Walking Buffalo, a Stoney Indian from Canada, explained the nature of the unity of creation and the possibility of communicating with any aspect of creation when he remarked:

> Did you know that trees talk? Well they do. They talk to each other, and they'll talk to you if you listen. Trouble is, white people don't listen. They never learned to listen to the Indians, so I don't suppose they'll listen to other voices in nature. But I have learned a lot from trees; sometimes about the weather, sometimes about animals, sometimes about the Great Spirit. [15]

Again we must return to the Christian idea of the complete alienation of nature and the world from man as a result of Adam's immediate postcreation act in determining the Western and Christian attitude toward nature. Some theologians have felt that man's alienation from nature is a natural result of his coming to a sense of self-consciousness, and people dealing with psychological problems seem to have a tendency to emphasize the sense in which man is alienated from nature by promulgating theories of childhood fears based on the unfolding of natural growth processes. Even Western poets have been articulating the Western fears of "I, a stranger and afraid, in a world I never made."[16]

By and large there was no fear of nature in the Indian view of the world. Chief Luther Standing Bear remarked on the "wildness" of nature in his autobiography:

> We did not think of the great open plains, the beautiful rolling hills, and winding streams with tangled growth as "wild." Only to the white men was nature a "wilderness" and only to him was the land "infested" with "wild" animals and "savage" people. To us it was tame. Earth was bountiful and we were surrounded with the blessings of the Great Mystery. Not until the hairy man from the east came and with brutal frenzy heaped injustices upon us and the families that we loved was it "wild" for us. When the very animals of the forest began fleeing from his approach, then it was that for us the "Wild West" began.[17]

In some sense, part of the alienation of man from nature is caused by the action of man against nature and not as the result of some obscure and corrupted relationship that came into being as a result of a man's inability to relate to the creator. It is doubtful if the Western Christian can change his understanding of creation at this point in his existence. His religion is firmly grounded in his escape from a "fallen" nature, and it is highly unlikely to suppose at this late date that he can find a reconciliation with nature while maintaining the remainder of his theological understanding of salvation.

We have one final subject to cover with respect to the creation. Whether it be considered as a specific event or as a basically unexplainable given that need not really be explained, certain empirical data exists today that was unavailable to mankind when tribal religions and Christianity originated. Modern science has in large part pierced the veil of nature. We are becoming increasingly aware of some of the basic processes of the universe to a much greater degree than we have ever done. With the explosion of the atomic bomb, mankind moved far beyond the speculations of earlier science and philosophy. It may be yet too soon to conclude that our science can determine everything about the universe. Yet the possibility of almost instantaneous destruction through misuse of science should indicate that we are fairly close to describing in a rough manner how the universe works.

Our further question, therefore, should concern how religious statements are to be made which are either broad enough or specific enough to parallel what we are discovering in nature through scientific experiments. Christian theology has traditionally fluctuated between the philosophical views of Plato and Aristotle. Occasionally some theologian will go to the ideas of Kant or Descartes to find a usable system to explain religious ideas in a scientific manner. Some theologians have gone so far as Alfred North Whitehead's view of the universe to find a way to describe religious ideas by the same basic form of articulation as followed in scientific circles.

Which religious atmosphere, Christian or Indian, would appear to be more compatible with contemporary scientific ideas? The question may appear absurd, but it has the highest relevance for a number of reasons. First, we must determine on what basis religious ideas are considered to be mere superstitions and on what basis religious ideas are said to be either valid or possible in the world in which we live. Indian dances for rain, for example, were said to be mere superstitions, songs to make corn grow were said to be even more absurd. Today men can make plants grow with music, and the whole nature of the power of sound vibrations has come into its own. The principles used by Indian tribal religions have tremendous parallels with contemporary scientific experiments. This can be either coincidental, which is very difficult to prove, or it can mean that the Indian tribal religions have been dealing at least partially with a fairly accurate conception of reality.

The second reason for determining compatibility of religion and science is to lay the groundwork for bringing our view of the world back to a unified whole, if at all possible. The competition between ministers and psychoanalysts, for example, to determine the sense of spiritual or psychological infirmity in effect promotes two distinct views of reality. As Karl Heim relates in his incisive book, *Christian Faith and Natural Science:*

> In cases of physiologically conditioned depression, in which the religious responses are often involved, modern medicine applies with great success the electric shock treatment, passing an electric current through leads placed in contact with the patient's temples. These are often people who in their state of depression also despaired of their spiritual salvation, who were a prey in other words to what has been called in theological literature 'certainty of damnation.' And lo and behold! What the minister of religion had tried in vain to achieve with comforting exhortations and encouraging words from the Bible and the Catechism has now been accomplished by the electric current! The depression has gone and the patient not only faces his life with new courage but is filled with a joyful belief in God's forgiveness and in his own eternal salvation.[18]

It would thus appear that unless some new effort in the field of religion is made to provide a more realistic understanding of the universe, there may be no solution to men's problems except manipulation by artificial means—the 1984 solution, which we all dread.

The Indian tribal religions would probably suggest that the unity of life is manifested in the existence of the tribal community, for it is only in the tribal community that any

Indian religions have relevance. James Jeans, in his book *Physics and Philosophy,* suggests a more profound view of nature lies in the concept of community:

> Space and time are inhabited by distinct individuals, but when we pass beyond space and time, from the world of phenomena towards reality, individuality is replaced by community.

> When we pass beyond space and time, they [separate individuals] may perhaps form ingredients of a single continuous stream of life. [19]

The parallel with conceptions of the basic unity of existence held by American Indian tribal religions is striking. If the nature of the world is a "single continuous stream of life," there is no reason to reject the idea that one can learn to hear the trees talk. It would be strange if they did not have the power to communicate.

R. G. Collingwood, in *The Idea of Nature,* attempts to sketch out Alexander's cosmology as it applies to a whole continuum of life:

> In the physical world before the emergence of life, there are already various orders of being, each consisting of a pattern composed of elements belonging to the order next below it: point-instants form a pattern which is the electron having physical qualities, electrons form an atom having higher chemical qualities of a new and higher order, molecules like those of air form wave-patterns having sonority and so on.

> Living organisms in their turn are patterns whose elements are bits of matter. In themselves these bits of matter are inorganic; it is only the whole pattern which they compose that is alive, and its life is the time-aspect or rhythmic process of its material parts. [20]

We apparently have order and orders. We have time but a time that is not a universal value, only a time internal to the complex relationships themselves. Above all, we have no disruption of the unity of the creation, only a variation on a general theme. If there is anything to the similarity of things, it is that a sense of alienation does not exist at a significant level that we can take as fundamental.

In conclusion, we have the rather startling statement of Alfred North Whitehead about the nature of God: "Not only does God [primordial nature] arrange the eternal objects; he also makes them available for use by other actual entities. This is God's function as the principle of concretion." [21] Again we are dealing with a complexity of relationships in which no particular object is given primacy over any other object or entity. While Whitehead cannot be said to be the last word on either theology or science, he is not an inconsiderable figure in Western thought, and even he goes beyond traditional Western religious thinking in an effort to find more compatible ideas for consideration.

The important thing is not an attempt to show that either Indian tribal religions or Christianity prefigured contemporary science, modern concern for ecological sanity, or a startingly new idea of what the universe might eventually be. Rather we should find what religious ideas can credibly encompass the broadest field of both our thoughts and actions. We must show that religious ideas are at least not tied to any particular view of man, nature, or the relationship of man and nature that is clearly in conflict with what we know. In this sense, American Indian tribal religions certainly appear to be more at home in the modern world than Christian ideas and Western man's traditional religious concepts.

Chapter 7

The Concept of History

ONE OF THE major distinctions that can be made between the tribal religions taken as a group and the Christian religion underlying Western thought is the extent to which the two views were dependent on the idea of history. Indian tribes had little use for recording past events; the idea of keeping a careful chronological record of events never seemed to impress the greater number of tribes of the continent. While the Indians who lived in Central America had extensive calendars, the practice of recording history was not a popular one further north.

On the other hand, Christianity has always placed a major emphasis on the idea of history. From the very beginning of the religion, it has been the Christian contention that the experiences of mankind could be recorded in a linear fashion, and when this was done the whole purpose of the creation event became clear, explaining not only the history of man but revealing the nature of the end of the world and the existence of a further world to which the faithful would be welcome. Again we have a familiar distinction. Time is regarded as all-important by Christians, and it has a casual importance, if any, among the tribal peoples.

111

The western preoccupation with history and a chronological description of reality was not a dominant factor in any tribal conception of either time or history. "The way I heard it" or "it was a long time ago" usually prefaces any Indian account of a past tribal experience, indicating that the story itself is important, not its precise chronological location. That is not to say that Indian tribes deliberately avoided chronology. In post-Discovery times, some tribes adopted the idea of recording specific sequences of time as a means of remembering the community's immediate past experiences. The best-known method of recording these experiences was the winter count of the Plains Indians. A large animal hide, usually buffalo, would be specially tanned, and each year a figure or symbol illustrating the most memorable event experienced by the community would be painted on the hide. Gradually the hide became filled with representations of the years, and it would be maintained as long as there were people who could remember what the figures and symbols meant.

One could not find a very accurate concept of history in the winter counts. In general they indicated the psychic life of the community—what was important to that group of people as a group. The chances of a continuous subject matter appearing on a winter count were nil. One year might be remembered as the year that horses came to the people, the next year might be the year when the berries were extremely large, the year after perhaps the tribe might have made peace with an enemy or visited a strange river on its migrations. The chances of a series of political or military events being recorded year after year as in the Western concept of history was so remote as to preclude the origination of history as a subject matter of importance. One recent Sioux winter count, for example, does not mention a number of important treaties, and one does not even mention the Custer massacre.

Other tribes devised methods of recording community

experiences similar to the winter counts. The Pimas and Papagos of Arizona had calendar sticks on which symbols were carved. By remembering what the symbols represented, a reader could recite a short chronology of recent years. But again the ability of the reader limited the extent to which the history could be recorded.[1]

The Delaware in post-Discovery times created a long chronology that had many political references called the Walum Olum. It mentioned the tribes immediately bordering the Delawares and with whom they shared a general political fate. In this sense, the Walum Olum can be said to be more complex than the Sioux and Pima/Papago systems. However the accuracy of Western European recounting and recording events was a distant goal for the most history-conscious of the American Indian tribes.[2]

Lacking a sense of rigid chronology, most tribal religions did not base their validity on any specific incident dividing man's time experience into a before and after. No Indian tribal religion was dependent on the belief that a certain thing happened in the past which required belief in itself in the occurrence of the event. Creation, gifts of powers and medicines, traumatic events, and the lives of great religious leaders were either events of the distant past and regarded as such or the memories of the tribe gave credence to the incident; however, salvation and religious participation in communal ceremonies did not depend on the event but on the ceremonies and powers used as a result of the event.

Culture heroes were plentiful in the tribes. Deganiwidah founded the Iroquois League some time in the pre-Discovery days. Iroquois religion and politics did not revolve around him in the usual religious sense, but the great law of the Iroquois held the major position in tribal religious and political life. Sweet Medicine, the Cheyenne religious figure, was believed to have received his powers in historical times, but the ceremonies he brought were important, not Sweet

Medicine himself. The story of the White Buffalo Calf Woman of the Sioux happened in the distant past. The importance in the story was the reception of the Sacred Pipe, not the woman herself as a personal object of salvation.

The tribal religions had one great benefit other religions did not and could not have. They had no religious controversy within their communities, because everyone shared a common historical experience, and cultural identity was not separated into religious, economic, sociological, political, and military spheres. It was never a case, therefore, of *having* to believe in certain things to sustain a tribal religion. One simply believed the stories of the elders, because the stories had been passed down to them from their elders.

No tribe, however, asserted its history as having primacy over the accounts of any other tribe. As we have seen, the recitation of stories by different peoples was regarded as a social event embodying civility. Differing tribal accounts were believed, since it was not a matter of trying to establish power over others. To be sure, tribes that had fallen under the wide-ranging military power of the various confederacies were reminded who ran things. Under the Iroquois and Creek alliances, weaker allies had no doubt about who was in charge. But there was no coercion to convert the smaller tribes to an Iroquois or Creek conception of past historical events and their efficacy.

In the turbulent period of conflict with the whites, speeches recorded at treaty sessions, statements made to the President to remind him of previous promises, and other statements of historical importance made use of chronological references. But one cannot say, on the basis of these speeches, that a fascination with historical reality was developed through contact with whites. Rather the speeches reflect negotiations and arguments over specific proposals made by the United States representatives.

Perhaps the best articulation of an Indian theory of history is found in the great speech by Chief Seattle at the signing of the Medicine Creek Treaty in Washington Territory in 1854. Recognizing that the loss of lands and establishment of reservations doomed his people, the Duwamish, Seattle sadly remarked:

> It matters little where we pass the remnant of our days. They will not be many. A few more moons; a few more win-ters—and not one of the descendants of the mighty hosts that once moved over this broad land or lived in happy homes, protected by the Great Spirit, will remain to mourn over the graves of a people once more powerful and hopeful than yours. But why should I mourn at the untimely fate of my people? Tribe follows tribe, nation follows nation, like the waves of the sea. It is the order of nature, and regret is useless. Your time of decay may be distant, but it will surely come, for even the White Man whose God walked and talked with him as friend with friend, cannot be exempted from the common destiny. We may be brothers after all. We shall see. [3]

Seattle's theory of history may be much more a recognition of life's cyclical nature than a statement of historical process. For many tribal religions the distinction would be academic. The recognition of growth and decay as limiting factors in a tribe or nation's existence is worthy of note; it runs contrary to the Western European conceptions of the Heavenly City of the Thousand Year Reich.

The idea of world ages, held by some tribes, is comparable in many ways to the world age concepts held by people in India. The flood stories, even the most remote, gave rise to the belief that the world is periodically destroyed by flood, fire, or other natural catastrophe, and this idea was held by a number of tribes with stories of some antiquity. Some substance was given to the belief in periodic destruction by particular stories, and in this sense the people could be said to have had a conception of history. For example, the Sioux explanation was framed in familiar terminology. They held that the world was protected by a huge buffalo which stood at the western gate of the universe and held back the waters that periodically flooded the world. Every year the buffalo lost a hair on one of its legs. Every age it lost a leg. When the buffalo had lost all its legs and was no longer able to hold back the waters, the world was flooded and renewed.

The Hopi had the most comprehensive understanding of world ages, as Frank Waters and White Bear recount in *The Book of the Hopi*. These people believed that they had survived three world destructions and that each world had been marked by peculiar circumstances. Before each destruction they were given special instructions for survival, and as each new world began they received songs and ceremonies designed for living in the new world. Their ceremonial life would end with each world destruction. Other tribes had legends of similar content, although a great many now appear to have had prophecies about the white man which now color efforts to come to any conclusions as to which stories were quasi-histories and which were later prophecies.

Suffice it to say, even the closest approach to the Western idea of history by an Indian tribe was yet a goodly distance from Western historical conceptions. What appears to have survived as a tribal conception of history almost everywhere was the description of conditions under which the people lived and the location in which they lived. Migrations from one place to another were phrased in terms descriptive of why they moved. Exactly when they moved was, again, "a long time ago." The scholars have had a difficult time piecing together the maps of pre-Discovery America because of the vague nature of tribal remembrances. The Iroquois, for example, relate that they once lived on the plains but then migrated eastward. When is not important to them, but their relative hardship on the plains and eventual prosperity in the East are important.

The result of this casual attitude toward history was, of

course, that history had virtually no place in the religious life of the tribe. The appearance of the various folk heroes who brought sacred ceremonies and medicines could often not be located in time at all. Only recent and specific events, such as the Cheyennes' loss of some of their sacred arrows to the Pawnees, were remembered and formed a conjunction of history and religion. But the ceremonies, beliefs, and great religious events of the tribes were distinct from history; they did not depend on history for their verification. If they worked for the community in the present, that was sufficient evidence of their validity.

The contrast between tribal religions and the Christian religion, therefore, can be made painfully clear with a brief and general sketch of the Christian religion itself. In a real sense, the Christian religion can be said to be dependent on the historical accuracy of the Hebrew religion as found in the sacred books of the Jews. After the death of Jesus the remaining disciples began to preach the doctrine that his crucifixion had been more than a simple execution. It was regarded by them as the culminating event in a direct sequence of events going back to the creation of the universe.

We have already seen in an earlier chapter how Paul made the connection between a historical man Adam and the historical man Jesus in such a way as to explain how the disobedience of Adam had been canceled with the death of Jesus. It was within the recorded experience of the Hebrew people and the remnant peoples of the tribe of Judah, then known as the Jews, that the Christian innovation of world history took place. Two of the Gospels written to interpret the life of Jesus and his teachings had as their introductory remarks genealogies of Jesus purporting to trace his ancestry back to Adam. That they are different is cause to wonder if a biological history of his family is the intent.

At any rate, the events of the Old Testament were seen as actual events of history in which a divine purpose was gradually unfolding. The idea had been inherent in Jewish religious circles prior to the advent of Christianity, but with the missionary explosion of the Christian religion, the events could be said to have taken on cosmic significance for believers of the new religion. For some time before the lifetime of Jesus, Jewish theological circles had seen the development of a curious type of literature. A large body of literature purporting to have been written by the major folk heros of the Hebrew past began to surface, and its concern with predictions about the end of the world and the salvation of the Jews appeared to be a common feature. Such writings were called apocalyptic writings, and it is from these sources perhaps more than any others that we derive the Christian idea of a divine purpose in history and a subsequent fascination by Westerners for history.

The religion that took form around the person of Jesus came to regard the events of the past as directly prefiguring his life and teachings. To arrive at such consequences, the books of the Old Testament were scoured for verses that might be interpreted as predicting certain events of his life. What we have in the four Gospels, therefore, is a curious mixture of historical events, parabolic teachings, and tortured proof texts from various sources in the Jewish writings. At best the Gospels, which can be said to be the first Christian effort to define the meaning of past events in terms of mankind's universal history, are exactly that—tortured.

The immediate followers who had known Jesus had come to the conclusion, apparently nurtured by Jesus himself, that their Lord would return within their own lifetime to restore the Kingdom of Israel to the glory known during the eras of David and Solomon. So impending was this feeling that the original commune in Jerusalem, headed by Jesus' brother James the Just, felt no desire or need to gather worldly goods. As a result they were soon bankrupt, and one of Paul's first acts was to take up collections from converts to bail them out of their financial difficulties.

The whole basis for the Christian belief in life after death was the alleged resurrection of Jesus after he had been dead for three days and his subsequent ascension into heaven. As the Gospels and the Acts of the Apostles were written, there can be little doubt that the primitive Christian community wished its converts to believe that Jesus in his physical body had risen upward to heaven in a cloud. Early converts saw visions in which he returned on the clouds. When Jesus failed to return within the lifetime of the men who had been his closest associates, the religion should have folded. But as the original group grew smaller and the religion spread to Asia Minor, the initial prediction was continually modified so that while the basic idea had been an immediate conclusion to history through divine intervention, its immediacy gradually became symbolic, not historic.

It is now nearly 2,000 years since Jesus lived and died, and there has been no return. New converts periodically become wildly enthusiastic about the impending return of Jesus, and evangelistic Christianity continuously phrases its message of mission and conversion in terms of a return of Jesus in the not-too-distant future. As the years have passed and certain milestones have been reached, Christianity has gone into traumas with the idea of imminent judgment. The arrival of the year 1000 was particularly disappointing for the thousands of people who sold their earthly goods and prepared to meet their maker. When the crisis passed and the Western world returned to normal, apologists for the religion trotted out their favorite Bible verses, attempting to smooth over the downhearted. "A thousand years is but a day·in Thy sight" and other comforting verses were used to cover over the failure of Jesus to reappear.

The Christian religion can be said to have a meaning because it looks toward a spectacular end of the world as a time of judgment and thus an end of history. It is thus theologically an open-ended proposition since it can at any time promote the idea that the world is ending; when such an event fails to occur, the contentions can easily be retracted by resorting to philosophical waffling about the nature of time. Time thus becomes a dualistic concept for Christians. It is both divine and human; prophecies given with respect to divine time are promptly canceled by reference to human time and its distinction from divine time.

At any rate the concept of history became a rather nebulous subject matter as Christianity continued to grow. The events of the Old Testament were regarded as actual historical events, and their miraculous nature was ascribed to divine intervention on behalf of the Hebrews. As the Old Testament came closer to the days of Jesus and the writings became closed to further prophecies, with Malachi the idea of divine intervention in men's affairs also appeared to slacken. The first several centuries of the Christian religion appear to have been filled with miraculous acts of God in direct as-sistance to the Christian martyrs. After several centuries, however, even this tendency ebbed, and with the estab-lishment of the organizational Church as a political power in the crumbling Roman Empire, Christianity adopted the temporary doctrine that Jesus had established a "church" to supervise the affairs of men until he decided to return.

This condition of nearly total Church control over the lives of men was strengthened during the centuries that followed, and for many centuries the political struggles of Western Europe had to have Christian approval to be considered valid. The Protestant Reformation was instrumental in breaking the control of the organized Church structure over the political and economic life of Europe. Since that time, while the political structures have continued to expand their power, the relative influence of the Church has declined.

The original doctrines of Christian expansion, however, did not decline with the waning influence of the Church organization. In the first several centuries of Christian existence, one of the most popular justifications for the failure of Jesus to return to earth was his alleged admonition to his disciples to preach the message of his life to "all nations." Thus a substantial portion of the Christians believed that until every nation had heard the message of Christianity, Jesus *could not come.* In almost every generation of Christians, there was somewhere a militant missionary force seeking to convert non-Christian peoples, and this propensity to expand the religion's influence meant in realistic terms an expansion of control by the Church structure over non-Christian peoples.

With the rise of secular governmental forms after the Protestant Reformation, the bitter competition between nations for lands in the newly discovered Western Hemisphere, and the very violent struggles between competing interpretations of the religion following the Reformation, missionary activity was seen as an arm of national politics, and the national imperialistic movements were justified on the basis of bringing the Christian religion to the heathen. This attitude is covered more thoroughly in a later chapter. What is important for our purposes here is to note that as secular goals became more important, they were clothed in familiar terms of Western cultural attitudes, not in terms of religious reality.

Christian theology also had a direct influence on the development of the manner in which Westerners conceived the nature of the world. In the development of Christian theology, the two Greeks Plato and Aristotle were highly influential. Both of their philosophical systems sought to bring order out of the chaos of the world, and as the two major theologians of Christian history, St. Augustine and St. Thomas Aquinas, sought to reconcile Greek philosophy with Christian ideas of history, people in the West became accustomed to thinking of natural processes in terms of uniformity. In the popular mind the Old Testament was filled with highly exciting supernatural events, while the story of mankind since the life of Jesus was filled with smaller miracles but lacked the spectacular nature of Old Testament happenings.

Western history as we now have it has failed to shake off its original Christian presuppositions. It has, in fact, extended its theory of uniformity to include Old Testament events so that the history of mankind appears as a rather tedious story of the rise and fall of nation after nation, and the sequence in which world history has been written shows amazing parallels to the expansion of the Christian religion. China with its history going back far beyond the days of Abraham thus does not appear as a significant factor in world history until it begins to have relations with the West. India with even more ancient records appears on the world scene only when the British decide to colonize it, despite its brief role as a conquest goal of Alexander the Great.

We are faced today with a concept of world history that lacks even the most basic appreciation of the experiences of mankind as a whole. Unless other cultures and nations have some important relationship with the nations of Western Europe, they have little or no status in the interpretation of world history. Indeed, world history as presently conceived in the Christian nations is the story of Western man's conquest of the remainder of the world and his subsequent rise to technological sophistication.

Because we cannot understand mankind from a more profound point of view, we have in recent years fallen into a number of easily avoidable difficulties. The original thrust of Christians opposing pagans translated itself many times in Christian history. Shortly after the discovery of the New World, Christianity was thought to be opposed on the one hand to the societies of the New World and on the other to the heretics of Europe. The peoples of the New World were virtually destroyed by the European invaders at the same time that Europe was being decimated by witch-hunts, the Inquisition, and religious wars.

The tendency of placing Christianity against the social or political forms of man's secular existence continues to this day. The original movement after the Second World War involved the opposition of godless Communism against the chosen people of God—the Christian nations. At least part of the involvement of the United States in Southeast Asia was at the request of an influential figure in the Roman Catholic Church, Cardinal Spellman, who sought to bolster the fortunes of the Church. Much of the misunderstanding of the place of the United States in the postwar worlds involves this tendency to reject the Russians because of their rejection of Christianity.

A major task remains for Western man. He must quickly come to grips with the breadth of man's experiences and understand these experiences from a world viewpoint, not simply a Western one. This shift will necessarily involve downgrading the ancient history of the Near East, thus serving to cut yet more subject matter away from the Christian religion. Louis Leakey's discoveries concerning early man in Africa would seem to indicate that we are reaching a point at which the history of the Old Testament must assume a rather minor importance in the whole scheme of development. In addition to surrendering the historical Adam and his successors, we must surrender the comfortable feeling that we can find a direct line from ancient times to the modern world via the Christian religion. This involves, of course, giving up the claim by Christianity of its universal truth and validity.

Already the field of history appears to be reaching a crisis. Ancient history is taken much too casually today, because it is assumed that whatever happened within man's experiences could not be much different than the mythology that has grown up to explain the relics of history. We have an apparent computer of great sophistication at Stonehenge in England, and yet traditional conceptions of life during the times when the massive structure was built continue to reflect the Western/Christian idea that nothing of major importance occurred until the advent of Western culture and its religion.

The experiences of the Hebrews do not really take precedence over the experiences and accomplishments of other peoples when viewed with an unjaundiced eye. The world abounds with ruins of incredible proportions relating hardly at all to the history of the Hebraic-Christian peoples. Yet these ruins are passed off with casual and hardly credible explanations based on the old theory of uniformity, which projects that the past had to be experienced in the way in which we have always conceived it.

The pyramids of Egypt are a case in point. In the popular mind of Western peoples, the pyramids were built *à la* Cecil B. De Mille with thousands of slaves tugging the large vine ropes up inclines to make a final resting place for the pharaoh. That the only reference to slave labor in the Old Testament which could be remotely connected with building involves the Hebrew slaves making mud bricks is difficult for the popular mind to assimilate. It is when we go to the scholarly mind that we find even greater confusion, so that our sense of man's accomplishments and the meaning of history are hardly enhanced by even the best of our educated minds. Walter Fairservis, for example, rejects the concept of slave labor in pyramid building in his book *The Ancient Kingdoms of the Nile:*

> We know that there were few slaves because foreign conquests were at a minimum. The labor for the pyramids came from the peasant farmers who, at times of high Nile, were comparatively idle and could be used for public projects. In such cases they were maintained at government expense, which in view of the job to be done could not have been meager. The number of pyramids, and the years it took to build each of them, indicates that a stable arrangement between government responsibility and peasant labor had been established.[4]

The picture appears to be idyllic. In times of unemployment the benevolent pharaoh provided work for his people by having them put together what must certainly be among the most massive structures in history. But is this even a realistic picture of what happened in earlier times? That the United States government put forward the make-work projects of the Great Depression years does not mean that the pharaoh did likewise. The very bulk of the pyramids precludes Fairservis' solution to the problem.

The Great Pyramid of Cheops, for example, is incredible. Its base covers "13 acres or 7 midtown blocks of the city of New York. From this broad area, leveled to within a fraction of an inch, more than *two-and-a-half-million blocks* of limestone and granite—weighing from 2 to 70 tons apiece —rise in 201 stepped tiers to the height of a modern forty-story building."[5] A construction project the size of this pyramid would have been a task of no mean proportions. Suppose that the workers had placed a minimum of 20 blocks of stone a day in the structure—a feat that would have been virtually impossible, yet, still conceivable. They would have assembled the 2.5 million stone blocks in about 125,000 days—working steadily—or 342 years. In this projection we have still not accounted for cutting the blocks, carrying them down the Nile, and bringing them to the assembly place. And we have projected a straight working project, not a summertime government make-work project as Fairservis and other scholars have assumed. If the Pilgrims had begun building a pyramid the size of the pyramid of Cheops to celebrate their safe landing in America, they would have finished the project in 1962—perhaps just in time to receive a government grant to celebrate. Is the traditional interpretation of history really an exercise in credibility?

Today at Aswan Dam in Egypt the people of many nations are trying to save four sandstone statutes from an ancient temple from being destroyed by the waters of the dam. Engineers from nearly 100 nations are working together to save these priceless treasures. They have the benefit of helicopters, the latest in hydraulic jacks, lifts, cranes, and other modern construction equipment. Yet they must cut the statues into smaller pieces to move them a mere sixty feet above the waters. In a quarry near Baalbek in Asia Minor, the Hadjar el Gouble stone lies squared and ready for removal. It weighs more than four million pounds. And primitive men are going to get their logs and ropes and move it? Hardly.

The world is, as we have noted, literally strewn with ruins of overwhelming proportions, structures that we cannot duplicate today if we wished to do so, yet the Western interpretation of world history is always skirting a straight-forward effort to incorporate theories about the origin of these ruins and structures. We are fixed on a rather staid reading of man's history, because we are emotionally and religiously tied to the assumption, today perhaps subconsciously at least, that everything is pretty much the way man once believed centuries ago.

Even the relatively short time period of American history has been influenced by our religious heritage. There is sufficient evidence that this continent was visited by numerous expeditions prior to the arrival of Columbus. Pottery discovered in South America suggests fairly early contact between Japan and this hemisphere. Ruins in Massachusetts and Arizona may be evidence of early visits by Phoenicians and Romans. Yet up to this time scholars have adamantly refused to believe that any pre-Columbian landing took place. Even the Viking ruins in Minnesota have been buffeted by tremendous criticism and the jeers of skeptics, while the Columbian primacy has prevailed.

Cyrus Gordon, noted scholar of Brandeis University, has recently taken a cautious stand in favor of pre-Columbian expeditions in his book *Before Columbus*.[6] He documents two possible pre-Columbian visits to the New World. In the immediate past scholars have had their reputations destroyed for suggesting less. Hopefully Gordon's prestige will give backbone to men of less renown who, lacking the courage of their convictions, have remained silent.

The reluctance of scholars to consider the possibility of pre-Columbian visits to the Western Hemisphere is but one example of the stranglehold that the one interpretation of history has had over the minds of men. There is, to a certain extent, a political justification in refusing to accept pre-Columbian discoveries. The land title of the United States relates back to the famous doctrine of Discovery, whereby Christian nations were allowed by the Pope to claim the discovered lands of non-Christian peoples. To accept a series of pre-Columbian visitations would mean that the lands of the Western Hemisphere were hardly "discovered" by Europeans. It would call into question the interpretations and justifications given to colonization, exploitation, and genocide committed by Europeans during the last five centuries.

Christian religion and the Western idea of history are inseparable and mutually self-supporting. To retrench the traditional concept of Western history at this point would mean to invalidate the justifications for conquering the Western Hemisphere. Americans in some manner will cling to the traditional idea that they suddenly came upon a vacant land on which they created the world's most affluent society. Not only is such an idea false, it is absurd. Yet without it both, Western man and his religion stand naked before the world.

It is said that one cannot judge Christianity by the actions of Western secular man. But such a contention judges Western man much too harshly. Where, if not from Christianity, did Western man get his ideas of divine right to conquest, of manifest destiny, of himself as the vanguard of true civilization, if not from Christianity? Having tied itself to history and maintained that its god controlled that history, Christianity must accept the consequences of its past. Secular history is now out of control and is becoming a rather demoniac, disruptive force among the nations of men, and this is part and parcel of the Christian religion. If the lack of a sense of history can be called a shortcoming of tribal religions, as indeed it can, overemphasis on historic reality and its attendant consequences can certainly be called a bad grade for the Christian religion.

Chapter 8
The Spatial Problem of History

WE HAVE SEEN that not all of mankind's experiences have been encompassed within the Christian idea of history. When one confines religious history to the Old Testament, the short period covered by the New Testament, and the two thousand years of Western European history, then obviously a majority of societies and religions have been left out of the schema. It remains to be seen if the portion of history covered by Christian history really justifies the faith placed in it.

If one were to take the last two thousand years and the events of that period as representative of the validity of the Christian religion in bringing peace on earth, then there would be little question that the religion is incapable of invoking any significant peaceful change in men or their societies. That period has been filled with continual warfare, conquest, bloodshed, and exploitation. In too many instances it was Christian pitted against Christian, leading one to conclude that the faith certainly played no favorites in choosing its victims. It has not been simply American Indians or other non-Christian peoples who have been the victims of Christian peoples. One crusade began by sacking Constantinople, a city filled with Christians at the time.

We can avoid prolonged examination of the Christian period; to recount the events would only appear as a deliberate indictment of the religion. It is far better to examine the nature of the Christian interpretation of history and seek to discover how and when it can be said that the Christian God does work in the affairs of men. At first glance it appears that God has not been as active in recent years as He once was. The Old Testament is filled with stories about the direct intervention of the Hebrew God in the affairs of men. These events were initially taken as actual historical facts, but in recent years an effort has been made to reinterpret them as representative of the spiritual quality of the Hebrew people and, by implication, the consequent spirituality of Christian peoples.

As Western people became more sophisticated about the nature of the universe, it became harder and harder to project exactly what the people of the Old Testament meant by seeing the action of their God in historic events. The victory of the English over the Spanish Armada (1588) was understood as an indication that God favored the Protestant English over the Catholic Spanish. While it did give rise to a plethora of religious poetry, prophecy, and theological development, it did not result in the establishment of a new religion. Even considered as a Christian renewal, Elizabethan England was not an exemplary Christian society.

Again, the victories of Russia over Napoleon and Hitler, aided each time by an unusually harsh Russian winter, might have in earlier times given rise to the idea that the Russians were especially chosen by God to be His people. Yet the theological development following those notable victories was practically nil. The American Civil War resulted in the banishment of slavery in the continental United States; yet as significant as this triumph was, it had practically no subsequent theological effect on the Christians of the land. Its major theological result could be said to have been the splitting of several major Protestant denominations into Northern and Southern branches, and thus if the war proved anything in a religious sphere, it proved damaging to the organizational churches.

Or we can ask what effect the numerous economic depressions in this country have had on the people's religious sensitivity. A depression as devastating as that of the 1930s visited on a nation in former times might have called forth a generation of repentant sinners and resulted in a renewal of religious faith of amazing intensity. Yet America's periodic depressions seem to call forth only bitter debates over the place and function of the federal government in the lives of citizens.

These are important questions to be asked, because of the contention of Christians that their God is specifically working in the events of mankind. In what specific way could God be said to be represented in the affairs of man's life? This question is a penetrating one; it is not easy to point to any specific event and find incontrovertible evidence of divine intervention. The problem puzzles theologians of all stripes, and some of them have made valiant efforts to derive a sound explanation of what is meant by the idea that God is working in history.

One of the significant efforts to recapture the Christian idea of history in the postwar era was the movement known as "demythologizing" history. Originally advocated by C. H. Dodd, an English theologian, the school of history demythologizers took on a broader aspect when Rudolf Bultmann began a systematic reinterpretation of the New Testament by using the framework of Heidegger's existential philosophy to eliminate the embarrassing eschatological sense of time from the New Testament. Bultmann felt that there was a basic Christian method and essence apart from any cultural values which might have crept into the text during New Testament days. His demythologizing thus involved an attempt to knock the Jewish apocalyptic flavor out of the Christian message. Under Bultmann's influence the idea grew that the events of the Bible were more symbolic than actual; the message of the coming of the Kingdom was primarily a psychological event, not an event of the real world.

In addition to Dodd and Bultmann, a movement known as the "death of God" philosophy attempted to revise and revitalize Christian theology. It was the child of Thomas J.J. Altizer. The "God Is Dead" theology flowered briefly during the social turmoil of the 1960s, enjoyed a brief day in the sun and apparently vanished quickly, much to the relief of other Christian theologians, who were not prepared to back Altizer and state that God had literally died on the cross and mankind had been godless ever since. Whatever else can be said about Altizer, one could only affirm that he took Western European history as a very valid reference point.

Other attempts have been made to realize, at least to some extent, the nature of God's activity in human history. Some Lutherans have been content to maintain that history is "His story," which is linguistically clever but does not tell us much. Other Christians, particularly those involved in the Civil Rights and other social movements of the last decade, have been willing to see the action of God reflected by the presence of the professional church in social movements. Nonclerical participants have also been very numerous in these movements, and thus the mere presence of clergy at antiwar rallies has not provided a startling renewal of theological doctrines.

Harvey Cox was among the most active clergymen in the movements of the 1960s, and if he did not have impeccable theological credentials, he at least made a significant effort to discover what was happening in modern society to which the

Christian peoples must attempt to speak. But even Cox with his Civil Rights experiences and work in the inner city was unable to derive a strong doctrine of God at work in history. In *The Secular City,* Cox finds that "the action of God occurs through what theologians have sometimes called 'historical events' but what might better be termed 'social change.'"[1]

Cox admonishes us to engage in social movements, in effect creating a "fervor" type of history—a qualitative, group type of historical reality. His empirical evidence that this is the correct Christian theory of history is singularly misty, however, since verification of the action of God depends on the ability of the Christian to "reflect." "Reflection," says Cox, "is that act by which the church scrutinizes the issues the society confronts in light of those decisive events of the past—Exodus and Easter—in which the intent of God has been apprehended by man in faith. Thus the church looks to the hints God has dropped in the past in order to make out what He is doing today."[2]

If we take the traditional conception of the events of history and attempt to locate the presence of theological dimensions, we basically arrive at Cox's conclusion. For traditional historical interpretation involves the premise that conditions were never much at variance with what we experience today. We have already seen the ridiculous conclusions attainable by applying a uniform method of arriving at descriptions of historical events. We find a benevolent pharaoh building pyramids on a part-time, make-work basis.

Yet the position which Cox takes, that the Christian God is somehow almost tiptoeing through history dropping sly hints that are to be discerned by a church critique based on the Exodus and Easter, presents even further problems. Do people believe that the Exodus actually happened as recorded in the Bible? Is the Bible a historically accurate book with respect to the events of major importance to both the Christians and Jews?

One would suppose that the Exodus would have been a

startling event in the experiences of the Hebrews. Slaves from their birth and with a heritage of slavery of nearly four centuries, they had no apparent reason whatsoever to expect release from their condition. Yet from the Exodus event can properly be said to have derived not only the modern Jewish religion but also Christianity and Islam—the two heretical offshoots of Jewish religious tradition.

What may be surprising to many people, particularly since theologians such as Cox depend so heavily on it for their verification, is that many significant theologians do not regard the Biblical accounts of the Exodus as historical. Theodore Gaster, for example, characterizes the events of the Exodus as recorded in the Old Testament as a flight of fancy of undiminished proportions:

> It is obvious to any unbiased reader that this story, with its markedly religious coloration and its emphasis on supernatural "signs and wonders," is more of a romantic saga or popular legend than an accurate record. Written down centuries later than the period which it describes, it is clearly more indebted to folklore than to sober fact.[3]

Theodore Gaster, while not the final authority on the Old Testament, is not an inconsiderable figure in the scholarly world. Yet he is unwilling to grant that the Bibilical record could be correct. Rather he understands the story as basically a romantic legend. Can Harvey Cox base his theology on a romantic legend? Can it be said then that God is not present in history at all or only within the poetic imagination that creates such romantic legends?

Gaster is a Jew, not a Christian. Johannes Pedersen is a noted Christian scholar who has specialized in Old Testament life and times. Almost every Protestant seminarian knows that *Israel: Its Life and Culture,* originally published in Swedish by Pedersen, is nearly *the* classic Christian study of early Israel. The book covers almost every aspect of Hebrew culture, illuminating many theological doctrines previously misunderstood or misinterpreted. In the book's appendix, Pedersen indicates that the Exodus is not history in the usual sense of the term but a highly colored legend meant to glorify the Jews.

> In forming an opinion of the story about the crossing of the Red Sea, it must be kept in mind, as we have remarked above, that this story, as well as the whole emigration legend, though inserted as part of an historical account, is quite obviously of a cultic character, for the whole narrative aims at glorifying the god of the people at the paschal feast though an exposition of the historical event that created the people. The object cannot have been to give a correct exposition of ordinary events but, on the contrary, to describe history on a higher plane, mythical exploits which make of the people a great people, nature subordinating itself to this purpose.[4]

In other words Pedersen finds the Exodus a historical event of no particular significance or relevance except as the Jews look backward into their past and attempt to glorify themselves. Again we have a form of historical interpretation employing modern forms as a basis for understanding events of the ancient past. The assumption that mankind's experiences have remained fairly uniform and constant dominates Pedersen's considerations.

Louis Dupré, a brilliant young Christian theologian at Georgetown University, devotes a chapter in his book *The Other Dimension* to an excellent review of the various Christian ideas on creation. Spinning away from traditional pitfalls of logic that maintain a benevolent god and the presence of evil in the world as a dualism, Dupré illustrates by a mention of the Exodus the idea that divine intervention can never eliminate the deficiencies of man's freedom: "The separation of the waters of the Red Sea may be seen as an affliction of physical evil for the Egyptians or a miraculous escape from it for the Hebrews, but it did not affect the moral or immoral intentions of either party."[5]

One would conclude from Dupré's sentence that here is one Christian theologian who is not afraid to contend that the Exodus was a real life, significant event of the ancient world featuring tidal waves, sweat, dust, blood, and all the grit of our existence. Where Harvey Cox and Pedersen—even Gaster, a Jew—fear to affirm God working in historic events, Dupré charges right in as a true believer. Such is not the case! After making this careful distinction between the morality of freedom and the goodness of God, Dupré has a little footnote stating: "Obviously in all this I do not take a position on the historical character of this event or of any particular miracle." [6]

Can this be? Can Christian theologians tell us that their God works in and dominates history while maintaining in their footnotes that they are not prepared to affirm that anything really happened? What about the resurrection? What kind of body did Jesus actually have? A "glorified body?" Or the body in which he walked on earth? Are Christian thinkers prepared to say? Popular Christianity, of course, is prepared to affirm almost everything it may happen to have called to its attention, including Jonah and Job, the subjects of two stories that seem to fall well within the categories of romantic legend these theologians advocated.

Yet the biblical stories of Jonah, Job, and others are not central to the Bible's major premise, that God specifically chose one people from out among the peoples of the world—or that the logical conclusion to the Exodus event was the crucifixion of Jesus and his ascension into heaven after being dead three days. If we narrow the historical requirements of the Christian religion to affirming only two of the infinite number of events which have taken place in time and space, even then, apparently, we are left with legend and folklore.

If the major events of the Bible are to be taken not as

actual events involving men, events of such significance that
they could be used later as patterns by which the subsequent
"church" could discern God dropping "hints" in the affairs
of men, then what do we make of the Christian religion? Can
we take it seriously? Even more, can we affirm that it is
superior to any other religion, and if so, on what basis?
Surely, at least, not on the basis that it tells us the true story
of mankind.

Behind the Christian theory of history lies a peculiar logic
of interpretation. One can see it clearly in the proposition put
forward by Paul Tillich in his *Systematic Theology:*

> It can be stated that in Christianity the decisive event occurs in
> the center of history and that it is precisely the event that gives
> history a center; that Christianity is also aware of the "not-
> yet," which is the main emphasis in Judaism; and that
> Christianity knows the revelatory possibilities in every
> moment of history. [7]

In other words the Christians ask us to accept that there is a
history, that there is a central event making the rest of the
history intelligible, and that because there is a central event,
there must necessarily be a history. The logic is clearly a
precursor of *Catch-22.* Whenever we focus on one of the very
important events of that line of history, we are told by Protestants, Roman Catholics, and Jews alike that what happened was really just the growth of legend, folklore, and
glorification, not a spectacular event.

This dilemma over the nature of history occurs and will
occur whenever a religion is divorced from space and made
an exclusive agent of time. Events become symbolic teaching
devices, and the actual sequence of physical action which
could indicate a divine intervention becomes unimportant;
what is important are the moral lessons and ethical choices
the legend illustrates. The Christians of another era believed
that their Bible was the real record of events. While they
could not geographically pinpoint the Garden of Eden, they

damn sure could find Mount Sinai and Jerusalem. So they took everything as historical fact.

The contrast between Christianity and its interpretation of history—the temporal dimension—and the American Indian tribal religions—basically spatially located—is clearly illustrated when we understand the nature of sacred mountains, sacred hills, sacred rivers, and other geographical features sacred to Indian tribes. The Navajo, for example, have sacred mountains where they believe that they rose from the underworld. Now there is no doubt in any Navajo's mind that these particular mountains are the exact mountains where it all took place. There is no beating around the bush on that. No one can say when the creation story of the Navajo happened, but everyone is fairly certain where the emergence took place.

The test of the extent to which a religion has a claim to historical validity, therefore, should as least partially involve its recognition of the lands upon which the religious event which created the community took place. And that religion should stand by the historical nature of the event; it should never back off and disclaim everything while becoming furious with other peoples for not believing its claim.

If the present interpretation of religious history which is accepted by many Christian theologians is maintained we are left with a religion devoid of any significance in either time or space. History becomes a series of glorified legends which teach ethical lessons and it becomes a demoniac thing to believe that the world operates one way for religious purposes and an entirely different way for secular purposes. Leaving aside popular Christianity, which has rarely questioned anything and remains comfortable in a three-dimensional universe while men walk on the moon, what effect would there be if we took the Exodus story, since it really triggers the creation of three world religions, and maintained that it in fact records a specific happening which occurred at a definite time and in a specific space. Do we have a problem?

The problem is that one man has dared to challenge the historians on their own grounds, and he is winning the battle. Immanuel Velikovsky,[8] a psychoanalyst and intellect of superstar magnitude, while doing research on a projected work encompassing three of Sigmund Freud's heroes, Moses, Oedipus, and Akhnaton, found evidence that Egypt had suffered a devastating catastrophe at one point in its history. The parallels between the Egyptian calamity and the accounts of Exodus were so startling that Velikovsky began to trace other evidence of natural disaster on a global scale in the legends of peoples around the globe. By 1950 he was ready to unveil his documented conclusions on the Exodus.

In 1950 Velikovsky published *Worlds in Collision,* in which he contends that global cataclysms fundamentally changed the face of the planet in historical times, the Exodus being the event most clearly documented, thanks in part to the religious interpretation given it by the Hebrews who had seized the chance to flee Egypt in the confusion and disorder. The major thesis of the book is that Venus was a recent addition to the groups of planets circling the sun, having been ejected from Jupiter sometime earlier and careening through our solar system for a period of centuries. During the time of the Exodus and later in the eighth century B.C., Venus came into near collision with Earth and Mars, disrupting the orbits of each and at one point saving Earth from a fatal collision with Mars.

Pointing out that prior to the second millenium B.C., there were no records of Venus as a planet by either the Hindus or Babylonians, Velikovsky asked why the most visible object in our night sky, outside of the moon, had not attracted the attention of the meticulous ancient astronomers. He replied that the only reasonable conclusion was that Venus could not be observed because it was not in the sky at that point.

Ancient tales describe Venus as coming from the head of Jupiter, and other ancient records describe the struggles between the dragon and the cultural hero. Combining these features of mankind's collective memory, Velikovsky concluded that the tail of a comet doubled back in an electric-field attraction with its head would appear to people as a struggle between a hero and a reptile of enormous length and strength.

The testimony of the peoples from around the globe was thus compared to see if the legends bore any resemblance to the description obtained from the Near Eastern region. The legends bore out the thesis, and where they appeared to vary, the variance only supported the thesis since the geographical location of the people changed the nature of the spectacle they would have been able to observe. Velikovsky thus unveiled a cosmic struggle between a comet and the two planets most familiar to mankind—Earth and Mars. In doing so, he naturally canceled psychological theories of religion as a fantasy of dream projections, raising the question of whether or not a substantial number of religions did not arise from activities taking place in the night sky.

The sequence developed by Velikovsky up to the Exodus explains a substantial number of lesser and more puzzling verses that theologians have always seen as evidence of the Hebrew prophets' extreme poetic pretensions. It is, as briefly and accurately as possible, the following: At some time, as yet not accurately identified but before 1500 B.C., Jupiter ejected a comet of planetary size, the red spot of the planet observed today being the scar remaining on Jupiter from this incident. The comet began to travel on a highly irregular path through our solar system, menacing Earth on a number of occasions. Its bright light was the initial indication of its presence.

Eventually, however, Venus began to intrude on Earth's presence as it passed its perihelion and began the long distance of its elliptical orbit. In or around 1500 B.C., Earth passed through the tail of the comet. The first indication that the planet was in trouble was a rusty iron dust that covered the globe, giving the land and waters a bloody hue. The miracle of Moses turning the waters bloody was, therefore, not a poetic flight of a later scribe but the comet's initial effect.

As Earth went deeper into the comet's tail, hydrocarbon gases covering parts of the planet exploded in great bursts of fire. Billions of gallons of hydrocarbons in the form of petroleum rained on parts of the planet, forming the oil fields we have tapped in recent years. Great pools of naphtha fell into depressions, caught fire, and burned for years giving the whole planet a twilight of nearly a generation. Then as Earth went even further into the comet's tail, it was caught in an electromagnetic vise and its axis tilted, resulting in the sudden destruction of the Near East's major cities.

The catastrophe was worldwide, traumatic, and highly destructive. Rivers reversed themselves. Islands disappeared into the sea, other islands emerged. Mountains crashed skyward where peaceful strata had lain for centuries. A global hurricane ensued, leveling forests in a moment. Monstrous lakes were formed when waters jumped mountains and could not return to the seas. Arabia, once a prosperous land, and the Sahara, then populated by several large cities, were turned into desolate wastes. Part of the world lay in utter darkness, part in extended but smoky light.

The Hebrew slaves fled from the smoking ruins of Egypt as the Middle Kingdom fell in a major catastrophe. Racing for the sea of reeds, they saw the comet as a pillar of smoke during the day and a pillar of fire at night. Reaching Pi-ha-Khiroth at the edge of the Red Sea, they were pursued by the Pharaoh Taoui-Thom and his army. The action of the comet temporarily pulled the waters from their bed, allowing the Hebrews to cross and destroying the pharaoh's army as the waters collapsed.

The hydrocarbons of the comet's tail formed, by precipitation every morning, a nourishing substance which the Hebrews ate, thus providing them with sustenance during their flight into the Sinai desert. This was the manna from heaven of which the Bible speaks. The sun, which had previously risen in the west and set in the east, appeared to have reversed itself, now setting in the west and rising in the east. Those societies that had survived relatively intact began the laborious task of locating the new directions, making up calendars, and determining the length of the year.

Earth had only begun to recover, however, when Venus made another close approach. It was some fifty years later and coincided with Joshua's conquest of Canaan. This time the first notice of calamity occurred just prior to a battle, when a rain of meteorites pelted the Near East. Again the sun appeared temporarily to stop in the sky, and Joshua, who was just beginning a battle, used this prolonged day to achieve victory in the valley of Beth-horon.

This sequence of events, as projected in Velikovsky's *Worlds in Collision,* was more precisely developed in his companion volume *Ages in Chaos,* published some years later. Where all previous historians proudly interpreted the books of the Old Testament as divine and sublime poetry of first-rank quality, the Velikovsky thesis explained the trauma and disasters suffered by the people of the Near East and gave startling new meaning to the Bible's descriptions. The verses celebrating the power of the Lord, taken as spectacular but impossible sequences of natural events by Christian scholars, began to leap from the pages as descriptions of natural phenomena.

Ravaged by the approach of Venus twice within a fifty-year period, the nations of the world decided that they had better find a way to appease and pacify the goddess of the comet before she destroyed everything. Religions began to emphasize rites and rituals to prevent the near approach of

Venus. Blood sacrifices were offered as peoples desperately sought ways to avoid continued destruction by the comet. Venus continued to cross Earth's orbit, beginning to come dangerously close to Mars so that the comet, while apparently appeased by the new religious ceremonies, was still feared by men as the initiator of destruction. A new conflict was building in the heavens as the orbits began to move closer toward a collision course.

In the days of King Uzziah, Venus missed Earth but managed to pull Mars from its orbit, sending it on a collision course with Earth. Mars was much smaller than Earth and did not have the velocity of Venus, so its approach to Earth did not result in the same degree of destruction that earlier passes of the comet had caused. Earth, which had earlier stabilized its calendar at 360 days, was forced farther out into space away from the sun, resulting in our present year of 365.25 days.

In 687 B.C. Sennacherib led his Assyrian army into Israel with the intent of conquering Jerusalem. On the evening of March 23, the first night of the Hebrew Passover, the Assyrians camped outside the city, ready to take it in the following morning. In what may have been history's most spectacular lightning bolt, the army, 185,000 strong, was destroyed when an electromagnetic charge was suddenly arched between Mars and Earth. The Hebrews had been saved twice on the same date by heavenly intervention. Is it any wonder that they used the most powerful, descriptive terms to praise their God?

Earth did not grind to a half again, but its rotation was slowed or halted for a number of hours—the prolonged night during which the Assyrian army was destroyed. The axis was somewhat shifted again, coming back closer to its original position before the start of the catastrophes. Mars and Venus then set up an electrical field between themselves, resulting in the repositioning of Mars away from its collision course with Earth. In the sky an immense drama was enacted, as Mars and Venus set and reset fields of incredible electrical energy with respect to each other. The struggle was recounted by the Greeks as the gods intervening in the battle to take Troy.

Mars finally achieved a release from Venus and settled in its present orbit. We have pictures today from our space probes showing the terrible extent of destruction suffered by Mars from the catastrophe. The planet, with heavy scars from the rain of meteorites, looks like the moon. Venus settled in its present orbit in a highly incandescent state, gathering up remnants of its tail as thick hydrocarbon clouds that space probes have disclosed cover the planet.

Now of course, all of this activity in the heavens was not new to Christians believing in the power of God and His role in history. They had read and believed it for centuries and had taught it as fact to generations of converts. When Velikovsky published his books documenting the catastrophes, however, Christians were not to be found defending the thesis or applauding his scholarly effort, which caused severe traumas in several sciences, including astronomy, geology, physics, and history. Rather they remained silent, while the academic community carried on what may have been history's most closed-minded, libelous attack against a thinker daring to ask separate academic fields to achieve a unity of knowledge.

Worlds in Collision was attacked by "respectable" scientists even before it was published. A concentrated effort was begun to force the Macmillan Company, Velikovsky's publisher, to stop the presses. Scholars began a boycott of Macmillan's textbook division, its most vulnerable place. Macmillan could not withstand the concerted attack and transferred the book's rights to Doubleday. A conspiracy of silence dropped over discussion of Velikovsky's works. He subsequently published *Earth in Upheaval,* which was an embarrassing revelation of geological shortcomings. The book simply took extant geological works and showed that the subject matter had been incorrectly interpreted and slanted by numerous geologists to make it conform to the then prevailing theories of geologic change based upon the interminably slow processes already defined by biologists to explain evolution.

This scientific basis of Velikovsky's work involved a recognition of the possibility that cosmic catastrophes could take place and had in historical times. These catastrophes were observed by men all over the globe and became part of their creation legends or myths explaining the origin of their sacrificial rites and rituals. Thus in the folklore of ancient men had been hidden important observations that were crucially important for an understanding of the nature of the universe. Scientists disagreed, however, and they began to produce facts and figures to refute Velikovsky. Fear set in among scholars, and no one stood up to demand that Velikovsky be allowed to present his views. He was subjected to bitter criticism by people who had not read his books but who had learned, from their earliest childhood, that the tales of non-Christian peoples about serpents swallowing the sun and prolonged nights of utter darkness were just pagan, hardly historical, superstitions, and probably the work of the devil.

As Velikovsky unveiled his concept of the solar system, respectable scholars guffawed at his apparently wild predictions and suppositions. Practically every point he suggested was derided as being totally contrary to what science had already "proved" to be true. Scholars in the major disciplines affected by the thesis ridiculed Velikovsky, announcing satirically that if his thesis were true, it would require certain phenomena to be present, which everyone knew was not the case. All of these wild predictions, made in 1950 by Velikovsky, were universally rejected.

Then the evidence began to come in. Science had new opportunities to conduct sophisticated experiments with the beginning of the space probes. New methods of dating materials began to be developed, the International Geophysical Year of 1958 was held to determine systematically certain facts about the planet, and eventually the Mars and Venus probes by space rockets were made. Universally and without exception Velikovsky's predictions and suggestions about the planets were confirmed. No other comprehensive explanation of the solar system had returned as many different accurate results as had the theory espoused in *Worlds in Collision*.

Naturally the scholars who had derided Velikovsky did not credit him with the results of his creative thought. They continued the curtain of silence while stealing his ideas as fast as they could read his books. Some of the more prominent scientists had made dramatic announcements that if Velikovsky were right, then Earth, the sun, Venus, the moon, Mars, and other heavenly bodies would have to have certain characteristics. When Velikovsky was proved correct, they promptly hedged rhetorically and dodged their embarrassment in double-talk, too chagrined or perhaps too stupid to apologize. Some of these memorable statements by noted scientists should be recorded for posterity's sake.

Velikovsky suggested that the sun was an electrically charged body. Donald Menzel, a Harvard astronomer and one of Velikovsky's most bitter critics, ridiculed the idea. He maintained that the sun cannot hold a charge above 1,800 volts if positive and a single volt if negative and said that Velikovsky's theory required a charge of 10^{19} volts which he assured everyone was patently impossible. This was in 1952. In 1960 V. A. Bailey of Australia discovered that the sun carries a negative charge of 10^{19} volts.

Cecilia Payne-Gaposchkin, another Harvard astronomer and the scientist who reviewed Velikovsky's first book by misquoting him and then ridiculing the misquotations, said in 1950 that the planets could not possibly possess electrostatic charges sufficient to produce the effects Velikovsky claimed for them. Three years later in an article in *Scientific American,* she advocated a universe that was essentially a gravitating electromagnet. She never mentioned that the idea had already been advanced by Velikovsky and rejected by herself as evidence of his instability as a scholar.

Velikovsky maintained that Venus, deriving from an erratic past as a comet, would be in an incandescent state. This was in direct opposition to what was "known" by science in 1950. Donald Menzel lost no time in ridiculing Velikovsky, since he was one of the leading proponents of the theory that Venus has an extremely low temperature. In 1955 he revised his estimate of the ground temperature of Venus, concluding that it was probably 50° C. The Venus probe of 1962 indicated that the surface temperature of Venus was some 800° F. Later probes showed that ground temperature was closer to 1,000° F.

Since Venus was believed by Velikovsky to have come from Jupiter, he predicted that Jupiter was probably a dark star giving off radio signals. This was in 1953 at Princeton during a talk to the graduate college. Less than two years later, two scientists found radio signals coming from Jupiter, and by 1965 Jupiter was declared a dark star. Velikovsky also predicted that Earth would have a magnetosphere reaching as far as the moon. In 1958 the Van Allen belts were discovered, named after James Van Allen who had only measured them, not after Velikovsky who had predicted them.

The May 1972 issue of *Pensée,* a journal published by the Student Academic Freedom Forum in Portland, Oregon, gives the complete story of Velikovsky's amazing predictions and his history of scientific persecution and derision. It devotes a considerable number of pages to a simple listing of his suggestions about the nature of the universe and the history of ancient peoples. Even a casual glance at the list of predictions made by Velikovsky in the face of then-accepted scientific theory, which it turned out was really dogma, is staggering to behold. There appears to be no doubt that Velikovsky has been vindicated and that we are on the verge of an incredible reordering of our conception of both the world and history.

Science and the academic community have revealed themselves as superstitious, dogmatic, narrow-minded, and spiteful little people as a result of their treatment of Immanuel Velikovsky. For nearly two and a half decades, they have refused to allow him to discuss the theories that have produced such a plentitude of newly verified facts about the universe as to make the basic theory the most revolutionary explanation of the creation we have ever seen. Some men have borrowed Velikovsky's ideas almost totally without giving him any credit or even mention. Others have reversed themselves completely without apologizing for their past errors or acknowledging Velikovsky's earlier and correct contentions.

The most common attack now leveled against Velikovsky is that he simply made a series of lucky guesses and hit on quite a few of them. The point that this attack misses is that every prediction that he made had to fit into his general interpretation of the nature of the solar system. He was not simply spinning a tale and casually throwing off unrelated predictions. Rather everything suggested by Velikovsky originated from the implications of his thesis. His predictions involve pulling together the meaning of numerous fields of interest to form a unified view of the universe. Taken together they give us a picture of a different kind of world and a different kind of history in which things of utmost significance happen—similar to the original Christian contention that God does work in the affairs of men.

Worlds in Collision has great relevance for religious thinkers. Velikovsky's original point of departure was the belief that the Exodus was an event of worldwide significance and experienced by peoples on a global basis. His search of many peoples' folklore and their religious and cultural myths and stories indicated that celestial events viewed from different places gave rise to different descriptions of phenomena which scientifically described a definite sequence. The religious interpretation of the events varied, of course, with the respective peoples' location, language, culture, and state of existence.

With the exception of Fulton Oursler, who wrote an article for the *Reader's Digest* correlating Velikovsky's thesis with the Old Testament—a duplication of effort considering that *Ages in Chaos* is a supreme demonstration of Velikovsky's skill as a biblical scholar and historian—no Christian theologian or Old Testament scholar of any note supported consideration of the thesis that the Old Testament might be historically accurate in many respects.

Christianity lost a chance to recoup its lost ground and assert the historical nature of its revelation. Instead, as we have seen, Christian scholars continued to view the Exodus as the glorification of romantic Hebraic legends. Was it perhaps the threat that the verification of the historical nature of the Old Testament on a world basis was also the verification of the legends of many of the competing religions? Did not the historical nature of religion frighten Christians who had not believed the Bible after all?

Granted that it is a severe rupture for the theological mind to go from a conception of God slyly dropping hints for the Church to discern to a conception of a cataclysmic event in which a number of religious are formed. But even today we have some indication that religions do not simply arise because the poets of a nation wish to glorify their past. The conflict in the Second World War brought Americans to parts of the world then unknown and unvisited by modern men. After the Americans had left certain islands in the

South Pacific, scholars discovered that a new religion had grown up that saw the Americans' airplanes and machinery as manifestations of their Gods. The cargo cults, as they have been called, would indicate that if an event is out of the ordinary and makes a sufficient impression on people, it can call forth a religion regardless of how correct that religion would appear to be to observers.

The Old Testament is probably extremely accurate in many respects, particularly in those events it described that involve specified sequences of natural events. The Old Testament may stand forth as our best record of man's ancient experience. But other religions covering the same event with different descriptions have an equal claim to validity. Our task, therefore, is not the affirmation of one religion as against any other, but an examination of the religious stories of all religions to determine to what extent they are memories of real events and to what extent they are elaborations of poetic and philosophical speculations.

It is for that reason that we have postponed discussion of American Indian tribal religions' creation stories. Can we determine to what extent they are remnants of tribal memories of a world catastrophe and to what extent they are actual tales about the creation as an event? For it is in the spatial dimension of tribal religions that we find their religious genius, not particularly in their recording of a linear time sequence. It is this spatial dimension that Christianity has lacked and misunderstood, which would appear to preclude it from becoming a realistic influence among mankind's societies.

Chapter 9
Origin of Religion

Suppose Immanuel Velikovsky is correct? Suppose that instead of the Exodus accounts being a poetic elaboration of religious doctrine of a later time, they are fairly well-remembered accounts of the phenomena encountered by the Hebrews as they left Egypt. How then do we approach religious writings? Are they to be understood as actual events, and do we take all religious stories as having been real events at some time and someplace in man's experience? It would seem that we have a major task of discovering to what extent we can accept the historical veracity of any story of ancient times. The fact that Immanuel Velikovsky's projections about the nature of the physical world continue to produce startling verifications would tend to make us back up and take another look at religious doctrines, symbolism, and beliefs.

The assumption apparently made by theologians when discussing religious writings and their symbols and images is that world events have followed a fairly homogeneous pattern and that no particular event has happened which we cannot observe in similar pattern today. Using this assumption the

Exodus does become simply another political revolt, which in later years had the fortune to be accepted as illustrating religious beliefs. But if we make this assumption, we are almost immediately faced with a more fundamental question about the origin of the religious beliefs illustrated in the stories that are found in religious traditions.

The Western conception of a homogeneous time experience apparently has many roots. Certainly one influence can be said to have been Greek philosophy and its insistence on the uniform operation of nature. This idea surfaces continually in Western thought, and it continually intrudes into theological doctrines about religion and the nature of God. So strong has this idea been that natural events have been forced into this interpretive pattern, even when the facts warranted otherwise.

For many centuries peoples of Western Europe believed that the heavens, being made by God at creation, were constant. The appearance of meteors and comets was thus a great embarrassment, since these phenomena seemed to indicate that the heavens were not all that stable. Was this possible in a divinely constructed universe? Present-day astronomers are searching the records of other societies for evidence of a supernova that occurred on July 4, 1054. It was one of the spectacular events of celestial history, and it apparently lasted some three weeks and was clearly observable at various parts of the planet, since it appeared quite close to the moon in its crescent phase.[1]

In at least one cave in California and on rock carvings and paintings in Arizona and New Mexico, there are representations of a crescent moon with a bright object quite near it. There are speculations that the early peoples of North America saw the supernova and made these records to verify for subsequent generations that such a thing had happened. There are very few references to this event in Europe, where the social science of history was fairly advanced. The reason that there are very few records in Europe is that everyone believed that the heavens were constant. Thus people did not really see what they were seeing.

In view of this startling victory of faith over experience, is it any wonder that contemporary theories of the nature of the Exodus fall apart whenever they are examined? If men become so blinded to their observations that their beliefs override their actual experiences, would it not seem possible that the whole method of interpreting events needs drastic revision?

In another day, perhaps, the rock paintings in the American Southwest would be taken as a primitive form of religious poetry. Theologians, historians of religion, psychoanalysts, and other wise men would pour forth books about the primitive ideas of the natives who could not know that no extremely bright star exists beside the moon at its crescent. Fortunately today we have sufficient fragmentation of knowledge so that astronomers can use Indian rock paintings as verifications that the supernova was observed.

Since it is possible, indeed highly probable, that American Indians observed and faithfully recorded a celestial event while their supposedly more civilized neighbors in Europe were gritting their teeth, reaffirming their faith in the Christian religion, and refusing to see the supernova, the whole question of the interpretation of religious symbols, doctrines, and beliefs should be reexamined. Suppose we find in the tribal traditions a memory that is not only more correct in many aspects than that of the Western religions, but suppose that we find in them the longer and more extensive history of mankind. That prospect has rarely been considered by Westerners. Yet it is precisely the consideration that must be made, if Western men are to be released from their religiously ethnocentric universe.

It is with this consideration in mind that we have postponed any discussion of American Indian tribal stories about creation. In the Western tradition we have been taught to regard all stories about beginnings as primitive efforts to understand how the world began. The obvious use of linear time as a determining factor in making sense of legends is so dominant in Western and Christian thought that it prevents legends being accepted on their terms.

We cannot necessarily project the thought that the early peoples in North America were any more concerned to describe the creation as an event than they were to explain any other facet of their experience as an event. The absence of a theological theory of history should be sufficient evidence of the Indians' refusal to use time as the determining factor when interpreting their experiences. Where we do have legends describing world conditions, the existence of other worlds, or the existence of catastrophic conditions caused by certain factors, we cannot assume that the people are concerned primarily with the sequence of events. They might much more be concerned with describing the actual life conditions, and the apparent sequence of activity in the legends might be a fairly accurate description of what actually took place rather than a poetic elaboration of events for theological purposes.

In short, what we have previously been pleased to call creation stories might not be such at all. They might be simply the collective memories of a great and catastrophic event through which people came to understand themselves and the universe they inhabited. Creation stories may simply be the survivors' memories of reasonably large and destructive events.

The tribal religion of the Hopi Indians of Arizona is a case in point. The legends of the Hopi relate that the world as they have known it has been destroyed three times and that our present world is now reaching a time of impending destruction. This religious tradition, which has tribal variations, appears as a spiral of religious insight rather than a rigid temporal or a totally spatial understanding. The ex-

istence of the Hopi in all worlds is predicated on a particular land being given to them over which they assume a
custodial function; in any specific world it involves deliberate
spatial considerations. The collective memory inherent in the
traditions combines time and space in a comprehensible
manner, however, and one which we may be working toward
today. [2]

The first Hopi world was called Topka, and it was characterized as a world of endless space. Topka was considered to be the original world, and the basic themes that are
found in some of the tribal legends about the nature of creation are found in descriptions of this world. The direction
of this world, according to the Hopi, was west. The living
things of the creation were congenial and lived without strife.
Eventually men became convinced that real differences
existed between the various life forms, and men became
increasingly wicked toward other species. This wickedness
was erased when the world was destroyed by a rain of fire.

The Hopi survived the end of this world by living underground with the ants. As the world cooled and men
were able to emerge, they discovered that the world had been
rearranged. Water now existed where land had formerly
been. Land stood where there had been waters. The direction
of the world was west, and it was called "dark midnight."

In the second world the men and animals were not allowed
to live together, so they lived separate lives. The fear that the
problems of the old world would return to plague them
caused this separation. Men came to learn the arts of trade
and commerce, but they used these talents to accumulate
more material goods than were needed. This greed eventually
led to the downfall of the second world. The earth's axis
tilted, and the world spun around rapidly, destroying the
natural features of the landscape. The world was stabilized
only by passing through an extremely cold part of space that
froze the waters into solid ice.

Everything was lifeless, and to survive the people lived

underground once again. Then the earth's axis changed again, and it resumed a more normal orbit of rotation around the sun. Revolution on nearly the same axis was eventually restored and the ice began to melt. The surface of the planet regained its original ability to sustain life. Men emerged once again. This third world was known to the Hopi as Kuskura, and its direction was east. The new world was the scene of much activity. Men had not forgotten the trade and commerce they had learned in the previous world, and substantial technology was developed. Men learned to fly through the air in *patuwvotas,* which were shields made from hide propelled by some unidentified power.

Using these flying shields, the various nations of men warred against one another. The warfare grew so intense that the third world was destroyed. Warned ahead of time that the world would be flooded, the Hopis appear to have constructed special cylinders of hollow reeds that floated on the flood waters. The descriptions of the flood bear close similarities with the flood stories of other nations. As the waters began to subside, the people sent out birds to find any lands remaining above the waters. Eventually the waters receded, and the various nations were assigned lands for themselves. The fourth world, the one in which we are presently living, began.

Could such a sequence of worlds have been made up in the imagination, no matter how religious that imagination, of a primitive mind that has been otherwise classified as relatively uninformed about the physical forces of the natural world? Could people have conceived the changing of directions of the world and made such a conception a primary part of their religious belief without something having happened that would justify such a belief? By "direction" of the world, we are basically talking about the rising and setting of the sun. In translating the meaning of the four Hopi worlds, we have the first two worlds in which the sun rises in the west and sets in the east, and the last two in which it rises in the east and sets in the west. All that is necessary to account for the difference in phenomena is a rotational change in direction.

Suppose that we break into this sequence and suggest that a nation of people comes into existence in one of the worlds. It begins to recognize itself as a people distinct from the other groups inhabiting the planet. A language comes into being that is relatively distinct from other languages. A religion comes into being that attempts to account for the creation of the world as the people either know it or can remember it from earlier legends. Their "creation" story involves the fact that the world was originally a cold and icy one. Gradually its rotation was changed, possibly by the assistance of hero figures, and the world began to warm. Eventually it warmed sufficiently to support life, and the various life forms came into being.

One day these people encounter a people who speak to them of two worlds. They are incredulous. Everyone knows that there is only one world and that it was created by changing the axis of the world, so that the ice, the original substance of the universe, gradually evolved ice. When they hear stories of how the first world was destroyed by rains of fire, they are livid. Pagans, they scream. The stories of the first world are interpreted as merely childish wish projections of a people refusing to believe that the ultimate nature of the world is ice. Measures are taken to be sure that the people who believe in the first world are converted to the belief that the stories of the world's origin as a large block of ice are the absolute truth as revealed by God Himself.

That is the precise position into which non-Christians are placed when the Christian religion insists that its story of creation is descriptive of the original creation event and that their stories are superstitions that have arisen because of a great psychological need which can be filled by accepting the Christian version. Forcing consideration of creation to be examined as if it were a specific event destroys the possibility of knowing the nature of the world with any certainty. It also presumes that the Christian account of the creation is either poetic ideology typical of a certain kind of people and that this kind of people is by definition the people of most ancient vintage. Such conclusions are not necessarily correct. That a religious tradition may contain references to more than one type of world should indicate that the tradition is at least older than traditions speaking of only one world.

Near Eastern religions, for example, appear to have only one recallable beginning. Both Genesis and the Enuma Elish of the Babylonian records indicate a beginning in a world of waters. Do these records extend only to the third world of the Hopi? Were there societies of men capable of passing on a longer history of mankind in the Near East, or were they destroyed by one of the earlier catastrophes visited on the planet? The basis of perpetuating religious knowledge would appear to be a spectacular event experienced by a people who subsequently survive sufficiently long to pass on the tradition. In the Near East we may have peoples surviving in an area where a catastrophe did not wreck total destruction.

The Enuma Elish begins with a description of the universe:

When a sky above had not (yet even) been mentioned
(And) the name of firm ground below had not (yet
    even) been thought of;
(When) only primeval Apsu, their begetter,
And Mummu and Ti'amat—she who gave birth to them all—
Were mingling their waters in one;
When no bog had formed (and) no island could be found;
When no god whosoever had appeared,
Had been named, had been determined as to (his) lot,
Then were gods formed within them. [3]

The Enuma Elish has sometimes been regarded as the

prototype of the Genesis story, sometimes as a parallel description of the creation as handed down in the Hebrew tradition. That it closely follows between Babylonian and Hebrew traditions is significant. Genesis appears to be concerned with much the same phenomena:

> In the beginning God created the heaven and earth.
> And the earth was without form, and void; and the darkness was upon the face of the deep. And the Spirit of God moved upon the face of the waters.
> And God said, Let there be light; and there was light.
> And God saw the light, that it was good: and God divided the light from the darkness.
> And God called the light Day, and the darkness he called Night. And the evening and the morning were the first day.[4]

If we closely examine these two traditions in a spatial sense rather than as a primeval event, we find that they rather specifically describe a particular condition in which there is extreme darkness. From our knowledge of the world in which we live, it would indicate extensive cloud cover. The concern of both stories would appear to be the separation of the waters so that the gods can determine and name the sky and the ground. When we understand that Genesis projects a much longer sequence of appearances, and if we understand the sequence as taking place in a particular place although not necessarily limited to seven days or extended for millions of years, we face a new sense of reality.

On the second day in Genesis the waters are divided between heaven and earth. The third day plant life is created. It is not until the fifth day that animal and fish life emerge, but on the fourth day the stars, the sun and moon are created. Clarence Darrow is supposed to have made Williams Jennings Bryan look foolish by asking him how the morning and evening of the first day could occur when the sun, moon, and stars were not created until the fourth day. If we view the emergence of each form mentioned in Genesis as the sequence in which things could be distinguished one from another following a monstrous flood with attendant cloud cover of unimaginable magnitude, the appearance of the sun, moon, and stars at that point at which the water vapor has allowed their light to be seen appears eminently reasonable.

The noteworthy factors in the Genesis account are that the sequence of action is not incompatible with the phenomena that would be expected in a catastrophe of major importance. Plant life, for example, develops prior to the creation of the heavens. We know that plant life would have an extremely difficult time originating without the conditions allowing photosynthesis being initiated before the origination of plants. But plants could survive for some time between periods of ordinary sunlight, if they were already in existence. While light itself is apparently present in the Genesis account prior to plant life, distinguishing the source of light comes after the emergence of plant life. We could find no better description of a planet emerging from a catastrophic event than to find light diffused in its atmosphere and people, unable to identify the source of light, still being able to recognize that somehow light and darkness had been separated.

We have an option that will apparently never be settled: Is the Genesis account a refined and somehow more sublime religious statement of creation that is secondary and derivative from the Enuma Elish; or are they really two accounts of two distinct peoples, bearing similarity to one another because of their geographic proximity to the event? Many scholars have simply foreclosed the second option, believing that the accounts are poetic attempts to describe the original creation event, instead of asking themselves whether these accounts are simply memories of one specific event in world history.

When we turn to American Indian tribal religions, we find a number of similarities also forming a pattern of interpretation. [The Navajo legends begin with an account of the emergence of the Navajos or First People from the underworlds. "The first three worlds were neither good nor healthful. They moved all the time and made the people dizzy. Upon ascending into this world, the Navajo found only darkness, and they said we must have light."[5] The Navajos then separate light into constituent colors of white, blue, yellow, and black representing the colors of the sky during the twenty-four-hour period of rotation.

The Pawnees and Arickara also speak of ancient people emerging from the darkness into a lighted world. The Pueblos are led by Mother Corn (plant life) into the new world of light from the world of darkness. The Mandans climb a vine rope from the underground until a large woman proves to be too heavy for the rope and breaks it, leaving some of the people remaining under the earth. Other tribes have had variations of this general theme of emerging from the underground, where they have survived a great catastrophe or at least begun their existence in this present world as a people. There would appear to be no reason for a number of tribes sharing this story, unless there was some event behind it even though very dimly recalled in tribal memory. Perhaps the disaster of which the Near East spoke did not affect the peoples of North America, who had prepared an underground shelter for themselves in anticipation of the event. At the least we can suggest that some common experience must be shared by some of the tribes, as emergence legends among other peoples of the globe appear to be rather sparse.

The tribal religions would serve to remind us that the scope of human history cannot be encompassed within a linear time sequence running from a creation event to the present-day world. The strong possibility that man's different societies recall in their religious traditions various geographical histories of the planet can lead us to remember the neglected dimension of religion that has appeared in nearly every religious tradition of man. If we recall the thrust of Jewish history and its eschatology in the time of Jesus, we come to recognize that land, the promised land, has remained as a constant and tangible element of religious experiences of communities of men.

While the theology of the Old Testament appears to focus on the Promised Land as early as the time of Abraham, it is with the emergence of the Hebrews as a migrating nation into Canaan that the community and the land merge into a psychic and religious unity. From that time on the people orient themselves around the idea that God has given them this particular piece of land. Even those people in Jesus' time who sought the return of the Son of Man as the Jewish Messiah looked for a military hero to restore their land ownership. The translation by Christians of the fanaticism of the Jewish resistance to the Romans in the days of Jesus into a "misunderstanding" by the Jews of the nature of the Messiah has always been a difficult interpretation for the Christians to make. By substituting heaven for the tangible restoration of Palestine to the Jews by driving the Romans out, Christians eliminated the dimension of land from religion, and necessarily their theology had to change Hebrew tribal memories of a particular land into a generalized statement about the origin of the world. Without the particularity of land on which it was intended that a particular people live, creation had to become an event of the beginnings of the world.

It is quite possible, therefore, that as we look for the origin of peoples, we must discover religious experiences; as we look for the origins of religions, we must discover nations of men, and whichever way we look, it is to the lands on which the men reside and in which the religions arise that is important. This possibility is what has dominated the concerns of

American Indian peoples from the very beginnings. The chance that lands would be lost meant that religious communities would be destroyed and individual identities forsaken. As sacred mountains became secularized, as tribal burial grounds became cornfields, as tribes no longer lived on the dust of their ancestors' bones, the people knew that they could not survive.

This feeling of the importance of land is also present in Western countries, but it has undergone a radical change. It has transformed itself into patriotism on the one hand and religious nationalism on the other. With this transformation, the whole nature of religion and land has been lost. Land is no longer a major element in Western religion but forms a tangential influence often manifesting itself whether or not the Christian religion intends that it do so.

The early Church centered itself in Italy in the city of Rome as surely as did the Hebrews center themselves in Jerusalem after they had conquered Canaan. Where the Jewish religion was and is centered in the Holy Land as *the* specific land of the religion, one cannot help but conclude that Rome is and has become the center of Christendom. With the Reformation the growth of national churches simply meant that each interpretation of the Christian religion had to find a home for itself. The peculiarities of European theology can be understood more easily by reference to countries than by abstract doctrinal analysis.

With the movement of Christianity to the North American continent and the subsequent freedom to develop offered in this land, the possibility of constituting a Christian culture or a unity of religion vanished. Christianity shattered on the shores of the continent, producing hundreds of sects in the same manner that the tribes continually split in an effort to relate to the land. It is probably in the nature of this land that divisiveness is one of its greatest characteristics, a virtually uncontrollable freedom of the spirit.

The land dimension of religion must inevitably wear itself out in respective religious traditions as they mature. What would be the nature of a religious tradition that has grown old and sophisticated on a land? The puzzlement of modern Europe would seem to indicate that the religious dimension of land is a factor that cannot be neglected. Germany was the scene of the Protestant Reformation in its most profound sense, for it was the home of Martin Luther, who claimed a doctrinal superiority to what had preceded him. If there were to be any land, therefore, in which Christianity could have entrenched itself outside of Italy, it would probably have been Germany.

Heinrich Heine in *Religion and Philosophy in Germany,* originally published in 1835, may have clearly foreseen the nature of the catastrophe occurring when a religion grows thin on a land to which it has become a stranger:

> Christianity—and this is the fairest merit—subdued to a certain extent the brutal warrior ardour of the Germans, but it could not entirely quench it; and when the Cross, that restraining talisman, falls to pieces, then will break forth again the ferocity of the old combatants, the frantic Berserker rage whereof Northern Poets have said and sung so much. The talisman has become rotten, and the day will surely come when it will pitifully crumble to dust. The old stone gods will arise then from the forgotten ruins and wipe from their eyes the dust of centuries, and Thor with his giant hammer will arise again, and he will shatter the Gothic cathedrals.[6]

Many people have remarked that the rise of National Socialism and its attendant sense of religious fervor fulfilled Heine's vision of a Christianity that was no longer able to contain the ancient Teutonic gods.

Carl Jung suggested the existence of a collective unconscious in which the archetypes and symbols of universal human experience were to be found. In his analysis of the nature of human spiritual problems, Jung suggested that the unconscious acted to structure solutions by presenting via dreams the archetypes representing familiar facets of our life in a type of drama of which we became aware. His system was based on the interpretation of the dream symbols and the story in which they were to be found in dreams. In the period before the rise of National Socialism, Jung said that he could see in the psychological problems of his German patients the symbols of the old Germanic religious myths that were to later mark part of the development of Nazi fanaticism among the young. [7] Do we attribute the ability of young Germans to dream in ancient religious symbols to a desire to escape from Christian rigidity or perhaps to a residual power in the land itself to produce certain religious mythologies and figures?

Additional pondering on this matter brings little relief. In England there appears to be the phenomenon of ghosts. It is estimated that some ten thousand ghosts inhabit the British islands, and it is a poor castle, manor house, or moor that does not have a full complement of ghosts. Germany has a proliferation of poltergeists. North America, however, is comparatively without spiritual phenomena of that kind. While we have ghosts, they are not a featured part of our folklore or present existence. How are we to account for the renewal of Druidism in England and the northern parts of France? Some people may deny that contemporary concern with witches and Druid religious practices does not conform with descriptions by scholars for ancient times. We must remember that scholars' descriptions of ancient times are primarily figments of their imaginations rather than accounts of reality.

How are we to catalog the existence of shrines of all faiths? The Shrine of Our Lady of Guadalupe Hildalgo, for example, rests on a spot already the site of ancient Indian religious practices centuries before the Christian version appeared on the scene. Why is there an absence of miracles and revelations in North America, when other parts of the

Christian world seem to have a plentitude of religious sites? Are Fatima and Lourdes uniquely Christian, or do they represent a religious site hoary with antiquity, whose earlier religions are unknown to us today?

What students of religion have failed to recognize is the unique nature of religious symbolism, its apparent correspondence with land masses, its vibrant ability to reassert itself in times of spiritual crisis, and the absence of a universal symbol system of religious experience. It is perhaps the clashing of religions on lands that has led to much of our social, political, and military conflict among peoples. It would appear to be difficult, therefore, simply to classify cultural competition and distinctions in community values as differentials on a time scale of social evolution. Rather careful examination should be given to the nature of disagreements and the origin of these differences in both the religious and geographical dimensions of men's lives.

If the old Germanic myths of Wotan can reassert themselves in a modern technical state, which Carl Jung believed happened in the rise of National Socialism in Germany, and if the practical political program of the ensuing movement is for additional lands and reunification of Germanic peoples in a genetic sense, we certainly cannot reject any consideration that might be given to the relationship between religion and land and how their interactions produce national identities.

Throughout the anthologies recording speeches of American Indian leaders, one finds a continual concern for preserving the homeland, the land where the fathers and grandfathers are buried. Curley, a Crow Indian chief, refused in 1912 to give any more of his land to the federal government when it proposed another land cession. Rejecting the government offer, Curley said:

> The soil you see is not ordinary soil—it is the dust of the blood, the flesh and the bones of our ancestors. We fought and

bled and died to keep other Indians from taking it, and we fought and bled and died helping the Whites. You will have to dig down through the surface before you can find nature's earth, as the upper portion is Crow.

The land as it is, is my blood and my dead; it is consecrated; and I do not want to give up any portion of it.[8]

A vital part of this attitude is certainly concerned with the nature of death, for it appears that for the American Indian death does not destroy the natural unity of creation that can be experienced and demonstrated in almost every facet of existence. Origination of religions, of peoples, and of ideas may thus be considered as part and parcel of the nature of lands if death itself becomes a function of lands. We do not really talk about the origination of anything but of the inherent structure of lands, which can periodically produce elements having a similarity of purpose. An examination of the conception of death may help us further to distinguish the differences between Indian and non-Indian conceptions of reality, so it is to that subject we will devote ourselves in the next chapter.

Chapter 10
Death and Religion

THE THEOLOGICAL PROBLEM of the Christian religion in regard to history has already been discussed. This religion is premised on the fact that human history is encompassed within the story of the Hebrew peoples and that the meaning of their history is in its preparation of the world for the coming of Jesus. The individual Christian believer is probably not very concerned about the validity or reality of this theological interpretation, however, since it is an abstraction not directly bearing on his individual existence or its meaning except peripherally.

What most probably concerns the individual Christian is its promise of eternal life. It is extremely difficult to discern exactly what the Christian religion has made central to its doctrine of eternal life. Popular Christianity has conjured up incredible visions of the life hereafter complete with streets of gold, angelic choirs singing hallelujahs and hosannas, and an existence totally devoid of pain and sorrow. While this picture shows great affinity for being a simple negation of life on earth as we confront it, its appeal has not lessened over the centuries. Popular Christianity even today promises a form of

169

existence after physical death of comparable conditions and dimensions. Especially in the fundamentalist churches on the right, heaven and the life hereafter forms a very potent part of the meaning of Christianity.[1]

Perhaps the most important feature of the Christian concept of life after death is its radical difference from life as we know it. There is no balance between the good and evil, pain and pleasure, and hardship and ease that form an important part of our present form of existence. Rather the conception of life after death emphasizes the benefits and pleasures of existence without the corresponding frustration and disadvantages. While a type of existence can be initially conceived in which all of these factors would be present, when they are translated into our familiar experiences certain problems arise. The old question of how we are to distinguish pain from pleasure in the absence of pain arises, as do other familiar and traditional facets of the problem of pain and suffering. No satisfactory explanation has been devised by Christian thinkers, and because popular Christianity's conceptions are so much apart from the ideas of theologians, it is doubtful if any solutions will be forthcoming.

The radical cleavage between the two forms of existence is notable because it results in a somewhat strange posture toward death among Christians. One would think that with the life after death so pleasant and the life here so difficult that the great majority of Christians would look forward to death as the final passage into a better world. If any religious people would not fear death, one would suppose, it would be Christians. But such is not the case. Of all the peoples in the world, perhaps Christians and the peoples they dominate fear death more than any other part of man's existence.

At least part of this fear of death derives from the message of Christianity itself. Death was early considered as unnatural to the creation and as an evil presence resulting from the disobedience of Adam in the Garden of Eden. We have seen earlier in the passage of Paul in Romans that death was the primary fact of human existence to be overcome by the obedience of Jesus. Throughout all of Christian history, death has formed a focal point for the tangible confrontation between the people of God of the other world and the reality and powers of this world. Traditional Roman Catholic doctrine built into the concept of confession an escape hatch from the terrors of death. Baptism was considered as the entrance into eternal life through the washing away of sins. So popular was the doctrine that for a while in Christian history people postponed baptism until their deathbed, so as to cancel all sins and proceed immediately to heaven on giving up the ghost.

Heavily involved in the Christian concept of death has been the assertion of judgment when the good and evil deeds of men would be evaluated, the good men going to heaven and the evil and unbaptised men going to hell. Perhaps it was this judgmental aspect of the religion that helped to create the fear of death, for if a person were not certain that he had lived a good life and had only a burning hell to look forward to, he was probably not particularly anxious to die. Exactly how much of the Christian description of the afterlife depended on Near Eastern conceptions of life after death is not certain. Many of the Near Eastern peoples had some version of judgment in their religious traditions, and the least that could be said was that judgment played an important part in the religious conception of the meaning of man's existence.

If the focus of the religion was concentrated on afterlife, the life of the present world necessarily took a secondary importance in the religions of the Near East. The world, instead of being real, had a "testing-ground" aspect to it which downgraded the events of this world in relation to the possibility of future existence. That such a concept would eventually de-sacralize history itself apparently never occurred to the Near Eastern peoples, yet from our previous discussion of history, we can see that the events of history when considered in a religious sense have become preaching parables for Christians rather than events of tangible nature.

One cannot emphasize too carefully this aspect of Western religious tradition, for it was in the developments of Western thought that man became severed from the earth in a final manner so that even death became a demoniac force to him. The Protestant Reformation hardly improved on the early Christian and contemporary Catholic conceptions of death. Salvation became intertwined with other doctrines in a strange manner, so that justification by faith had to find a tangible point of reference in the real everyday world. When coupled with predestination, which determined which individuals should be saved, the emergence of the doctrine of afterlife manifested itself in the material wealth of this world and its accumulation by those who were saved. Salvation meant that those people predestined from the foundations of the world to enter eternal life manifested their blessed state by enjoying material prosperity in this world.

The Protestants early embarked on a program to demonstrate to their neighbors that they had been saved, and many writers have commented that the Protestant ethic is at least partially dependent on theological considerations of the afterlife. With the demythologization of the afterlife as Western science became more sophisticated and projected evolutionary explanations of man's existence, the habit of accumulating material possessions continued in the West, while its symbolic value—that the accumulator was able to gather material wealth because he was a chosen person—vanished as a meaningful explanation of wealth and poverty.

The Christian doctrine of life after death had another and extremely unfortunate aspect. The soul was believed to live on while the body, which was considered evil and gross, decayed although it would apparently be glorified during the turmoil of the Second Coming. At any rate, by conceiving that it was possible to separate soul from body, Christians then created the most terrible tortures to be perpetrated on those suspected of heresy. Theologians felt that it was proper to crush the body if it meant saving the soul. Thus the Inquisition spared no torture conceivable to man to force admissions of sin and heresy from its victims with the sure and steady assurance that they were in fact saving the person's soul. Many of the genocidal acts of the Europeans against American Indian peoples can certainly be laid directly at the door of Christians who sought only to convert the natives yet killed millions of peoples to gain those few who converted as they expired.

If the Christian religion has any promise of life after death, it certainly has had a checkered record with respect to fulfilling this promise. Of the various sins committed by Christians against mankind and non-Christian peoples, forced conversions have been the most detrimental, thoughtless, and frequent.

In the field of secular knowledge, we have seen the impact of the Christian conception of life after death. Ancient ruins are almost always considered to be the efforts of primitive peoples to ensure an afterlife. Thus the pyramids have traditionally been interpreted as efforts of the pharaohs to achieve immortality. While some of the smaller structures of the later Egyptian period might have been used as tombs, the period of time required to build the larger structures would appear to exclude them as burial places. The most complete Egyptian tomb discovered was that of Tutankhamen, which was uncovered in 1922 by Howard Carter and Lord Carnarvon. Tutankhamen was buried, like most Egyptian pharaohs, in a tomb cut into living rock in the Valley of the Kings and not in a pyramid. [2]

Perhaps of more importance in attempting to align Christian and other non-Indian religious conceptions of death is the fact that even the Egyptian tombs would indicate that the people saw death and the afterlife as an extension of this life. Many of the objects found in the tomb were familiar possessions of the dead pharaoh, indicating the belief that he would need them in the life to come. It has been only with the Christian religion that life after death was not considered a natural continuation of this life. At the least we can consider death as a fearful thing to be common to peoples of Western Europe and the Christian tradition.

When we move into the American Indian tribal religions, we find a notable absence of the fear of death. Burial mounds indicate a belief that life after death was a continuation of the life already experienced. Scholars who interpret the presence of weapons, foods, artifacts of daily existence, and ornaments as indicating a primitive conception of life after death are in fact simply reflecting a less sophisticated Christian concept of the radical distinction between life in its various forms. To accept a basic unity of life continuing through many phases, as these artifacts would indicate, would seem to be a more mature attitude toward life and death.

It is this aspect, the fundamental relationship between life and death, that can be said to characterize many tribal religions. Rather than make a radical distinction between two ways of life, many tribal religions see a basic continuity of life in which the various states of existence form a history that many times includes the very land on which people live. At a treaty-signing session in the Illinois country in 1821, the Potawatomi chief, Metea, spoke of this continuity as the basic reason for his reluctance to cede the tribal lands:

> A long time has passed since first we came upon our lands, and our people have all sunk into their graves. They had sense. We are all young and foolish, and do not wish to do anything that they would not approve, were they living. We are fearful we shall offend their spirits if we sell our lands; and we are fearful we shall offend you if we do not sell them. This has caused us great perplexity of thought, because we have counselled among ourselves, and do not know how we can part with our lands.

My father, our country was given us by the Great Spirit, who gave it to us to hunt upon, to make our cornfields upon, to live upon, and to make our beds upon when we die. [3]

This idea of identity and continuity of life lay behind the posture of many of the tribes as they approached the white men. It could be said to be a more fundamental reason than any other for the Indian resistance to white invasions of tribal land a century ago and even today. Young Chief Joseph, the famous Nez Percé leader, remained at peace with the white settlers until they began to invade his valley. When he was finally forced to fight to protect himself, he recalled the promise he had made to his father as the older Joseph lay dying. The old chief told his son:

My son, my body is returning to my mother earth, and my spirit is going very soon to see the Great Spirit Chief. When I am gone, think of your country. You are the chief of these people. They look to you to guide them. Always remember that your father never sold his country.

You must stop your ears whenever you are asked to sign a treaty selling your home. A few more years and the white men will be all around you. They have their eyes on this land. My son, never forget my dying words. This country holds your father's body. Never sell the bones of your father and your mother. [4]

Some people have regarded this speech of the old Joseph as merely symbolic of Indian religion, but we must recall that for tribal people symbolism is not the communicative image of Western man but the expression of a reality that Western man often refuses to acknowledge. This conception of land as holding the bodies of the tribe in a basic sense pervaded tribal religions across the country. It testified in a stronger sense to the underlying unity of the Indian conception of the universe as a life system in which everything had its part.

It is doubtful, however, if any of the tribal religions considered life after death to be radically changed from the life they were living. Chief Seattle, on signing the Treaty of Medicine Creek in 1854, gave a famous speech in which he summarized his beliefs about the nature of the lands his tribe had given up. If ever an Indian could have been said to have anticipated D. H. Lawrence, Albert Camus, and William Carlos Williams, Seattle's speech would certainly merit first consideration. In it he distinguished between tribal beliefs and the attitude of the Christians who were taking control of the land—at least in a legal sense:

> To us the ashes of our ancestors are sacred and their resting place is hallowed ground. You wander far from the graves of your ancestors and seemingly without regret. . . .
>
> Your dead cease to love you and the land of their nativity as soon as they pass the portals of the tomb and wander way beyond the stars. They are soon forgotten and never return. Our dead never forget the beautiful world that gave them being. . . .
>
> Every part of this soil is sacred in the estimation of my people. Every hillside, every valley, every plain and grove, has been hallowed by some sad or happy event in days long vanished. The very dust upon which you now stand responds more lovingly to their footsteps than to yours, because it is rich with the blood of our ancestors and our bare feet are conscious of the sympathetic touch. Even the little children who lived here and rejoiced here for a brief season will love these somber solitudes and at eventide they greet shadowy returning spirits. And when the last Red Man shall have perished, and the memory of my tribe shall have become a myth among the White Men, these shores will swarm with the invisible dead of my tribe, and when your children's children think themselves alone in the field, the store, the shop, upon the highway, or in the silence of the pathless woods, they will not be alone. At night when the streets of your cities and villages are silent and you think them deserted, they will throng with the returning hosts that once filled and still love this beautiful land. The White Man will never be alone.

Let him be just and deal kindly with my people, for the dead are not powerless. Dead, did I say? There is no death, only a change of worlds.[5]

Again we see the fundamental conception of life as a continuing unity involving land and people. One might be tempted to suggest that as land is held by the community, the psychic unity of all the worlds is made real. We are not faced with formless and homeless spirits in this idea but with an ordered and purposeful creation in which death merely marks a passage from one form of experience to another. Rather than fearing death, tribal religions see it as an affirmation of life's reality.

A story of rather recent vintage from the Cheyenne people will enable us to see more fully the communal nature of death in the tribal context.

A young man named Hugh Boyle had been killed by the Cheyennes. The authorities demanded that the Indians give up the murderers to justice. The Indians tried to settle the matter. According to their ideas, the death of Boyle might be compensated by the payment of ponies. They offered to give up a great number of horses, raising each bid as it was rejected, until the payment proposed was calculated to beggar them if it was accepted. To the ponies they added all their wealth in blankets and such other evidences of riches as an Indian may possess. They were finally made to understand that the white man did not accept a property atonement for the spilling of blood. The negotiations were carried on for some time and with difficulty, for the reason that few white men know the Cheyenne language.... The intercourse with the people was carried on through mixed-bloods of the tribe, and it was finally made clear to them that they must give up the slayers of Boyle. But they could not give them up to die the death that kills the soul as well as the body. They believed, in common with most Indians, that when a man died his soul left the body with his last breath, and that in case a person was hanged, the soul was confined in the body with the rope. They would defend their young men from such an awful fate as was involved in the hanging by the white man's justice. The crime they neither denied nor defended. An ultimatum being sent them that they must bring in the murderers, they sent word back that a Cheyenne was not afraid to die, but would not submit to being hanged; that the two young men, Head Chief and Young Mule, would show the whites how a Cheyenne could die.

They appointed a date for the affair, September 13, 1890, and they intended that it should be magnificently spectacular. They were to bend their necks to the white man's justice, but they proposed doing it in a fashion that would impress the soldiers and the people at the agency. Special Indian Agent James A. Cooper had asked for troops, and one troop of the First Cavalry had been sent to the agency to make the arrest of the two men by force if necessary. The Cheyennes gave up diplomacy when the troops arrived, and word was sent that the two Indians would give themselves up and be ready to die. They appointed to die with their weapons in their hands. They would shoot at the soldiers, and the latter would have to kill them in defending themselves. The proposition was a rather startling one, but there was nothing to do but accept it. An attempt to arrest the men in their camps would assuredly have precipitated a bloody conflict. The proposition of the Cheyennes was for a spectacular form of suicide, and the matter was arranged on this basis. The Cheyennes accepted it all as a matter of course. The young men went about their affairs as usual, unmolested, and spent much time in visiting with and saying good-bye to their relatives. The night before the date set for the finish, there were solemn dances, in which the Indians all took part. They were to meet death as warriors and there was no reason why they should be mourned for.

The morning of the appointed day the two men were anointed by the medicine men. They painted and decorated themselves with great care, and wore all their finery. Their best horses were chosen for the ride to death, and the animals were devoted to the same fate that was to be meted out to their masters; for it was unlikely that they could escape the hail of bullets that would be sent at the doomed men. Thus, attired and mounted as warriors should be, the two rode down the slope from the northeast to the agency, where the troops were drawn up.

The agency is located on a flat, with a rather sharp declivity across Lame Deer River. The flat is almost surrounded by elevations, and on the ridge to the west the Indians, probably every one on the reservation, were assembled to see the young men demonstrate to the whites how a Cheyenne could die. Beside the agency office the troop of cavalry was drawn up; alongside of them stood the agency Indian police, close to their headquarters. The agency people were scattered about, out of what might be the line of fire when the shooting began. Never was a stage so set for so spectacular a tragedy.

At the time appointed for the coming of the men, they appeared at the top of the hill to the northeast, and dashed down the hill at the best pace their horses could make. As they rode they sang the death-song of their people, and before reaching the level ground they began shooting into the ranks of the soldiery and Indian police.

The fire was answered at once, the cavalrymen firing rapidly, but ineffectively. The Indian police, or one of them, made better practice, for one of the Indians went down with his horse in a heap just as he reached a little clump of bushes. The bullets of the police and soldiers could not find the other man. They fired at almost point-blank range, but his life was charmed. He rode shooting and singing past the cordon of troops and policemen, out beyond the agency, then turned and rode deliberately back. He had passed the troops a second time before the fire of the soldiers and the police was effective. [6]

The primary concern of the Cheyenne community was the preservation of life. When, however, it was evident that the men could not be saved, the concern shifted to preserving human dignity. The young men perfectly reflected the tribal belief, for they did not fear death, only a meaningless death that would discredit their community and violate their religious beliefs. The symbolism of dying as warriors was not something that extended beyond the grave as in the Germanic vision of the afterlife in which warriors were rewarded for their exploits by continual feasting and access to beautiful and pliant maidens. The Cheyenne response can only be understood as an affirmation of life, not as preparation for a radically different type of existence. Immortality is secondary to integrity of tribal existence in the present, and we find not a cringing fear of death but a religious community so strong as to virtually shrug off death as an enemy.

It is probably in the idea of the death song, which was found in many of the tribal religions, that the idea of death can adequately be understood. The death song was a special song sung as a man faced certain death. Often it taunted his enemies who were in the act of killing him. More often it acted as a benedictory statement by the individual to summarize and conclude his time of existence. Rather than being a feverish preparation for death it was the final affirmation of the meaning of individual existence, for it glorified the personal integrity of the person. It individualized his tribal membership in a manner bringing credit and meaning to his life as a tribal member.

One of the most famous death songs was that of Satank, the famous Kiowa chief who was being taken as a prisoner to Texas for trial after a raid against the Army. As he tore the manacles from his wrists and stabbed one of his guards, Satank chanted:

O sun, you remain forever, but we Kaitsenko must die.
O earth, you remain forever, but we Kaitsenko must die. [7]

Here we find no cringing to confess sins and imagined failures. The specific events of a man's life as judged by external standards pale beside this basic affirmation and acknowledgment to the rest of creation that finitude is but a role drawn by man in this form of existence.

The singular aspect of Indian tribal religions was that almost universally they produced people unafraid of death. It was not simply the status of warrior in the tribal life that created a fearlessness of death. Rather the integrity of communal life did not create an artificial sense of personal identity that had to be protected and preserved at all costs. Many other examples could be used to show the Indians' attitude toward death. The Five Civilized Tribes of Oklahoma had their own courts in the last decades of the nineteenth century. Occasionally a member of the tribe was sentenced to death. Upon the passage of the death sentence, the condemned would be informed when and where the execution would take place. He was then released to spend his remaining days with his relatives. As the day approached he would perform any obligatory religious ceremonies, say goodbye to his relatives, and on the appointed day report to the place of execution to be killed. While this behavior was common among Indian tribes, how many Christians fully believing in the hereafter would act in comparable manner?

Some tribes had special ceremonies to be used in conjunction with the dead. The Lakota, or Sioux, for example, had a ceremony in which the sacred pipe was used, and the souls of the recently departed were kept with the tribal community to be purified and eventually released.[8] In a tragic interference with the tribal religion, the government banned this ceremony in the 1890s, causing a great trauma among the people. The Iroquois had special ceremonies in conjunction with their New Year's celebration in which the dead of the past year were remembered.[9]

In general we could say that the afterlife was not of overwhelming concern to people of the tribal religions. Vague references to the lands of the spirits, descriptions of the Milky Way as the path over which souls traveled, and concern for the departed spirits remaining, which was prevented in some tribes by burning of personal possessions, probably indicated distinct beliefs of certain tribes. No highly articulated or developed theories of the afterlife were ever necessary, and certainly none projected a life radically different than that experienced on Earth.

The possibility that departed spirits would or could remain in the immediate vicinity to act malevolently was probably based on experiences of ghosts of tribal members manifesting themselves to individuals. Whether they were all automatically shunned is yet another question. The occurrence of ghosts cannot be said to be a peculiarly Indian superstition as the Christian world apparently abounds with ghosts, and the appearance of departed spirits appears to be a planetary phenomenon.

Some additional distinctions between tribal conceptions of the afterlife and Christian ideas can be drawn that will be particularly helpful. It is very difficult to distinguish between ideas that are primarily Christian and those that are the result of the speculations of Greek philosophy, and perhaps by reviewing one of the more recent controversies in Christian theology, we can find a way to understand the Christian posture toward death.

Oscar Cullmann, a brilliant Christian thinker, wrote a little book entitled *Immortality of the Soul or Resurrection of the Dead?* [10] He was bitterly attacked by his fellow Christians for having introduced somber and defeatist ideas into the Christian doctrine of the life to come. What Cullmann did was draw the necessary distinctions and conclusions from an examination of ideas that were primarily Christian and those primarily Greek. The differences had been blurred by generations of Christian ministers who preached popular sermons of reassurance to their congregations and used the framework of Greek philosophy to engage in speculative ventures about the afterlife.

The distinction between immortality of the soul and the peculiarly Christian ideal of the resurrection of the dead is a vital one. Immortality is a Greek philosophical idea that originates primarily from the thought and teachings of

Socrates. The Greeks regarded the body as only the outer garment of the soul. As a mutable part of man, the body prevented the soul from moving freely into the realm of eternal essence that for Socrates, and even more so for his disciple Plato, constituted the real world beyond that of sense perceptions. The soul was thus basically imprisoned in the body and became tainted with materialistic things, because it was unable to remember its previous existence in the world of pure ideas.

For the Greek philosophers the task of the individual was to free his soul from its bondage to the body. This release could be effected in a number of ways, the pursuit of knowledge of the world of ideas being the most sublime, and every approach seemed to be based on the conception of man as the rational animal. Upon death, for the Greeks, the soul was released from the body. Cullmann placed a great deal of emphasis in his book on the distinction between the deaths of Jesus and Socrates, pointed out that death was a welcome visitor for Socrates, a hated and tormenting experience for Jesus.

Cullman found that death, in the Christian context, was a feared foe. Death was an event to be avoided at all costs, because it meant the cessation of identity. Cullman suggested that all men naturally fear death, and that the Greek rational approach to the termination of life functions served only a select few, who had become so enamoured of their philosophy that they could welcome death as a natural conclusion to the journey of the soul in a world in which it was a stranger.

The great innovation of Christianity, according to Cullmann, was that it preached a message of bodily resurrection in which the totality of human personality was to be reconstituted. Death was understood as the destruction of all life created by God, not the shedding of the body by an indestructible soul. Jesus' resurrection meant that God had prepared a special type of existence for his followers, which was apparently not available to those who had not heard or those who had but did not believe. Resurrection at the last day was therefore a singularly revolutionary concept in religion. Other religions had foreseen a continuous existence after the death experience and purported that the spirits or souls of individuals had some measure of permanency beyond the grave. Christianity was the only religion to confront directly the question of total personality survival, and it found in the fact of Jesus' resurrection a basis for overcoming the agony of death experienced by the majority of men.

Cullmann's thesis is as revolutionary today as it was when first published nearly two decades ago. It is, perhaps, the most strenuous analysis of the problem, and Cullmann grounded it well in Biblical thought, using a minimum of philosophical argument and analogy for his conclusions. It is doubtful if the majority of contemporary Christians would support or believe Cullmann's distinction between immortality of the soul and resurrection of the dead. Most people who believe themselves to be Christians are thoroughly Greek in their beliefs concerning life after death.

Tribal religions show an almost total absence of concern about either doctrine. Both doctrines would appear to tribal peoples as separating the body and the spirit of man in a detrimental manner. A majority of the tribal religions simply assume some form of personal survival beyond the grave. As Chief Seattle remarked, death is merely a changing of worlds.

Christian cemeteries reflect a curious mixture of belief, and one cannot say for certain whether they are based on the premise of the bodily resurrection or on the idea of the immortality of the soul. The use of stone gravestones indicates a determination not to allow the body to become a part of the soil. Waterproof caskets and other devices designed to preserve the body for as long as possible may indicate a belief in the resurrection of the actual body of the departed. The monuments to great men may mean, on the other hand, that there is a desire to perpetuate people of stature in the memories of men which could be interpreted as honors to great souls.

Lame Deer, in his autobiography, remarks that the old Indian graveyards had markers of wood, because it was felt that the body and the wood would both return to the earth as intended.[11] He contrasted this attitude with the granite headstones to illustrate the distinction between Christian and Indian attitudes toward death. In the very old days many of the tribes employed various means of burial; almost all of them aiming at the return of the body to the earth.

Strangely enough there has been habitual conflict over the internment in Christian cemeteries of nonwhite peoples. During the Korean War, a Winnebago Indian, Sergeant Rice, was killed in action, and his body was returned to Sioux City, Iowa, for burial. But the good Christians in Sioux City forbade his burial in a cemetery reserved for whites. To the great embarrassment and grief of the family, the body remained unburied until finally accepted for burial in Arlington National Cemetery. The newspapers frequently feature stories of similar incidents involving blacks, Indians, Chicanos, and Asians. One can only conclude that the Christian religion and its promise of the afterlife is not meant for nonwhites; Christians either do not believe in resurrection, or they exclude nonwhites from their heaven.

According to Oscar Cullmann, death has been conquered by Jesus on behalf of all mankind. As the belief in the afterlife has eroded in Western civilization, a further twist has been added to the concept of death. Western peoples avoid mention of death at all costs. Insurance peddlers always speak of taking out insurance "in case something happens." The implication, of course, is that pending an irrational and arbitrary action of God, every good tax-paying white citizen will live forever. This belief is rarely articulated as a formal doctrine, but we cannot help but recognize it as the fundamental approach of contemporary Western peoples toward death. If the Christian religion is a victory over death, why do Western peoples who have had the benefits of the Christian religion for 2,000 years fear death? Arnold Toynbee once described death as totally "unAmerican," an infringement of each individual's right to life, liberty, and the pursuit of happiness. [12] As a subversive activity, death has recently come under examination by Western thinkers attempting to chart out the possible parameters of the problem. Rollo May, for example, suggests that the American preoccupation with sexual activity may in part be a response to the finality of death and the incessant concern for new sexual freedoms might be efforts directed toward a deliverance from death anxiety.

Regardless of how we attempt to explain it, the fundamental distinction between tribal religions and the Christian religion and secular Western attitude toward death must revolve around the conception of creation. For the tribal person, death in a sense fulfills his destiny, for as his body becomes dust once again he contributes to the ongoing life cycle of creation. For the Christian, the estrangement from nature, his religion's central theme, makes this most natural of conclusions fraught with danger. Believing that he is saved and interpreting this salvation by accumulating material possessions, Western man cannot accept death except as a form of punishment by his god. The Christian facing death often cries out to his god, "what have I done?" His priest or clergyman has only the relentless logic of theology to present. Death is feared and rarely understood.

It is in the face of death that Indian tribal religions have their greatest magnificence. Big Elk, an Omaha chief, delivered a funeral oration in 1815 at the death of Black Buffalo, a fellow Omaha, and counseled his fellow chiefs:

Do not grieve. Misfortunes will happen to the wisest and best of men. Death will come and always out of season. It is the command of the Great Spirit, and all nations and people must obey. What is past and cannot be prevented should not be grieved for.... Misfortunes do not flourish particularly in our path. They grow everywhere.[13]

Thus while death is truly a saddening event for people of tribal religious traditions, it is an event with which every person and nation is faced, not an arbitrary, capricious exercise of divine wrath. Even today this attitude persists in Indian societies, and the natural grief occurring with the loss of a loved one is rarely translated into personal feelings of guilt, inadequacy, or sin, which appear to plague Western man. The community regroups and continues to exist, and while individuals are lonely, they are not alone.

Chapter 11

Human Personality

WESTERN PEOPLES HAVE become accustomed to thinking of religious activity as involving a radical change of human personality. This attitude is ingrained in European peoples and finds its greatest following in the United States, where a substantial number of people believe that becoming a Christian involves a radical change in the human being's constitution. In contrast to this attitude, the Indian tribal religions do not necessarily involve any significant change in human personality but encompass within the tribal cultural context many of the behavioral patterns spoken about by Christians.

The basis for Christian beliefs must certainly originate in the days of the early church. Arising in the days of turmoil of the Jewish eschatological hopes, the message of the early church was one of impending doom, the arrival of the day of judgment, and the consequent salvation of those people who believed the Christian message. The chief message of Jesus seems to have been a call for repentence by the Jews, so that the Messiah could come, throw the Romans out, and reinstall the Jewish state. In this respect, Jesus and John stood well within the Zealot tradition of Jewish sects, which looked for a radical intervention by God in the history of men.

In the very early Christian community, the message of Jesus was transformed into a message about Jesus having been the Messiah who had come to earth, been rejected, and would return almost immediately with an angelic army to judge the world. This message was further transformed with the conversion of Paul, who later articulated a theory of cosmic redemption based on the crucifixion of Jesus, and the subsequent beliefs that he had risen from the dead and appeared to his disciples and then to Paul on the road to Damascus.

The impending end of the world did not occur within the lifetime of even the longest-lived immediate disciple of Jesus, and the doctrine changed once again to provide that missing explanation to hold the religious community together. One explanation of the failure of Jesus to return was that he could not come until all nations had heard the message of the Christians about the meaning of Jesus' death. Another explanation was that Jesus had intended to found a church and had given supernatural powers to the representatives of this church to exercise until his return. An even better explanation was that if men persisted in attempting to discover when the end of the world would occur, they would preempt God's options. In spite of what the Bible said it was therefore wrong to speculate on the time of the return; people simply had to wait it out and behave in the meantime.

The changing time element in these various theories of the meaning of the life and message of Jesus is extremely important in understanding the nature of the Christian conception of the human personality, because it indicates that the various theories were fundamentally accommodations to the incidents in the life of the early Christian community and not intended to reflect a reasoned, mature, or even rational understanding of human beings.

If we refer to the immediate urgency felt by Jesus and John in gaining the confidence of the Jews that they in fact knew that the Kingdom of Heaven was at hand, the initial demand for repentence appears as quite similar to recent power movements in American society. These power movements anticipated a violent revolution in the United States that was to be followed by a prolonged period of peace and justice during which minority groups would control the nation and not make any of the mistakes made up to that point in American history.

In the same manner, Jesus and John called for a general repentence of the Jews, so that the Messiah could come and restore the Jewish people to international sovereignty by driving out the Romans. Repentence was thus a short-term shifting of alliances of individual Jews from one religious sect of Judaism to another before the impending arrival of the last days. Their call was not an effort to bring into fruition another manner of viewing life, but an attempt to restore to the Jews a sense of national pride and group integrity before the peoples of the world were judged. The Dead Sea Scrolls have made it fairly clear that Palestine at that time seemed to abound with religious communities; many of them looked forward to divine military intervention on behalf of the Jews. In this respect, the Ghost Dance of the American Indians of the last decade of the last century looked forward to the same type of divine intervention.

The activity of the early church was centered on continuing this activity of calling the Jews to repentence. The Jerusalem community headed by Jesus' brother James thought the arrival of the kingdom so imminent that they were soon destitute of funds, since everyone had stopped working because of the momentary expectation of the world's end. Paul, in one of his earliest efforts to reconcile the Jerusalem community with his new doctrines, collected money to help the disciples survive. Conversion at that point must have involved simply an acknowledgment that Jesus had been the Messiah and that he was expected to return soon.

It was with the theological speculations of Paul that the Christian religion was expanded far beyond its original intent or scope. Paul viewed Jesus as representing a cosmic christ standing as an obedient son of the deity and as a sacrificial gift atoning to God for the disobedience of Adam, presumably a historical figure who had originally corrupted man's relationship with God. Paul believed in the idea of original sin, because he had provided the solution to it with his theories of cosmic atonement. Yet even with Paul, the expectation of the imminent end of the world was reflected in his efforts at counseling his new congregations as to their interim behavior.

From this initial series of concepts, additional Christian doctrines evolved; a totally coherent process of repentence, conversion, redemption, salvation, confession, absolution, and eternal life was constructed as the Christian description of the effect of the sect's religious beliefs on the human personality. Almost every category of human behavior appears to have been set into a system of distinguishing good deeds, sins, and penances through the offices of the organizational church. Sin, for example, could at least be classified into original sin, mortal sins, and venial sins, although in some Christian denominations there may be additional categories.

As Christianity gained political control over the lives of Western men, the Western theories of human personality began to develop, and while Christianity has recently declined in its importance in the West, many of its original premises continue to exert influence over the way men think of themselves, especially in the field of religious experiences. Preaching and teaching, the fundamental form of religious activity set down by John and Jesus and emphasized by Paul, has dominated Western peoples ever since. As preaching in the Roman world was thought to be the key to man's salvation, so education, its secularized counterpart in the contemporary world, is thought to be the final answer to social ills.

Once the various Christian doctrines are taken from their original time dimension and used to form a theory of human personality coupled with the identification of sins in anticipation of the final judgment that is apparently still to come, they can be said to form the basic posture of Western peoples toward this world, the world to come, and the world's institutions. Human personality has been forced into these predetermined categories without regard to the reality of human experience. Other religious systems have been detrimentally explained in terms of the basic Christian categories of explanation. As we have previously seen, the Christian concern with death has been used to project a universal fear of death by all men when such was not necessarily the case.

The great variety of Christian denominations that now confronts us in the religious sphere makes it virtually impossible to gain a concensus among Christians as to the meaning of the respective doctrines. Conversion may mean a quasi-miraculous event in which instant salvation is made available to the convert, or it may mean only the beginnings of an intention to live a Christian life as defined by a particular denomination. Baptism may be seen as the almost magical washing away of original and accumulated sins or as a gesture of initiation into the religious community. One can hardly determine what interpretation of any Christian doctrine would receive the support of a majority of Christian believers, since it is doctrinal disagreement that creates the Christian denominations.

What we are more interested in, however, is what effect in practical terms the various sequences of the Christian life—from initial conversion to eventual salvation—have on individuals and societies. What peculiarly distinguishes a Christian from any other person is difficult to determine. The track record of individual Christians and Christian nations is not so spectacular as to warrant anyone seriously considering becoming a Christian. From pope to pauper, Protestant to Catholic, Constantinople to the United States, the record is filled with atrocities, misunderstandings, persecutions, genocides, and oppressions so numerous as to bring fear into the hearts and minds of non-Christian peoples.

One aspect of Christian history that is so appalling is the almost continuous warfare between Christians. Heresy hunters seem to abound in Christian history as a regular part of its religious experience. Persecutions for religious purposes appear to dominate many periods of Christian existence. The first settlements on the shores of North America's East Coast were apparently made by people fleeing religious persecution, while settlements in the Southwest featured religious persecution of the native inhabitants, especially after their conversion.

The response of many Christians to the reminder that their religion has failed to bring peace on earth, or even a semblance of it, has been that the people who committed the numerous sins filling the pages of Western and world history were not really Christians. If we eliminate those perpetrators of criminal activity from the Western world, we are left with a very small percentage of people who were really Christians. Why did these people remain silent while the various abuses were being committed in the name of their religion? There is apparently no answer to that question, unless we conclude that there have never really been any outstanding Christians since the early days. If such is the case, then we must only conclude that the purported ability of the Christian religion to change men's hearts and minds has been a gigantic hoax, perpetrated for an unknown purpose by unknown people. We are thus confronted with accepting the reality of Christian history and attempting to understand how it conceives its message and impact, so as to warrant considering religion in the categories it has chosen to express itself. Probably a great many Christians of recent vintage would demand that Christianity be defined as establishing a personal relationship with God via a belief that Jesus the Jewish carpenter of the first century was his son. Certainly the multitudes of contemporary Christians who follow the evangelical and fundamentalist versions of Christianity would make such a demand.

What does this interpretation mean in human terms? Through preaching, a general description of Christian beliefs is presented to the listener. If he decides to accept the validity of this explanation of mankind's existence, he apparently affirms his consent and, depending upon the denominational interpretation, is saved or well on his way. He is then expected to follow a Christian life which generally has great affinity to his society's cultural mores.

In some denominations the initial conversion appears to effect the guarantee of eternal life as partially described in the discussion on death and featuring denominational variations which have developed over the years. Other denominations relate that the conversion allows the individual perfect freedom, but strangely the perfect freedom is almost immediately circumscribed with rules and regulations of great specificity. In practically every version of Christianity, the conversion experience or decision is followed by the exercise of individual will to act differently with respect to practical problems. One could almost say that the whole of the Christian conversion and salvation doctrines are dependent on the exercise of individual will to achieve certain standards of behavior or to make a record with respect to good and evil deeds. The degree to which the religion itself provides more than a high standard of behavior, in an external sense, is highly questionable.

Aside from the conversion experience and the exercise of individual will to follow behavior standards, the problem with the Christian conception of human behavior is that it apparently depends on the cultural context in which it exists to determine what standard of behavior the will shall follow. With only a preliminary examination of some of the positions understood as Christian over the years, one could conclude that Christianity attempts to dominate cultures and does so initially but eventually falls victim to cultural values. For a long time, for example, Christians, eschewing political involvement, were among the most persecuted peoples in the Roman world. The message emphasized that Christ's kingdom was "not of this world." Spotting the weakness in the European political structures, the doctrines suddenly changed to support the theory that Christ had given the pope total power over men's lives as his vicar on earth. No king could be crowned, no emperor installed without the pope's approval.

Expecting the momentary return of Jesus, Paul discouraged marriage among his converts but appeared to relent if it meant that they would be living in even greater sin by having intercourse in an unblessed state. From that position, marriage apparently evolved into one of the church's sacraments. The church held that position for a very long time, and monogamy became a European cultural value. The state of monogamy was held to be a Christian ideal, with marriage considered to be sealed sacramentally and divorce, which banned one from communion, sinful.

In recent years as both American and European societies have come to a greater understanding of the nature and needs of human beings, divorce has taken on a new status in Christendom. It is still frowned upon, but the wrinkles are not nearly as deep. Second, third, and fourth marriages often receive denominational blessings, and annulments for influential members of the Roman Catholic Church are not a rare occurrence. We may yet see the day when it becomes a Christian doctrine that no man or woman can have more than one wife or husband *at the same time.*

Sexual intercourse was once considered as sinful; the act was permissible only for purposes of procreation. Today a number of ministers advocate more sexual freedom, and premarital sex, for many people, is not the mortal sin that it formerly was. Marital sexual activity is now defined by a substantial number of Christians as an activity anticipated by God and encouraged by the clergy. Homosexuality, once the bane of Christianity, is now considered by some clergy as an expression of human needs, and the stigma is gradually fading in those denominations which at present do not advocate its sinlessness.

Poverty was once considered a Christian virtue for it was meant to indicate a lack of concern for the values of this world and a concentration on the life to come. In the centuries after the Protestant Reformation, poverty was considered indicative of the fact of sin, sloth, and other sins, and its appearance was seen as proof of the individual's degeneracy. The expression "poor but honest man" meant that a person was poor because he was dishonest and God had refused to bless his labors. As the white populace of Christian America has become more affluent, the concept of stewardship has been developed to explain the embarrassingly rapid growth of wealth of a substantial number of peoples. The theory goes that we are not really greedy, God has simply blessed us by giving us wealth over which we are to exercise good stewardship, i.e., the organizational church must have its cut for us to be good stewards.

These examples and many others that we can think of illustrate at least two points. One is that once the decision is made to exercise the human will to live a Christian life, the content of that life is rapidly determined by the cultural values of the society in which the convert finds himself. As the cultural values change, the doctrines also change; it becomes impossible to determine exactly how a Christian does behave.

The other point is that as conversion is regarded as an individual concern, so determination of the hallmarks of the Christian life is also regarded as an individual concern. Individuals thus follow that version of the religion that appears to be the most comforting to them. Shopping for prestige churches as an individual climbs the social, political, or economic ladder is not unheard of. In its practical sense, Christianity is a religion almost wholly determined by the culture in which it finds itself. It brings to that culture some of its ideas, including a comforting sense of history. But in practical terms it quickly bends to whatever forces are most dominant in that culture, as individual Christians are forced to follow a course that they would imagine to be most religious in a cultural context strange to the world of Roman-dominated Palestine.

Because the Christian religion is conceived as personal, the individual is both victim and victor of the religion. It is to his personal evaluation of events and values that the religion responds. It never allows him to forget the impossibility of ultimate success for he is, after all, a sinner among sinners, but it allows him to escape the consequences of that sin by making him the sole determining factor of what he shall do and what he shall consider religious activity. Ambrose Bierce once defined a Christian as one who follows Christ's teachings insofar as they are not incompatible with a life of sin. Bierce was not underestimating the practical side of the Christian religion.

Today we are suffering the impact of two thousand years of Christian individualism. Social problems continue to mount with no apparent solution to any of them in sight. Yet the United States appears to have a substantial number of devout Christians inhabiting it. We have just finished a long war in Asia, which was prolonged primarily for political considerations by two Presidents and yet both of these men were apparently Christians in good standing. At least prominent churchmen such as Dr. Graham have not called them to account as being anti-Christian or non-Christians for the wastage of human life.

The rising rate of mental illness, especially the alarming rise in multiple murders and brutality in civil disorders on the part of police and demonstrators, would indicate that there is something amiss. The continued proliferation of psychologists, psychoanalysts, group therapy, psychodramas, and other phenomena indicative of attempts to heal the spiritual problems of modern man should tell us that at least part of our conception of the nature of religion has been mistaken. If Christianity saves the individual, and the evidence that it does appears to be decreasing, it must certainly be determined a failure when societies or even large numbers of human beings are concerned.

In terms of philosophical analysis, what Christian doctrines purport to do is to isolate the individual human being in a vacuum where he is confronted with a deity who is, by definition, angry. Every consideration that he could conceivably make, based on his relationships with the world of daily experience, are negated as factors to be considered as part of his religious experience. He is then asked to make a theoretical choice on whether certain factual happenings on this planet indicated a radical change of cosmic significance to the deity. Upon giving his assent, he must exercise his will to prevent the commission of further disobedience toward the deity when he faces the world of daily experience. Then he is once again placed in that world and expected to respond to novel situations in a manner consistent with the concept of obedience to divine commands and purposes which remain obscured if not invisible to him.

Is there such an individual? Does the individual exist apart from his nation, his language, his family, his culture, his wealth, his knowledge of the world, his problems, his secular beliefs, his immediate situation? Traditionally Protestant theologians could conceive of such an individual. "Sinners in the hands of an angry God" characterized the sermons of such a conception, and today's evangelists who carefully orchestrate their crusades with hymns, angry sermons, threats of judgment, soothing words of comfort, efforts at healing, and mass psychology of getting the reluctant to the front row kneeling in fear and trembling are their successors. Without the ability to invoke emotion, to create fear and anxiety, to promise instantaneous relief from such fear, they are helpless. It is by artificially creating that solitary individual through deliberate manipulation of his emotions that they give credence to their version of the Christian religion. They are notably absent in the solutions of social problems, in the ongoing work of local communities, and in the examination of the nature of human personality and its problems.

When we turn from Christian religious beliefs to Indian tribal beliefs in this area, the contrast is remarkable. Religion is not conceived as a personal relationship between the deity and each individual person. It is rather a covenant between a particular god and a particular community. The people of the community are the primary residue of the religion's legends, practices, and beliefs. Ceremonies of communitywide scope are the chief characteristic feature of religious activity. Religion dominates the tribal culture, and distinctions existing in Western civilization no longer present themselves. Political activity and religious actively are barely distinguishable. History is not divided into categories of explanation. It is simultaneously religious, political, economic, social, and intellectual.

There is no salvation in tribal religions apart from the continuance of the tribe itself. Being a tribal religion, there are no deviations of doctrine. Doctrine is not needed and heresies are virtually unknown. Theology is part of communal experiences needing no elaboration, abstraction, or articulation of principles. Every factor of human experience is seen in a religious light as part of the meaning of life. Tribal customs structuring relationships found to be proper for people are continued. Preconceived standards of conduct are unimportant and the assumption of the innate sinfulness of man is impossible, for the individual is judged instantaneously by his fellows as useful or useless, according to his degree of participation in community affairs.

The possibility of conceiving of an individual alone in a tribal religious sense is ridiculous. The very complexity of tribal life and the interdependence of people on one another makes this conception improbable at best, a terrifying loss of identity at worst. It is this tribal religious man who causes reaction among Christians whenever Indian and white men meet. Harvey Cox, for example, in *The Secular City* remarks that "tribal man is hardly a personal 'self' in our modern sense of the word. He does not so much live in a tribe; the tribe lives in him. He is the tribe's subjective expression."[1] Cox concludes that "tribal naiveté must be laid to rest everywhere, and everyone must be made a citizen of the land of broken symbols."[2] In other words, if a religion or a person is different, it or he must be destroyed.

The fact of religion being a tribal phenomenon can be found in Indian life in many respects. There is no demand for a personal relationship with a personal savior. Cultural heros are representative of community experience. They may stand as classic figures, such as Deganiwidah, Sweet Medicine, Black Elk, Smohalla, and even Wovoka, but they never become the object of individual attention as to the efficacy in either the facts of their existence or their present supratemporal ability to affect events. The revelation that establishes the tribal community or brings to it the sacred pipes, the sacred arrows, the sacred hats, and other sacred objects is a communal affair in which the community participates but in which no individual claims exclusive franchise.

It is virtually impossible to "join" a tribal religion by agreeing to its doctrines. People could not care less whether an outsider believes anything. No separate religious standard of behavior is imposed on followers of the religious tradition outside of the requirements for the ceremonies—who shall do what, who may participate, who is excluded from which parts of the ceremony, who is needed for other parts of the ceremony. The customs of the tribe and the religious responsibilities to the group are practically identical, and the existence of two sets of values side by side is unthinkable. Contrast this state of affairs with Richard Nixon's stand against abortion based on his Christian reverence for life and his continuation of the Vietnam War in which thousands of lives were taken so that he would not be the first American president "to lose a war."

The fears that Harvey Cox and others express as to the lack of a personal self among tribal peoples is unwarranted, and they indicate a lack of understanding of tribal religious beliefs and practices. One of the most notable features of Indian tribal cultures is the custom of naming individuals. Indian names stand for certain qualities, for exploits, for unusual abilities, for unique physical characteristics, and for the individual's unusual religious experiences. Every person has a name given in religious ceremonies in which his uniqueness is recognized. Harvey Cox, as a name, indicates that for an undetermined number of generations the male member of the genetic line has been called Cox and Harvey's parents happened to like the name Harvey. Such a name hardly indicates a personal self but at least partially denotes a breeding line.

To be sure, Indian tribal religions have an individual

dimension. The Vision Quest of many of the tribes indicates that a major responsibility of the individual is to remain open and keenly aware that he might be chosen by the Great Mystery as a holy man, as a great and heroic warrior, as one cursed with a handicap, or as any number of other functions. Depending on the tribe and its traditions, the vision quest may be a relatively short-term experience. It may indicate nothing at all. Or it may require the most arduous type of life, requiring the greatest of personal sacrifices. There is no emotional aspect of the evangelistic crusades present in this aspect of Indian individual religious experience, however. No ranting and raving preacher threatens everlasting hellfire and damnation unless an immediate decision is forthcoming.

Not only are names and religious experiences highly personalized, but the individual is enabled to relate to all phases of his life experience through tribal religions. The Iroquois and Cherokee, for example, had sophisticated systems for dream interpretation that were part of their religious beliefs. A great majority of the tribes recognized the religious aspect of dreams and made some provision for understanding them. Western psychoanalysis has only recently come to understand the uncharted field of dream analysis as an indication of personal mental health. The Christian theologians have yet to attempt to understand the reality of dreams, in spite of the appearance of dreams in both Old and New Testaments. At least in Matthew dreams played a vital part in Christian experiences.

Individual worth was also recognized in other ways in the tribal religions. The keepers of the sacred medicine bundles, for example, were people who had been carefully watched for their personal characteristics and were chosen to share some of the tribal mysteries and responsibilities in a religious sense. The priesthoods of some of the tribes were filled with people who had been carefully trained after they had demonstrated their personal integrity. These people were chosen by the men and women responsible for maintaining the tribal religions. Young people and casual participants did not choose a religious office within the tribe as a career "because they liked people," as the Christian clergy are today so often inspired to become ministers.

In almost every way, tribal religions supported the individual in his community context, because they were community religions and not dependent on abstracting a hypothetical individual from his community context. One could say that the tribal religions created the tribal community, which, in turn, made a place for every tribal individual. Christianity, on the other hand, appears to have created the solitary individual who, gathered together every seven days, constitutes the "church," which then defines the extent to which the religion is to be understood and followed. With the individual as the primary focal point and his relationship with the deity as his primary concern, the group is never on certain ground as to its existence but must continually change its doctrines and beliefs to attract a maximum number of followers. It is always subject to horrendous fragmentation over doctrinal interpretations, whenever two strong-minded individuals clash.

The anthologies of Indian speeches reflect the basic Indian religious attitudes toward the nature of religion in a great many instances. As we review them, we find a rejection of the whole conception of religion as found in Western Christian understanding.

Red Cloud, for example, when told that he must become as the white men, remarked:

> You must begin anew and put away the wisdom of your fathers. You must lay up food and forget the hungry. When your house is built, your storeroom filled, then look around for a neighbor whom you can take advantage of and seize all he has.[3]

Sitting Bull, asked in Canada why he did not surrender

and return to the United States to live on a reservation, replied:

> Because I am a red man. If the Great Spirit had desired me to be a white man he would have made me so in the first place. He put in your heart certain wishes and plans, in my heart he put other and different desires. Each man is good in his sight. It is not necessary for eagles to be crows.[4]

Chief Joseph once met with a United States commission that wanted him to cede the Wallowa valley in Oregon, which the Nez Percé owned. During the negotiations he was asked why the Nez Percé had banned missionaries from their lands. Joseph answered:

> They will teach us to quarrel about God, as Catholics and Protestants do on the Nez Percé Reservation (in Idaho) and other places. We do not want to do that. We may quarrel with men sometimes about things on earth, but we never quarrel about the Great Spirit. We do not want to learn that.[5]

A Delaware chief complained about the Gnadenhutten massacre in 1782 when 90 Christian Indians had been killed by whites because two Indians, not of the group, had injured a white man some miles away from the settlement:

> And yet these white men would be always telling us of their great Book which God had given them. They would persuade us that every man was bad who did not believe in it. They told us a great many things which they said were written in the Book; and wanted us to believe it. We would likely have done so, if we had seen them practice what they pretended to believe—and acted according to the good words which they told us. But no! While they held the big Book in one hand, in the other they held murderous weapons—guns and swords—wherewith to kill us poor Indians. Ah! And they did too. They killed those who believed in their Book as well as those who did not. They made no distinctions.[6]

Old Tassel, the famous Cherokee leader of the eighteenth

century, remarked on the continuous demand by the whites that the Cherokees accept the white civilization:

> Much has been said of the want of what you term 'civilization' among the Indians. Many proposals have been made to us to adopt your laws, your religion, your manner and your customs. We do not see the propriety of such a reformation. We should be better pleased with beholding the good effects of these doctrines in your own practices than with hearing you talk about them, or of reading your newspapers on such subjects. [7]

Red Jacket, the great Seneca orator, encountered a young missionary named Cram, who was sent by the Evangelical Missionary Society of Massachusetts to visit and convert the Iroquois. His reply to Cram's speech advocating that the Senecas accept Christianity best summarizes the tribal attitude toward the overtures of Christianity:

> You say there is but one way to worship and serve the Great Spirit. If there is but one religion, why do you white people differ so much about it? Why not all agree, as you can all read the book?

> Brother, we do not understand these things. We are told that your religion was given to your forefathers, and has been handed down from father to son. We also, have a religion which was given to our forefathers, and has been handed down to us, their children. We worship in that way. It teaches us to be thankful for all favors we receive; to love each other, and be united. We never quarrel about religion, because it is a matter which concerns each man and the Great Spirit.

> Brother, we have been told that you have been preaching to the white people in this place. These people are our neighbors: We are acquainted with them. We will wait a little while and see what effect your preaching has upon them. If we find it does them good, makes them honest and less disposed to cheat Indians, we will consider again of what you have said. [8]

Ernest Thompson Seton compiled a series of quotations on

American Indian religious behavior entitled *The Gospel of the Red Man: An Indian Bible.* The selection is designed to indicate the spiritual qualities of the various tribes and so naturally presents the best side of Indian life. One selection, however, seems to be so typical and universal an example of the nature of tribal life that is reproduced here to show how the tribal religious system worked with respect to the most modest of tribal members. Seton cites Tom Newcomb, who had been his guide in 1912 and 1914 in his travels in the West:

> I tell you I never saw more kindness or real Christianity anywhere. The poor, the sick, the aged, the widows and the orphans were always looked after first. Whenever we moved camp, someone took care that the widow's lodges were moved first and set up first. After every hunt, a good-sized chunk of meat was dropped at each door where it was most needed. I was treated like a brother; and I tell you I have never seen any community of church people that was as really truly Christians as that band of Indians.[9]

The question that arises, of course, is how the tribal religions were able to produce behavior that surpassed the actions of the Christians, if Christianity was to be considered as the one and true religion. Why does Christianity give rise to perpetual bickering and arguments over God and religion, which became anathema to the Indians who observed it? One cannot say that a fundamental defect is inherent in the genes of Europeans that makes them unable to follow their religious beliefs. One can only conclude that while Christianity can describe what is considered as perfect human behavior, it cannot produce such behavior.

Perhaps the closest approach that any Christian community has made to the type of behavior described by countless observers of Indian religion is that of the Amish communities of the midwest. By every criteria which measures social integrity, the Amish appear to rank far above other communities and other denominations of Christianity. Hardly a Christian denomination can approach the record of the Amish for lack of delinquency, lack of idleness, lack of alcoholism, lack of divorce, lack of any statistic that would indicate social disintegration. Need it be noted that the Amish have settled on and related to definite lands, that they hold themselves in a tight communal setting, and that they adhere to customs with the tenacity of belief that amazes outsiders and brings them to as many clashes with civil authority as any group in the nation.

That the Amish can make their religion work indicates not so much the validity of their religion, but the fact that they have created a specific community which relates land, community, and religion into one integrated whole. To a lesser degree, the Mormons have also accomplished this task. The proper response of human personality to religious experience would seem to involve the factors that Indian tribal religions have traditionally emphasized, which the Amish and Mormons at least partially emphasize or practice, and which has distinguished American Indian people from the rest of America. In a sense then, religion must relate to land, and it must dominate and structure culture. It must not be separated from a particular piece of land and a particular community, and it must not be determined by culture.

Chapter 12

The Group

THE CHRISTIAN RELIGION's doctrine of creation was developed very early and is fundamental to the articulation of the basic Christian theology. It has since been absorbed into the general set of assumptions about the nature of the world, so that few people concern themselves with the idea's implications. The subsequent expansion of the Christological doctrines has been so extensive that their relationship to the doctrine of creation has been largely ignored or forgotten.

It may be unnecessary also to place much expectation on a renewal of the examination of history by adherents of the Christian religion. The linear conception of history as an exclusively European franchise has been so secularized and in recent years so militarized that it is no longer a wholly Christian phenomenon. While Christians abstractly maintain that God rules history, as we have seen there is no great tendency to identify exact events in which this control of history is exercised. Rather the more Christians appear to confront the problems involved with historical interpretations, the more they shy away from maintaining that any specific event has been the scene of divine activity. History, at least in its most concrete sense, has become largely a symbolic and parabolic matter.

Of more concern for the present situation with which we are confronted may be the community context in which religions arise. The present trend in Christian religion is to interpret religion and religious experience as a wholly individual phenomenon. The right wing of Christianity has embarked on a Jesus movement in which the major focus is "getting right with God" on a personal basis and an almost total neglect of the social conditions of the various nations and communities in which these believers live. In large measure, this tendency is opposed to another tradition of the Christian religion that has always placed a heavy emphasis on the existence of the church as a community of the saved and quasi-saved. The final spasm of individualism may be the logical conclusion of Christian ideas but cannot by any means be said to represent fairly the historical roots and experiences of Christiantity.

The Old Testament laid down the definitions of the existence of a religious community in a number of related and rather significant doctrines. From the experience in Egypt and the ensuing trauma of the desert came the conception of the Hebrews as the Chosen People of God. In a historical sense, we can well understand that having survived a disastrous natural holocaust fairly intact would tend to make people believe that they had been particularly chosen by a deity to represent his interests here on earth. The development of an ethical system requiring the people to act responsibly toward one another and toward the strangers in their midst may be an added feature of the conception of the Chosen People. However, the idea that religion was conceived as initially designed for a particular people relating to a specific god falls well within the experiences of the rest of mankind and may conceivably be considered a basic factor in the existence of religion.

Even within the ethical systems of the later prophets of the Hebrew religion, however, the Chosen People concept did not spill out from its ethnic boundaries. Isaiah and Jeremiah are concerned more with Israel's example as a people to the nations of the world than with a universal ethical humanism into which secular Judaism has lapsed. The absence of missionaries indicates that while the conception of God, particularly the God of Israel, may have narrowed in the centuries before the advent of Christianity, there is no impelling reason within the Hebrew religion to convert non-Hebrews to the religion of the nation.

The crisis that ensued in the doctrine of the Chosen People with the advent of Christianity was profound. If Jesus were really the Messiah and John the Baptist were Elijah, then the day of judgment should have come with the death of Jesus or shortly thereafter. Such was not the case. The community of Jesus' followers lingered on in Jerusalem for many years after his death, and it was apparently on the edge of starvation when Paul discovered their plight and sought contributions for them in Asia Minor. Inherent in the Jerusalem community's state was the problem of the salvation of a few of the Jews who had followed Jesus, and the subsequent damnation of the remainder of the Jews who had not heeded his preaching. It was essential to hold the Jerusalem community intact to maintain that the Jews had rejected their status as Chosen People, and that the *real* meaning of Jesus' life and death had been to open the gates of salvation to non-Jews.

This struggle began as Paul developed his theology and the subsequent doctrines of creation, history, and atonement. Without these doctrines, preaching to the Gentiles would have been futile, as they could not have been saved at any cost. The Christian God thus became dislocated not only in time and space but also ethnically. In opening the religion to Gentiles, the whole conception of the Chosen People was radically changed from an identifiable group or nation to a mysterious conglomerate of people who could not be identified with any degree of accuracy.

Granted that during the first few centuries of Christian existence, the followers of the religion could be readily identified. It was not as religious people that they received identity, however, but as subversives, political malcontents, and enemies of the Roman Empire. The long-haired peace protesters of today and the Christians of the early Christian era share at least that peculiar feature. They both spoke of concepts totally foreign to the political structures of the society in which they lived, and both were persecuted for their beliefs. Fortunately for our day, the peace protesters did not have the exclusive concept of the invisible community that the early Christians maintained.

The existence of fellow travelers as well as identifiable Christians thrown into the arena made it necessary to develop the conception of the community of saints as a body of believers that could not be readily identified—the Church. Perhaps the most standard definition of the "Church" that has been advanced by Christian theologians is the "Body of Christ." That is to say, the historical aspects of Jesus as an identifiable human being were early consumed by the development of the idea of the Church as the invisible body of the Christ. No one knew or could know who belonged to it until the final judgment, when everything would be revealed. As a community, then, and as a community to be identified as the Jews had once identified themselves nationally, the Christian Church was virtually invisible during its ascendency to political equality in the Roman Empire.

As the empire began to disintegrate, the only institution to which people could cling was the Christian Church. It had adopted the basic political structure of the old Roman administrative apparatus and transformed it into an ecclesiastical hierarchy; the transition from a social milieu primarily political to one that emphasized religious certitude was fairly smooth. In the absence of strong political leaders, Christian bishops and clergy often handled problems of local importance and concern.

By the end of the first Christian millenium, the Church hierarchy had established itself as the supreme ruler of Europe. By cleverly combining a claim to divine sanction with the ambitions of rising European political leaders and the need of these leaders for divine sanctions to their authority, the professional clergy was able to solidify itself as a favored group within the continent's dominant feudal system. As the trend toward strong national governments increased, the Church was able to protect itself by expanding its functions to account for the changing conditions. Ecclesiastical courts were thus set up to maintain a favored position for Church officials in the face of the development of the kingdoms' secular courts.

The high point in Church influence was probably the insistence that God had specifically given the governments of the world to the Pope. Whom the Pope recognized, therefore, was rightful ruler of the nation. The clash over this doctrine invokes familiar pictures of Henry of Germany kneeling in the snows, begging the Pope's pardon for his arrogance in attempting to claim heirship of the Roman Empire without the blessing of the Holy Father. For Europe, the Christian Church had become the first overt conspiracy.

With the Protestant Reformation, the Christian Church was shattered into a number of national organizations, each claiming a direct relationship with the essential teachings of the Christian religion to the others' detriment and degradation. Again the conception of the Church as the Body of Christ was emphasized as the symbol of the community of believers, but again the most important aspect of the Church was the visible organization assuming command of men's religious lives. To the degree that each church claimed primacy in delivering divine commands, it also placed less emphasis on religious experience itself and concentrated on the discipline needed to maintain itself politically and economically. Today we inherit nearly five hundred years of Church growth and organizational control over the religious lives of men. The multitude of Christian churches in America testifies to the misplaced energy that has gone into maintaining special doctrinal divergencies by disciplined organizational groups. The Lutherans in America, for example, trace themselves back to national origins in Europe rather than to any profound doctrinal differences although doctrinal differences do occur. Among the Presbyterians, the American Civil War resulted in the creation of two churches which took opposing sides in the conflict. If, as each ecclesiastical structure would maintain, the church is the Body of Christ, Christianity is indeed in sad shape. If it is in any shape at all.

The Christian religion's traditional claim to validity in regard to its obvious disunity is to return to the days of the early Christian Church and maintain that the Church is in fact invisible and made up of those who truly believe in Jesus as the Christ. It therefore becomes virtually impossible to discuss the conception of a religious community in terms of Christianity, since no visible community can or does exist. Any efforts to identify failures with any of the organized denominations brings the response that the particular denomination under consideration is not really the Church. Yet that denomination collects money in the name of God, it issues pronouncements in His name, it protects its tax exemption because it is a religious group, and it plays an active part in the political decisions of the country be they the Vietnam issue, abortion, capital punishment, welfare, or whatever happens to arouse citizens' emotional involvement.

The tendency among Christian theologians is also to speak as if the denomination were in fact the Church that exists invisibly and sinlessly off stage. After carefully defining the

Church as the Body of Christ containing true believers, true followers, and the saved or the baptized, theologians then promptly launch into exhaustive analyses of social conditions, the state of sin, the nature of the life to come, and other exotic topics with countless suggestions as to what each particular denomination can or should do about them. The abstraction that existed momentarily when conceptualizing "the Church" generally fades in favor of budgets, fund-raising efforts, new programs of social relevancy, and new theologies of program and mission that the denomination's corporate organization must undertake if it is to carry out its ancient task of dictating to the world the conditions by which the world must exist.

The unhappy result of this practice is to make the career employees of each denomination believe that *they* are the Church and that where they appear, what they believe, how they act, and what they do constitutes the Christian religion. One need scarcely comment on the egotism that this behavior indicates.

In the last decade the churches have certainly given impetus to badly needed political reforms that could not have been made without their active participation. The justification of church denominational involvement in social issues has been that the message of Chrisitanity is one of concern for all men in all conditions of life with a special concern for those who, for one reason or another, have been particularly deprived of a chance to fulfill themselves.

One cannot fault the premise of social involvement of corporate Christianity, yet one must take deep exception to both the procedures used to accomplish this end and the priorities such a path indicates. Without a continuing self-examination and reflection by the people of the respective denominations as to the nature of their involvement in social movement, the members of the churches have become increasingly alienated from their own organizations. The result of church staff and career employees delegating to themselves the power and authority to act for the whole membership has been to reduce some major denominations to a shadow of their former strength. Thus even the most tangible indication of the existence of the Christian Church, the denomination, may be disappearing in our day.

One might conclude that the departure of Christianity from its Jewish ethnicity to a universal religion maintaining that its existence is invisible and unknown while constructing elaborate organizations capable of manipulating political and economic power at a significant level has been one of the major reasons for its decline in recent years. Formal organizations seem to have an inevitable direction downward in their development, as they become incapable of maintaining the original emotional commitments present at their creation. The history of Christianity would seem to indicate that attempts to form a religious community capable of maintaining an arena for religious experiences are doomed to become involved in everything but religious experiences.

The breakup of Christianity during the Reformation into national churches and the proliferation of denominations today would seem to indicate that a religious universality cannot be successfully maintained across racial and ethnic lines. The types of Christianity enjoying success in the southern United States today are hardly within the traditional experiences of two millenia of Christians. Rather they tend to reflect the cultural and political biases of the people of the religion, thus indicating that instead of the message of universal salvation and/or brotherhood, ethnicity will almost always triumph. Until contemporary Christian denominations recognize the human reality of ethnicity, they will continue to blunder into and out of contemporary situations and emerge worse for the experience.

It is in the conception of the community that Indian tribal religions have an edge on Christianity. Most tribal religions make no pretense as to their universality or exclusiveness. They came to the Indian community in the distant past and have always been in the community as a distinct social and cultural force. They integrate the respective communities as particular people chosen for particular religious knowledge and experiences. A substantial number of tribal names indicate the fundamental belief that the tribe is a chosen people distinct from the other peoples of mankind. *Dine,* the Navajo word for themselves, means the people. The Biloxi called themselves *taneks aya*—first people; Kiowas noted that they were the principal people. Washoes relate that *washui* means person, and Klamaths called themselves *maklaks*—the people or the community. The concern in almost every instance is to identify the community and distinguish its uniqueness from the rest of the creation.

Once having made this identification, the other aspects of life are then determined as a function of the community identity. Death, for example, in the Cheyenne sense, is a demonstration of a belief in the community's continuity. No imperative to conduct religious warfare or missionary activity exists, because it would mean altering the identity of the community by diluting its cultural, political, and social loyalties with the introduction of foreign elements. In the history of the early Hebrew people, we find the same concern for the maintenance of national identity as a religious function. And in both groups we find the same concern for the stranger taking on an aspect of religious duty.

It is with respect to the attitude displayed toward strangers that a community's psychic identity can be determined. A community that is uncertain about itself must destroy in self-defense to prevent any conceivable threat to its existence, whereas a community that has a stable identity accords to other communities the dignity of distinct existence, which it wishes to receive itself. The admonition of the early Hebrews to honor the stranger in their midst because they were once strangers in Egypt indicates the degree of community security enjoyed by the people. Their faith in the continuity of their nation precluded the destruction of others simply because they had different customs and beliefs. Logan, the Mingo chief, appealed to the Virginians for justice at the peace council following the back country war of 1774: "I appeal to any white man to say if he ever entered Logan's cabin hungry and he gave him not meat; if he ever came cold and naked and he clothed him not."[1] Such hospitality characterized the tribal religious communities precisely because they were communities limited to specific groups, identifiable to the world in which they lived and responsible for maintaining a minimum standard of hospitality and integrity.

The obvious benefit of a tribal religion is its co-extensiveness with other functions of the community. Instead of a struggle between church and state, the two become complementary aspects of community life. The necessity of expanding the political functions of government into the social welfare field is avoided as religious duties cover the informal aspects of community concern, and the coercive side of community life as we have traditionally seen it in Western democracies is blunted by its correspondence with religious understandings of life. Yet religious wars are avoided because of the recognition that other peoples have special powers and medicines given to them, thus precluding an exclusive franchise being issued to any one group of people.

In the closing decades of the last century, the Indian tribes could not be broken politically until they had been destroyed religiously, as the two functions supported each other to an amazing degree. Some Indians agents were able to keep control of reservations because of their use of Indian police. The tribal members would not kill their own people, and those Indians still resisting the Army refused to kill the tribal policemen. When religious ceremonies were banned and the reservations turned over to missionaries and political patronage appointees, the decline of both the traditional political leaders and the religious solidarity of the people was accomplished in a very short time. The Indian Reorganization Act made some restoration of tribal religion possible by abolishing the rules and regulations that forbade the practice of tribal religions on the reservations. By creating corporate forms of government for political and economic ends, however, the federal government created the same problems of religious confusion in the Indian tribes that existed in America at large.

Today with tribal governments severed from the tribal religious life, the integrity of the governments is dependent only on the ability of outside forces to punish wrongdoers. If the people of the reservation see no wrong in the actions of their tribal government in a political sense, they generally keep them in office in spite of constant failures of that government or council to act on behalf of the reservation community.

Even with large defections of the tribal members to Christianity and Mormonism and with the political structure of the respective tribes frozen into quasi-corporate forms of activity, Indian tribes have shown amazing resilience in meeting catastrophes visited on them by government policies and outside interference. The primary identity of the group remains and in many cases has been perpetuated by the government with its incessant concern for administration and distribution of individual and tribal trust property. The major difference between Christianity and tribal religions thus remains active. Tribal members know who they are, and for better or for worse the whole tribe is involved in its relations with the rest of the world.

The opposite is true for Christianity. Mention the failures of either the religion or Western culture as influenced by Christian thinking, and the average Christian will tell you that Christians were not really responsible. Question any outstanding evangelist, theologian, or church leader today as to the orthodoxy of his theology or practice, and people will deny that he is remotely related to Christianity. The self-critical mechanism for analyzing behavior is thus missing from Christianity, whereas it is consumed within the tribal communities. No one will reject a tribal member as not belonging to the tribe. He may be viciously attacked as corrupt, as having assimilated, or as being a stupid tradition-al. He is never disclaimed as a tribal member. (This, of course, refers to tribal members and not to those such as Chief Red Fox who make claims on Indian ancestry without any Indian knowing that they have made such a claim.)

Another phenomenon existing in tribal religions that does not exist in Christianity is the absence of a paid professional religious staff. Tribal religions do not have the massive institutions which Christianity requires to perpetuate itself. While the Indian religious leader may receive gifts for his work in conducting ceremonies, he does not have pension plans, regular working hours, vacations and the other benefits the professional Christian clergyman enjoys. The Indian religious man looks at his religious powers as partly a blessing and partly a curse of added burdens of social responsibility. The Christian clergyman looks up the church hierarchical scale and begins plotting from the time of his ordination how quickly he can reach the apex of the pyramid. The scramble for rich parishes, seats on seminary faculties, appointments to church national staff positions, and boards of directors is quite irreligious and could only take place in direct opposition to the concept of religion, not as a part of it.

Indian religions consequently do not need the massive buildings, expensive pipe organs, fund-raising drives, publi-cations, and other activities that the Christian denominations need to perpetuate themselves. The religious ceremonies of the tribal religions are carried out with a minimum of distracting activities. Many take place in sacred locations, where the people can be in contact with the spiritual powers who have always guided the tribe. Other ceremonies can be performed as the occasion arises, and wherever the need is shown. Many Indian religious ceremonies have been held in apartments within the large urban areas far from the sacred lands of the tribe. Take away the large buildings and other secular achievements of Christianity, and it would vanish within a decade. Unless the Christian God is confined within a quasi-Gothic stone structure, He cannot operate. Needless to say, He does not do very well even with His real estate.

The two concepts of community are carried over into secular life. Today the land is dotted with towns, cities, suburbs, and the like. Yet very very few of these political subdivisions are in fact communities. They are rather transitory locations for the temporary existence of wage earners. People come and go as the economics of the situation demand. They join churches and change churches as their business and economic successes dictate. Lawyers and doctors climbing the ladders of affluence will eventually become Episcopalians and Presbyterians. Businessmen will gravitate to those churches in which their level of secular concern is best manifested.

Within each town and city exist many denominational branches of Christianity; each competes with the others for financial and political control over an extensive portion of community affairs. People may live side by side for years having in common only their property boundaries and their status as property taxpayers. At no point do the various denominations serve to integrate cities, suburbs, or even neighborhoods. The most recent development, sharing church facilities by a number of weak denominations, and community churches, too often reflect what would otherwise be regarded as community secular concerns and the perpetuation of secular ethical values.

Outside of ethnicity, no unique thing distinguishes one

group of Christians from another in the same manner as tribal groups are distinguishable. In the first place, the tribes have a discernible history, both religious and political. The various Indian languages have in the past acted to bind each tribe even closer, and in this respect they have been paralleled by the Roman Catholic use of Latin and the ethnic use of European languages as liturgical languages. Latin early became artificial, but the use of German, Swedish, and other languages in services meant solidification of the religious community to a real degree. In this respect some denominations of Christianity were closer to Indian tribes than they would have cared to elaborate.

Only with the use of Hebrew by the Jewish community, which in so many ways perpetuates the Indian tribal religious conceptions of community, do we find contemporary similarities. Again the conception of group identity is very strong among the Jews, and the phenomenon of having been born into a complete cultural and religious tradition is present, though many Jews, like many Indians, refuse to acknowledge their membership in an exclusive community.

Today many of the Indian tribes are undergoing profound changes with respect to their traditional solidarity. Employment opportunities away from the reservations have caused nearly half of the members of Indian communities to remove themselves from the reservations for work and educational programs leading to work. Massive economic development programs on the reservations have caused population shifts that have tended to break down traditional living groups and to cause severe strains in the old clan structure. And the tragedy of the Indian power movement is that it avoids looking realistically at this obvious change in living conditions. While Indian tribes have been able to maintain themselves in the face of sweeping technological changes, the day may be fast approaching when they too will fall before the complexity of modern life.

For that reason the future may be already a threat to Indian tribal and religious existence as it has never before appeared to be. New social, political, and religious forms must be found to enable the tribal religions to exist in a religious sense, in spite of the inroads being made by the conditions of modern life. In a few selected communities, this transition is being made. In Christian perspective the Amish and perhaps the Mormons show how successfully communities can be established and maintained, when they are restricted to ethnic communities residing in specific locations and preserving specific religious doctrines and ceremonial forms. The rest of Christendom and Indian religious and political leadership would do well to look at these groups as having made a realistic decision to perpetuate themselves as a community.

Surveying the past and looking to the future, the question of religion and its relationship to the social structures of mankind becomes more important. The universal and hardly identifiable conception of a religion for everyone as articulated by Christianity no longer appears to have validity. Where Christianity has most successfully entrenched itself into the lives of people, it has been on an ethnic or racial basis and has had to adopt the cultural and political outlook of the people of the land in which it has chosen to exist. In America it has become virtually impossible for Christianity to have positive effects on our society's movements. Lacking a specific people to which it could relate, Christianity has simply become a captive of the novelty of American life. Then to protect itself it has had to support the political structure of secular America, for without that structure the whole content of American Christianity would be meaningless.

The conflict over tax exemption of Christian churches and church property is a point in question. Would American Christianity be able to continue without its tax exemption? If there were no deductions allowed for contributions to church programs, what would the effect be on church income and programs? How would individual Christians respond to annual taxes on their massive churches, cathedrals, and investments? The fact that the churches are not willing to risk such a tax is indication enough that without a favored position in the secular world and its political and economic structures, most of what we now know as American Christianity would not and could not exist.[2]

The fundamental question of the nature of religion, therefore, must certainly involve a rejection of the structures Christianity has traditionally used to perpetuate itself and promulgate its message. For without the alliance with political structures that lend it credence and protection, Christianity would have vanished long since. It lives today because it has become so intimate a part of Western culture that its existence or reason for existence is rarely questioned. Is this condition necessarily a feature of religion as it has been experienced by mankind at various times and in various places? Is institutionalism necessary to religion in any sense? American society must honestly face and answer that question before it can understand the nature of the problems it faces.

Chapter 13
Christianity and Contemporary American Culture

WE HAVE NOTED quite frequently that it often appears as if Christianity is defined by the cultural context in which it appears, and that with few exceptions it is unable to influence that culture to accept its doctrines. Intertwined with cultural and religious change is certainly the historical era in which the contact is made between a religion and a culture. Christianity may have done yeoman's service in calming the Germanic tribes and enticing them away from barbarism. But the ferocity with which Nazi ideology wreaked its havoc on Europe should cause us to wonder how much savagery Christianity actually abolished from the psychological makeup of European man.

American Christianity in particular appears to be a willing captive of American culture. The trend of recent years has only accentuated the traditional role of Christianity in American society as one of buttressing official folklore and patriotism. It is extremely difficult to discern whether American Christianity follows the culture, expressing its variations religiously, or whether it really does open up new avenues of social reality for consideration. At best we can worry that when a religion finds it necessary to make itself attractive to a society in the hopes that the society will consider it worthy of its attention, that religion is in deep trouble.

Perhaps the most publicized movement of recent years among Christians has been the Jesus movement. Theories abound as to the exact origin of this movement, but at least one reputable theory is that it came as a desperate effort by young people to get off drugs. Whether these young people were tired of drugs or whether drugs were in such short supply that they were forced to find a substitute may be a thesis of a future sociologist. At any rate, Jesus became a drug substitute for a significant number of people. Recounting how Jesus was a perpetual "high," numerous young people adopted the complete fanaticism that had characterized the earlier flower children, Civil Rights, and anti-war movements.

There does not seem to have been a theological basis of any depth within the Jesus movement. Evangelists hailed it as the greatest development in religion in recent years, foreseeing a new generation of the clean-shaven, white-buck-wearing Christians with whom they became familiar in the 1950s. Strangely, the chief characteristic of the Jesus movement was its absolutism, which led to violent intolerance of other ideas. While many of its followers proclaimed their faith in Jesus, few knew any of the details of the life of Jesus the Jewish carpenter. The ironic aspect of this move from drugs to a hypnotic belief in Jesus was the appearance of a book that attempted to show that the original Christians were more interested in psychedelic mushrooms than in Jesus as a cosmic messiah. While the book and the movement were not formally connected, their simultaneous emergence may indicate a psychic need of unsuspected proportions in our society.

The most recent development of the Jesus movement has

been the organization of parents to kidnap the youngsters involved in the movement and take them to de-briefing stations where they are gradually returned to normal secular values and concerns. The possibility of psychic injury to participants of the movement has probably not occurred to the parents of these young people. But an additional, more serious question plagues us. How can these parents keep up the pretense of being Christians, celebrating Christmas, and doing all those other fun things that adult Christians do? Christianity is apparently something that can be taken seriously—but not *too* seriously.

While the Jesus experience has been described by ex-addicts as a "trip," only one man thus far has elaborated on this theme. The Reverend Wesley Seeliger, an Episcopalian chaplain at Texas A & M, views Christianity as a trip in his new frontier theology. The church, according to Seeliger, is a battered covered wagon, and God is a determined and driving trail boss. Jesus is the scout who rides out in front of the wagon train. Seeliger's theology has been published initially in a fifteen-cent cartoon format—which sold more than 12,000 copies at Texas A & M, a noted center of philosophical and theological study.

Against the frontier theology Seeliger sees the temptation of Christianity to form a settlers' theology, and this tension between rolling wagons headed westward and the sedate and comfortable life in the frontier town is apparently what has been causing a lot of our problems. In the settlers' theology, God is seen as the mayor of the old frontier town. The citizens never see Him, but they are certain He exists because they have law and order. The townsmen are scared to death of the mayor, but he keeps the old payroll coming in, and after all that's what made America great.

Meanwhile out on the prairie the old wagon train keeps rolling along. We are presently in the age of the spirit, and sure enough, there he is, the Holy Spirit as the old buffalo hunter, bringing in fresh meat to the people on the wagon train every morning. The clergy appears as the cast of characters like Wishbone and Hey Soos used to complement Mr. Favor and Rowdy Yates of the old television "Rawhide" series. They serve up that old buffalo meat whenever the people have a hankering for food. One need not comment on how this particular theology will be received on the Indian reservations.

A theological development of recent vintage approaching the Western violence-prone trend of frontier theology is the new emphasis on judo, karate, and other Oriental fighting skills. The Reverend Mr. Mike Crain of Brownsville, Kentucky, runs a Judo and Karate for Christ Camp. Karate is, according to Mr. Crain, useful in fighting off the devil. "We are teaching young people how to defend themselves against man," the good pastor has said. "Then we talk to them about how to defend themselves against Satan." Mr. Crain travels around the nation giving demonstrations and preaching sermons. To emphasize his point he often shatters a 300-pound block of ice.

Mr. Crain is not unique, however, because karate is the coming thing in Christian theology. Dean Blakeney, a fellow Christian who studied karate at North Georgia College and Tennessee Temple Theological Seminary, is also using karate to bring home the message of God's reconciliation with a sinful world. Blakeney apparently is further advanced in the Christian life, for besides karate he uses swords and curved Turkish Gurkha knives in his ministry. Recently he placed a potato on the stomach of one of the faithful and split it with a sword without harming the fellow Christian, whom, he noted, had already been saved. Then he cleaved a watermelon into two pieces with his Gurkha knife to the amazement of his audience. His final knife act on behalf of the Lord was severing a banana, which was placed near the neck of one of his disciples.

Blakeney performed all of these Christian feats in the cafeteria of the New Testament Baptist Church in Miami in the fall of 1972. His performance was clearly superior to the feats recorded in the New Testament, since you will recall Peter attempted the same feat and bungled, severing the ear of the servant of the High Priest of the temple in the Garden of Gethsemane. Blakeney lined up four concrete blocks an inch and a half thick and drove his head through them, shattering them. He explained: "These concrete blocks represent your life and one day the devil is going to try to break your life just like I did these blocks."

Dean Blakeney's final sermonette left something to be imagined. He had four men place a 150-pound slab of ice on the stage. "I'd like to do to the devil what I'm about to do to this ice," he chanted as he gave the ice a massive and highly religious karate chop. The block of ice remained firm as Blakeney lost his first encounter with the devil. Had he had a sudden lapse of faith? Was his faith half as strong as that of Mike Crain, who splits 300-pound blocks of ice with little emotion and considerably less pain? Or was it simply denomination differences that allowed Crain to vanquish the devil but tore victory from Blakeney's grasp?

Christians Crain and Blakeney are not alone in their belief that Christianity is relevant to athletic ability. Paul Anderson, an Olympic weightlifting champion, preached a sermon a couple of years back in which he credited his strength to his religious faith. During this historic revelation, Anderson lifted 200 pounds with one arm. Not one of his devout audience apparently felt religious enough to duplicate the feat, immediately raising the question of the relative effectiveness of the Christian faith as opposed to simple athletic training.

Other signs of the efficacy of the Christian faith were noted by the Reverend Noel Street, a British spiritual healer who visited the United States in 1970. He noted that to have a good spiritual life with mental and physical health, one must live a Christian life. Later he elaborated on this prescription, adding that one should also be a strict vegetarian, do yoga or any good regular exercise, and avoid smoking and alcohol. Like Christian karate, yoga is a difficult word to find in either the Greek or Latin versions of the Bible.

Some Christian churches have refused to venture into the new realms of religious realism with new theologies, remaining fairly close to familiar American traditions. The Cathedral of Tomorrow, for example, has followed the New Testament teachings on the talents, wisely investing its earnings in businesses. It owns the Unity Electronic Company of New Jersey, the Nassau Plastic and Wire Company of Long Island, land for a shopping center near its headquarters in Cuyahoga Falls, Ohio. Its best investment thus far, however, is the Real Form Girdle Company of Brooklyn, New York. Knowing this we can conclude that Christianity is in good shape in Cuyahoga Falls, Ohio.

The Cathedral of Tomorrow did not stop with mere business investment, however, but launched into the sale of bonds for Mackinac College, gift annuity plans, life income agreements and other security deposit agreements. The Ohio Department of Commerce, as well as six other states, has ordered a halt to these sales. Whether the Cathedral was religious or not, it was plainly an enterprising group—and that, after all, is what made America great.

The prize for merging religion and business must go, however, to the promoters of Holyland USA, a proposed 50-million-dollar Biblical "Disney-type theme park" that is being built on the Alabama Gulf coast. The original promoter of Holyland USA, a man named Bill Caywood, convinced a number of devout fundamentalists that the park would bring in an extra three million souls. Plans are being made to erect a 157-foot statue of Jesus on a 57-foot base. The sculpture will be taller than the Statue of Liberty and will be visible for miles down the highway each way.

A 4,000-seat amphitheatre will be built for the production of passion plays, but the features that surround the central theme of the park are really what makes it noteworthy. There will be a Noah's Ark Kiddy Petting Zoo, a Biblical wax museum, Biblical story tellers and a 100-foot replica of Jonah's whale. Roman chariots and drivers will be featured in daily rides for the devout believers. A Tower of Babel, Herod's Palace, Wailing Wall, a Red Sea actually able to divide, a Golden Calf (for the disbelievers?), Solomon's Temple, and a Roman catacomb will all be built in the park. Finally, plans were being made to develop an actual trip through Heaven and Hell for the more venturesome of the park's visitors. One can but speculate on the outpouring of devotion that this project will inspire.

Other churches have not invested in businesses or developed Holyland Parks, but they have adopted modern business methods. The Congregational Church in Vergennes, Vermont provided a credit card machine at the entrance of the church to allow parishioners to charge their gifts to the Lord. "Vergennes is literally flooded with credit cards," The Reverend Richard Ogden stated, "and since we are moving into a credit card age, there's no reason the church should remain aloof." Theologically, perhaps, Master Charge would be most suitable.

The First Baptist Church in Hammond, Indiana did not get its credit card machine in time, but it did get a fleet of buses to bring people right to the church door. It owns a fleet of 108 buses, which weekly carry some 2,500 worshipers to the church. The fleet covers seventy-six different routes, and the church employs a full-time mechanic. The annual budget runs close to 80,000 dollars for the fleet of buses, which includes 6,000 gallons of gas a month and about 5,000 dollars worth of tires annually. The minister, who has obviously found peace with the Lord, remarked, "I think so much of building church growth through transportation that I'm spending my life working with buses rather than pastoring a church. And I have no regrets." At least, he must figure, when you save a bus, it stays saved. Hopefully the church will survive the energy crisis.

Christian churches in the Seattle, Washington area preferred to dance instead of ride. In 1970 they sponsored a course on "soul," which was designed to teach Afro-American culture to white parishioners. For sixteen dollars, an eight-week course was offered that involved learning how to move to sound blasted forth on stereophonic equipment. The idea was to get whites used to moving their bodies in conjunction with the rhythm. Many of the participants dug the course, although one lady said that she did it just to torture her husband. Christianity, as we know from the New Testament, will pit father against son, mother against daughter, husband against wife.

Other Christian churches have recently been involved in an exciting affirmation of the efficacy of the faith. Prior to the diocesan convention of the Episcopal Church in Colorado in 1970, the young priests of the diocese petitioned then-Bishop Thayer for permission to hold a peace mass for those who wanted peace in Vietnam. Bishop Thayer, a direct lineal descendent of the Apostles according to official Episcopal doctrine, is reported to have told them that there are other ways of achieving peace besides praying for it.

Sometimes even when prayer works in its mysterious ways, it places a tremendous strain on the recipients of its benefits. Oral Roberts, long-time minister of the Pentacostal Holiness Church and nationally known faith healer, recently joined the Methodist Church. His success in the healing arts was unparalleled in modern times, since it enabled him to build Oral Roberts University in Tulsa, Oklahoma, which now has a fine basketball team with national ratings. Roberts is also a director of the Tulsa Chamber of Commerce and a director of one of the city's largest banks. Where the Lord chose martyrdom for Peter and Paul, He obviously had bigger things in mind for Oral.

Life has not been a bed of roses for Roberts in spite of his recent rise to prominence in Oklahoma. He told a Denver *Post* reporter of the great relief he had in joining the Methodist Church and leaving behind the great burden of faith healing. Faith healing was a great burden, Oral commented to the reporter, because people expected miracles!!!

Perhaps the most important Christian event of our day was Explo 72, a giant rally held in June 1972 at the Cotton Bowl in Dallas, Texas, a city of brotherly love. It was conceived and carried out by Bill Bright of the Campus Crusade for Christ International, one of the many fundamentalist-oriented groups working on college campuses. More than 75,000 gospel-preaching, sure-enough young Christians came to Dallas to conduct a historic rally on behalf of fundamentalist Christianity.

Bill Bright is something of a wonder himself, for he surpassed all previous expositors of the gospel except Jesus himself by reducing the Christian faith to four spiritual principles: God has a plan for everyone; everyone sins; Jesus is God's method of correcting sin; and everyone must individually receive Jesus as savior. To emphasize these four spiritual principles, Bright collected a group of Christian athletes, most notably Roger Staubach, quarterback of the Dallas Cowboys. Outside of Jesus, Roger was apparently the hit of the event by comparing life to a football game with salvation as the goal line and the Christian as being in good field position because of Christianity. It remained uncertain whether the Christians needed a touchdown or a field goal to win the game.

Unlike the feeding of the five thousand, Explo 72 had a budget of 2.7 million dollars and charged participants a twenty-five-dollar entrance fee, which was certainly an improvement over the New Testament way of doing things. But for the entrance fee enough potato chips were served to make a "one-ton potato chip," although apparently the Lord did not do so, preferring to serve individual portions. The event was billed as a religious Woodstock, and it was advertised on 800 billboards, 100,000 bumper stickers, and 5,000 T-shirts.

The festival featured all of the famous Christian personalities, including Don Wilkerson of the "Cross and Switchblade" fame, the Chaplain of Bourdon Street, the Chaplain of Hollywood, and Dr. Billy Graham, who was honorary chairman of the great event. Graham expressed his confidence in the ability of the participants to distinguish false prophets from true ones. Folksingers Johnny Cash and Kris Kristofferson were present to serenade the assembled multitude of faithful and a band, the Armageddon Experience, helped to keep the assembled saints at a fever pitch.

The climax to Explo 72 came when the 75,000 assembled young Christians broke forth in a frenzy of religious devotion and began chanting football cheers. Gimme a J, "JJJJJAY," Gimme an E, "EEEEE," Gimme an S, "ESSSSSS," Gimme a U, "UUUUUUU," Gimme an S, "ESSSSS." Whatta ya got? "JESUS!!!!" The Sermon on the Mount must have seemed pale in comparison.

Anyone who could not distinguish between Christianity and contemporary American culture on the basis of Explo 72 was simply not receiving God's signals in the great football game of life. Had not the Reverend Billy Graham himself been present as honorary chairman people might have had cause to wonder. But Dr. Graham had given his whole life to an exposition of the gospel and although he had previously been unable to reduce it to the four spiritual principles, he was still highly regarded. Among Dr. Graham's achievements is his informal chaplaincy at the White House, which aroused the ire of Reinhold Neibuhr, who could very possibly not distinguish between true and false prophets—being a liberal and all. Neibuhr protested that Dr. Graham and the White House prophets were reducing religion to a civil obedience course that helped to cover problems, not solve them.

Dr. Graham was very hurt at this charge, remarking that he was simply a personal friend of the President and not a political man. He later said that he would vote for Richard Nixon, basing his choice on the President's obvious morality and integrity. Perhaps Dr. Graham felt that a man who could remain oblivious to Watergate, the ITT affair, the Lockheed loan, the Hughes loan to his brother, and who would maintain a committee to re-elect him months after his reelection must have the highest morals in the nation. Dr. Graham felt that his presence at the White House in no way endorsed the policies of the President. When asked to comment on the Vietnam situation Dr. Graham replied that he spoke out only on the moral issues. We can suppose, then, that Dr. Graham has been present at the White House in his role as one of America's Best Dressed Men of 1970, a Christian calling of singular importance.

Dr. Billy Graham's role in contemporary Christian thinking is buttressed by his lack of doubt. Having never attended a seminary, he did not have the opportunity to study Christian history or doctrine and thus had no chance to be led astray by the facts. He once related that he had no doubts whatsoever about Christianity since 1949 when he was converted on a golf course in Florida—calling into question, perhaps, Roger Staubach's theology, which viewed Christianity and life as football games. Some years ago when Dr. Graham addressed a men's group in England, he compared life to a golf course in which one need only follow the rules to be greeted by the Lord after the game was over. (Perhaps the greatest golfer of them all?)

While Dr. Graham is probably the most admired Christian in the modern world, distinguishing his theological position as a religious leader and judge of morality from his

participation in American cultural forms appears to be very
difficult. He apparently swallows almost all of the traditional
mythologies of American life without any critical analysis of
whether they in fact relate to the Christian religion. In 1971
he was the grand marshal of the Rose Bowl parade, and he
has consistently used sports metaphors as vehicles for his
preaching. Dr. Graham supports athletics because "the Bible
says leisure and lying around are morally dangerous for us."
But "sports," Graham contends, "keeps us busy; athletes,
you notice, don't take drugs." How any adult in this day and
age can make that statement is perhaps the most incredible
aspect of Dr. Graham's view of the world.

In the political arena it is virtually impossible to tell Dr.
Graham from the rest of Mr. Nixon's aides. When the
President came to the University of Tennessee in 1970—one
of the few campuses he dared to visit—to address Dr.
Graham's revival meeting, a choir of 5,500 voices sang
"How Great Thou Art" as Mr. Nixon was seated awaiting
Billy's introduction. There remains some question as to
which "thou" the choir was trumpeting. The avowed
purpose of inviting Mr. Nixon to speak in Tennessee was to
"show the younger generation that the President is listening
to them." This attitude meshes with his interpretation of
religion as a buttress of civil and political structures. "I'm for
change, he was reported in *Newsweek* to have said, "but the
Bible teaches us to obey authority."

Dr. Graham's crusade frequently is held in conjunction
with other events of less theological stature. During his
appearance at Madison Square Garden in 1969, a special
hall was set up near the Garden where rock and roll in-
terspersed with confessions of faith continued all night after
the famous evangelist's sessions. Poor Dr. Graham was thus
connected with at least some of those who did not take the
command to obey seriously. But the participants apparently
dug the session. "It's amazing to hear those band members

talk about Christ," one young visitor to the hall was heard to remark. The Reverend John Guest, leader of the sessions, called it "getting back to the biblical principle of going where the people are." He probably could have added that the Christian church itself was founded on a rock.

The confusion between Christianity and American culture is not simply a phenomenon of evangelical and right-wing Christianity. The liberal counterpart has made its contribution to making Christianity relevant to the modern world. The Lutheran Youth Congress meeting in San Diego in 1972 originated the Jesus cheer later repeated at the Cotton Bowl. In 1970 the United Church of Christ in Chicago held an unusual ordination ceremony which indicated that it also had seen the light and was trying to make religion relevant to American culture.

The ordinand wore a multicolored vest with seventeen symbols representing "his concerns" sewn on it. Included were symbols of joy and sorrow, a black fist, a Star of David, a peace symbol, a herald's trumpet, and wheat seeds. Two leotarded dancers conducted a "moving prayer" against a background of shifting images projected on the walls of the museum in which the service was held. Kent Schneider, the newly ordained minister, "celebrated." He is director of the Chicago Center for Contemporary Celebration and will teach others to celebrate. "Celebration," he noted, "is an idea whose time has come." We'll drink to that.

Celebration may be the name of the game over on the left wing of the Christian spectrum as football cheers seem to characterize the right wing. The Reverend Harvey Cox of *Secular City* fame, who is the liberal guru of the Boston area, decided in 1970 to combine all the elements of religion into one massive presentation. Choosing a congruence of holy days, Jewish Passover and Orthodox Easter, Cox gathered his disciples in "The Boston Tea Party," a converted warehouse discotheque near Fenway Park. A projector flashed images on the walls to represent pictorially the agony of Vietnam, while participants wrote graffiti on the walls of the building. A rock band called the Apocrypha played "I Can't Get No Satisfaction," and at daybreak the crowd rushed into the streets, chanting, "sun, sun, sun." Liberal Christianity had finally come of age. Right on, as the liturgy of the day related.

Women's Liberation, a big movement on the left, has even intruded itself into what has normally been a man's exclusive domain. In November 1972 a group of women from the Roman Catholic, Presbyterian, Methodist, Episcopal, United Church of Christ, and other denominations held a "sister celebration" at the Washington Square Methodist Church in New York City. Choosing Reformation Day, the traditional commemoration of Martin Luther's nailing of his 95 Theses on the church door, the women wrote their own unique service. It featured the "liberation of apples."

The service began with the reading of the Genesis account of the creation and fall but rapidly assumed a relevant status. "We were told that we were agents of evil, corrupters of perfect creation," the leader chanted. "We fell for all that," the congregation replied in unison. "We were told that we were subordinate beings, derived from man, not uniquely created," the leader continued. "We fell for all that," the faithful responded. The service featured apple juice, which was tagged the "ferment of freedom." The women added a new myth of Lilith, who was first created co-equal with Adam but abandoned him because she refused to be subservient to him. God, a male chauvinist if ever there was one, then created Eve for Adam, a more compliant female who would minister to Adam's needs. Then Eve apparently climbed the apple tree, jumped over the garden wall, and left Adam standing there. This version does add a dimension to the traditional Christian story of the creation.

The flexibility of the conception of Jesus appears to be another feature of contemporary Christianity. The Reverend

Cecil Maxey of Parker, Colorado, for example, believes that Jesus wore short hair, not long hair, and has preached sermons against long hair. He was asked why the portraits of Jesus show him with long hair. "That's just an artist's conception, and you know how artists are," he replied. The Reverend stated that the first paintings of Jesus were done "hundreds of years" after his death, and he is convinced that Jesus had short hair. The Reverend, in charge of the First Baptist Church, is installing swimming pools, tennis courts, and a minature golf course to provide an "opportunity to witness."

It is very unfortunate that the Reverend Maxey has discredited the portraits of Jesus, for that raises a serious problem for the people in Jerusalem. The Rockefeller Museum there has a skeleton whose anklebone has a steel nail driven through it. The relic was discovered in 1969, but its existence was kept secret until 1971. The relic is called the Yehochanan bone, because it was found in a coffin with that title inscribed on it. When the discovery became known, scholars from around the world wrote to ask if the skeleton was that of Jesus. The Jerusalem scholars, on the basis of anthropologist Nico Haas' report of his findings on the structure of the skull, have determined that the skeleton is not that of Jesus. The skull, according to Haas, bore no resemblance to "Christ as we know him from portraits." Perhaps the anthropologist should join Pastor Maxey's congregation.

From Jesus freaks to portraits of Jesus, contemporary Christianity rocks with efforts to clarify its faith, define its beliefs, and make itself relevant to the modern world. Yet the tensions existing in its divergent branches, and its cancerous growth of splinter sects via television and radio evangelism, make it virtually impossible to understand. The advent of electronic communications has made radio and television religious programs so popular and lucrative that a significant number of evangelists have done very well financially in building up their own private denominations. Younger evangelists are now pushing Dr. Graham and Oral Roberts into the past, creating gaudier, more spectacular programs for bringing the faithful into the fold.

The evangelical world was recently shattered when Marjoe Gortner, a well-known evangelist, became the subject of a documentary movie based on his experiences as a traveling evangelist. He had been brought up from early childhood as a religious prodigy, gaining great fame as a prototype of Christian youth. Then the fascination grew thin, and Marjoe decided to blow the whistle on the circuit that had proven so lucrative to his fellow evangelists. The movie revealed the money-mad preacher casually and perhaps cynically shearing his sheep. The greatest fears of the fundamentalists are thus realized, and the old Elmer Gantry image they have carried seems doomed to follow them.

The movie *Marjoe* appeared perhaps at an auspicious time. Revivalists have been getting somewhat out of hand, as witness Reverend Ike. Better known as the Reverend Frederick J. Eikerenkoetter II in respectable Christian circles, Reverend Ike likes money. For a time he was simply another poor evangelist, but he soon developed a theology second to none in the modern world. Discovering that most people were already in hell, Reverend Ike began telling his congregations to give him money, basing his message on the belief that the Bible says "all things are possible." Combining a fascinating style with the propensity for greed found scattered among the unsaved, Ike is reported to have said he spends one thousand dollars a week on clothes, and since this is rather expensive overhead to maintain, he asks his congregations for money with which to pay the bills. They cough up. As for Jesus, who is the standard product of other evangelists, "One thing even Jesus didn't do," Ike preaches, "he didn't save the world."

As the various branches of American Christianity gather to

karate the devil, to celebrate, or to collect money, religious problems continue to grow. Dr. Carl F.H. Henry, a noted Christian theologian, sees a rise of atheism on a world basis. "Without a recovery of those lively spiritual convictions and vitalities through which the church itself came into historical existence," Henry maintains, "Christianity is unlikely long to remain either a serious contender among world religions or an effective alternative to Communist or any other ideology."

Therein lies the problem. Christians continue to view their religion as an alternative to personally disliked political, social, and economic theories. The alternative to the pot-smoking environs of Woodstock is, for right-wing Christianity, a crewcut, weightlifting, quarterbacking, and Christian folksinging rally in the Cotton Bowl with Jesus cheers. A religious Woodstock, as the promoters called it.

Contemporary American Christianity can quite possibly be understood as having two major, apparently mutually exclusive, emphases. The right-wing, evangelical, and fundamentalist spectrum of Christianity dwells almost exclusively and fanatically on the figure of Jesus, and on the familiar theology of the old-time religion. Its actual scholarly knowledge of Jesus and his times, the nature of the Roman world, and the movement of the early Church is practically nil. The less it knows about the human being Jesus, the more comfortable it is, since it is the idealized, law-abiding, goody-goody projections of themselves, which they call Jesus, that forms the object of their devotion.

The predominance of white men in the right wing of Christianity and their perpetual identification of Christianity as the opponent and mortal enemy of Communism, Social-ism, freethinking, long hair, and other symbolic foes makes their version of Christianity little more than a sacred patriotism seeking to restore the imagined elegance of the last century to American society. Their position with respect to social problems is generally to ignore them. Dr. Billy Graham, their leading spokesman, sees poverty and race problems as indications of the coming of the end of the world. He already finds twenty-eight signs that the end is imminent, and he speculates that he would perhaps receive a favored place in the universe after Judgment Day as his reward, as ruler of a planet perhaps. He notoriously avoids the Bible verses having to do with Christ being present in the prisons, among the hungry and poor, and living with the oppressed.

The left wing is almost the opposite of its counterpart. It is probably best represented by the more traditional denominations such as the Presbyterians, Methodists, United Church of Christ, Episcopalians, and Roman Catholics. Perhaps the Greek Orthodox church should also be included in this category. For such denominations the mention of Jesus is both an embarrassment and a disappointment. Their primary theology can be summarized as a church theology. Every theological question presenting itself is solved by asking what the church should do about it. Inherent in their attitude is the presumption that they are by definition the world's religious and respectable people. They feel the only task remaining in the field of religion is to find a way to make their church relevant to the outside world. Most of them would take the Second Coming of Jesus as a personal affront indicating that God had lost confidence in their ability to solve problems.

The left wing thrives on social movements and fads of all kinds. Let someone advocate the use of hoola hoops to illustrate a theological point, and they swarm to his corner. These churches see their task as making American society respond to people, not as making American society change its basic presuppositions. They have thus set aside large amounts of money for self-determination of minority groups and for studies to determine how to assist the wealthy of the world in filling their leisure time. Planning new liturgies and new ministries, they feel impelled to issue a pronouncement on each and every event occurring on the planet. Much of the social movement of the past two decades has been made possible by the work of these churches, and in that respect they are probably more in tune with the state of American society than their fellow Christians on the right.

Today we find that the right wing of Christianity is growing quite fast, while the left wing, battered from indiscriminate support of demagogues in the power movements, is losing both members and financial support. Gary Wills in *Bare Ruined Choirs* has outlined the extent of internal dissension within the Roman Catholic branch of Christendom, and one might only note that its basic problem is that of reconciling itself to the world of the nineteenth century. In spite of its most optimistic emotions, it has not yet begun to comprehend the twentieth century or its most advanced twentieth-century man, Teilhard de Chardin.

Intertwined in both branches of Christendom is the fast-rising pentacostal movement, which finds its meaning in the underground church of the left and in some of the healing evangelicals on the right. Walter Hollenwerger has compiled a four-thousand-page handbook on pentacostalism that discusses the phenomena to be encountered in this movement. Speaking in tongues, healing, and other activities can be found among pentacostals of all persuasions, and if anything, the movement testifies to the human need for experience in religion.

While Christians are tearing themselves apart on the left or avoiding contact with the real world on the right, we are witnessing the rather frightening revival of demonism, devil worship, the astrological and numerological sciences, and other manifestations of the occult. Both the pope and Billy Graham agree that this is the devil's work, but the persistence of such ancient forms of religious experience in the modern world can testify more to the desperate nature of the spiritual crisis rather than the active work of the devil. Even the devil can certainly think up something new in two thousand years.

Theologies come and go. Black theology apparently attempts to interpret the black experience in American society in religious terms. Carl McIntyre, right-wing Christian, sponsors rallies in the nation's capital extolling the Christian virtues of killing one's enemies. Women's theologies, gay theologies, frontier theologies, and especially athletic theologies abound. At what point does America echo the plaintive cry of the Boston policeman who was assigned to guard Harvey Cox's Easter celebration: "This is not religion, it is chaos."

It is chaos. The world in which Christianity arose no longer exists in its social and political sense. Even the world in which most of today's theologians grew to adulthood no longer exists. The old certainties have become stumbling blocks and the question is not whether one can make Christianity relevant in the modern world. The question is whether the modern world can have any valid religious experiences or knowledge whatsoever. The traditional assumption that Christianity represented the highest form of evolved religion can no longer be considered valid. Nor can the contention that it is the revealed truth of God, perhaps the only revealed truth.

The majority of Christian leaders today do not derive their claim to the office of religious leader from their ability to project spiritual values. More often they have been educated and trained to assume the reins of church leadership. Or they have attracted large followings by simplifying the nature of religion into "four spiritual principles" or other formulas that are eagerly sought by people as a divine form of life insurance. The old charisma that attached to the truly religious man has been negated by the rapid pace of the modern world and is an extreme rarity today.

Instead of observing other religions and finding that they

are "close" to Christianity, Christians would be wise to begin a search for religious experience and certainty itself regardless of the consequences. If there is no means by which the modern world can come into religious integrity, we should accept our condition and shoulder our responsibility of humane treatment of one another as victims of an incomprehensible universe. But if we find our way religiously we should have the courage to accept the revelation that comes and live in the manner it commands us.

Chapter 14
Tribal Religions and Contemporary American Culture

WE HAVE SEEN some examples of the deviations created in religious activity when a culture defines a religion. In a great many areas, tribal religion defined culture. This aspect of Indian life can be seen fairly clearly in the speeches and attitudes of the old chiefs and warriors. Their refusal to consider land as a commodity to be sold, and their insistence that the lands held a great and sacred place in their hearts and the hearts of their people, must be understood in its context of the last century, when they faced the momentous decisions of giving up some of their lands in an effort to preserve the remainder of it for themselves and their children.

There can be no doubt that not only times have changed but cultures also since the white man first set foot on the continent. Tribal cultures have shifted to confront the changes forced on the people by the tidal wave of white settlement. The recent Indian activist movement has attempted to recoup the lost ground and return to the culture, outlook, and values of the old days. The fundamental question facing tribal religions is whether the old days can be relived—whether, in fact the very presence of an Indian

247

community in the modern electronic world does not require a massive task of relating traditional religious values and beliefs to the phenomena presenting themselves.

One small example might indicate the extent to which this problem is a daily irritation to Indian people. In some of the traditional pueblos, modern conveniences are rejected, even electricity. The children of the pueblo attend the public school system, however, and have become accustomed to having cold milk. For the children to have cold milk at home, the pueblo must install electricity. But this innovation will violate the people's religious beliefs. A generation gap of no small distance emerges. What decision do the tribal elders make about the nature of the tribal religion and the demand of the little children for cold milk?

Again and again Indian people are faced with a puzzling unveiling of the distinctions between the Western Christian world and themselves. Sacred bundles of the tribe reside in the state museum; for centuries they were revered by the people, serving to focus their attentions on their religious experience as a people. During the period of religious oppression, the government forbade the practice of Indian religions, and one day the sacred bundle was given or sold to the museum. Everyone had given up on the idea that they would ever again be allowed to practice their own religion, and the sacred bundles were considered as the remaining artifacts of paganism. Today the younger people of the tribe, trying to revive the tribal religion, need the sacred bundles. An old man has been found who has preserved the tribal religion. He is old, and unless he can train the young men, the religion will be lost. What can be done? The sacred bundles are no longer in Indian hands. Do we storm the museum? Will the whites understand why we need the sacred bundles back?

We have been taught to look at American history as a series of land transactions involving some three hundred

Indian tribes and a growing United States government. This conception is certainly the picture that emerges when tribal officials are forced to deal with federal officials, claims commissioners, state highway departments, game wardens, county sheriffs, and private corporations. Yet it is hardly the whole picture. Perhaps nearly as accurate would be the picture of settlement phrased as a continuous conflict of two mutually exclusive religious views of the world. The validity of these two religious views is yet to be determined. One, Christianity, appears to be in its death throes. The other, the tribal religion, is attempting to make a comeback in a world as different from the world of its origin as is the present world different from the world of Christian origins. Can tribal religions survive? Can they even make a comeback?

Even where the two religious systems have clashed, the picture is not clear as to villain and hero. Father A.M. Beede, a missionary to the Sioux at Fort Yates, North Dakota, told Ernest Thompson Seton, "I am convinced now that the Medicine Lodge of the Sioux is a true Church of God, and we have no right to stamp it out." [1] Yet they did try to stamp it out, even recognizing the wrong they were doing.

Some Christian missionaries successfully bridged the cultural gap and became more important to the tribes than most of their own members. The Reverend Samuel Worcester, a missionary to the Cherokees in the 1830s, remained a faithful friend to the tribe in defiance of the State of Georgia. He persisted in his recognition of the Cherokees as a people, following their cultural development, obeying their laws, and giving continual assistance. For his loyalty he was imprisoned by Georgia, and his appeal for release was heard in the United States Supreme Court in the famous case *Worcester v. Georgia* [2] in which Chief Justice John Marshall gave the definitive statement on the status of Indian tribes under the Constitution.

At the opposite end of the spectrum is the Reverend John

M. Chivington, an infamous Methodist minister from Denver, Colorado. Chivington served briefly as a colonel in the Colorado Volunteers during the Civil War. Finding no Johnny Rebs to fight, he turned his attentions to the Indians. He planned, led, justified, and celebrated the massacre at Sand Creek, Colorado in which, in an unexpected dawn attack on a friendly band of Cheyenne and Arapaho Indians, hundreds of helpless people were needlessly slaughtered. The actions of the Colorado Volunteers remain, even today, as one of the most barbaric examples of human behavior.

Between these two extremes are hundreds of cases of Christian people who reflected generous portions of both their religious beliefs and their cultural values in their relationships with Indians. Some were staunch defenders of the tribes they knew; others behaved in a rigid, authoritarian manner without a trace of human feeling. In fairness one cannot judge the religion of the whites as either good or bad when it came into contact with the tribal religions, but only conclude that no consistent set of values ever emerged as peculiarly and gloriously Christian.

Under four centuries of pressure and religious imperialism, many tribal religions disappeared. Some disappeared bacause the tribes were destroyed or were reduced to such few members that the survivors, dropping their own religion, joined larger tribes and accepted the practices of the host tribe. It has only been in fairly recent times that a number of religions have emerged that cross tribal lines. Foremost of these has been the Native American Church, which uses peyote in its ceremonies. Nearly ninety years ago the Ghost Dance spread across the Rockies and high plains with disastrous results.

The Ghost Dance was not the first Indian religious movement to spark resistance to the white invaders. At a major confrontation between red and white, Indian tribal religions were sure to be involved. The Alliance of Pontiac was spurred by an Indian prophet who advocated a return to the original life-style of the tribes and a rejection of the white man's new technology. The brilliant plan of Tecumseh to drive the Americans from the Ohio and Mississippi valleys was thwarted by the premature attack initiated by his brother The Prophet. The delivery of General Custer to the alliance of Northern tribes was in large measure due to the successful medicine of Sitting Bull and other holy men of the tribes.

The establishment of reservations generally involved the creation of mission stations at agency headquarters. Some of the treaties gave to the missionaries lands on which they promised to build schools, houses for teachers, hospitals, and farms. The tribes failed in many cases to appreciate that allowing the missionaries to enter the tribal lands would inevitably result in religious conflict and dissension among tribal members. We have already seen how Chief Joseph refused to have missionaries around, fearing that they would teach the people to quarrel about God.

As the reservations became more permanent, the churches devoted themselves whole-heartedly to converting the people. Religious controversies increased, and missionaries soon became one of the most vocal forces in demanding that tribal political activity be suppressed, since it was apparent to them that the religious and political forms of tribal life could not be separated. Soon plans were underfoot to ban tribal religious ceremonies. The ignorance of the Indian agents assisted the missionaries in their endeavors, since they interpreted any Indian ceremonial as a "war dance."

By the time of the Allotment Act, almost every form of Indian religion was banned on the reservations. In the schools the children were punished for speaking their own language. Anglo-Saxon customs were made the norm for Indian people; their efforts to maintain their own practices were frowned on, and stern measures were taken to discourage them from continuing tribal customs. Even Indian funeral ceremonies were declared to be illegal, and drumming and any form of dancing had to be held for the most artificial of reasons. The Lummi Indians from western Washington, for example, continued some of their tribal dances under the guise of celebrating the signing of their treaty. The Plains Indians eagerly celebrated the Fourth of July, for it meant that they could often perform Indian dances and ceremonies by pretending to celebrate the signing of the Declaration of Independence.

In 1934 under the Indian Reorganization Act, Indian people were finally allowed religious freedom. The missionaries howled in protest, but the ban on Indian religious ceremonies was lifted. Traditional Indians could no longer be placed in prison for practicing old tribal ways. Ceremonies began to be practiced openly, and there were still enough older Indians alive that a great deal of tribal religious traditions were regained. The great Black Elk, today perhaps the best-remembered of the Sioux holy men, was still alive in 1934, and it is said that he had frequent conferences with the holy men from other parts of the tribe living on different reservations.

For several decades the tribal religions held their own in competition with the efforts of the Christian missionaries. But a whole new generation had grown up, educated in mission and government schools and living according to the bureaucrats' dictates; these young Indians rigorously rejected old religious activities as a continuation of paganism. Yet as more Indians went off the reservation, went to war, attended college, and lived in the cities, the situation began to change. The Indian people had always been somewhat in awe of the white man's technology. It had seemed to imply that his god was more powerful than their tribal religions and medicine. The great expansion of the American Indian horizon in the 1950s had a tremendous effect on attitudes toward tribal religions, which provided a very important link with the tribal past. Often through healing ceremonies performed by the holy men of the tribe, sicknesses were cured that urban white doctors could not cure. In one decade many American Indians began to see that white men and their Christian religion had fatal flaws.

In the last several years tribal religions have seen a renewal of interest that astounds many people. The Pueblos of New Mexico and the Navajos of Arizona had managed to retain much of their ceremonial life throughout the period of religious suppression. The Hopi in particular preserved many of their ceremonies with relative purity. The Apaches also had kept a number of their tribal ceremonies. In the Northwest some of the tribes kept their ceremonies by holding them in secret on the isolated reservations lacking sufficient federal resident staff to prohibit them. These tribes simply and frankly continued their ceremonies by making them once again a total community affair to which everyone was expected to come.

Other tribes have seen an increasing interest in recent years as specific ceremonies became the objects of people's affection. Naming ceremonies in some tribes appear to have become much more numerous, as urban Indians seeking a means of preserving an Indian identity within the confusion of the city have asked reservation people to sponsor naming ceremonies for them. They have traveled sometimes thousands of miles and spent thousands of dollars to be able to participate in such events.

Religious conflict has become pronounced on some reservations as Christian Indians have had to make room for traditional Indians in tribal affairs. The continuous conflict on the St. Regis Mohawk Reservation in upper New York State is a classic example of such strife. For nearly two centuries the Roman Catholic Church dominated the affairs of the Mohawks who remained on this side of the border after the Revolutionary War. Edmund Wilson recounts how he visited a cemetery where many of the Christian Mohawks sat silently in the night, listening to the songs and activities of the traditional Mohawks being held a short distance away. Such was the overt situation until recently.

In 1972 open conflict broke out at St. Regis as the impending wave of traditionalism threatened the political stability of a few figurehead Christian Mohawks who had been dominating tribal affairs for nearly a generation. The largest Indian newspaper in North America, *Akwesasne Notes,* operated by traditional Mohawks on a sharing-the-cost-by-contribution basis, has been harassed continuously. Questions have been raised about whether Canadian Mohawks and their adopted friends can be allowed to live on the reserve. The fundamental question is that of defining contemporary Mohawk culture and outlook. The traditionals appear to be strongly appealing to the rest of the people.

As tribal religions emerge and begin to attract younger Indians, problems of immense magnitude appear. Many people are trapped between tribal values constituting their unconscious behavior responses and the values that they have been taught in schools and churches, which primarily demand conforming to seemingly foreign ideals. Alcoholism and suicide mark this tragic fact of reservation life. People are not allowed to be Indians and cannot become whites. They have been educated, as the old-timers would say, to think with their heads instead of their hearts.

Additional problems face any revival of tribal religions originated in times when the tribes were very small and compact. Whenever a band got too large to support itself and required a large game source to feed everyone, it simply broke into smaller bands of people. The two bands would remain in contact with each other. Often they would share war parties and ceremonials of some importance. At treaty-signing times they would congregate and act as a national unit. Their primary characteristic, however, was their manageability. For political decisions, religious ceremonies, hunting and fishing activities, and general community life both the political and religious outlook of the tribe was designed for a small group of people. It was a very rare tribal group that was larger than a thousand people for any extended period of time.

Today tribal membership is figured on a legal basis, which is quite foreign to the accustomed tribal way of determining its constituency. The property interests of descendants of the original enrollees or allottees have become determining factors in compiling tribal membership. People of small Indian blood quantum descended from people who were tribal members a century ago are thus included in the tribal membership roll. Tribes can no longer form and reform on sociological, religious, or cultural bases. They are restricted in membership by federal officials responsible for administering trust properties who demand that the rights of every person be respected whether or not that person presently appears in an active and recognized role in the tribal community. Indian tribal membership today is a fiction created by the federal government, not a creation of the Indian people themselves.

In the 1860s the Navajo bands who were gathered up and marched to New Mexico to be imprisoned by Kit Carson numbered some 4,000 people. The basis of their unity as a people was similarity of language and occupation of a commonly defined area. It was not a political unity. When they were returned to Arizona and given a reservation in the most desolate part of the state, they then fictionally became a distinct tribe, although they had previously composed several distinct independent bands. Today that same tribe numbers close to 150,000 people. The Navajo have not had sufficient time to develop an expanded religious or political structure to account for this tremendous population explosion.

The Oglala Sioux once formed a numerous tribe, but one that was dominated by a series of brilliant and charismatic chiefs such as Red Cloud, Crazy Horse, American Horse, Standing Bear, and Little Wound. They had a number of bands virtually acting independently of each other. Thus Crazy Horse and his people spent most of their time in Montana with the Cheyennes fighting Custer while Red Cloud and his people were living in South Dakota several hundred miles away from that scene. It would have been absurd for Red Cloud to have signed a treaty for the Oglala Sioux without having Crazy Horse and the other chiefs also signing for the tribe.

Today the Oglala Sioux number at least fifteen thousand people, perhaps twenty thousand. A substantial number live off the reservation and participate only sporadically in community life. Yet the people must find a way to define what it means to be an Oglala Sioux in today's world. When such a process is-rigidly controlled by federal officials fearful that the Sioux may gain control over their lives, then incidents such as the recent confrontation at Wounded Knee are inevitable.

While the American Indian Movement received a lion's share of the publicity at Wounded Knee, it was merely the external symbolic group of which the public was made aware. AIM had been asked to come to the reservation to mount the protest by members of the Oglala Sioux Civil Rights Association, a group formed a year earlier to protest conditions on the reservation brought about by the tribal council's refusal to guarantee civil rights to individual Indians. Cooperating with the two groups was the Black Hills Treaty Rights Council. This council was composed of the elder traditional statesmen on the reservation who have tried to preserve the older form of tribal political organization. They have been working all their lives to see that the federal government fulfills its commitments to the Oglalas as promised in the Treaty of 1868 and the Agreement of 1876.

The situation was even more complicated by two other organizations supporting the protest. One, the Landowner's Association, was composed of individual Indians who owned allotments of land and wished to use their lands in community cooperatives to form grazing units for the local communities. The Bureau of Indian Affairs, with the concurrence of the tribal council, had placed their lands in larger grazing units and leased these large units to white cattlemen. The individual Indians were thus deprived of the use of their lands and were given small rental checks by the federal government. They were kept in a perpetual state of poverty while the white cattlemen enjoyed the benefits of economic prosperity during the great rise in the price of beef.

The fourth group involved in the protest was the Inter-District Council. As the conditions on the reservation grew worse during 1972 the people of the different reservation districts formed their own shadow government, known as the Inter-District Council. They had representatives from every one of the eight districts on the reservation and were discussing ways to get a federal law passed to give the people of the local communities political control over their lives through a new constitution. Naturally the present tribal council and the Bureau of Indian Affairs were violently opposed to such a reform as it would have unseated the tribal council and reduced the power of the bureaucrats. During the Wounded Knee confrontation the Inter-District Council tried valiantly to get the federal government to understand how the conditions on the reservation had led to the protest and how the protest could be peacefully resolved.

Perhaps the most important aspect of the Wounded Knee protest was the fact that the holy men of the tribe and the traditional chiefs all supported the AIM activists and younger people on the issues that were being raised. Some were fearful of the violence that threatened their lives, but the strong ceremonial life and the presence of medicine men in the Wounded Knee compound defused a great deal of the criticism that would have been forthcoming from members of the other Indian tribes. No Indian worth his salt could keep up a sustained criticism of the confrontation when he knew that the people at Wounded Knee had their sacred pipes and that the medicine men from both Pine Ridge and the neighboring Rosebud Sioux reservation were performing the ceremonies.

The Wounded Knee protest was dreaded by Indians but it was not unexpected. The federal government had taken the original rolls of the allotment period and insisted that the descendants of those original allottees be considered members of the tribe whether they had sufficient Indian blood to qualify for membership or whether they lived in the communities of the reservation. The internal social mechanisms that ordinarily would have operated to define community membership were forbidden by federal law—and if they operated they were given no legal status or recognition.

We have just begun to see the revival of Indian tribal religions at a time when the central value of Indian life—its land—is under incredible attack from all sides. Tribal councils are strapped for funds to solve pressing social problems. Leasing and development of tribal lands is a natural source of good income. But leasing of tribal lands involves selling the major object of tribal religion for funds to solve problems that are ultimately religious in nature. The best example of this dilemma is the struggle over the strip-mining at Black Mesa on the Navajo and Hopi reservations. Traditional Indians of both tribes are fighting desperately against any additional strip-mining of the lands. Tribal councils are continuing to lease the lands for development to encourage employment and to make possible more tribal programs for the rehabilitation of the tribal members.

A substantial portion of every tribe remains solidly within the Christian tradition by having attended mission schools. They grew up in a period of time when any mention of tribal religious beliefs was forbidden, and they have been taught that Indian values and beliefs are superstitions and pagan beliefs, which must be surrendered before they can be truly civilized. They stand, therefore, in much the same relationship to the tribal religion as educated, liberal people now stand to the Christian and Jewish religions. Both groups have lost their faith in the mysterious, the transcendent, the communal nature of religious experience. They depend on a learned set of ethical principles to maintain some semblance of order in their lives.

A great many Indians reflect the same religious problem as do the young whites who struggled through the last decade of social disorder. They are somehow forced to hold in tension beliefs that are not easily reconciled. They have learned that some things are true because they have experienced them, that others are true because everyone seems to agree that they are true, and some things they feel are insoluble and cannot be solved by any stretch of the imagination.

One of the primary aspects of traditional tribal religions has been the secret ceremonies, particularly the vision quests, the fasting in the wilderness, and the isolation of the individual for religious purposes. This type of practice is nearly impossible today. The places currently available to people for vision quests are hardly isolated. Jet planes pass overhead. Some traditional holy places are the scene of strip-mining, others are adjacent to superhighways, others are parts of ranches, farms, shopping centers, and national parks and forests. The struggle of the Taos people to get their sacred Blue Lake away from the Department of Agriculture indicates the tenuous nature of some tribal religious practices in a world of complicated transportation services and radio and television.

Education itself is a barrier to a permanent revival of tribal religions. Young people on reservations have available an increasingly complicated educational system. Perhaps like conservative Christians, older Indians see the educational system as basically godless and tending to destroy communities rather than create them. As more Indians fight their way through the education system in search of job skills, the tendency of their education will be to concentrate on the tangible and technical aspects of contemporary society and away from the sense of wonder and mystery, which has traditionally characterized religious experiences. In almost the same way as young whites have rejected religion once they have made strides in education, young Indians who have received solid educations have rejected religious experiences. Education and religion apparently do not mix.

Tribal religions thus face the task of entrenching themselves in a contemporary Indian society that is becoming increasingly accustomed to the life-style of contemporary America. While traditional Indians speak of a reverence for the earth, Indian reservations continue to pile up junk cars and beer cans at an alarming rate. While traditional Indians speak of sharing the structure of jobs, insurance, and tribal politics, education prohibits a realistic sharing. To survive, people must in effect feed off one another, not share with each other.

In the old days leadership depended on the personal prestige of the men whom the community chose as its leaders. Their generosity, service to the people, integrity, and honesty had to be above question. Today tribal constitutions define who shall represent the tribe in its relationships with the outside world. No quality is needed to assume leadership, except the ability to win elections. Consequently tribal elections have become one of the dirtiest forms of human activity in existence. Corruption runs rampant during tribal elections, and people deliberately vote in scoundrels over honest men for the personal benefits they can receive. Much of the formal resistance to federal programs for increasing tribal independence comes from the Indian people's mistrust of their own leadership, present and future. Many tribes want the tribal lands and assets so restricted that no one can use them to the tribe's detriment—or benefit.

One of the greatest hindrances to the reestablishment of tribal religions is the failure of Indian people to understand their own history. The period of cultural oppression in its most severe form (1887-1934) served to create a collective amnesia in contemporary people. Too many Indians look backward to the treaties, neglecting the many laws and executive orders that have come to define their lives in the period since the first relationship with the United States was formed. Tribal people are in the unenviable position of dealing with problems the origins of which remain obscured to them.

The disruptions of tribal religions for a period of fifty years have resulted in the loss of a well-accepted recent tradition of ceremonies, religious leaders, and other ongoing developments characterizing a living religion. Contemporary efforts to reestablish tribal religions have come at too rapid a rate to be absorbed on many reservations. In some instances ceremonials are considered part of the tribal social identity rather than religious events. This attitude undercuts the original function of the ceremony and prevents people from reintegrating community life on a religious basis.

Most tribal religions, as we have seen, have not felt that history is an important aspect of religious life. Today as changes continue to occur in tribal peoples, the immediate past history of the group is vitally important in maintaining the nature of the ceremonies. The necessary shift in emphasis to a more historical approach can be seen in the various Indian studies programs, which have attempted to fill in the missing tribal history. Indian tribal religions thus find themselves in the position of earlier Christian communities that were forced to derive historical interpretations to account for unfulfilled prophecies.

We may find the incongruous situation of many Indian people leaving Christianity to return to traditional religions, creating a tribal history to solve social problems, and falling into the historical trap that has plagued Christianity. It would seem that history itself is a deceremonial process, which continues to strip away the mystery of human existence and replace it with intellectual propositions. As the mainstream of Christianity begins to face ecology and the problems inherent in its traditional doctrine of creation, tribal religions are running the risk of abandoning the traditional Indian concerns about the creation in favor of a more historical and intellectual religion.

Tribal religions in the old days did not create an external ethical system. Cultural considerations involving total tribal life enabled people to merge all societal functions into a unity from which all forms of behavior derived. With tribal members spread across the country today and the conditions on the reservations subject to radical shifting at every change of federal policy, there is not that continuity of experience or homogeneous community of people present that would enable Indian people to avoid creating ethical systems based on traditional values.

The closest parallel that we find in history to the present condition of Indians is the Diaspora of the Jews following the destruction of the temple. A surprising number of Indian activists have made this comparison, without considering that the exile of the Jews was for a significant period of time and that the Jewish people almost immediately developed a strong scholarly tradition to preserve their ceremonies and beliefs in exile. The Indian exile is in a sense more drastic. The people often live less than a hundred miles away from their traditional homelands, yet in the relative complexities of reservation and urban life, they might be two thousand or more years apart. It is not simply a spatial separation that has occurred but a temporal one as well.

Many traditional leaders have recognized this problem. In recent years an intertribal ecumenical council has been formed to meet every summer to discuss ways of keeping the people focused on the nature of tribal religions and their meaning for the future of the tribes. The ecumenical council has met the last two years on a reserve in Canada. In the summer of 1972 some five hundred people attended the sessions, and the number of participants has grown each year. There is, however, an extreme danger that such meetings can deteriorate into pleasant sessions of reviewing the past, because of an unwillingness to forge into the future.

One of the chief past functions of tribal religions was to perform healing ceremonies. This function was impaired by lack of any rights to train new people to perform the ceremonies and a general lessening of dependence on tribal medicine men, because of the presence of Public Health hospitals on the larger reservations. Indian healers were generally considered as superstitious magicians by the missionaries and government officials, and healing arts were lost in many tribes.

Today healing remains one of the major strengths of tribal religions. Christian missionaries are unable to perform comparable healing ceremonies, and a great many still regard Indian healers as fakers and charlatans. This particular field is thus open for Indian religious figures who have received particular healing powers, and it is being recognized by the Public Health Service as competent to perform certain ceremonies. A special grant has been given to train more medicine men and to have them work closely with doctors trained in internal medicine.

The modern world has lost a large number of healing medicines, because of the arbitrary rejection of Indian religions. Some tribes had special roots and herbs that had amazing properties. Only a few have remained in use in some tribes, while the vast majority have been lost for a number of reasons. Restriction of Indian people to the reservations has meant that long trips to particular places to gather specific kinds of roots and herbs have been stopped. Gradually people have forgotten which plants were used for what purpose. As the older people have died off, a substantial number of medicinal plants has also been lost.

The great orgasm of dam building which hit the West following the Second World War also destroyed a number of Indian medicines. The dams flooded the smaller creek and river bottom lands where many plants grew, leaving only the higher reservation land above water. Even those plants and herbs that had been remembered and used regularly by the people were thus sometimes lost, because the places where they grew are now under water. A comparable situation exists on the land that has been reduced to farmland from its original state. Some medicinal plants grew wild on certain parts of the prairie or in certain places in the forests. The prairie in large part has now been reduced to erosion-ridden wheat and corn fields, and in most places the forests have given way to farmlands and cities.

When one remembers that a substantial number of people of each tribe lives in urban areas away from the reservation, the problems faced by Indian healers come into sharper focus. Only rather hopeless cases or those presenting an extreme problem will reach Indian medicine men from people outside the reservation. The task of healing will thus take on an Oral Roberts dimension in the future. People will indeed expect miracles. Unless there is a determined effort to gather individual knowledge of healing plants, herbs, and earths as well as a general acceptance of the necessity of rebuilding tribal use of healing people, the impact of healing on Indian religions will continue to decline in spite of temporary successes and may perhaps lose its ultimate validity as a ceremonial experience.

A counterpart of the healing ceremonies are the rites performed by religious people of the various tribes that allow them to predict the future in part or in whole, to give advice on courses of action, and to give general advice and admonitions on a variety of subjects. Divination and foretelling the future were once major parts of religion; with the coming of Christianity, they appear to have lost their respectability. The result of this loss has been the survival of astrology, fortunetelling through cards, and the use of the I Ching in recent years in Western civilization. Discovering the future was once a major function of tribal religious leaders. It remains today as one of the major strengths of traditional religious people.

One can hardly speculate on either the problems or changes this field will experience in the immediate future. The most important aspect that stands out is the insufficient number of people who can perform this special function. In many tribes it is a power given to people only after special ceremonies have been undertaken, and it is a power not always given. It would seem to be a gift most urgently needed by Indian people, as decisions of crucial importance are being forced on Indian people daily, particularly on tribal governments. Yet one can be forewarned and do nothing. Julius Caesar was an example of failure to listen to predictions. Learning the future will probably suffer the same general fate as the rest of tribal religions—if the people return to their old ways, it will be important; if not, it will also fade. The distinction to be made is simply that as a particular gift, it cannot be developed to the exclusion of other gifts but must remain a community-centered experience. If communities cannot produce these kinds of people, they cannot have the benefit of this type of religious experience.

The nature of Indian tribal religions brings to contemporary America a new type of legal problem. Religious freedom has existed as a matter of allowing differing beliefs to exist in people's minds. It has not, thus far, involved consecration and setting aside of lands for religious purposes. This issue, as we have seen, was successfully raised in the case of the Taos Pueblo people. A great deal remains to be done to guarantee to Indian people the right to practice their own religion. A number of other tribes have sacred sanctuaries in lands that have been taken by the United States government for purposes other than religion. These lands must be returned to the concerned Indian tribes for their ceremonial purposes.

New Mexico is the state in which the greatest number of Indian shrines are located and in which the tribal religions have remained comparatively strong. The Cochiti Pueblo needs some 24,000 acres of land for access and use of religious shrines in what is now Bandelier National Monument, where the people go every year for religious ceremonies. The people also have shrines in the Tetilla Peak area. San Juan Pueblo has also been trying to get lands returned for religious purposes. Santa Clara Pueblo requested the Indian Claims Commission to set aside 30,000 acres of the land that have religious and ceremonial importance to the people but are presently in the hands of the National Forest Service and Atomic Energy Commission.

In Arizona the Hopi people have a number of shrines which are of vital importance to their religion. There is, of course, the Black Mesa area, which is regarded by traditionals as sacred, but which is being leased out to Peabody Coal by the more assimilative tribal council. The San Francisco Peaks within the Cococino National Forest are regarded as sacred, because they are believed to be the homes of the Kachinas, who play a major part in the religion of the Hopi. The Navajo have a number of sacred mountains now within federal lands. Mount Taylor in the Cibola National Forest,

Blanca Peak in southern Colorado, Hesperus Peak in the San Juan National Forest, Huerfano Mountain in public domain lands, and Oak Creek Canyon in the Cococino National Forest. Part of the Navajo religion involves the "Mountain Chant," which describes the seven sacred mountains and a sacred lake located within the region of these mountains. From this area the Navajo believe that their ancestors arose at the creation.

In other states sacred places occur with less frequency but hold no less tribal importance. The best-known of Indian religious places is, of course, the Black Hills. Mount Adams, a mountain of particular religious significance to the Yakimas, was restored to them by President Nixon in 1972. The Pipestone Quarry in Minnesota holds particular religious significance to many tribes as the place where they gathered the sacred red stone for their pipes. Some of these lands could be returned to the tribes involved, since they border present tribal lands. Others have passed into private ownership and could be purchased from the present owners.

The question that arises, however, is the extent to which the tribal religions can maintain themselves if sacred lands are restored. Would restoration of the sacred pipestone quarries result in more men seeking to follow the religious life, or would it result in use of the stone for tourism and other purposes? This question can only be answered by the various tribes during the next decade. To what extent can they reinstitute traditional religious values in a world gone mad with development, electronics, almost instantaneous transportation facilities, and intellectually grounded in a rejection of spiritual and mysterious events?

A highly difficult task lies ahead for people believing in the old tribal religions. The ridicule that these religions have suffered must be overcome. This means that in some instances the beliefs of tribal peoples must be reexamined in scientific terms in self-defense. People discovering the variety

of rain, corn, and other dances poked fun at the tribal
religions. Yet today it has been shown that praying and
playing music for growing plants helps them to grow faster.
This is a scientific observation and can be done with
experiments, yet in the religious sphere, the dances to ensure
that the corn grows plentifully appear to cover the same
behavior. A way must be found to reinterpret tribal religions
in terms of how they support, parallel, or oppose knowledge
of the world now available.

Such a suggestion is counter to accepted conceptions of
religion held by many tribal people. They believe, and
rightly, that religion is something particular that cannot be
treated as if it were another subject matter. Yet for a
substantial portion of the tribal communities, no other form
of proof would be acceptable. Tribal religions thus face two
distinct types of movement in their effort to reclaim for
themselves the people's allegiance. They must answer the
questions of those people who have already traveled down the
road of American education and whose needs initially are for
a rational exposition of beliefs. They must also provide the
experiences needed by the people who have always followed
traditional beliefs and practices.

An almost total translation of tribal beliefs into contemporary terms must be accomplished today by Indians of this
generation. The forfeiting of respectability in the intellectual
and academic worlds will only foredoom the comeback of
tribal religions to the status of a fad. It is not simply enough
for Indian people to claim a validity for their religion as
against Christianity and other religions. Rather they must be
always on guard to ensure that their religion is taken seriously as a religion by others with a conception of the world
that is different than other conceptions, but which has a high
degree of potential validity.

The translation of tribal beliefs is itself a singularly
difficult task simply on an academic basis. The Senecas, for
example, believed that the spirits of corn and beans were

highly compatible, and they therefore grew the two plants together. Modern science has shown that of all the kinds of plants grown together that maintain the soil in proper condition, corn and beans supplement each other to the greatest degree. Can this Indian belief be simply a superstition happily arrived at and coincidentally confirmed by experiments in agricultural research projects? Or did the Senecas have a theory of creation that was rooted in many ways in the world in which we live? Did they have sufficient insights into the nature of things to discern this particular relationship and perhaps many others?

The whole question that emerges with the broad reappearance of the Indian tribal religions is the nature of the world and the knowledge that we have of it—what is superstition, and what is insight into the nature of things. No one would seriously contend that Indians of any tribe had an exclusive franchise on religious experiences to the detriment of the insights of other religions. Nor could anyone say that the respective tribal religions were not riddled with superstitions with some fairly crude conceptions being accepted as descriptions of the nature of ultimate reality. To attempt to bring tribal religions back as a social force determining the actions of the people would appear to be foolhardy, and a great danger exists that some Indian people will attempt precisely this task.

On the other hand, tribal beliefs were not all superstitions, and not all actions and customs preserved by Indian people were the product of a primitive people lacking vision of the world's nature. The problem is distinguishing the insights from the superstitions, while maintaining the ceremonials and practices that prove most helpful to small communities in our day. The constant temptation to make religion an objective set of beliefs and logical propositions as Christianity has become may doom the tribal groups that do not take their task seriously enough.

The primary thesis of tribal religions, the relationship of a particular people with a particular land, and the belief of many tribal religions that certain places have special sacred significance must itself be tested in the years ahead. Young Indians must once again take up the vision quests, the search of revelations and dreams, and the responsibility to make the tribal community come alive as a community even with the tremendous hurdles that exist in the modern world.

The non-Christian peoples of other races that live on the continent also have a responsibility to bring into being a new type of religion that does not view our world as lifeless and inimical to human existence. Whether or not this will be patterned after tribal religions, the movement of non-Indians into new religious forms appears inevitable and in many ways welcome. Without a substantial change in understanding of the world (and ecologists warn of the consequences of continued exploitation of the world), it would appear that mankind is approaching a catastrophe of undetermined dimensions.

Christianity can no longer provide a comprehensible picture of either man or the world, and a surprising number of people are turning to other religions trying to find the answers they seek. Among the movements attracting people are witchcraft, demonism, nature worship, Eastern religions, and reincarnation. Among the peoples clamoring for religious certitude are American Indians. As they search for religious experiences to help make them whole once again, they discover the fascination and familiarity of tribal religions.

This is not the kind of world in which tribal religions arose and prospered. It is a world largely determined by other, more complex considerations. If the modern world shows us a world that does not coincide with traditional Christian beliefs and indicates that the problems of the world and the manner in which solutions can be conceived appear compatible with the old Indian tribal religions, the tendency to attempt to return to old ways will continue.

The recent struggle between the various elements of the Indian community over the occupation of the Bureau of Indian Affairs building in Washington gives us an indication of how deeply the Indian community is split in its outlook, value system, and political beliefs. It could be fairly said that Indians now stand on the threshold of success. They have in their tribal religions a comprehensive understanding of the creation far superior to the speculations of the white man and far more coherent than that of the Christian. But they have fallen into the trap of Western education. Sun Chief, a Hopi, wrote in his autobiography:

> As I lay on the blanket I thought about my school days and all I had learned. I could talk like a gentleman, read, write, and cipher. I could name all the States of the Union, with the capitals, repeat the names of all of the books of the Bible, one hundred verses of Scripture, sing more than two dozen hymns, debate, shout football yells, swing my partners, and tell dirty stories by the hour. It was important that I had learned how to get along with the white man. But my experience had taught me that I had a Hopi Spirit Guide, whom I must follow if I wish to live and I want to become a real Hopi again, to sing the old songs and to feel free to make love without the fear of sin or rawhide.[3]

The American Indian of today is in the same predicament. If the tribal religious leaders cannot help Indian people make that necessary connection with the real spirit of Indian religious life, Indians will become simply another academic subject, a relic of a rather thrilling past.

Chapter 15

The Aboriginal World and Christian History

HAD THE WORLD been a three-story finite universe, the Christian doctrine of history might have maintained itself and been a valid consideration of modern people. The simple story of mankind growing out of the Garden of Eden and populating the world might have been sufficient for all men in their own times. The world did not remain as the early prophets conceived it. By 300 B.C. Alexander the Great had shown the Near Eastern peoples the wonders of India. Explorations by Europeans over a 1,000-year period indicated that the globe was much larger than the writer of Genesis had figured. Columbus demonstrated that it was indeed a globe.

The trauma of Discovery of the New World for the Christian theologians was immense. It had not yet been adequately understood by them. What were devout thinkers to make of the existence of millions of people living on lands larger than Europe? What was their status with respect to Christianity—the one true religion? Did God have a purpose for these people? Could Jesus return until all of these nations had been preached the gospel? What was the responsibility of God's chosen nations in the face of this revelation of the tremendous scope of mankind?

The reaction of the Christian nations to the Discovery of the New World and its potential riches was one of unmitigated greed. Having been repulsed by the Muslims in their efforts to subjugate the Near East and nearly prostrated after the wars to establish the divine right monarchies, the kings of Europe badly needed an inexhaustible source of income to maintain themselves. Visualizing a steady stream of wealth from the Indies, which would allow them to avoid giving benefits to the rising commercial classes in return for financial support to the Crown, the heads of the European states saw in the New World the only hope of maintaining themselves.

The Christian Church was even more eager to exploit the new lands. Its political power beginning to wane with the rise of strong European political leaders, the Christian Church saw a means of directing the invasion of the new lands by placing its imprimatur on exploitation, in effect thus taking a percentage of the loot in return for blessing the enterprise. In 1493 Pope Alexander VI issued his *Inter Caetera* bull, which laid down the basic Christian attitude toward the New World. "Among other works well pleasing to the Divine Majesty and cherished of our heart, this assuredly ranks highest, that in our times especially the Catholic faith and the Christian religion be exalted and everywhere increased and spread, that the health of souls be cared for and that barbarous nations be overthrown and brought to the faith itself."[1]

What this pious language meant in practical terms was that if confiscation of lands were couched in quasi-religious sentiments, the nations of Europe could proceed. In an immensely practical gesture the Pope noted that he did thereby "give, grant, and assign forever to you and your heirs and successors, kings of Castile and Leon, all singular the aforesaid countries and islands . . . hitherto discovered . . . and to be discovered . . . together with all their dominions, cities, camps, places, and villages, and all rights, jurisdictions, and appurtenances of the same." [2]

The lands and villages were not, of course, the Pope's to give, unless the understanding of the universe, history, and the planet promulgated by Christianity were correct. If such were the case then it would have followed that, the entire planet being a franchise of the Holy Father, he could distribute it to whomever he found in need of rewarding. Regardless of the later totally secular exploitations of the native peoples conducted by the secular governments of Europe, this papal bull of 1493 marked the attitude of Christianity toward peoples it had not previously thought to exist.

The controversy over the place of the newly discovered natives continued to rage, however, as more information on the New World was made available to the people of Europe. The Treaty of Tordesillas in the following year divided South America neatly between Spain and Portugal, allowing each primacy over portions of the continent which neither had explored or conquered. Plainly the Pope was supervising not the divinely ordered division of the world's lands but national hunting licenses for rape and pillage.

The status of native peoples around the globe was firmly cemented by the intervention of Christianity into the political affairs of exploration and colonization. They were regarded as not having ownership of their lands, but as merely existing on them at the pleasure of the Christian God who had now given them to the nations of Europe. Upon encountering a tribe or nation of native peoples, the Spanish used to read their Requirement, which basically recited the Christian interpretation of history beginning with the Garden of Eden and ending with the pope then enthroned in Rome. The natives were then asked to pledge their allegiance to the pope and the king of Spain. Failing to surrender to Christianity and the expanding Spanish empire meant that it was then legal and an act of religious piety for the Europeans to wage war to wrest the lands from the people.

Again the use of Christian doctrines served to justify the actions of the Christian nations. For centuries Christian theologians debated the conception of the nature of the "just war," in much the same manner as Protestant theologians used to debate the morality of killing people trying to get in your home bomb shelter during an atomic attack back in the days when America was paranoid over Russian missile attacks. The natives refusing to accept the gospel were thus made subjects of the just Christian war, since they had refused to accept the truth which had been revealed some 1,500 years before.

As exploration and colonization continued, the debate expanded about the native peoples and their rights. The only available philosophical system purporting to explain the world of daily events was that of Aristotle, who had once divided mankind into men and slaves. The anti-Indian theologians relied heavily upon Aristotelian thinking to support their thesis that natives could be enslaved. Even pro-native theologians admitted that the natives should be subjected to force until they were converted to the true faith.

In 1526 Francisco de Vitoria at Salamanca attacked the use of Aristotle to deny Indians of the New World their rights to property and liberty. Vitoria denied the right of the Christians to convert the natives forcibly, since he was aware of the mistreatment that had been the lot of the natives resisting conversion. But he then justified conquest of the natives and their lands on the basis of Christian trade rights, finding that God had intended all nations to trade with one another. Any nation or group that prevented trade could then be conquered so that uninhibited trade might continue. Preventive conquest to protect commercial rights was then the basis on which the Spanish and Portuguese made complete their mastery of the new lands and their peoples.

By 1550 two camps of theologians had developed, each with its own version of the legal and theological status of the peoples of the New World. Each theory, incidentally, led to justifying the peoples' exploitation and conquest. Father Las Casas took the side of the natives, while Juan de Sepulveda took the opposing view and justified extinction and enslavement. Las Casas interprepted the Christian position and the 1493 papal bull as giving a right to Spain only to preach the Christian doctrine peaceably; the natives' existing property rights were to be recognized.

Sepulveda, a rigorous Aristotelian philosopher, simply classified the natives as among those who had been meant to be subjugated. Their opposition to Spanish enslavement was thus morally wrong, since it violated the purpose for which God had intended the natives. For Sepulveda pure Christian chauvinism was the answer to the problems of the Old World meeting the New World. While he did not totally win the debate, his views were eagerly accepted by those Europeans going to the New World, thus winning his point in fact in what came after him.

By the time that the other European nations got into the business of discovering lands and peoples in the Western Hemisphere, the struggle for recognition of native legal rights had for all practical purposes vanished. The European nations were more concerned with their wars for control of distant lands than they were in acknowledging the rights of the peoples over whom they asserted control. The doctrine that the pope had been given total control over the planet by God was soon secularized into justification for European nations, definitively Christian, to conquer and subdue the peoples of the lands which they entered. Once the doctrine became secularized, it was impossible for anyone to question its validity; its impact was obvious, and the results were satisfactory to European political heads of state.

Gradually, then, the colonizing European powers began to

define their rights with respect to other nations of non-Christian peoples. The natives had rights to occupy the lands on which they had traditionally lived, until such time as those lands were needed by the invading Europeans. At that time the European nation could extinguish the natives' title by purchase or conquest. With respect to each other, the European nations respected the claims of the nation that first explored new lands and had sufficient military power to protect its claim. With respect to the natives who happened to occupy the lands, they were completely at the mercy of the claiming Christian nation.

The wars for control of the North American continent saw the claims of the various European nations dwindle as England consistently defeated the other nations and succeeded to their claims as each gave up its territory on the continent as part of the peace terms. While European wars raged between England and France, Spain, Holland, and other countries, the natives' legal rights were bounced back and forth as concessions made in wars that had little to do with the people of the continent. England had no sooner achieved dominance in North America than the English colonists revolted against the mother country. Aided by France, which was still smarting over the defeat handed them by England a decade before, they succeeded in freeing themselves from English control.

Almost the first claim put forth by the new nation after the successful break with England was that the colonies had succeeded to the claims made by the mother country under the doctrine of Discovery. The United States was therefore under no obligation to deal justly with the continent's interior tribes. Rather it stood well within the tradition of Christian nations that had previously looted Central and South America and were then in the process of conquering India and Africa. The basic legal policy of the United States government became one of tentative recognition of the Indian interest in the land combined with the assertion that the lands could be taken from the people at any time they were needed by the federal government.

The first articulation of the Christian attitude toward the native peoples and their rights came in the Northwest Ordinance of 1787, in which the Congress of the United States proclaimed that it would never take the Indian lands except in just wars.[3] As it turned out, there were no unjust wars, and the lands were systematically taken. After a century of conflict and systematic oppression, the tribes were lucky to survive with a fragment of their former homelands as reservations for those who had not been killed.

The story is not simply that of the American Indians, however, since the history of Christian nations around the globe has been less than religious. England and France fought titanic struggles for control of the Indian subcontinent, for parts of Africa, and for trade rights in North Africa and Asia. As late as the First World War the nations of the planet were being given to dominant European nations as League of Nations "mandates" and "protectorates," and colonialism has still not vanished. It now shows itself as the American political crusade against Communism, or as the operational results of the giant supranational corporations of Western peoples.

When Canada and Australia achieved independence from the British Crown, they allegedly stepped into the shoes of the Queen insofar as the natives of the lands were concerned. The Queen had been the trustee for Indian lands in Canada, and a substantial portion of the Canadian lands had been held by the Queen on behalf of the native Indian tribes. After the British North American Act, Canada refused to accept its responsibilities with respect to native land rights. Today the Trudeau government refuses to recognize the land titles of the Canadian Indian tribes, and thus even the veneer of protection which aboriginal title has given to natives of the United States has been denied to Canadian Indians.

The aborigines of Australia are in worse shape. Since they

are by definition without rights, they cannot enter the courts of that land to defend their rights to lands on which they have lived for thousands of years. Australia simultaneously claims a legal right to the lands of the continent as derived from Great Britain, while denying the Australian aborigines the right to demand from the Australian government the protection in land occupancy such a derived title implies.

The South American countries make no bones about simply exterminating their Indians. Brazil has carried on systematic genocide against the interior native tribes for many years. The atrocities committed against these people have been well documented by numerous groups and promptly denied by Brazilian officials. Not the slightest pretense has been made that the natives could have any rights to land. They are simply moved or killed whenever land is needed by the Brazilian government. Almost all of the South American nations are predominantly Catholic and reflect the same attitude once promulgated by Sepulveda—some men are meant to be slaves, and it is immoral for them to resist enslavement.

Even smaller nations that should have lands and rights protected have been denied any voice in the matter. Sweden simply moved into Lapland some centuries ago and now denies that the Lapps may have any rights in their lands. In a situation similar to Canada, changes in Swedish national law and status have erased any mention of the rights and property that the Lapps may have had. At present the Swedish government is busy finishing the cultural genocide of the Lapp or Same people through the travesty of court procedures which have already been arranged to divest the Lapps or any rights to their lands and national status.

The final arena of degradation is what is now known as the "Trust Territories" of the Pacific. During the period before the Second World War, Japan fortified those islands received as protectorates following the peace ending the First

World War. As the Second World War got under way, the American forces invaded many of the islands Japan had occupied and many Japan had not occupied. As the war progressed a substantial number of peaceful islands got in the way of the two superpowers and were taken by one side or the other. The peaceful Pacific was soon divided between the United States and Japan.

After the Japanese surrender all the islands came under what may be euphemistically called a United States trust. That is to say, the United States now holds the islands and will continue to do so until it feels like disposing of them. Little effort has been made to give the islands political freedom, and they are now being prepared for large excursions of affluent American tourists. The peaceful Pacific will shortly be America's vacation land, and its people will be servants to rich vacationing Americans. They will never receive even the degree of independence they enjoyed prior to the Second World War. Even worse, their lives are administered by the Department of the Interior, a bureaucracy hopelessly inept and unconcerned.

The responsibility of Christianity for this state of affairs must certainly be heavy. Without the initial Christian doctrines giving Europeans free reign over the rest of the world, much of the exploitation would not have occurred. It was only when people were able to combine Western greed with religious fanaticism that the type and extent of exploitation that history has recorded was made possible. Even today the Christian missionaries search the jungles of the Amazon looking for Indian tribes to convert. In their wake come the professional killers to exterminate the tribes, and following them the government bureaucracies and road builders to subdue the lands of the interior for world commerce.

In almost every generation trade and conversion for religious purposes have gone hand in hand to destroy nations of the world on behalf of Western commercial interests and Christianity. Where the cross goes, there is never life more abundantly—only death, destruction, and ultimately betrayal. As among all the nations of the world the United States, because of its secular concern for justice, has created the best record in dealing with aboriginal peoples. The checks and balances of the American political system have slowed the rate of exploitation of American Indians, so that for many tribes at least a portion of legal status exists. The United States, for example, is the only nation to establish a claims commission to attempt to rectify treaty wrongs with the native inhabitants. Canada refuses to discuss such a commission; Australia loathes the suggestion.

The average Christian when hearing of the disasters wreaked on aboriginal peoples by his religion and its adherents is quick to state: "But the people who did this were not really Christians." In point of fact they really were Christians. In their day they enjoyed all the benefits and prestige Christendom could confer. They were cheered as heroes of the faith, enduring hardships that a Christian society might be built on the ruins of pagan villages. They were featured in Sunday school lessons as saints of the Christian Church. Cities, rivers, mountains and seas were named after them.

And if the exploiters of old were not Christians, why did not the true Christians rise up in defiance of the derogation of their religious heritage and faith? If Pierre Trudeau is today not a Christian in his attitudes toward the Indians of Canada, where are the Christians in Canada who prophetically denounced his actions? If the leaders of the Brazilian government are not Christians, where are the Christians coming forth to disclaim their actions? If exploitation of the Amazon for commercial purposes by American investors results in the un-Christian activity of poisoning thousands of

Indians, why are not the true Christians demanding the resignations of the heads of American corporations supporting Amazon development?

At this point in the clash between Western industrialism and the planet's aboriginal peoples we find little or no voice coming from the true Christians to prevent continued exploitation. Instead we find rhetorical assertions that the Christian God is controlling history and fulfilling His divine plan for all mankind. In the face of world events this assertion is fraudulent at best, an insult to the intelligence of mankind at worst. It is time to call a halt to the unchallenged assumptions of the Christian conception of history. This conception is even breaking apart in the national strongholds of Christianity. The various tribal peoples of Europe that were bludgeoned into accepting super-nationalism a century or more ago are flexing their muscles in resistance to continued oppression. The Irish, Welsh, and Celts are demanding freedom. In France the Bretons have a national movement, the Flemish are reviving their ancient customs, Italy is a virtual conglomerate rebelling at the continued supremacy of the national government. Even Russia has problems of ethnic restlessness and the desire for freedom. Not only is Christian history at an end but quite possibly the end is in sight for its secular manifestation—manifest destiny of Europeans to rule the world.

The first step in this process should not be recitals by sincere followers of the Christian religion admitting their guilt for past wrongs. We have already seen a multitude of tears fall over the demise of Dee Brown's Indians, for example, without a corresponding change in attitude or treatment of American Indians. Further confession of sins is useless and avoids the central question of history: Why must men repeat past mistakes? Being guilty for remote sins is easy, accepting responsibilities for current and future sins is difficult. It is this contemporary attitude toward aboriginal peoples that must be changed rather than compensation for past wrongs.

Christians must disclaim the use of history as a weapon of conquest today. In doing so they must support the fight of the aboriginal peoples wherever it exists. They must demand a new status for native peoples around the planet. They must demand protection of natives and of their lands, cultures, and religions. They must honestly face the problems of the Western societies and consider what real alternatives now exist for those societies to survive in a world that is growing smaller—a world that must contain a great number of smaller groups whose existence is guaranteed and whose rights are not to be trampled underfoot.

The justification of past exploitations of native peoples has been that the gospel had to be preached to them and that a newer and better civilization had to rise from the native peoples' primitive hovels. Such a gospel of peace has been notoriously lacking as an element in Western civilization, and it is very questionable whether the present state of decay, corruption, and exploitation is better than what had existed before the coming of the Western Christian to the nations of the world. When ecologists find a predictable life-span of a generation separating us from total extinction, it would seem that we have a duty to search for another interpretation of mankind's life story instead of the traditional Christian view of the world and what it means. Unless we solve some of our problems, God will *have to intervene* to save any of us.

The present state of affairs cannot conceivably be justified. It cannot be justified at least religiously, and one must conclude that in Christianity mankind has at best been deluded. While the religion appeared to give comfort and solace to people in all ages, its resultant impact on the world as a whole has been anything but comforting. It has been used by its followers to justify their most dastardly deeds, and it has focused our concern on the life hereafter, so that we have refused to believe what our experiences tell us is true. We must now undertake to find a more profound explanation of ourselves and the planet on which we live.

Already in our secular society we are finding indications that, given a degree of concern for the land, people, and solving problems, changes can be made in our understanding of the world. We now recognize that the command of Genesis is not to be taken literally. We simply cannot continue to be fruitful and multiply without destroying everything. We need some relevant form of birth control. In recent years the legal status of abortion has been changed, and we are finally offered some relief from the medieval conception of woman as breeding stock and society as a growing and expanding cancer on the land, which appears to have been the traditional Christian response to overpopulation problems forced upon us in defiance of reality as we have known it.

We have seen this past year the rejection of the death penalty by the Supreme Court and are now faced with the responsibility of acting as a mature society in relation to those who defy our laws. While a substantial number of Christians supported abolition of the death penalty, an even greater number opposed abolition on biblical grounds. The fact that each Justice of the Supreme Court felt it necessary to outline his own position on the subject indicates that we are not far over the threshold of barbarity. No sooner had the Supreme Court decision been announced than the nation's conservatives rose up to find ways to overcome the decision. In California a referendum was placed on the ballot in 1972 and was passed into law. It required the dealth penalty on a mandatory basis for a specific list of crimes, thereby making an effort to circumvent the reasoning of the justices.

In recent years Congress has considered forms of compensation for victims of violent crimes. This development is a return to old Anglo-Saxon law and finds its natural roots in the beliefs of tribal religions. The reward for suffering, in Christianity, has always been in heaven, and the idea that a society has a responsibility to compensate those whom it failed to adequately defend has not been a major thrust of Christian nations. Such a societal conception has always dominated Indian tribal groups. Beyond that, however, the idea of social compensation means that we have taken a major step in the conceptualization of America as a society with a potential for integrity. It is, perhaps, the most important aspect of the problem.

We are now ridding ourselves of a fear of sex imposed upon us by Christian theologians of the past, beginning with the theology of St. Paul. Whether this society can complete the transition from thinking of sexual activity as inherently sinful to considering it as a normal part of the existence of a life species is yet a question to be resolved. At the very least the subject is brought out for consideration instead of being hidden in the closets of our minds. The rather lame efforts of Christian theologians to ride the crest of sexual freedom indicates that even for them the matter is here to stay.

On almost every hand, therefore, we find the old mythologies of Christianity being intellectually and often emotionally rejected by contemporary society. The rejection is not always for the better. Jumping from Christianity to devil worship can hardly be called an improvement. But the willingness to explore the unknown forces in man's spiritual frontier can be called an improvement.

We cannot reject the Christian religion piecemeal. The importance of the decline of the specific doctrines of the Christian religion is that this decline means that the whole religion has been wrong from its inception. Merely canceling the belief in the Christian afterlife does not free us from the necessity of finding out the nature of that life, if such exists. Rejecting the Christian interpretation of creation means a responsibility to find a better conception of a religion as it relates to creation. Or creation as it testifies to religion or religious experiences.

Having changed and rejected Christian interpretations of many of mankind's experiences, we must in our generation reject the concept of history as an inevitable and controlled or controllable process. Our little adventure in Vietnam should surely testify to the fact that we cannot control history and that what appears inevitable is only a projection of our wishes, not a future event. We need to take a new look at what the experiences of mankind have been, and from our best conclusions begin to describe what we feel the whole nature of historical existence on the planet has meant.

Stabilizing the societies of men so that further societal exploitation cannot exist is the first step in determining a new idea of history for mankind. The planet was not given to the pope, and his subsequent division of it to his favorite European kings may have ultimately been illegal in the most fundamental sense of the term. Present unhampered exploitation of the lands and peoples of the world by post-Christian supranational corporations may have been the logical result of Western history, but it does not have to be its final result.

Christianity itself may find the strength to survive, if it honestly faces the necessity to surrender its narrow interpretation of history and embark on a determined search for the true meaning of man's life on this planet. Even surrendering a belief in a god who exercises supremacy over world events becomes possible, if in surrendering the belief, one comes to a greater understanding of the nature of religion and religious experiences. For a divinity, if indeed one exists, cannot even be bound in doctrines and beliefs in any ultimate sense. To restrict one's god then to a particular mode of operation and sequence of appearance would seem to be irreligious and the utmost folly.

Chapter 16

Religion Today

IN PRECEDING CHAPTERS we have made tentative comparisons between Christian doctrines and beliefs and some of the beliefs of Indian tribal groups, which appear to stand in direct opposition. The opposition is more than merely conceptual; it colors the manner in which non-Indians view the world and the people they deal with in that world, particularly Indians. While many Christian doctrines have now passed into the sphere of Western civilization's general beliefs, others continue to form the basis of Christian belief and determine in large measure the manner in which Christians understand the world and form their responses to its events.

Opposing tribal concepts to Christian concepts exist does not mean that tribal conceptions are necessarily correct because Christianity is wrong. Rather the fact that Christianity is unable to speak to certain problems without facing internal collapse of its doctrinal structure means that of the possible alternative answers, one starting point must certainly be the ideas found in American Indian tribal religions. Balanced against the tribal religions, however, is the fact that for the most part these religions provided for a meaningful existence for a people facing a world far different than the one presently experienced. Whether the old tribal religions can survive prolonged exposure to modern conditions is yet to be demonstrated.

In our present situation, we therefore, face a most difficult question of meaning. Ecologists project a world crisis of severe intensity within our lifetime, whereas the religious mythologies projecting the existence and eventual salvation of another world had better be correct in their beliefs. It is becoming increasingly apparent that we shall not have the benefits of this world for much longer. The imminent and expected destruction of the life cycle of world ecology can be prevented by a radical shift in outlook from our present naive conception of this world as a testing ground to a more mature view of the universe as a comprehensive matrix of life forms. Making this shift in viewpoint is essentially religious, not economic or political.

The problem of contemporary man, whatever his ethnic or cultural background, lies in finding the means by which he can once again pierce the veil of unreality, in a religious sense, to grasp the essential meaning of his existence. For people from a Western European background or deeply embued with Christian beliefs, the task is virtually impossible. The interpretation of religion has always been regarded the exclusive property of Western man, and the explanatory categories used in studying religious phenomena have been derived from the doctrines of the Christian religion. The minds and eyes of Western man have thus been rather permanently closed to understanding or observing religious experiences. Religion has become a comfortable ethic for Western man, not a force of undetermined intensity and unsuspected origin that may break in on him.

Many thoughtful and useful systems of belief of ancient peoples have been simply rejected *a priori* by Western thinkers in the religious sphere. This attitude has intruded into Western science and then emerged as criteria by which the world of our experience is judged, condemned, and too often sentenced to death. Many people, for example, have developed astrological systems by which they have charted the nature of relationships between the lives of men and the movement of the planets and stars. Given that modern science now views the universe as an extremely sophisticated electromagnetic complex, the contentions of astrologers as to the influence of the heavens on individual propensities to behave in certain ways may not be as superstitious as it would at first appear. Yet astrology is rejected out of hand by many followers of Western religious thinking, because it conflicts with the philosophical problem of free will.

For centuries the Chinese have used and practiced acupuncture as a regular part of their religious and cultural beliefs. The very idea that there might be centers of feeling within the human body that can block off pain and sensation if properly understood was virtually anathema to many Westerners. The same situation exists today with respect to the conception of Chakras, as defined by some of the Eastern religions. Apparently such conceptions collide with Western beliefs about the human being composed of body, mind, and spirit—the neo-Greek beliefs about the "soul" of man which have intruded into Christianity or the Western conceptions of psychology and psychological problems.

A number of religions have concentrated on the development of beliefs covering the spirits of places; the relationship of man to animal, bird, and reptile forms of life; and the nature of religious healing. Again these beliefs have been rejected on dogmatic grounds, not because they were not suitable for the communities which held them as beliefs. The usual answer given to questions about the nature of religion is highly unsatisfactory. Other religions have been given credibility to the extent to which they conformed or paralleled certain Christian doctrines. To the extent to which they varied or were in direct opposition to Christian doctrines, they have been regarded as false and sometimes as deliberate attempts on the part of the Christian devil to mislead people.

All of these things have been excluded from our consideration. We have been taught to consider problems using logic and concepts that ignore certain facets of existence. Religious experiences are not nearly as important to Western man as his creeds, theologies, and speculations—all products of the intellect and not necessarily based on experiences. Regardless of the experience of a multitude of gods, monotheism has come to be regarded as the highest form of religious knowledge. Yet religions that have achieved a monotheistic doctrine are often rapidly intruded upon by a development of lesser spiritual beings forming a pantheon. When a religion is based in experience whether it be theological or popular, it seems to be of a polytheistic or pantheon-oriented nature.

We cannot be absolutely certain that we are dealing with only one god. The fact that monotheism is logically pleasing does not mean that it is an accurate description of reality. The universe, being somewhat discontinuous in other respects, may also conceivably be discontinuous with respect to divinity. Wotan appears to have amazing resiliency; Yahweh's rainbow still shines in the sky; ghosts prowl the British Isles; the picture of Jesus is appearing more frequently in unexpected places—and the Hopi have rain.

A more basic question about man's psychological processes must be resolved before we begin to understand the breadth of the nature of religious questions. What are religious experiences? Are they of such a nature that they can only be described in terms of the Western peoples, or do they properly belong in non-Western categories? It is a fact that many societies of man have had definable and satisfactory relationships with some form of divinity almost from the beginning of mankind's journey on the planet. Traditional Western thought, and more specifically traditional Christian thought, has been based on the assumption that these religions have often been cruel delusions perpetrated against primitive societies by religious leaders, *shamans*, and medicine men seeking personal gain or additional powers, or men forced into trickery to preserve their place in society.

We cannot conclude that other peoples spent centuries in a state of delusion simply because their experiences of God were so different than those of Western peoples. That their experiences could not be either described accurately by Westerners or understood in Western categories of thought does not make them false. The least we can do is to understand that it is in the nature of religion to exert a profound influence within societies and groups and sustain the community or national group over a period of time. Having retreated even that much, the Western world must be prepared to analyze religion as a phenomenon that does not necessarily explain the unanswered questions posed by the philosophical mind, but which may, in itself, cause such questions to occur to all manner of men in a great variety of situations.

As we find religion in the societies of men, there are a number of factors that appear generally to be present as preconditions to religious experiences. While religious experiences may be individual in specific events, the impact of them is generally quickly felt by respective groups of men, so that the individualistic nature of religion is not that emphasized in Christianity but that given credence in tribal religions. That is to say, whatever else a particular experience may be, religion itself exists in specific groups and is probably more a national or tribal affair than either an individual or universal affair. Universal ethics, however, generally do arise during the course of a religion's growth, and rules for conduct of lives and general theories of salvation seem to appear as religions become more mature. The religions that grow in these ways also lose those aspects that give religion its special importance to a society—healing and divination powers.

Many Christians will vehemently argue that the places at which religious experiences take place are of no consequence. God, they maintain, was released from the bounds of time and space with the revelation of Christianity. God is thus everywhere at all times, and to define divinity according to sacred or holy places is to limit His powers beyond reason, reducing Him to a facade of power and intelligence. The impact of Christianity on the questions of time and space, however, was to transfer the problem to "another world" thus initially sidestepping the question. The final result of the emphasis was to banish God from any possibility of relating to time and space, thus in effect precluding Him from interference with this world.

The major step to be taken to understand religion today is to understand the nature of religion as it occurs in specific places. There is a reason why shrines exist over and above the piety of the uneducated religious person who has visions while tending sheep. Mount Sinai, for example, has been a holy mountain for a considerable length of time, thus indicating that it has a religious existence over and above any temporary belief held by particular people. If this concept is true then economics cannot and should not be the sole determinant of land use. Unless the sacred places are discovered and protected and used as religious places, there is no possibility of a nation ever coming to grips with the land itself. Without this basic relationship, national psychic stability is impossible.

A corollary of this concept is the possibility that each land projects a particular religious spirit, which largely determines what types of religious beliefs will arise on it. Judaism, Islam, and Christianity do not radically differ about the nature of creation and the final days, when even nature is to be renewed. Arising as they did from the desert of the Middle East, it may be that concern with a renewal of that particular land has preformed their religious conceptions. The fact that Druidism is once again rising in parts of Europe may indicate that those lands, in largely determining the shape and beliefs of religious experiences, are Druid lands.

The effort to shift religious thinking so as to examine this theory appears ludicrous to Western men when first proposed. We do not have any exact knowledge of what Druid religious beliefs and practices were. Whether present practitioners are precisely following ancient religious practices is less important than the fact that the religion has contemporary followers, who are attempting to make the proper connections with what has gone before. That religions change is a foregone conclusion. To go from Jesus on the hillside advocating the message of the Beatitudes to a Cotton Bowl filled with Jesus freaks chanting "two bits, four bits, six bits, a dollar, all those for Jesus stand up and holler" indicates that anything can occur in a religious tradition.

Nearly as important may be the fact that lands can apparently be consecrated by a particular religious group wishing to place its roots in the land. The persistence of some religions on originally foreign lands would appear to testify to the fact that peoples and lands can relate to each other in a very powerful manner to develop a spiritual unity. It may be this possibility that will prove the salvation of Christianity in the modern world. Once having developed roots as did the Five Nations at the Great Tree of Peace at Onondaga, the land and the religion apparently become as one. The Hopi also established themselves on a land.

Rather than attempt to graft contemporary ecological concern onto basic Christian doctrines and avoid blame for the current planetary disaster, Christians would be well advised to surrender many of their doctrines and come to grips with the lands now occupied. That certain lands will create divergent beliefs and practices is certainly preferable to extinction. The problem of relating to a place's spirit or alternatively bringing a spiritual reality to a particular place is yet to be understood in the sphere of religious thought. That a fundamental element of religion is an intimate relationship with the land on which the religion is practiced should be a major premise of future theological concern.

Given a specific land on which a religion can grow, the problem then shifts to the nature of the people adhering to that religion. Is religion necessarily a universal condition for all men, or is it a phenomenon that can manifest itself to different groups of men in different ways? The very conception of a Chosen People implies a lost religious ethnicity. Most probably religions do not in fact cross national and ethnic lines without losing their power and identity. It is probably more in the nature of things to have different groups with different religions. The traditional objection to this concept is that it would create religious wars. If the number of important religious experiences occurring in a specific community were supported by homogeneous cultural and political factors, the religion would probably have more impact, and religious wars would not occur. At present we have wars fought with religious justification as well as religious wars. The past history of the West is eloquent testimony to the fact that a universal religion crossing ethnic lines does not lessen wars; it tends to increase them until one particular ethnic group comes to dominate the religious beliefs of the whole group with its own cultural values.

Besides the importance of land in religion, the existence of a specific religion among a distinct group of people is probably a fundamental element of man's experience. Once religion becomes specific to a group, its nature also appears to change, being directed to the internal mechanics of the group, not to grandiose schemes of world conquest or the afterlife. What a religion does to a group of people on a distinct land is thus a vital question for future analysis. The phenomenon that is most clearly seen among the non-Western religions is the element of healing ceremonies. It is this fact of religious life, Oral Roberts excepted, that appears to dominate land-based religions of particular peoples.

One cannot separate the spiritual problems of people from their religion; particularly the tribal religions treat healing as a major part of religious life. Inherent in ceremonial healing practices are powers given to religious men in their visions and religious experiences. The tribal religions look at healing in an entirely different manner than do Christian religious healers. The predictable Christian religious healer builds his audience to a fever pitch, hoping that supreme acts of willpower will release the person from his infirmities. No consideration is given to the people's cultural practices or the particular spirit of the lands on which they live. In a very real way healing is an abstract process, dependent as much on the self-motivation of the infirm as it is on the healer's powers.

Tribal religions do not place as much emphasis on the infirm's rigorous willpower. Rather, specific ceremonies and healing songs and practices are used to cure specific types of sicknesses. Many Indian religious healers can tell at a glance if they can heal a particular illness. No pretense is made if it appears that the medicine cannot be used for a particular illness. And the healers do not pretend to be able to cure any sickness. The individual medicine man has specific powers—his own gifts received through his experiences. The counterpart of healing is a recognition of his healing powers' limitations.

Almost all of the healing disciplines came originally from religious beliefs and the religious men's practices. The severance of medicine and psychology from religion has only been a recent event in the histories of religious people. In the West it has taken extreme forms, and the rising number of psychoanalysts coupled with the declining number of professional clergy testifies to the fact that the religious crisis of Western civilization is taking extreme forms of alienation within itself. The phenomenon of a substantial number of clergymen suffering psychological problems indicates that religious and mental problems are not being solved as Christianity is presently practiced.

Again in the field of healing, relationships already seen as crucial to tribal religions are prerequisites for receiving healing powers. Healing may indeed be a means of determining the extent to which a religion is strong or weak, declining or growing. In none of the three areas of land, ethnicity, or healing is any set of beliefs required in the traditional sense which Western religious thinkers have defined beliefs. The transition from traditional Western and Christian categories to tribal and non-Western categories of religious experience is not then a matter of learning new facts about life, the world, or mankind's history. It is primarily a matter of participation in terms of the real factors of existence—land, a specific community, and religious men with special powers existing within that community.

It is the nonphilosophical quality of tribal religions that makes them important for this day and age. Modern society has now reached the stage at which any particular proposition is viewed as partially or relatively true but most probably not ultimately true. Truth, in the Western scientific sense, is what can be verified. In tribal religions no effort is made to define religion as a system of doctrinal truths about the nature of the world. It cannot, therefore, be verified, and only in a certain sense can it be experienced by a certain community.

The analytical error of contemporary man is that he has not understood, in religious terms, the meaning of what he has already accomplished scientifically by revealing the world of sensory perceptions. In seeking an ultimate answer to the meaning of existence, that is, reading God's mind as early scientists considered their work, modern man has foreclosed the possibility of experiencing life in favor of explaining it. Even in explaining the world, however, Western man has misunderstood it.

Harvey Cox in *The Secular City* relates, "In our time the Copernican revolution has reached out to incorporate everything into its sweep. All things are relative. Everything depends on how you look at it."[1] In this statement Cox echoes the profound confusion of modern Western man and his inability to comprehend how far from his origins he has really come. The theory of relativity, in this sense, hardly means that all things are relative. It rather means that all things are related. This fundamental premise undergirds all Indian tribal religions and determines the relationships of all parts of creation one to another.

As between the two theories of interpreting the world, the impact and implications of the differences are tremendous. All things being relative, no particular thing has an existence of its own for its own sake but is finite in the worst sense of the term: It lacks identity. Everything becomes an object for scientific scrutiny in the same way in which Christian theology early relegated the world, the life forms of the world, and God himself to philosophical analysis. Given this type of world the only conceivable answer to problems was the sermon admonishing, threatening, cajoling, and enticing entities to become what they were not. Self-generated change induced by additional information then became the only solution to the problems of existence.

If all things are related the unity of creation demands that each life form contribute its intended contribution. Entities are themselves, because they had been made to be so. Any violation of another entity's right to existence in and of itself is a violation of the nature of the creation and a degradation of religious reality itself. Admonitions to generate self-change are a form of insanity, violating the whole nature of reality. There are, consequently, few sermons preached in the tribal religions.

We stand today at a series of crossroads. Rather than revolutionary movements we may have possibly lapsed into a prolonged period of respectable boredom from which we will never recover. Clearly the current tendency is to attempt to reclaim the nineteenth-century roots of social existence that can give us a sense of permanency in a world of increasing change. But the stability of that era was at best a mythological memory of a golden age. Our very refusal to acknowledge the failures of both American and world history and our patriotic effort to make it into a golden age show how pathetic and inadequate our tools for confronting change really are.

Within the traditions, beliefs, and customs of the American Indian people are the guidelines for mankind's future. It is this spirit of the continent, of all continents, that shines through the Indian anthologies and glimmers in the Indian communities in grotesque and tortured forms. The vision of stability of the community is found by non-Indians who venture into the reservations, and yet in viewing the remnants of Indian religion they understand neither Indians nor themselves. White America and Western industrial societies have not heard the call of either the lands or the aboriginal peoples. In the appalling indices of social disorder of the tribal peoples Westerners see only continued disruption and, being unaccustomed to viewing life as a totality, cannot understand the persistence of the tribal peoples in preserving their communities, lands, and religions.

The lands of the planets call to mankind for redemption. But it is a redemption of sanity, not a supernatural reclamation project at the end of history. The planet itself calls to the other living species for relief. Religion cannot be kept within the bounds of sermons and scriptures. It is a force in itself and it calls for the integration of lands and peoples in harmonious unity. The lands wait for those who can discern their rhythms. The peculiar genius of each continent, each river valley, the rugged mountains, the placid lakes, all call for relief from the constant burden of exploitation.

Who will find peace with the lands? The future of mankind lies waiting for those who will come to understand their lives and take up their responsibilities to all living things. Who will listen to the trees, the animals and birds, the voices of the places of the land? As the long-forgotten peoples of the respective continents rise and begin to reclaim their ancient heritage, they will discover the meaning of the lands of their ancestors. That is when the invaders of the North American continent will finally discover that for this land, God is Red.

Notes and Commentary

Chapter 1

1. Various newspapers gave different evaluations of the damage. Often the downtime of employees whose offices were damaged was listed as part of the total damage. I have taken the figure reported in the *Washington Post* several times and used that as illustrative of the accounts of the extent of the occupation.

2. Many people have personal disagreements with Richard Nixon, and I find many of his positions distasteful; however, credit should be given where credit is due. All reports that have leaked out of the White House indicate that President Nixon made a major effort to restore Blue Lake to the Taos people, and this should not be forgotten in any evaluation of him.

3. Senator Goldwater is generally regarded as very conservative, but his Indian record is consistently good. Blue Lake was an instance where he played a major part in helping Indians obtain justice.

4. The Cornwall Bridge incident has deep religious roots in that traditional Iroquois peoples were involved in the incident. This account is basically a summary of a series of different news stories reported in *Akwesasne Notes*.

5. More information on this running conflict between young Navajo people and the white power structure of Gallup, New Mexico, can be obtained from: Southwest Indian Development, Inc., Window Rock, New Mexico.

6. More information on the Quinault action to close their beaches and a copy of their tribal ordinance can be obtained from the Quinault Tribal Council, Taholah, Washington.

7. A copy of the proclamation issued upon the successful landing on Alcatraz is included as Appendix I to this book.

8. A film has been made about the Pitt River Indians, and information about them and the film can be obtained from the California Indian Legal Services, 2727 Dwight Way, Berkeley, California. In the fall of 1972 they filed a major lawsuit to determine their rights. It had the support of many of the California Indians who had received settlement under other claims awards.

9. The Indians of All Tribes organization held on and successfully negotiated with the federal government and the city of Seattle to receive a lease on the western part of the Fort Lawton lands, where a cultural center is being planned. The most important figure in this action was probably Bernie Whitebear, who led the Indian negotiating teams.

10. Restoration of the belts is dependent, however, on the construction of a tribal museum at Onondaga, and the people are currently making plans for such a museum. A very important figure in getting the belts returned was Kenneth Dewey, who worked for the New York Council on the Arts and gave his wholehearted support to the Iroquois. Ken was killed in an airplane crash in August, 1972.

11. The American Indian Movement initiated many other activist protests, but I have chosen those that seemed most to the point, most representative of their attitude, and those that appeared to be skillfully planned and executed and produced some results.

12. Lame Deer gives a better account of the takeover of Mount Rushmore since he was there. People interested in this aspect of the movement should read *Lame Deer, Seeker of Visions* by John (Fire) Lame Deer, Simon and Schuster, 1972.

Chapter 2

1. Jennings Wise covers this burial of the California treaties in his *Red Man in the New World Drama,* Macmillan, 1971. I have brought his account up to date. Aubrey Grossman, attorney for the Pitt River people, has done a monograph on the treatment of the California Indians. Copies can be obtained from him in San Francisco or from the California Intertribal Council in Sacramento.

2. The Indian fishermen of the Washington State area have an organization known as the "Survival of American Indians," P.O. Box 719, Tacoma, Washington. They have made a film entitled *As Long As the Rivers Run,* which includes shots of the police brutality. In 1973 the Washington State national guard used the Nisqually Indians as the "enemy" during a practice war games. When the Governor was asked about it, he gave a lame apology as to how he didn't realize that it would be offensive to the Indians.

3. As this book goes to press the federal government has done virtually nothing to get the case tried. Part of the Northwest Indian participation in the Trail of Broken Treaties was caused by Indian desires to get the Justice Department to move on this lawsuit.

4. Tax suits from these three states went to the United States Supreme Court in the fall term 1972. The suits all involved an interpretation of the right of a state to tax Indians and their income from the sales of goods on the reservations or on income derived from reservation activities. The cases are: *State vs. Tonasket* (Washington), *State vs. McClanahan* (Arizona) and *State vs. Mescalero Apache Tribe* (New Mexico). The *McClanahan* case was decided in favor of the Indians, the *Mescalero* case was lost.

5. The Survival of American Indians, Inc., Tacoma, Washington, is able to furnish a list of the cases in which no convictions have been made for Indians allegedly fishing.

6. Survival of American Indians has documents showing a close cooperative effort by the state, the Bureau of Indian Affairs, and the U.S. Army in keeping the Indians under surveillance.

7. All of the incidents listed below that involve grave-robbing or excavation of Indian burial sites have been taken from newspaper reports originally published in *Akwesasne Notes*. Anyone wishing to check out the accounts need only get the newspapers from 1971.

8. The American Indian Press Association, 1346 Connecticut Ave. N.W., Washington, D.C., covered the Yellow Thunder incident thoroughly, and its press releases to the Indian newspapers are available in its files. The incident continued to cause a great deal of concern for months afterward, and this death can probably be said to be one of the major causes of the Trail of Broken Treaties. The Sioux made a number of pleas to then Attorney General John Mitchell without any response. As the Trail of Broken Treaties was being planned, Indians decided to ask for a law making it a federal crime to kill an Indian. Had the Justice Department supported the Sioux and made a thorough investigation, there would doubtless have been no Trail of Broken Treaties.

9. The American Indian Press Association has good material on the Oakes case. At last report Mrs. Oakes had filed a suit against the camp and the guard concerned.

10. As this book goes to press one Congressional hearing has been held on the incident. Senator Kennedy originally promised hearings also, but the subject matter got too hot for him and he dropped his plans. Then the Wounded Knee incident began and the matter of the Bureau occupation became one of secondary importance.

Chapter 3

1. Stan Steiner, author of *The New Indians*, the book that really opened up modern Indians as a subject matter for publishing, has a series of now-humorous anecdotes verifying the attitude of publishers toward Indians as outlined in both points. Any publisher taking offense can contact Mr. Steiner for information.

2. I presented these same ideas in *Natural History Magazine* in

a book review of *Seven Arrows* by Storm and received a barely rational letter informing me of the greatness of the books listed in this paragraph. I have basically summarized the feelings of the letter writer in this paragraph.

3. Peter Farb is more keenly aware of contemporary events than appears from his book. He is far and away one of the most perceptive people ever to look at Indian affairs from an observer's point of view. Too many people become emotionally involved in the subject to be objective, but Farb is much fairer and more incisive in his short articles and book reviews as to what is happening to Indians than almost any other observer, white or Indian.

4. *The New York Times* did an investigation of Red Fox and found that almost every fact he had presented did not check out. A significant number of people still believe that he is an Indian, although he is unable to name any relatives at all on any of the Sioux reservations. Believe me, there is not a Sioux Indian in the world who does not know who his relatives are. By asking for relatives and settlements on any reservation, any Indian remotely acquainted with Indian country can tell in five minutes whether a person is Indian or not. See *The New York Times*, Friday, March 10, 1972, pp. 1 and 22.

5. All of these books are excellent studies of Indian religions. Powell's book on the Cheyenne is perhaps the most thorough, but the two Black Elk books are almost verbatim accounts by Black Elk, and so form a very important unity as to Sioux religious beliefs.

6. People appear to be split on the authenticity of the Yaqui theology presented by Castenada. Yaquis, as a rule, are Mexican Indians with only a small American settlement in Arizona. The absence of references to sacred lands causes me to wonder.

Chapter 4

1. This attitude is discussed more precisely in my book *We Talk, You Listen*, published in 1970, which was written during the

time I was trying to get the churches to stop their flirtation with confrontation and fund solid and badly needed projects for Indian communities. I have all of my correspondence from those days in case any church official wishes to dispute my interpretation of events. I also have a number of letters from the planning stages of the Trail of Broken Treaties, which show heavy church involvement at various stages.

2. I have met several young Colville Indians who reject some of the popular activists because they did not assist the antitermination people in their fight. Among those who did help the Colvilles were Chuck Trimble, then head of the American Indian Press Association, now director of the National Congress of American Indians; Elnathan Davis of the Klamath tribe; Bernie Whitebear, head of Indians of All Tribes in Seattle; Jim White, head of DRUMS of the Menominees; and Ada Deer of the Menominees.

3. Cited in *I Have Spoken*, compiled by Virginia Irving Armstrong, Swallow Press, Chicago, 1971, p. xviii. It seemed to be a startling prediction of what I had thought was developing for years, and when combined with the series of grave-robbing incidents is little short of prophetic.

4. Camus, Albert, *The Rebel*, Vintage Books, 1956 (Alfred A. Knopf, 1956), p. 299.

5. Quotation is cited from the back cover of *I Have Spoken*, and is also found in *Touch the Earth* by T. C. McLuhan; it originally comes from *Land of the Spotted Eagle* by Luther Standing Bear, Houghton Mifflin, Boston, 1933, p. 248.

Chapter 5

I do not pretend to make a complete analysis of the problems involved here, but I feel that it is necessary to redefine at least one problem which seems to me to be of utmost importance. If they occur, events must occur *someplace*. That Ardrey finds so much evidence for the importance of territory in animal behavior seems to me indicative of the fact that living organisms do respond to their immediate environment. The Second World War being triggered by the Nazi desire for living room for the Germanic peoples, it seemed to me that an effort should be made to force consideration of land itself, places, and finally space as a vital factor in our lives, experiences, and our perceptions of the meanings of things.

Chapter 6

1. Hodge, Frederick W., *Handbook of American Indians,* Rowman and Littlefield, 1965, vol. II, p. 366.

2. See, for example, Brown, Joseph Epes, *The Sacred Pipe,* University of Oklahoma Press, 1953, pp. 3-6 for Black Elk's discussion of this relationship.

3. Augustine, *The Confessions.*

4. Tillich, Paul, *Systematic Theology,* Vol. II, University of Chicago Press, 1957, pp. 41-42.

5. *Touch the Earth,* compiled by T. C. McLuhan, Outerbridge and Dienstfrey, 1971, p. 8.

6. Cox, Harvey, *The Secular City,* Macmillan, 1965, p. 20.

7. White, Lynn, Jr. "The Historical Roots of Our Ecological Crisis"

8. Dubos' address is published as a small booklet by the Smithsonian Institution, Washington, D.C.

9. Quoted in the Religion Section, *Denver Post,* Saturday, March 7, 1970, in article by Louis Cassels.

10. The Creation Science Research Center in San Diego, California, has been extremely active in submitting textbooks to the State Board of Education which allege to give equal treatment to both Darwin and Genesis. There has apparently been some talk by people who support the center of forcing acceptance of their textbooks by court action. (Reported in the *Denver Post* Religion Section, Saturday, August 12, 1972.)

11. Eastman, Charles, *The Soul of the Indian,* Houghton Mifflin, 1911, 11. 119-120.

12. Romans 5: 13-19.

13. *Touch the Earth,* p. 18.

14. The ceremony is briefly described in *The Book of the Hopi* by Frank Waters and White Bear Fredericks.

15. *Touch the Earth,* p. 23.

16. Houseman, A. E. *A Shropshire Lad.*

17. Standing Bear, Chief Luther, *Land of the Spotted Eagle,* p. xix.

18. Heim, Karl, *Christian Faith and Natural Science,* Harper Torchbooks, 1957, p. 15.

19. Jeans, James, Sir, *Physics and Philosophy,* Ann Arbor Paperbacks, University of Michigan, 1958, p. 204.

20. Collingwood, R. G. *The Idea of Nature,* Oxford University Press, London, 1945, p. 160.

21. Johnson, A.H., *Whitehead's Theory of Reality,* Dover Publications, New York, 1962, p. 60-61

Chapter 7

1. Edward Spicer reproduces a Papago calendar stick recording in his book, *A Short History of the Indians of the United States,* Van Nostrand Reinhold Company, 1969.

2. Spicer also gives a fragment of the Walum Olum.

3. *Uncommon Controversy,* A Report Prepared for the American Friends Service Committee, University of Washington Press, 1970, p. 29.

4. Fairservis, Walter, *The Ancient Kingdoms of the Nile,* A Mentor Paperback, Thomas Y. Crowell Company, 1962, p. 89.

5. Tompkins, Peter, *Secrets of the Great Pyramid,* Harper and Row, 1971, p. 1.

6. Many of the scholars I have asked about this book ridicule it for their own emotional reasons. When I asked one scholar about it, I was told that no one believed it. I asked why not,

and the scholar simply said that everyone knows that it is impossible. I personally think Gordon has a good point to illustrate, and if scholars have determined *a priori* that his thesis is impossible, that is probably the best testimonial he can get as to its ultimate validity. Remember the flat earth that was obvious to anyone who looked?

Chapter 8

1. *The Secular City,* p. 91.

2. *Ibid.,* p. 222.

3. Gaster, Theodore, *Passover,* Henry Schuman, 1949, p. 29.

4. Pedersen, Johannes, *Israel: Its Life and Culture,* Geoffrey Cumberledge, Oxford University Press, London, 1959, vol. III-IV, p. 728.

5. Dupré, Louis, *The Other Dimension,* Doubleday, 1972, p. 395.

6. *Ibid.,* footnote.

7. Tillich, Paul, *Systematic Theology,* vol. II, p. 88.

8. Attempting to cite the extensive material on Immanuel Velikovsky's work, the vicious attacks leveled against him, and the results of his predictions would take many books to accomplish. Two sources do a fairly presentable job of showing the abuse that Velikovsky received at the hands of the academic and scientific community. *Pensées,* a student journal published in Oregon, did a special issue on the thought of Velikovsky. A book entitled *The Velikovsky Affair,* edited by Alfred de Grazia, was published by University Books in 1966.

   I have followed the battle between Immanuel Velikovsky and his critics for some time, the better part of two decades. His reception by the academic community has convinced me that he is probably correct. To wit: I had dinner one night with a very well-known archeologist, and I asked her about Velikovsky's writings. She nearly collapsed with emotion, telling me that he was a wild man, that he had been refuted, and that he was considered a crank. When I asked if she had read his books, she told me that she would never read his books.

I have consulted with numerous scholars to see if anyone would refute even one point that Velikovsky makes in his books, knowing that scholars are objective, that they mull over the facts and do not make hasty decisions. I have been taught all my life that we can trust scientists and scholars for they are impartial truth seekers.

Almost universally in my questioning of scholars, I have met two basic attitudes toward Immanuel Velikovsky. The first attitude is that he is wrong and that the scholar will not read any of his books or examine any of the theories he presents because he is wrong. I have rarely met a scholar who has even read any of the books, I have never met a scholar who can refute any specific point, and I am reminded of the churchmen who refused to look through Galileo's telescope to see the moons of Mars.

The second attitude is one of virtually paralyzing fear that anyone would ask a scholar to admit that perhaps Velikovsky has been right in numerous instances. After reading off an almost endless list of Velikovsky's predictions that have proved true, I have been met with the suggestion that he made a lot of lucky guesses. All right, let's see any other man alive today make a series of lucky guesses that have proved so accurate; if he is not correct in his theory he has such a superior batting average in lucky guesses that we should let him have his way.

I would heartily recommend his works to one and all. When I have discussed using his theories in this book and people have discovered what the theories are, I have been universally warned that mentioning his name would discredit whatever I might say. Probably the reverse is true; I have nevertheless used many of his ideas with the confidence in mind that ten years hence the same scholars who warned me about mentioning Velikovsky will be lecturing piously about the great break-through that has been made in our conception of the world. Like any other superior mind, people are waiting for him to die before they mention his name.

His theory of the Exodus is at least more credible than that of Gaster, Dupré, and Pedersen, for whom the event never occurred.

Chapter 9

1. *Washington Post,* January 14, 1973 discusses the present investigation of the visibility of the Crab nebula supernova explosion and its possible observation by the Indians of North America.

2. The best exposition of the Hopi history of the four worlds is probably Frank Waters and White Bear Fredericks' *The Book of the Hopi.*

3. *Theories of the Universe,* edited by Milton K. Munitz, The Free Press, 1957, p. 9.

4. Genesis: 1.

5. Alexander, Hartley Burr, *The World's Rim,* Bison Books, The University of Nebraska, 1953, p. 13.

6. Heine, Heinrich, *Religion and Philosophy in Germany,* Beacon Press, 1959, pp. 159-160.

7. See Carl Jung's essay "Wotan" in *Civilization in Transition,* vol. X, published by the Bollingen Foundation through Pantheon Books.

8. Seton, Ernest Thompson, *The Gospel of the Red Man,* Doubleday Doran, 1936, pp. 58-59.

Chapter 10

1. Dr. Billy Graham, for example, frequently speculates on how we will all look in heaven. A feature story on him in *Newsweek* (July 20, 1970) quotes him as saying, "I believe in the resurrection of the body and I have in mind that in heaven we will look like what we were at our best on earth." If so, Joe Namath and Paul Newman have it made here and in the life to come.

2. See Immanuel Velikovsky's *Oedipus and Akhnaton* if you want an eye-opening account of Tutankhamen's tomb and why Carter and Lord Carnarvon found it so filled with wealth.

3. *I Have Spoken,* p. 51.

4. *I Have Spoken,* pp. 94-95.

5. *Uncommon Controversy,* p. 29.

6. McLaughlin, James, *My Friend the Indian,* Salisbury Press Book, 1970, pp. 81-82.

7. *I Have Spoken,* p. 95.

8. See *The Sacred Pipe* for a description of these ceremonies.

9. See *The Iroquois Ceremonial of Midwinter* by Elisabeth Tooker, Syracuse University Press, 1970, for more information on this type of ceremonial.

10. Macmillan, 1958.

11. Almost every facet of which we have been speaking is covered on one way or another in Lame Deer's book, and rather than use extensive citations from the book, I have simply suggested it as a fundamental source of information on tribal religious experiences.

12. As quoted by *Newsweek,* April 6, 1970.

13. *I Have Spoken,* p. 49.

Chapter 11

1. *The Secular City,* p. 9.

2. *Ibid.,* p. 30.

3. Andrist, Ralph K. *The Long Death,* Macmillan, 1964, p. 134.

4. *I Have Spoken,* p. 112.

5. *Ibid.,* p. 95.

6. *Ibid.,* p. 33.

7. *Ibid.,* p. 30.

8. Washburn, Wilcomb, *The Indian and the White Man,* Doubleday, New York, 1964, pp. 209-214 cites Red Jacket's reply to Cramm.

9. Seton, Ernest Thompson, *The Gospel of the Red Man,* pp. 26-27.

Chapter 12

1. *I Have Spoken,* p. 28.

2. When the case on church tax exemption came to court, the attorneys general of 39 states filed *amicus curiae* briefs supporting continued exemption of the churches. The alleged separation between church and state does not seem so separate after all.

Chapter 13

I have been collecting clippings on religion for years, and from the multitude of stories I have selected the stories in this chapter. I have no doubt that most of the efforts described herein were sincere or well-meaning efforts. That is precisely the problem I am talking about. If even Christians cannot distinguish between American culture and their own religious doctrines, who can?

Chapter 14

1. Seton, Ernest Thompson, *The Gospel of the Red Man,* Doubleday, Doran & Company, Garden City, New York, 1936, p. 4.

2. 6 Pet. 515 (1832)

3. *I Have Spoken,* p. 157.

Chapter 15

1. Washburn, Wilcomb, *Red Man's Land, White Man's Law*, Scribner, New York, 1971, p. 5.

2. *Ibid.*, p. 5.

3. This statute has always been regarded as the basic affirmation of Congressional policy toward American Indians.

Chapter 16

1. *The Secular City*, p. 27.

Appendix I

Proclamation to the Great White Father and to All *His* People, 1969

We, the native Americans, re-claim the land known as Alcatraz Island in the name of all American Indians by right of discovery.

We wish to be fair and honorable in our dealings with the Caucasian inhabitants of this land, and hereby offer the following treaty:

We will purchase said Alcatraz Island for twenty-four dollars (24) in glass beads and red cloth, a precedent set by the white man's purchase of a similar island about 300 years ago. We know that $24 in trade goods for these 16 acres is more than was paid when Manhattan Island was sold, but we know that land values have risen over the years. Our offer of $1.24 per acre is greater than the 47¢ per acre the white men are now paying the California Indians for their land.

We will give to the inhabitants of this island a portion of the land for their own to be held in trust by the American Indian Affairs and by the bureau of Caucasian Affairs to hold in perpetuity—for as long as the sun shall rise and the rivers go down to the sea. We will further guide the inhabitants in the proper way of living. We will offer them our religion, our education, our life-ways, in order to help them achieve our level of civilization and thus raise them and all their white brothers up from their savage and unhappy state.

We offer this treaty in good faith and wish to be fair and honorable in our dealings with all white men.

We feel that this so-called Alcatraz Island is more than suitable for an Indian Reservation, as determined by the white man's own standards. By this we mean that this place resembles most Indian reservations in that:

1. It is isolated from modern facilities, and without adequate means of transportation.
2. It has no fresh running water.
3. It has inadequate sanitation facilities.
4. There are no oil or mineral rights.
5. There is no industry and so unemployment is very great.
6. There are no health care facilities.
7. The soil is rocky and non-productive; and the land does not support game.
8. There are no educational facilities.
9. The population has always exceeded the land base.
10. The population has always been held as prisoners and kept dependent upon others.

Further, it would be fitting and symbolic that ships from all over the world, entering the Golden Gate, would first see Indian land, and thus be reminded of the true history of this nation. This tiny island would be a symbol of the great lands once ruled by free and noble Indians.

American Indian Center

Appendix II

The Last Message of the Indians of Alcatraz

TO THE CITIZENS OF THE UNITED STATES:

We, Indians of All Tribes, having held the island of Alcatraz for 19 months, were forcibly removed by Federal marshals. Despite all the injustices we American Indians have suffered, we hold a hope that you will at last hear our words.

We propose:

That the deed of the island of Alcatraz be given to the Indians of All Tribes, with the stipulation that they act as guardians of the island in the name of the Great Spirit, and for the benefit of all men and women who respect our earth mother.

We propose that work begin immediately to level all man-made structures so that nature can once more return to this island, and that it be declared as sacred ground to remain as such forever. We propose that a small roundhouse be erected for an annual ceremony of earth renewal and purification to re-dedicate it to all who respect our earth.

This proposal, then, we offer to the citizens of this country, hoping that by its acceptance, a new era of understanding and cooperation between a people of varied cultural backgrounds can at least begin.

Appendix III

Sierra Club vs. Morton involved federal approval of the extensive ski development in the Mineral King Valley in the Sequoia National Forest. In this suit Justice William O. Douglas dissented from the majority and wrote what may come to be regarded in later years as the first major effort in the history of American jurisprudence to incorporate a contemporary understanding of nature into law. Douglas' effort to redefine man's relationship with nature by recognizing the standing of a particular feature of nature to sue is a fascinating review of the many nonhuman entities that have been recognized in law for commercial and criminal purposes. It would have, or at least should have, according to Justice Douglas, been a natural step to come full circle and vest in the lands and rivers themselves a legal power to be represented in the courts of the land. Douglas' opinion is reproduced in full below:

MR. JUSTICE DOUGLAS, dissenting.

I share the views of my Brother Blackmun and would reverse the judgment below.

The critical question of "standing" would be simplified and also put neatly in focus if we fashioned a federal rule that allowed environmental issues to be litigated before federal agencies or federal courts in the name of the inanimate object about to be despoiled, defaced, or invaded by roads and bulldozers and where injury is the subject of public outrage. Contemporary public concern for protecting nature's ecological equilibrium should lead

321

to the conferral of standing upon environmental objects to sue for their own preservation. See Stone, "Should Trees Have Standing?" 45 Southern California Law Revision 450 (1972). This suit would therefore be more properly labeled as *Mineral King vs. Morton.*

Inanimate objects are sometimes parties in litigation. A ship has a legal personality, a fiction found useful for maritime purposes. The corporation soul—a creature of ecclesiastical law—is an acceptable adversary, and large fortunes ride on its cases. The ordinary corporation is a "person" for purposes of the adjudicatory process, whether it represents proprietary, spiritual, esthetic, or charitable causes.

So it should be as respects valleys, alpine meadows, rivers, lakes, estuaries, beaches, ridges, groves of trees, swampland, or even air that feels the destructive pressures of modern technology and modern life. The river, for example, is the living symbol of all the life it sustains or nourishes—fish, aquatic insects, water ouzels, otter, fisher, deer, elk, bear, and all other animals, including man, who are dependent on it or who enjoy it for its sight, its sound, or its life. The river as plaintiff speaks for the ecological unit of life that is part of it. Those people who have a meaningful relation to that body of water—whether it be a fisherman, a canoeist, a zoologist, or a logger—must be able to speak for the values which the river represents and which are threatened with destruction.

I do not know Mineral King. I have never seen it nor travelled it, though I have seen articles describing its proposed "development," notably Hano, "Protectionists *vs.* Recreationists—The Battle of Mineral King," *New York Times Magazine,* Aug. 17, 1969, and Browning, "Mickey Mouse in the Mountains," *Harper's,* March 1972, p. 65. The Sierra Club in its complaint alleges that,"One of the principal purposes of the Sierra Club is to protect and conserve the national resources of the Sierra Nevada Mountains." The District Court held that this uncontested allegation made the Sierra Club "sufficiently aggrieved" to have "standing" to sue on behalf of Mineral King.

Mineral King is doubtless like other wonders of the Sierra Nevada such as Tuolumne Meadows and the John Muir Trail. Those who hike it, fish it, hunt it, camp in it, or frequent it, or visit it merely to sit in solitude and wonderment are legitimate spokesmen for it, whether they may be a few or many. Those who have that intimate relation with the inanimate object about to be injured, polluted, or otherwise despoiled are its legitimate spokesmen.

The Solicitor General, whose views on this subject are in the Appendix to this opinion, takes a wholly different approach. He considers the problem in terms of "government by the Judiciary". With all respect, the problem is to make certain that the inanimate objects, which are the very core of America's beauty, have spokesmen before they are destroyed. It is, of course, true that most of them are under the control of a federal or state agency. The standards given those agencies are usually expressed in terms of the "public interest." Yet "public interest" has so many differing shades of meaning as to be quite meaningless on the environmental front. Congress accordingly has adopted ecological standards in the National Environmental Policy Act of 1969, Pub. L. 91-90, 83 Stat. 852, 42 U.S.C. s 4321, et seq., and guidelines for agency action have been provided by the Council on Environmental Quality of which Russell E. Train is Chairman. See 36 Fed. Reg. 7724.

Yet the pressures on agencies for favorable action one way or the other are enormous. The suggestion that Congress can stop action which is undesirable is true in theory; yet even Congress is too remote to give meaningful direction, and its machinery is too ponderous to use very often. The federal agencies of which I speak are not venal or corrupt. But they are notoriously under the control of powerful interests who manipulate them through advisory committees, or friendly working relations, or who have that natural affinity with the agency which in time develops between the regulator and the regulated. As early as 1894, Attorney General Olney predicted that regulatory agencies might become "industry-minded," as illustrated by his forecast concerning the Interstate Commerce Commission:

> The Commission is or can be made of great use to the railroads. It satisfies the public clamor for supervision of the railroads, at the same time that supervision is almost entirely nominal. Moreover, the older the Commission gets to be, the more likely it is to take a business and railroad view of things. (M. Josephson, *The Politicos* 526 (1938).)

Years later a court of appeals observed, "The recurring question which has plagued public regulation of industry (is) whether the regulatory agency is unduly oriented toward the interests of the industry it is designed to regulate, rather than the public interest it is supposed to protect."

The Forest Service—one of the federal agencies behind the scheme to despoil Mineral King—has been notorious for its alignment with lumber companies, although its mandate from Congress directs it to consider the various aspects of multiple use in its supervision of the national forests.

The voice of the inanimate object, therefore, should not be stilled. That does not mean that the judiciary takes over the managerial functions from the federal agency. It merely means that before these priceless bits of Americana (such as a valley, an alpine meadow, a river, or a lake) are forever lost or are so transformed as to be reduced to the eventual rubble of our urban environment, the voice of the existing beneficiaries of these environmental wonders should be heard.

Perhaps they will not win. Perhaps the bulldozers of "progress" will plow under all the esthetic wonders of this beautiful land. That is not the present question. The sole question is, who has standing to be heard?

Those who hike the Appalachian Trail into Sunfish Pond, New Jersey, and camp or sleep there, or run the Allagash in Maine, or climb the Guadalupes in West Texas, or who canoe and portage the Quetico Superior in Minnesota, certainly should have standing to defend those natural wonders before courts or agencies, though they live 3,000 miles away. Those who merely are caught up in environmental news or propaganda and flock to defend these waters or areas may be treated differently. That is why these environmental issues should be tendered by the inanimate object itself. Then there will be assurances that all of the forms of life which it represents will stand before the court—the pileated woodpecker as well as the coyote and bear, the lemmings as well as the trout in the streams. Those inarticulate members of the ecological group cannot speak. But those people who have so frequented the place as to know its values and wonders will be able to speak for the entire ecological community.

Ecology reflects the land ethic; and Aldo Leopold wrote in *A Sand County Almanac* 204 (1949), "The land ethic simply enlarges the boundaries of the community to include soils, waters, plants, and animals, or collectively, the land."

That, as I see it, is the issue of "standing" in the present case and controversy.

Appendix IV

REPLY TO THE WHITE HOUSE RESPONSE

TO

THE TWENTY POINTS
OF THE TRAIL OF BROKEN TREATIES

POINT ONE—RESTORATION OF CONSTITUTIONAL TREATY-MAKING AUTHORITY: The U.S. President should propose by executive message, and the Congress should consider and enact legislation to repeal the provision in the 1871 Indian Appropriation Act, which withdrew federal recognition from Indian tribes and Nations as political entities which could be contracted by treaties with the United States, in order that the President may resume the exercise of his full constitutional authority for acting in the matters of Indian Affairs—and in order that Indian Nations may represent their own interests in the manner and method envisioned and provided in the Federal Constitution.

The Response

The first proposal is that Indian nations should again become sovereign political entities which would contract treaties with the United States—the purpose being "in order that Indian Nations may represent their own interests."

Over one hundred years ago the Congress decided that it was no longer appropriate for the United States to make treaties with Indian tribes. By 1924, all Indians were citizens of the United States and of the states in which they resided. The citizenship relationship with one's government and the treaty relationship are mutually exclusive; a government makes treaties with foreign nations, not with its own citizens. If renunciation of citizenship is implied here, or secession, these are wholly backward steps, inappropriate for a nation which is a Union.

Indians do need to "represent their own interests" and Indian tribes, groups and communities are finding increasingly effective ways of expressing these interests. There are several active and vocal nationwide Indian organizations; there are many tribal governments and these are being strengthened with full Administration support and endorsement. The President has even proposed that the administration and control of most BIA and HEW Indian programs be transferred to Indian tribal governments, at the latter's option, but the Congress has not yet approved this legislative proposal.

The President has proposed the creation of an Indian Trust Counsel Authority to represent Indian interests in the vital field of natural resources rights, but the Congress has not enacted this legislation.

The White House and every Department in this Administration meets frequently with Indian leaders and groups, listens to and pays attention to Indian recommendations and, as for example, in the development of the Alaska Native Claims legislation, works with Indian representatives on matters vitally affecting Indian people. We will continue to go forward with these many, close relationships.

The Reply

The Reply to Point One is totally inadequate and inaccurate on a number of points. The 1924 Indian Citizenship Act expressly preserves to Indian members of Indian tribes the right to tribal citizenship:

BE IT ENACTED BY THE SENATE AND HOUSE OF REPRESENTATIVES OF THE UNITED STATES OF AMERICA IN CONGRESS ASSEMBLED, That all non-citizen Indians born within the territorial limits of the United

States be, and they are hereby, declared to be citizens of the United States: PROVIDED, *That the granting of such citizenship shall not in any manner impair or otherwise affect the right of any Indian to tribal or other property.* Approved, June 2, 1924, 68th Congress, Session 1, Chapter 233.

The right to maintain tribal property in common is a citizenship right of a tribal member *(Choate v. Trapp),* and for the Task Force to maintain that a treaty relationship is incompatible with citizenship is legally incorrect since treaties are signed with Indian tribes, not Indian individuals. The point made by the Trail of Broken Treaties is that treaty-making should be restored to Indian tribes, not to extend it to Indian individuals.

While Congress may have decided that "it was no longer appropriate for the United States to make treaties with Indian tribes" in 1871, it apparently failed to inform the executive branch. From 1871 to 1906 the Executive Branch continued to make what are now known as "Agreements" (see Jerome Agreement, Curtis Agreement, etc.) with Indian tribes which have been interpreted by the court as "treaties" (see *Waldron v. United States).* Even after the formal agreement-making period Congress has generally made sure that there is some form of Indian consent to major changes in the Indian legal status. The Indian Reorganization Act, for example, requires that the members of each tribe accept its provisions and agree to organize according to the act before it can be applied to the tribe. The termination legislation made provision for either withdrawal or Indian consent and Congress recently made a point of informing the Menominees that they had agreed to termination (when they hadn't) as an argument for refusing to repeal their termination act. (See testimony and questioning on Senator Jackson's Policy Resolution July 1971.)

The fact that the President has proposed certain changes in regard to administration of BIA and HEW programs by tribal groups does not mean that the President has given more than lip service to the concepts. His proposal, for example, of an Indian Trust Counsel Authority, has been characterized by his unwillingness to support the program in Congress. It is regarded by the national American Indian community as a constructive proposal but also as a rhetorical concern of the administration, not a programatic concern.

Consultation with Indian groups was fairly good at the beginning of the present administration but it has since lapsed into a desperate game of favoritism, cronyism, and co-optation with the creation of a number of national Indian organizations which are little more than publicity arms of the federal government advocating either the President's or the Vice-President's views on Indian policy. Obviously such a development belies the serious phraseology of the response and appears ludicrous in retrospect.

POINT TWO—ESTABLISHMENT OF TREATY COMMISSION TO MAKE NEW TREATIES: The President should impanel and the Congress establish, within the next year, a Treaty Commission to contract a security and assistance treaty, or treaties, with Indian people to negotiate a national commitment to the future of Indian people for the last quarter of the Twentieth Century. Authority should be granted to allow Tribes to contract by separate and individual treaty, multitribal or religional groupings, or national collective, respecting general or limited subject matter—and provide that no provisions of existing treaty agreement may be withdrawn or in any manner affected without the explicit consent and agreement of any particularly related Indian nation.

The Response
The points stated in the first response apply to this proposal also.

The Reply
The United States does not hold its land title, in a legal sense, as against the Indian tribes of this continent. It holds its legal title against the European nations of the Christian world according to the Doctrine of Discovery. It has only the right, as against other western European nations, to extinguish Indian title. It therefore is in no legal position to forbid treaties with the Indian tribes at any time except insofar as its Congress forbids new treaties in a domestic sense. In an international sense if the United States is to dwell among the civilized nations of the world, and its present policy towards American Indians and Asians places it outside the family of civilized nations, the United States is legally and morally bound to revive the treaty-making process with the Indian tribes.

Chief Justice John Marshall, in his famous opinion in *Cherokee Nation v. Georgia,* did not say that Indian tribes were not nations with whom the United States could contract by treaty. He simply classified them as "dependent, domestic nations" in that they would be jealously considered by the United States should another nation attempt to deal with them by treaty. In this respect the Indian tribes of this country stand on the same footing with respect to the United States as does Monaco toward France, San Marino toward Italy, and Liechtenstein toward Switzerland and Austria. At least five Indian tribes in this nation are giants compared to the aforementioned nations with respect to population and land base. France signed a treaty with Monaco in 1918 to provide for sucession to the throne of the country. Liechtenstein contracted with the Swiss government in 1924 to become a member of the Swiss Customs Union, and Switzerland administers Liechtenstein's currency, telegraph and postal service, and its foreign affairs.

The United States purports to belong to the family of civilized nations, yet with respect to its treaty commitments to the tribes of American Indians it is notoriously suspect. No national or international rule of law has extinguished the sovereign nature of American Indian tribes and we ought not be deprived through accident of history of privileges of sovereignty simply because we are not small European nations. Justice Johnson, voting with the majority in *Cherokee Nation v. Georgia,* described the legal status of the American Indian tribes thus:

> Their condition is something like that of the Israelites when inhabiting the deserts. Though without land that they can call theirs in the sense of property, their right of personal self-government has never been taken from them; and such a form of government may exist though the land occupied be in fact that of another. The right to expel them may exist in that other, but the alternative of departing and retaining the right of self-government may exist in them. And such they certainly do possess; it has never been questioned, nor any attempt made at subjugating them as a people, or restraining their personal liberty except as to their land and trade.

The United States, in its answer to the British in the Cayuga arbitration case concerning the War of 1812, alleged that it made no effort to restrict or interfere with the rights and self-government of domestic Indian tribes. If the United States is telling other nations of the world that it is doing one thing and in fact doing another thing, it must correct this inconsistency before the family of civilized nations. To continue to deny the possibility of making new treaties with American Indian tribes is maintain to the world in fact that the United States is not as civilized as Italy, France, Switzerland and Austria, and that it cannot protect a small nation without in fact exploiting it also.

POINT THREE—AN ADDRESS TO THE AMERICAN PEOPLE AND JOINT SESSION OF CONGRESS. The President and the leadership of Congress should make commitment now and next January to request and arrange for four Native Americans—selected by Indian people at a future date—the President of the United States and any designated U.S. Senators and U.S. Representatives to address a Joint Session of Congress and the American people through national communications media, regarding the Indian future within the American Nation, and relationships between the Federal Government and Indian Nations—on or before June 2, 1974, the half-century anniversary of the 1924 "Indian Citizenship Act."

The Response

The Congress has been addressed—two and one-half years ago—when the President sent the Congress a Special Message on July 8, 1970 dealing exclusively with American Indian matters. Indian advice about those program proposals was sought and obtained at that time in a series of meetings held throughout Indian country. With two exceptions, none of the President's legislative proposals made in that Message have been enacted by the Congress; some have not even been given hearings.

What is needed is not more addresses and messages; the President will again submit in 1973 legislative proposals to implement his progressive policy for Indians. What is needed is congressional action.

It would be up to the Congress to determine whether it would like to invite four Indians to address a Joint Session. As important, or more so, will be the appearance of Indian representatives at congressional committee sessions which hopefully will be called soon to take up the bills the President has proposed. Administration witnesses will be on hand and fully ready to explain the President's program.

At the present time, the Administration, as well as congressional committees, is again open to any specific Indian suggestions as to how our proposals could be improved or strengthened.

The Reply
   The President need only officially inform the Congress of the United States in his State of the Nation address that he has received a proposal from the American Indian tribes and peoples of the nation that they would like to jointly address the Congress with him concerning the future of American Indians. Such an action would speak much louder than additional words.

POINT FOUR—COMMISSION TO REVIEW TREATY COMMITMENTS AND VIOLATIONS: The President should immediately create a multi-lateral, Indian and non-Indian, Commission to review domestic treaty commitments and complaints of chronic violations and to recommend or act for corrective actions, including the imposition of mandatory sanctions or interim restraints upon violative activities, and including formulation of legislation designed to protect the jeopardized Indian rights and eliminate the unending patterns of prohibitively expensive lawsuits and legal defenses—which habitually have produced indecisive and indeterminate results, only too frequently forming guidelines for more court battles, or additional challenges and attacks against Indian rights. (Indians have paid attorneys and lawyers more than $40,000,000 since 1962. Yet many Indian people are virtually imprisoned in the nation's courtrooms in being forced constantly to defend their rights, and while many Tribes are forced to maintain a multitude of suits in numerous jurisdictions relating to the same or a single issue, or a few similar issues. There is less need for more attorneys' assistances than there is for institution of protections that reduce violations and minimize the possibilities for attacks upon Indian rights.)

The Response
   We already have a Commission: the Indian Claims Commission, a quasi-judicial agency created by the Congress in 1946. Its mandate is to settle finally any and all legal, equitable and moral obligations the United States might owe to the Indians, including the loss of aboriginal lands or inadequate payment for them through awards, and has certified $424 million for appropriation as award payments. There are about 250 dockets still pending

before the Commission, and in the last Congress the Commission's life was extended another five years.

It is asked that a new Commission formulate legislation to protect jeopardized Indian rights. This legislation has already been formulated and the President proposed it to the Congress two and one-half years ago; the creation of an Indian Trust Counsel Authority. The Authority would be a quasi-independent part of the Executive Branch of the United States Government, would be governed by a three-man Board of Directors, two of whom would be Indians, would have the right to bring suit against the United States or otherwise to intervene in any State or Federal regulatory proceeding to protect Indian natural resources rights, speaking for the United States as trustee for those rights. The Congress has not enacted this legislation; it will be resubmitted to the new Congress and this Administration will again defend and support it, and we are confident we will again have the endorsement and assistance of Indian witnesses also.

Pending the enactment of the Trust Counsel Authority, this Administration has actively defended Indian treaty and trust rights. We have persuaded Congress to restore the Blue Lake lands to the Taos Pueblo; the President has acted to restore to the Yakima Nation the 21,000 acres of land mistakenly alienated from their control 66 years ago; the Administration has filed a number of suits to protect Indian water rights including a suit in the Supreme Court to protect the rights of Indians in Pyramid Lake; the Administration has initiated a procedure whereby, on the request of the Secretary of the Interior, briefs stating the United States' position as trustee of Indian land and water rights will be filed in any Court cases in which the Department of Justice takes a position contrary to those trust interests, so that no Court is ever unaware of the trustee position of the United States concerning these rights.

Briefs supporting Indian trust rights have been filed in the *McClanahan, Kahn, Mescalero,* and *Tonasket* Supreme Court tax cases, the *Stevens* tax case was won in the Ninth Circuit on the strength of the Interior Department's brief as trustee for the Indian defendant.

The Secretary of the Interior has established a special Water Rights Office in the Department of the Interior to give special attention to any Indian water rights problems and allegations of invasion of rights. This Office is headed by an Indian Lawyer.

With respect to the stated wish to "eliminate the unending patterns" of lawsuits and legal defenses, this desire is rather theoretical, since public life today is full of controversy; what we are trying to guarantee is effective defense, in those controversies, of Indian trust rights by the United States which is itself the trustee of those rights.

The Departments of the Interior and Justice are and will continue to be alert to any specific allegations of violations of Indian trust rights, and will continue to work with Indian leaders and their representatives to ensure effective defense of Indian trust interests.

The Reply

The characterization of the Indian Claims Commission as the commission to review treaty commitments and violations borders on fantasy and indicates an ignorance of the commission and its work short of inbecilic. The Indian Claims Commission litigates the old violations of values received for lands ceded and accounting claims involving misuse of tribal funds by the United States as trustee. It does NOT litigate equitable and moral claims of Indian tribes; it does not allow land claims for much of the east coast; it does not handle depredations committed by the United States in violation of Indian treaties. It frequently violates all principles of fair play as in the California Indians case and the Pit River Indians.

To portray the Indian Claims Commission as more than an old realty arbitration board is absurd. Presently the Fort Sill Apaches, made prisoners of war illegally by the United States from 1886 to 1906, were thrown out of the Indian Claims Commission because their case against the United States for suffering did not involve the cession of land. The case is presently on appeal to the Court of Claims. Their claim is at least equitable, perhaps the best moral claim of any Indian tribe against the United States. It was rejected by the Indian Claims Commission.

The state of Washington continually and ruthlessly violates six treaties with the tribes of that state concerning the right to fish at usual and accustomed places. The United States is casually and haphazardly engaged in a law suit that has taken over three years already and is nowhere near solution. The western states are continually violating Indian tax and water rights and it is only at the Supreme Court level that the United States becomes involved, not at the trial court level.

Part of the reason for the Trail of Broken Treaties was the series of wanton murders of American Indians in Nebraska, Pennsylvania, Arizona, and California. Almost without exception treaties assure tribal members that the United States will protect them from depredations committed by its citizens, part of the Code of Federal Regulations makes it a duty of the United States Justice Department to protect the rights of Indians. This duty is rarely if ever exercised and practically never in the case of murders of American Indians. Papers taken during the occupation indicate the extent to which the murders of Indian women in Wisconsin were punished by the United States in the exercise of its trusteeship.

The new Indian Water Rights Office is continually overruled by its superiors in the Interior Department. In a water rights case involving the Salt River of Arizona last year, the Indian Water Rights Office developed the facts to show that approval of a compromise agreement on water rights on the river would be detrimental to the protection of Indian water rights. Authorities in the Interior Department overruled the Indian Water Rights Office and made them send a telegram to the Phoenix Area Office approving and recommending for approval the water compact. Even in this relatively enlightened administration the treatment of Indian water rights borders on deceit and fraud as indicated by the position taken in the *Eagle River* case with respect to Indian water rights.

As pointed out above, while the President has proposed the Indian Trust Counsel Authority he has done little or nothing to see that the legislation is written into law. The American Indian community has seen little assurance that the Indian Trust Counsel Authority will not become another NCIO in its petty political stance toward the majority of Indian people.

With regard to the restoration of lands illegally taken from Indian tribes, fairness demands that the present administration be given the highest marks in this subject. It has without a doubt been the most responsive administration, with the exception of the first term of Franklin Roosevelt, of any administration in American history. If this administration was as concerned and efficient in other fields as it has been in this particular field it would certainly stand out as the best period in American Indian history.

Controversy does exist in modern life and American Indians do not shirk from social problems. However, the tribes of the Pacific Northwest have been forced to litigate the treaty phrase "usual and accustomed places" for 118 years—ever since the treaties were signed. It is this endless pattern of litigation that must be resolved. Indian tribes have been continually forced to litigate their tax immunities ever since the *Kansas Indians* case in the 1850s. Three Indian tax cases are presently in the Supreme Court; none of them were brought by the Department of Justice on behalf of the Indian tribes. It is this pattern of endless litigation that must be stopped.

A new commission must be formed to prevent the continual state encroachment on Indian treaty rights such as is presently occurring in Washington, Oregon, Idaho, Montana, North and South Dakota, Minnesota, Arizona, Wisconsin, Michigan, New York, and Oklahoma. Treaty rights are legal rights. The passage of years does not void them. Treaty rights are presently being violated by both the United States government and the several states. A new commission must be formed to prevent this according to the nearly uniform promise of the treaties that the United States will not itself commit depredations against members of Indian tribes nor will it allow the several states or their citizens to commit such depredations.

POINT FIVE—RESUBMISSION OF UNRATIFIED TREATIES TO THE SENATE: The President should resubmit to the U.S. Senate of the next Congress those treaties negotiated with Indian Nations or their representatives, but never heretofore ratified nor rendered moot by subsequent treaty contract with such Indians not having ratified treaties with the United States. The primary purpose to be served shall be that of restoring the rule of law to the relationships between such Indians and the United States, and resuming a recognition of rights controlled by treaty regulations. Where the failure to ratify prior treaties operated to affirm the cessions and loss of title to Indian lands and territory, but failed to secure and protect the reservations of lands, rights, and resources reserved against cession, relinquishment or loss, the Senate should adopt resolutions certifying that a prior *de facto* ratification has been effected by the Government of the United States and direct that appropriate actions be undertaken to restore to such Indians an equitable measure of their reserved rights and

ownership in lands, resources and rights of self-government. Additionally, the President and Congress should direct that reports be concluded upon the disposition of land rights and title which were to be protected, when such rights and land title were lawfully vested or held, for people of Native Indian Blood under the 1848 Treaty of Guadalupe Hidalgo with Mexico.

The Response

As was explained under Point 1, we are now a Union and we have a citizenship rather than a treaty relationship with the people who make up that Union, American Indians included.

The injustices and inequities which were in fact suffered by Indian tribes and peoples because of either unfair or unratified treaties are being dealt with as the Congress has provided in the Indian Claims Commission. This is particularly true in the case of many California Indians, the treaties with whom were negotiated but not ratified, and whose claims have been decided by the Indian Claims Commission and confirmed by the Congress, with award payments even now being disbursed totaling $29,100,000.

The Claims Commission will continue to be diligent and fair as it moves through the remainder of the 250 dockets still pending.

The Reply

Again the response neglects the whole area of treaty rights in favor of individual citizenship. The fact is that the Indian Claims Commission often refuses to recognize the rights of Indian tribes which appear in unratified treaties. In the case of the California Indian treaties which remained unratified, they were kept in a secret file in the United States Senate for nearly three quarters of a century by undetermined but admittedly powerful influences in order that the land titles recognized in them not be given official recognition. It did not prevent the United States from taking the lands of the California Indians, however.

The supposedly favorable decision returned by the Indian Claims Commission in the California Indians case was marked with a great many irregularities in that some tribal groups did not want to join the litigation but wanted to pursue their own claims for aboriginal homelands and were prevented from doing so by the artificial creation of the legal fiction known as the "California Indians." The intervention by the Bureau of Indians Affairs in the voting of the California Indians on whether or not to accept the settlement was so blatant and crude as to call for separate investigation.

On the whole this answer is no more satisfactory than are the other answers involving treaty rights. The administration appears determined to overlook the development of four centuries of legal doctrines involving Indian treaty rights and the legal status of Indian tribes as political communities.

POINT SIX— ALL INDIANS TO BE GOVERNED BY TREATY RELATIONS: The Congress should enact a Joint Resolution declaring that, as a matter of public policy and good faith, all Indian people in the United States shall be considered to be in treaty relations with the Federal Government and governed by the doctrines of such relationship.

The Response

The Treaties that were concluded and ratified with Indian tribes are still in force and will be respected by the United States. But as explained in Points One and Five, we are a Union and, since 1871, no longer negotiate new treaties with our citizens as if they were foreign entities.

American Indian people have many needs and concerns; these needs and concerns are being addressed and must be addressed further by both the Executive and Legislative branches of our government. We, in this administration, want Indian people to continue to work with us in formulating and carrying out specific proposals and actions to meet the pressing economic, legal, educational, health, and housing problems of Indian people.

To call for new treaties is to raise a false issue, unconstitutional in concept, misleading to Indian people, and diversionary from the real problems that do need our combined energies.

The Reply

This response obviously overlooks the fact that Point Four asked for a commission to determine violations of treaty rights and the response to that point was that the administration was doing everything possible and that the Indian Claims Commission was litigating treaty violations. If the administration sees that the existing treaties should be respected, then quite obviously a substantial number of Indian people should be already living under treaty relationships—except that the government is not now recognizing or enforcing the provisions of the treaties.

To indicate the depth of ignorance of the authors of the administration response with respect to the nature of treaties, the United States never, at any point, made treaties with its own individual citizens—or with individual Indians. Treaties were made with tribal governments and the whole intent of the points in the Twenty Points relating to treaties is that they be once again used as the formal instrument for negotiations between an Indian tribe and the United States government. Far from being unconstitutional, this demand is well within the provisions of the Interstate Commerce Clause. The real question posed by Point Six is whether or not the 1871 act prohibiting further treaties with the Indian tribes is constitutional since no other means of dealing with Indian tribes is given in the Constitution of the United States.

POINT SEVEN—MANDATORY RELIEF AGAINST TREATY RIGHTS VIOLATIONS: The Congress should add a new section to Title 28 of the United States Code to provide for the judicial enforcement and protection of Indian Treaty Rights. Such section should direct that, upon petition of an Indian tribe or prescribed Indian groups and individuals claiming substantial injury to, or interference in the equitable and good faith exercise of any rights, governing authority, or utilization and preservation of resources, secured by Treaty, mandatorily the Federal District Courts shall grant immediate enjoinder or injunctive relief against any non-Indian party or defendants, including state governments and their subdivisions or officers, alleged to be engaged in such injurious or interfering actions, until such time as the U.S. District Court may reasonably be satisfied that a Treaty violation is not being committed, or otherwise satisfied that the Indians' interests and rights, in equity and in law, are preserved and protected from jeopardy and secure from harm.

The Response

This demand apparently is based upon a misunderstanding of the judicial process. It is proposed that mandatory injunctions be granted upon the mere filing of an Indian complaint that a treaty right is being violated and that such injunctions continue until the court is satisfied a violation is not being committed. It is not clear what is meant by a "mandatory" injunction, although there is a clear implication that concepts of due process should not apply to litigation to enforce treaty rights.

As near as can be determined from the demand, much of what is desired is attainable through existing judicial process, by use of temporary restraining orders (and subsequent injunctive relief) whenever a citizen can show that he will suffer irreparable harm. The courts now give priority to requests for temporary restraining orders and injunctions. It seems highly unlikely that the Congress would pass such legislation, and it is questionable as to the authority to do so under the constitution.

The Reply

The administration response makes it appear as if very difficult questions are involved when asking the federal courts to determine if a treaty rights violation has occurred. Even a preliminary glance at the almost countless series on fishing rights, water rights, taxation, trespass, and mismanagement of natural resources would indicate that in a very short time a document could be drawn up outlining for courts and laymen concerned the potential treaty violations possible, the fact situations under which they can be said to have occurred, and the remedies that can be immediately available. To call for an action of mandamus in which the court can command the state, county, city or private citizen from violating treaty rights does not seem to be an unreasonable request.

Treaty rights are special legal rights guaranteed to a specific group of people by action of the United States government. To classify them along with ordinary civil rights violations and to impose the usual civil rights procedural requirements upon them is to negate them. Violation of the treaty should be legally the presumption of damage as an incident is the presumption of damage in international law calling for some type of arbitration. Too often temporary restraining orders have been dropped because of the willingness of the Bureau of Indian Affairs to promise the federal courts to handle the problem administratively. Nothing then happens to remedy the treaty violation except that bureaucratic bungling replaces some more efficient form of legal relief.

It is indeed ironic for an administration that unconstitutionally arrested thousands of demonstrators in the nation's capitol a couple of years ago to speak of due process. In a land in which airline passengers are presumed to be hijackers and must prove their innocence, in which the news media is constantly harrassed until they take a pro-administration stance, in which the no-knock law is the major tool of harrassment of young people and in which the concept of "preventive detention" is a favorite, the concern of the administration that due process and constitutional protections should be carefully followed when dealing with Indian treaty rights violations can not be taken seriously; the rhetoric is at best hollow, at worst a sardonic form of humor.

POINT EIGHT—JUDICIAL RECOGNITION OF INDIAN RIGHT TO INTERPRET TREATIES: The Congress should by law provide for a new system of federal court jurisdiction and procedure, when Indian treaty or governmental rights are at issue, and when there are non-Indian parties involved in the controversy, whereby an Indian Tribe or Indian party may by motion advance the case from a federal District Court for hearing and decision by the related U.S. Circuit Court of Appeals. The law should provide that, once an interpretation upon the matter has been rendered by either a federal district or circuit court, an Indian nation may, on its own behalf or on behalf of any of its members, if dissatisfied with the federal court ruling or regarding it in error respecting treaty or tribal rights, certify directly to the United States Supreme Court a "Declaratory Judgment of Interpretation", regarding the contested rights and drawn at the direction or under the auspices of the affected Indian Nation, which that Court shall be mandated to receive with the contested decision for hearing and final judgment and resolution of the controversy—except and unless any new treaties which might be contracted may provide for some other impartial body for making ultimate and final interpretations of treaty provisions and their application. In addition, the law should provide that an Indian Nation, to protect its exercise of rights or the exercise of treaty or tribal rights by its members, or when engaging in new activities based upon sovereign or treaty rights, may issue an interim "Declaratory Opinion on Interpretation of Rights" which shall be controlling upon the exercise of police powers of administrative authorities of that Indian Nation, the United States or any State(s) unless or until successfully challenged or modified upon certification to and decision by the United States Supreme Court—and notwithstanding any contrary U.S. Attorney General's Opinion(s), Solicitor's Opinion(s), or Attorney General's Opinion(s) for any of the States.

The Response

This proposal would require the fundamental revision of our judicial processes in order to give Indian groups highly preferential positions in controversies about their treaty rights. To the extent the revision would impinge on the judicial review powers of the courts, it would present constitutional problems. Granting a right of appeal to the Supreme Court in Indian cases would necessitate amendment of 28 U.S.C. 1254 and 1257.

At present, all Indian tribes have the right to take a position in any case or controversy on the meaning of their own treaties and to advocate their interpretation through the courts, as any State, locality, citizen, or group of citizens can press for favorable judicial interpretation of their rights. Due process and equal access, however, must be accorded to all citizens involved.

We would reemphasize here the matters stressed in Point 4: this Administration, more than any other in American history, has been alert to defend Indian natural resources rights and to urge both the Legislative and Judicial branches to do the same. What is needed from now on is not the skewing of America's judicial principles or the creation of any new built-in preferences for or against specific groups or institutions. What is needed is a continuing alterness by the Executive Branch, which we pledge, and in addition perhaps a better system by which Indian leaders can bring alleged trust violations more promptly to the Government's attention.

The Reply

Even a basic knowledge of cases involving Indian treaty rights will indicate that problems of interpretation of treaty phraseology are litigated perpetually and with deadening repetition. The phrase "usual and accustomed places" in regard to fishing rights, for example, has been the source of continual controversy in the state courts of this land. In Supreme Court cases too numerous to mention (examples are *Winans, Tulee, Seufert Bros.*) the treaty has been interpreted in favor of Indian readings of the phraseology. In the field of taxation from *Kansas Indians* to *Capoeman*, the Indian version has prevailed, in cases involving tribal sovereignty the Indian version has prevailed, and yet a glance at the current active cases will indicate that the same issues are being litigated once again by zealous state governments hoping that the placement of Nixon appointees on the Supreme Court will result in the overturning of established Indian law.

The administration makes it clear that it wants to continue the present situation in which the Indians always bear the burden of proof as to their interpretation of the treaty phraseology. In the appeals from the federal district courts in Washington State alone enactment of this proposal could save both the federal government and the Indian tribes thousands of dollars as the court almost always rules against the Indians at the district level and is almost always overturned at the circuit level. Why continue this harrassment and wasteful expenditure of funds?

If the Indian tribe were able to certify the issue of treaty interpretation immediately, state governments would cease their harrassment of Indians since the law clearly favors the Indians. In almost every case involving interpretation of treaty rights the doctrine is promulgated that treaty interpretation must be "liberally construed" in favor of a defenseless people. (See *Jones v. Meehan, U.S. v. Winans, U.S. v. Cutler, U.S. v. Brookfield Fisheries, Choate v. Trapp, U.S. v. Kagama* and dozens of other important cases.)

The administration response states that 28 U.S.C. 1254 and 1257 would have to be amended. Amendments are being made to laws in every Congress that sits. What the administration apparently wants to keep is the unilateral right of the United States government to interpret the treaties since it apparently supports the theory that Indians would be biased in their interpretation of the treaties. Yet the United States already has an unfair advantage—it drew up the treaties and in drawing up the treaties it could have put into them almost everything it wanted. Now it wants to continue its unfair advantage of interpreting its own words to its own advantage. No concept of Anglo-Saxon, Roman, or Germanic law allows one party the privilege of exclusive interpretation of a document which both parties have agreed on in mutual bargaining.

The purpose of this proposal is to eliminate frivolous suits of harrassment by state governments, fish and game departments, and county governments who have even less knowledge of Indian treaties than the administration and who continually have a vested interest in destroying legally vested treaty property rights by use of overwhelming force and unfair interpretation of treaty documents.

POINT NINE—CREATION OF CONGRESSIONAL JOINT COMMITTEE ON RECONSTRUCTION OF INDIAN RELATIONS: The next Congress of the United States and its respective houses should agree at its outset and in its organization to withdraw jurisdiction over Indian Affairs and Indian-related program authorizations from all existing Committees, except Appropriations, of the House and Senate, and create a Joint House-Senate "Committee on Reconstruction of Indian Relations and Programs" to assume such jurisdiction and responsibilities for recommending new legislation and program authorizations to both houses of Congress—including consideration and action upon all proposals presented herewith by the "Trail of Broken Treaties Caravan," as well as matters originating from other sources. The Joint Committee membership should consist of Senators and Representatives who would be willing to commit considerable amounts of time and labors and conscientious thought to an exhaustive review and examining evaluation of past and present policies, programs and practices of the Federal Government relating to Indian people; to the development of a comprehensive, broadly-inclusive "American Indian Community Reconstruction Act," which shall provide for certain of the measures herein proposed, repeal numerous laws which have oppressively disallowed the existence of a viable "Indian life" in this country, and effect the purposes while constructing the provisions which shall allow and ensure a secure Indian future in America.

The Response
This proposal, to create a new joint congressional committee, should be addressed to the Congress, and would not be appropriate for Executive Branch comment.

The Reply
True.

POINT TEN—LAND REFORM AND RESTORATION OF AN 110 MILLION ACRE NATIVE LAND BASE: The next Congress and Administration should commit themselves and effect a national commitment, implement by statutes or executive and administrative actions, to restore a permanent non-diminishing Native American land base of not less than 110 million acres by July 4, 1976. This land base, and its separate parts, should be

vested with the recognized rights and conditions of being perpetually non-taxable, except by autonomous and sovereign Indian
authorities, and should never again be permitted to be alienated
from Native American or Indian ownership and control.

The Response

The Federal Government now holds in trust about 40 million
acres of tribal land owned in common, plus approximately 10
million acres of land held in trust for individual tribal members. In
addition, the title to 40 million acres has been confirmed by the
Congress as belonging to Alaska Natives. In accordance with their
wishes, it will not be held in trust but will be under their full
control and inalienable for twenty years.

Assuming that the above land is included in the suggested 110
million acres land base, this proposal calls for giving to Indians an
additional 20 million acres of land. But what is omitted is the fact
that claims concerning some of this additional land (it is difficult to
know how much since the 110 million acres are not identified) are
undoubtedly involved in the 250 cases now pending before the
Indian Claims Commission.

The proposal that this 110 million acres be perpetually non-
taxable and inalienable would be in part repetitive of existing
rights, would deprive Indians of their right to deal with their lands
for the benefit of all their people, and is a legal impossibility as one
Congress cannot bind future Congresses amending or repealing
such a law. With the consent of the Secretary of the Interior as
trustee, individual Indians may exchange or sell their land when it
is to their advantage to do so for a worthy purpose. These land
owners might not want this right eliminated. Alienation of tribal
land requires an Act of Congress. Some tribes for special reasons
have obtained this right with the approval of the Secretary of
Interior and would probably be opposed to its being withdrawn
from them.

The Reply

It is indeed surprising that this administration should refuse to
consider this proposal since it has an excellent record with respect
to the preservation of the tribal land base. In the answer to another
Point the respondents mention the record in the past of restoring
Blue Lake, Mount Adams, and other pieces of land.

A telephone call to the Bureau of Indian Affairs would indicate that with tribal lands, Alaskan lands, and individual allotments the present Indian land base is nearly 95 million acres. A process of selective land restoration to tribal groups and the placing of Indian lands beyond the reach of hungry land speculators and future Congresses should not be so difficult. Purchase of fee lands within or adjoining existing reservations, purchase of allotments, restoration of submarginal lands and surplus lands could easily make up the remaining 15 million acres.

As to the legal impossibility of future Congresses amending or repealing the new land policy, it is more likely that such a policy is a moral impossibility both for future administrations and future congresses. The question is whether the concept is a moral impossibility for the present administration and the present congress.

POINT TEN A—PRIORITIES IN RESTORATION OF THE NATIVE AMERICAN LAND BASE: (Lists a formula for arriving at the figure and recommends landless groups, urban Indians, and non-reservation peoples.)

The Response

The proposal is that the following priorities be followed in connection with the requested 20 million acres of land:

1. The Indian Nations landless because of unratified treaties or unfulfilled treaty provisions.
2. Indian Nations landless because of abuse of trust responsibilities.
3. Urban Indians and non-reservation Indians in some groupings who are landless.

There would be considerable differences of opinion on the proposed priorities. The Federally-recognized tribes with reservations are also interested in obtaining additional land.

In the light of the many individual, piecemeal proposals for the creation of additional parcels of trust land for specific Indian groups, a study of trust land status and eligibility policy has been begun in the Department of the Interior. The study has been delayed by the disruption of the building and records of the Bureau of Indian Affairs during the occupation by the Trail of Broken Treaties two months ago, but it is now resuming.

As the Washington Conference of Eastern Indian peoples recently made clear, the process of identifying these options and costs is going to require a great deal of research: which Indian groups not now federally recognized live on what land now; what is the status of that land, what services are available and not available to them from what source, etc.

In the end it is the Congress that must set the policy and provide the additional resources, if any. We shall be working with Indian leaders in giving these questions the thorough and detailed attention they deserve. We solicit the cooperation of Indian people, especially those not now federally recognized, in helping us with the rigorous economic and financial research which will be a prerequisite of any conclusions or recommendations.

The Reply

While there would indeed be considerable differences of opinion on which lands should be restored, the present administration had no problems in choosing Blue Lake, Mount Adams, and the Warm Springs for restoration. The choice is not that difficult.

The alleged "study" of trust land status and eligibility policy will be a very unique study. Its conclusion is already contained in the famous letter from Brad Patterson to William Rogers in which it is said that no further groups can be recognized because that would mean giving preference to a particular ethnic group. With this attitude firmly in mind the study is merely a frantic effort to find justification for the view and to produce a thick report filled with rhetoric and obscure footnotes.

The alleged exhaustive costs of recognizing additional groups and giving them rights are minimal if reforms are made in the existing administrative structure of the Bureau of Indian Affairs. The research is not necessary if one follows the dictates of the U.S. Supreme Court which notes in *United States v. Sandoval:*

> The power and duty of the United States under the Constitution to regulate commerce with the Indian tribes includes the duty to care for and protect all dependent Indian communities within its borders, whether within the original limits or territory subsequently acquired and whether within or without the limits of a state.

POINT TEN B—CONSOLIDATION OF INDIANS' LAND, WATER, NATURAL AND ECONOMIC RESOURCES.

The Response

Land owned in common by a number of heirs has long been a difficult unresolved problem. The separate essay promised to the Government on this subject will be given careful study.

The Reply

(Apparently a separate essay on land consolidation will be forthcoming.)

POINT TEN C—TERMINATION OF LEASES & CONDEMNATION OF NON-INDIAN LAND TITLE. (Calls for selective and rapid phasing out of leases on Indian lands and condemnation of non-Indian lands within the reservation boundaries and restoration to tribes.)

The Response

Indian land owners, as individuals or tribes, decide themselves how they want to use their land or whether to lease it to others to obtain income. The Indian owners have to approve any lease. They and the trustee jointly determine the particular way in which the land is to be used. The Indian land owners are being encouraged to use their land themselves whenever they can and whenever it is to their advantage to do so. In many instances, it is impractical for the elderly, a child or woman, or those who are not interested in working on the land to do so. In other instances, because of the size or location of the land or the capital required, a greater return is obtained by lease than self-operation.

The Trail of Broken Treaties representatives are free to recommend to their Indian colleagues who are land owners that there should be a large-scale program of lease cancellations and non-renewals. However, some questions need to be faced. Who would pay the lessees who would certainly seek damages for cancellation of leases without cause?

It is also proposed here that tribes be given the authority by Congress to condemn any land owned by non-Indians within reservation boundaries, the cost to be borne by the Federal Government. No mention is made of repaying any monies already received for the lands. Such condemnation would involve a large amount of land and money, particularly for the checkerboarded reservations of the plains states. It is doubtful that the Federal Government could or should delegate its powers of eminent domain to non-Federal entities, even if this amount of money were available under present stringent budget strictures.

Enactment of the President's credit legislation would give Indians a further basis for obtaining land necessary for economic development; we look forward to early Congressional hearings on this legislation.

The study referred to under point 10 A will also pertain to the recommendation made here concerning the resecuring of alienated lands within reservation boundaries.

The Reply

In general the Administration response is surprisingly mild. A question arises as to the relative freedom of both tribes and individuals to lease their lands and the degree to which the Bureau of Indian Affairs and other government agencies fulfill their trust responsibility of Indian lands in the area of leasing. The recent lease at Papago, signed under this administration, the leasing of Cochiti Pueblo, Black Mesa, and the Tesque Pueblo lands under the previous administration, and the current leasing and selling practices of the timber management in the Pacific Northwest all call into question the rather optimistic description given by the administration as to the relative ease with which land problems are presently approached.

POINT TEN D—REPEAL OF THE MENOMINEE, KLA-MATH & OTHER TERMINATION ACTS.

The Response

The Administration has expressed very firmly its strong opposition to any forced termination of the special relationship between the United States of America and Indian tribes involving the trusteeship of tribal land and the providing of special services. The President has specifically asked the Congress to rescind the outdated Termination Resolution of 1953, but the Congress has not yet taken the action the President recommended. Some years ago, Congress did terminate certain tribes based on its conclusion that they were prepared and able to manage their own affairs. Whether the Federal Government should now attempt to unscramble all of the situations that have since intervened and somehow restore the land that was conveyed in fee to the tribes and individuals and the numerous other matters that would be involved will have to be considered at greater length and, in fact, is part of the study referred to under section 10 A.

With respect to the Menominees specifically, we repeat the pledge made by our convention in the Republican Platform:

> We are fully aware of the severe problems facing the Menominee Indians in seeking to have federal recognition restored to their tribe, and promise a complete and sympathetic examination of their pleas.

The Reply

This response is vague but will be understood by the American Indian community as a pledge to assist in repealing the Menominee Termination Act to the same extent to which the administration gave assistance in restoring Blue Lake, Mount Adams, and other land problems which were difficult to "unscramble."

POINT ELEVEN—REVISION OF 25 U.S.C.: RESTORATION OF RIGHTS OF INDIANS TERMINATED BY ENROLLMENT AND REVOCATION OF PROHIBITIONS AGAINST 'DUAL BENEFITS.' (Concerns enrollment in more than one tribe.)

The Response

This proposal urges Congressional recognition of complete and unfettered authority of a tribe to determine its own membership for all purposes, including membership in more than one tribe resulting in dual federal and tribal benefits. Only in a very few special situations has the Congress enacted legislation affecting the requirements for tribal membership. On occasions when bills have been introduced in Congress that would define tribal membership, the Department has generally opposed enactment as an invasion of tribal rights to self-determination.

It has long been the policy and practice, supported by the courts, to permit tribes by the adoption of their own constitutional provisions or special membership ordinances to determine the qualificiations for membership in their tribes. Often a tribe will require that a member may not be enrolled in another tribe. While the Department of the Interior does not have a prohibition against dual membership in tribes, it does not permit individuals to receive distribution of tribal assets held in trust, usually in the form of a per capita payment, from more than one tribe. The Trail of Broken Treaties' authors recognize that their recommendation is contrary to the position taken by the members of tribes in their referendums adopting constitutions setting forth their membership requirements. The TBT argument is really with the tribes who prescribe their membership provisions pursuant to constitutions and by-laws that have been adopted.

The Reply

How did it become the Department of the Interior policy not to allow an individual to receive per capitas from those tribes in which he has either membership or descent? The recent controversy concerning the Osage judgment distribution should indicate that this is a more serious federal problem than it is a tribal problem. Granted that some of Point Eleven is in conflict with the regulations of some tribes, the matter should be exclusively tribal in all respects without any Interior interference or policy on the matter.

POINT TWELVE—REPEAL OF STATE LAWS ENACTED UNDER PUBLIC LAW 280 (1953): State enactments under the authority conferred by the Congress in Public Law 280 has posed the most serious threat to Indian sovereignty and local self-government of any measure in recent decades. Congress must now nullify those state statutes. Represented as a "law enforcement" measure, PL 280 robs Indian communities of the core of their governing authority and operates to convert Reservation areas into refuges from responsibilities, where many people, not restricted by race, can take full advantage of a veritable vacuum of controlling law, or law which commands its first respect for justice by encouraging an absence of offenses. These states' acceptance of condition for their own statehood in their Enabling Acts—that they forever disclaim sovereignty and jurisdiction over Indian lands and Indian people—should be binding upon them and that restrictive condition upon their sovereignty be reinstated. They should not be permitted further to gain from the conflict of interest engaged by such States' participation in enactment of Public Law 280—at the expense of the future of Indian people in our communities, as well as our present welfare and well-being.

The Response

Public Law 280 permits a State to acquire civil and criminal jurisdictions in Indian areas but only with the consent of the involved tribe. A State's assumption of jurisdiction under P.L. 280 is voluntary and whether a State repeals the law involved (or any other State law) is also with the discretion of the State. There is a provision in the Indian Civil Rights Act of 1968 which permits States which have acquired jurisdiction under PL 280 to retrocede their jurisdiction back to the U.S. They are not required to do so at the request of the tribe.

It is not true that P.L. 280 deprived any Indian tribe of any of its civil or criminal jurisdiction over its members. The jurisdiction of the Federal Government over "major crimes" and under the Assimilated Crimes Act was divided and transferred to the States, but nothing in the Act strips the tribe of its powers.

The Congress possesses the power to provide for the reassuming of Federal jurisdiction in Indian country where the States have acquired it under P.L. 280. The Congress, no doubt, would want to have the views of the tribes which had consented to State jurisdiction before taking the action recommended under this proposal.

The Reply

The problem is that few states have made clear whether or not they have in fact taken jurisdiction under P.L. 280. The state of Washington, for example, is attempting to tax cigarette sales made on those reservations where they *did not* assume jurisdiction. Arizona is attempting to levy and collect an income tax over the Navajo Reservation residents even though it did not follow the procedures set up in P.L. 280 for assuming jurisdiction. Since the states are acting almost at whim with respect to the specific authority they have in civil and criminal matters on Indian reservations, the most obvious and simple solution is for the federal government to withdraw all authority of any kind from state governments and make provisions for each state and tribe to specifically negotiate for any assumption of jurisdiction over persons and subject matter upon which they can agree.

While the proper place for this legislative solution may be

Congress, the administration can introduce such legislation and give it support.

POINT THIRTEEN—RESUME FEDERAL PROTECTIVE JURISDICTION FOR OFFENSES AGAINST INDIANS: The Congress should enact and the Administration support and seek passage of new provisions under Titles 18 and 25 of the U.S. Code, which shall extend the protective jurisdiction of the United States over Indian persons wherever situated in its territory and the territory of the several states, outside of Indian Reservations or Country, and provide that prescribed offenses of violence against Indian persons shall be federal crimes, punishable by prescribed penalties through prosecutions in the federal judiciary, and enforced in arrest actions by the Federal Bureau of Investigation, U.S. Marshalls, and other commissioned police agents of the United States—who shall be compelled to act upon the commission of such crimes, and upon any written complaint or sworn request alleging an offense, which by itself would be deemed probable cause for arresting actions.

The Response

We have difficulty with the constitutionality of the concept that Congress can, by statute, require the judiciary to issue warrants for arrest on the basis of a "written complaint or sworn statement," since, in our view, "probably cause" is determined by constitutional rather than legislative standards.

The Reply

Procedural requirements can be worked out. However, the basic intent of this Point is to prevent the continued unpunished crimes of violence against American Indian people. The response is a cop-out, a cheap shot at the language of the demand and not a confrontation with the issue raised. Can the murders of Richard Oakes, Leon Shenandoah, and Raymond Yellow Thunder be condoned? Must American Indians continue to march into a thousand border towns to demand justice and make continued appeals for protection from violent acts by non-Indians. The treaties provide that the United States will protect Indians from violence by its own citizens, yet there is virtually no protection offered. To make violence against an Indian a federal crime would eliminate a lot of mysterious and unsolved Indian deaths in the western states.

POINT THIRTEEN A—ESTABLISHMENT OF A NATIONAL FEDERAL INDIAN GRAND JURY. (A grand jury to monitor acts of violence and corruption in tribal affairs.)

The Response

In the first 13 lines of this proposal, one would substitute in place of "Indian" the categories "black", "Asian", "Chicano", etc. It would be a misguided choice indeed to subdivide our American system of justice into ethnic slices, each skewed to give special attention on a racial basis. Our task is to improve our local and Federal systems so that they function in a manner utterly devoid of considerations of race or creed or culture.

Insofar as the proposed Grand Jury would be permitted to return indictments for prosecution in tribal courts and also against tribal officials, the proposal seems to conflict with the idea of tribal self-determination. Congress would also have to make an alteration in the existing concepts of the immunity of Federal officials from criminal actions arising from duties performed under color of their Federal authority.

The Reply

As long as people are being killed on a racial basis there would appear to be no objection to bring the murderers to justice to face the racial community which suffered the loss. The substitution of ethnic names for "Indian" would be perfectly permissible if each group had treaties with the United States which promised them federal protection from the white citizens of the United States. Since they do not, to bring up the ethnic confusion is just a smokescreen to hide the fact that the administration refuses to admit that a problem exists.

Insofar as amending existing concepts of immunity of Federal officials from criminal action arising from duties performed under color of their Federal authority, this should have been done a long time ago and not simply in the field of Indian Affairs.

POINT THIRTEEN B—JURISDICTION OVER NON-INDIANS WITHIN INDIAN RESERVATIONS: The Congress should eliminate the immunity of non-Indians to the general application of law and law enforcement within Reservation Boundaries, without regard to land or property title. Title 18 of the U.S. Code should be amended to clarify and compel that all persons

within the originally-established boundaries of an Indian Reservation are subject to the laws of the sovereign Indian Nation in the exercise of its autonomous governing authority. A system of concurrent jurisdiction should be minimum requirement in incorporated towns.

The Response

Before taking any action in the direction of this recommendation, we would wish to have the views of the elected Tribal Chairmen and Tribal Councils, since they are the most competent representatives of Indian Reservation people.

Indian tribal courts currently, we contend, have no judicial jurisdiction over non-Indians in criminal matters and have jurisdiction in civil matters only where the non-Indian consents to jurisdiction. A tribe may have legislative jurisdiction over non-Indians on a reservation, but whether tribal laws can be enforced against non-Indians remains unsettled.

The proposal would, therefore, affect the rights of non-Indians who reside within the "originally-established" exterior boundaries of a reservation and present severe problems of whether it would deprive them of the rights of citizenship in the States in which they reside. Further, it would affect those who are merely travelling through a reservation and arguably could deprive such persons of their immunity and privileges as citizens of the United States.

Finally, it must be noted that the 1968 Civil Rights Act requires that a tribe afford every person under its jurisdiction the fundamental rights of due process and equal protection of the laws. The greater the extent of tribal jurisdiction over non-Indians, the greater claim they have to the right to participate in tribal affairs, i.e., not only would they have a right to protection in judicial proceedings, but they might also have a valid claim to participate in the tribal legislative process.

The Reply

This response characterizes the nature of the relationship which has existed between Indians and whites throughout American history. It is presumed that Indians will be unfair to any whites who happen to fall under their jurisdiction and that whites will be scrupulously fair to any Indians who come under their jurisdiction. Thus the idea of Indians carrying their tribal-treaty citizenship into areas controlled by states as suggested in Point Thirteen is the counterpart of this proposal since if the administration response is taken seriously it means that the problem of tribes having jurisdiction over whites on the reservation will not be changed.

The present situation with continual trespass on tribal lands in cattle grazing, hunting and fishing, and other areas goes practically unnoticed by the Bureau of Indian Affairs. When whites are caught hunting on Indian lands without permission they generally receive a "warning" that it is illegal. Even when Indians are at their usual and accustomed fishing sites they are harrassed and arrested on spurious charges.

If the administration is serious about this proposal it should do a survey of elected tribal officials and at least issue a report on their attitudes.

POINT THIRTEEN C—ACCELERATED REHABILITATION & RELEASE PROGRAM FOR STATE & FEDERAL INDIAN PRISONERS. (Asks for new Commission of Review on Rehabilitation of Indian Prisoners in Federal and State Institutions, a new release program.)

The Response

A new cooperative program has been in effect between Interior and Justice for the past two years under which contracts are entered into with tribes for them to provide a rehabilitation program, including vocational training and counselling for Indians in Federal and State prisons.

The Reply

Why no comment on the suggestion for a national Commission to carry out a systematic program in this area?

POINT FOURTEEN—ABOLITION OF THE BUREAU OF INDIAN AFFAIRS BY 1976: A NEW STRUCTURE: The Congress working through the proposed Senate-House "Joint Committee on Reconstruction of Indian Relations and Programs," in formulation of an Indian Community Reconstruction Act, should direct that the Bureau of Indian Affairs shall be abolished as an agency on or before July 4, 1976; provide for an alternative structure of government for sustaining and revitalizing the federal-Indian relationship between the President and Congress of the United States respectively, and the respective Indian Nations and

Indian people at large consistent with constitutional criteria, national treaty commitments, and Indian sovereignty; and provide for tranformation and transition into the new system as rapidly as possible prior to abolition of the BIA.

The Response

Two and one-half years ago, the President's message foreshadowed the longer-term nature of the Bureau of Indian Affairs: it will become, in effect, an Indian Trust and Technical Assistance Agency, responding to requests from elected Indian tribal leaders who will themselves be taking over the management and operation of the Federal programs which serve their reservations. The pace of this change, i.e., the degree of transfer of control over program operations, will be at Indian option; the President specifically does not intend to force Indian groups into running their Reservation affairs on any time-table except each Tribe's own.

The trust responsibility will, of course, remain—as long as each Tribe wishes it; the President has repudiated termination.

Whether the changed Bureau would remain within the Department of the Interior, or within a new Department of Natural Resources, or be placed in another Cabinet Department would be a matter which the President would not propose to the Congress until after close consultation with Indian leaders themselves.

The Reply

Partial reform of the BIA without the corresponding changes in legal status as suggested by the first nine points in the Trail of Broken Treaties proposal would be useless. As long as the BIA can have final say on the matter of Indian treaty rights, on the use of Indian lands, and on determining tribal memberships and programs there is no use in changing the name of the BIA and expecting it to change its attitudes or forsake its traditional dictatorial powers over Indian communities.

The administration response parallels the response of the Johnson administration. When told that Indians disliked the Relocation Program, the Johnson administration began to call it "Employment Assistance" instead.

POINT FIFTEEN—CREATION OF AN "OFFICE OF FED-
ERAL INDIAN RELATIONS & COMMUNITY RECON-
STRUCTION." (Suggests an alternate structure to the BIA.)

The Response

This proposal would create a three-headed agency in the
Executive Office, one head being a Presidential appointee, another
a Congressional appointee and the third appointed by Indian
people; it would be directly responsible to all three sources, would
be authorized a seven year budget of $15,000,000,000 and would
have few if any restrictions on its program or operation from
OMB, the Congress or the Civil Service Commission

This suggestion may have come from the best of intentions, but it
would create a helpless, irresponsible administrative mechanism
able to spend vast sums without any clear accountability. Indian
people, no less than the President and Congress, could and would
be defrauded by such an institution; neither the President nor the
Congress would permit it to be created.

What the administration favors is an effective trust protection
and service-delivery system, which makes sure that every dollar of
the more than $1 billion in the federal government's current overall
budget for Indians actually is put to work directly helping Indian
people. To get this requires perhaps tighter rather than looser
Department management and OMB review, may require closer
scrutiny by the Congress or the General Accounting Office or the
Civil Rights Commission. In any case it requires unified direction
and clear responsibility to the officer to whom the Constitution
gives the Executive power: the President.

The Reply

It is indeed strange that the administration has no questions on
the present inability of the federal government to solve some of the
pressing problems of Indian people while spending an un-
precedented $1 billion a year in funds. To continue to support the
same structure and the same personnel and to use the same methods
which presently do not work appears to be using an "Avis" concept
of problem-solving, "We try harder."

Rejection of some of the ideas hitherto presented in the Twenty
Points eliminates the possibility of solving some of the problems
and reducing the cost of Indian administration overall. The land
proposal, for example, would eliminate the need for countless

employees tediously keeping track of heirship lands, leases, and individual Indian moneys with considerable savings. Recognition of all Indians having a basic treaty relationship would allow for the use of computers in the fields of educational scholarships, eligibility for health services, and protection of civil rights allowing for massive savings in the administrative costs of the present structure.

In view of the administration's present cut of $50 million in the budget without a corresponding structural change that would help to eliminate the red tape, the advocacy of a more efficient delivery-system appears rhetorical. Impoundment of $18 million in Indian education funds only adds to the administration credibility gap in the field of Indian affairs.

POINT SIXTEEN—PRIORITIES & PURPOSE OF THE PROPOSED NEW OFFICE. (Advocates setting priorities according to a "regulation of commerce theory" of federal relationship.)

The Response

Most of this section in the Trail of Broken Treaties paper seems to be directed at the Congress and it would seem appropriate to let the response be primarily from the Congress.

We would add that the principal thrust of the President's own legislative proposals for Indians is toward self-determination and self-government for Indian tribes. If problems have arisen concerning the responsibility and accountability of tribal governments to their people, these should be brought to our attention in the Task Force which was set up to explore this among several other aspects of Indian needs and problems. We would welcome specific legislative or administrative proposals.

The Reply

While the response should come directly from Congress, it is the executive branch through its newly discovered power to impound funds that must accept responsibility for determining Indian policy in fact. Recent impoundment of Indian education moneys shows that even when Contress does give direction the current administration feels that it can safely ignore the directives of Congress.

More important, the ideology presented in this point should be understood if the administration is actually serious about reform in Indian policies and programs. It is alright to refer people to their tribal leaders, but when the government has corralled all the tribal leaders in its own organization and makes them support the administration line, then it becomes impossible to accept the words of the administration at face value.

POINT SEVENTEEN—INDIAN COMMERCE & TAX IM-MUNITIES. (Asks for clarification of Indian tax immunities.)

The Response

Indian land held in trust, either for tribes or individuals, may not be taxed by the States or their subdivisions. States can tax non-Indians within Indian reservations, except licensed Indian traders on sales to Indians. Tribes do have the authority to levy taxes within their reservations. Indian trust lands and proceeds from them are immune from property taxation. Unless current litigation changes this, Indian owners must pay all other taxes such as that on their earned income unrelated to their tax exempt property. No justification is offered as to why as citizens of a State they should be set apart from their fellow citizens in matters not related to the trust relationship, even if Congress had the authority to give them this exemption.

Having the advantage of the special tax exemption, Indians will want to take the steps necessary to enforce it. Indians, like others, will have to employ attorneys and undertake the burden and expense of litigation to assert their rights, although the access to courts to enforce rights is a precious right in itself. The tribes, however, have the additional benefit of being able to call on the legal services of the Departments of Justice and Interior in certain kinds of actions.

The proposal that tribes be treated as sovereign nations in relation to trade with foreign nations by removal of barriers of "borders, customs, duties, or tax" is entirely inconsistent with their status as American citizens and could lead to erosion of their special relationship with the Federal Government.

The Reply

What the point called for was congressional action to clarify the tax status of American Indians with respect to state and federal taxation. It may be true that Indians have access to the courts to defend their rights to tax immunities, but why should they have to defend these rights over and over and over again?

To refer to the whites in the several states as "fellow citizens" is high satire of the best tradition but it is not an accurate description of the actual situation. In *U.S. v. Kagama* the Supreme Court noted that:

> These Indian tribes are wards of the nation. They are communities dependent on the United States. Dependent largely for their daily food. Dependent for their political rights. They owe no allegiance to the States, and receive from them no protection. Because of the local ill feeling, the people of the States where they are found are often their deadliest enemies. From their very weakness and helplessness, so largely due to the course of dealing of the Federal Government with them and the treaties in which it has been promised, there arises a duty of protection, and with it the power. This has always been recognized by the Executive and by Congress and by this court, whenever the question has arisen.

As outlined above, Monaco, Liechtenstein, and San Marino, all very small countries in Europe, have the privileges which are demanded in the Twenty Points. Indian tribes should stand in the same legal status as these nations which are in fact smaller in population and area than several Indian tribes.

POINT EIGHTEEN—PROTECTION OF INDIANS' RELIGIOUS FREEDOM AND CULTURAL INTEGRITY: The Congress should proclaim its insistence that the religious freedom and cultural integrity of Indian people shall be respected and protected throughout the United States, and provide that Indian religion and culture, even in regenerating or renaissance or developing stages or when manifested in the personal character and treatment of one's own body, shall not be interfered with, disrespected or denied. (No Indian should be forced to cut his hair by any institution or public agency or official, including military authority or prison regulation, for example.) It should be an insistence by Congress that imposes strict penalty for its violation.

The Response

The American people and their government are particularly concerned that the Indians' religious and culture be protected, and there is no policy or program to remove this protection. Indians, like all citizens, are protected in their religious rights by the First

Amendment. If Congress attempts to secure for Indians greater religious rights than the First Amendment itself provides, it runs the danger of conflicting with the establishment clause, particularly when it is remembered that Indians, like all Americans, belong to different faiths.

The Supreme Court so far has refused to review, and the Courts of Appeal are divided on the question of whether public schools can require students to cut their hair. However, the cases have focused on the issue of the First Amendment freedom of expression rather than that of religion, and the latter argument would seem to present a stronger case.

The Reply

The Administration response is precisely why this point was raised. Winning the right to wear hair long on freedom of expression grounds avoids the question of Indians having their own religious practices that are respected. The Constitutional question of establishment of religion is spurious since the constitution only allows the United States to have relationships with Indians on the Interstate Commerce Clause basis. It would simply be in keeping with the treaties to forbid discrimination against Indian religions specifically. At the least there is no indication that the administration has supported the Indian cases on long hair and religious freedom.

POINT NINETEEN—NATIONAL REFERENDA, LO-CAL OPTIONS & FORMS OF INDIAN ORGANIZATION (Recommends new forms of national referenda for Indian interest groups.)

The Response

The Federal Government recognizes the elected tribal governing bodies as the principal spokesmen for the members of their tribes. It is also willing to hear and interested in obtaining the views of individual Indians or groups, such as school boards, Indian women's organizations, Indian professional organizations, etc., and giving them due consideration. (The Trail of Broken Treaties authors seem to be addressing themselves under this point to various privately organized associations and groups of Indians rather than to the Federal Government.)

Certainly not now and probably never will one Indian group

have a monopoly of being "the spokesman" for all Indian people.

The Reply

The administration's co-optation of tribal officials via the tribal chairmen's association is well known by everybody. A glance at the multitude of Indian organizations reveals that many were created by federal agencies desirous of having an Indian front group to work behind. The recent establishment of an alleged Indian board to supervise the Roswell Training Center is a case in point. So long as this ruthless manipulation of Indians is made a standard practice of the federal government there will be complaints about it.

Why not an elective process to determine which Indians are members of NCIO instead of having the director choose his own Indians for his own purposes?

POINT TWENTY—HEALTH, HOUSING, EMPLOY-MENT, ECONOMIC DEVELOPMENT, & EDUCATION. (Examination of how the proposed $15 billion seven year budget would be spent and description of the present situation.)

The Response

This is a request for $15 billion in Federal funds to be appropriated for Indians in the remaining years of the 1970's for the enumerated purposes. There is also a very generally stated objection to the manner in which past appropriated funds have been spent.

The Trail of Broken Treaties paper makes no acknowledgement of the fact that under this President and the last two Congresses, the budget for the Bureau of Indian Affairs alone has increased from $261.3 to $571.4 millions, or 218.6%.

The question is not whether Indian people have acute needs in education, housing, health, and economic development. The question is whether pumping more money in the direction of those problems in the same old way is the best method of solving them.

This Administration had doubled the Indian budget—but it has done something much more important: it has proposed new and more effective ways of bringing to bear the resources that are available. We want Indian control of the programs operating on reservations; we want Indian parents to have a say in the off-reservation schools which their children attend; we want to see reservation hospitals staffed and managed by responsible Indian officials.

The watchword in the Federal Human Resources budgets of the second term is not "more" but "more effective"—and we solicit the cooperation and suggestions of all Indian groups and leaders as to how to ensure that the available resources do in fact accomplish the results for which those resources are invested.

It is urged here that Indian communities reclaim their authority over the education process and that Indian operated schools be recognized by all other school systems through a mandatory accreditation system. It is the President's policy to encourage Indian communities to take over the control and operation of the BIA schools. The movement toward contract schools is a visible commitment to this policy. With the passage of recommended legislation providing for taking over of BIA programs by tribes and permitting Federal employees employed by tribal governments to retain their Civil Service benefits, the move to Indian community control and operation will accelerate.

Accreditation of a school is accomplished by a school joining the privately supported accreditation system and seeking accreditation. Indian schools wanting their students to be prepared to enter accredited schools elsewhere should adhere to certain minimum standards in order to adequately serve their students. It would seem inappropriate for Congress, even if it could, to require on a blanket basis the accreditation of Indian operated schools.

The Reply

While the present administration has indeed boosted funds for Indian programs somewhat over 200%, it is this very expansion that has raised the question of federal expenditures. Programs do not appear to be making much progress and the structural changes suggested in many of the Twenty Points having been ideologically rejected by the administration because of its insistence on over-looking treaty rights and federal protections due to Indians in favor of a nebulous "citizenship" which is not remotely fulfilled foreshadows another four years of failure.

The present administrative monstrosity which confronts Indian people is made necessary because of the lip-service paid to Indian treaty rights. Educational problems are the result of nearly a century of dictatorial federal policies which have eroded the Indian culture, land base, legal status, tax immunity, and resources rights and which now make it necessary to have thousands of employees to direct programs to bandage the wounded who are created by the failure of the federal government to protect Indian rights and live up to the treaties.

Many of the administrative practices of the BIA would be made unnecessary if the treaty rights were made more specific in federal law. Litigation over Indian rights would be greatly reduced and tribal funds could be put to new forms of development, not the legal and political struggle to defend what is left.

The Administration's response should be rejected and it is suggested that the authors of it read several legal histories of the nature of the relationship between American Indians and the United States government. Then a new response which incorporates treaty rights into a new and contemporary legal relationship between the federal government and Indian tribes and people should be issued.

The Nixon Administration stands on the threshhold of achieving the best record on Indian problems in the history of the nation. It must, however, reject the "citizenship" theories of its employees and develop a fully operative theory of contemporary treaty rights which give Indian people the direction and protection promised in the treaties and statutes which bind the United States government to American Indian peoples before the family of civilized nations of the world.

Appendix V

The tribe was known to the white man as:	The people called themselves:	The name meant:
Abnaki (Maine)	Alnanbai	men or people
Iroquois (New York)	Ongwanosionni	we are of the extended lodge
Delaware (New Jersey)	Lenni Lenape	true men
Biloxi (Mississippi)	taneks aya	first people
Tunica (Mississippi)	Yoron	those who are people
Cherokee (Georgia)	ani yun wiya	real people
Illinois (Illinois)	Illinois	men or people
Winnebago (Wisconsin)	Hotcangara	people of the real speech
Chippewa (Minnesota)	anish inaubag	spontaneous men
Arikara (North Dakota)	Tanish	the people

The tribe was known to the white man as:	The people called themselves:	The name meant:
Mandan (North Dakota)	Numakaki	people
Sioux (South Dakota)	Lakota	the allies
Pawnee (Nebraska)	Chahiksichahiks	men of men
Kiowa (Oklahoma)	Kiowa	principal people
Wichita (Oklahoma)	wits	man
Comanche (Oklahoma)	nemene	people
Navajo (Arizona)	Dine	the people
Zuni (New Mexico)	a shiwi	the flesh
Hopi (Arizona)	hopitu	the peaceful ones
Maricopa (Arizona)	Pipatsje	people
Pima (Arizona)	a atam	people
Yavapai (Arizona)	enyaeva	sun people
Washo (Nevada)	washui	person
Arapaho (Wyoming)	Inuna-ina	our people
Nez Percé (Idaho)	Nimipu	the people
Clallam (Washington)	Nu-sklaim	strong people
Skagit (Washington)	Hum-a-luh	the people

Index

Abernathy, Ralph, 60
Abnaki Archaeological Society, 33
Aboriginal title, 278-83
Acupuncture, 291
Afterlife, 88, 119, 170-74, 181-82, 286
Ages in Chaos, 142, 149
Akwesasne Notes, 254
Alcatraz Island, occupation of 1964, 15
    occupation of 1969, 15-18, 20, 25, 65
Alliance of Pontiac, 251
Allotment Act, 251
Altizer, Thomas J. J., 132
American Horse, 256
American Indian Movement (AIM), 21, 30, 31, 35, 58, 66, 256-57
American Indians and Federal Aid, 45
Amish, 207-8, 223
Ancient Kingdoms of the Nile, The, 124
Anderson, Clinton P., 8, 9, 10
Anderson, Paul, 229
Apache, 253

Apocalyptic writings, 118
Arapaho, 250
Ardrey, Robert, 74
Arickora, 161
Aristotle, 106, 121, 276
Armstrong, Virginia, 44
Astrology, 243, 291
Atheism, 241
Augustana College, 21, 58
Australian aborigines, 280

Bailey, V. A., 146
Baldwin, James, 47
Bandelier National Monument, 266
Banyaca, Thomas, 67
Bare Ruined Choirs, 69, 243
Barker, Ernest, 32
Beede, Fr. A. M., 249
Before Columbus, 126-27
Bellecourt, Vernon (Clyde), 3, 30
Benson, Michael, 13
Berger, Thomas, 40
Bernal, Paul, 9, 10
Bible, Alan, 10
Bierce, Ambrose, 198

*Big Brother's Indian Programs**
    With Reservations, 45
Big Elk, 186-87
Biloxi, 217
Black Buffalo, 186-87
Black Elk, 51, 201, 252
Black Elk Speaks, 51
Black Hawk, 42
Black Hills, 267
Black Hills Treaty Rights Council, 256
Black Mesa, 258, 266
Black theology, 244
Blakeney, Dean, 228-29
Blanca Peak, 267
Blatchford, Herb, 13
Blue Eagle, Acee, 6
Blue Lake controversy, 7-11, 15, 21, 259, 266
Book of the Hopi, The, 116
Borland, Hal, 40
Boyd, Malcolm, 62
Bridges, Allison, 26
Bright, Bill, 233
Brinkley, David, 22
Brookings Institution, 45
Brown, Dee, 29, 35, 44, 49, 284
Brown, Joseph Epes, 51
Bryan, William Jennings, 159-60
Bultmann, Rudolf, 131-32
Bureau of Indian Affairs, 1972
    takeover of, 3-7, 36-37, 45-46, 56-60, 65, 66, 271
    and California Indians, 24
    and Wounded Knee, 257
Bury My Heart at Wounded Knee, 35, 44, 49

Calendar stick, 113
California Indians, 23-24, 25, 42
Calley, Lt., 72
Camus, Albert, 70, 71, 176
Canadian Mohawks, 11, 12, 253-54

Cardinal, Harold, 44
Cargo cults, 150
Carmichael, Stokely, 63
Carnarvon, Lord, 173
Carson National Forest, 8
Carter, Howard, 173
Cash, Johnny, 234
Casteneda, Carlos, 52-53
Cathedral of Tomorrow, 230
Cavett, Dick, 11, 35
Cayuse, 95
Caywood, Bill, 230
Chakras, 291
Chardin, Teilhard de, 243
Cherokee, 203, 205-6, 249
Cheyenne, 52, 113, 117, 177-80, 217, 250, 256
Chicago Center for Contemporary Celebration, 237
Chivington, Rev. John, 249-50
Christian Faith and Natural Science, 107
Christian religion, and aboriginal right, 274-87
    and alienation from nature, 104-6
    and American culture, 196-98, 225-45
    and atheism, 241
    and baptism, 171, 192
    and church power, 20-21, 212-13
    clergy of, 216, 220
    and conception of God, 93, 199-200
    confession in, 171
    and conversion, 96-97, 121, 173, 193-196
    and creation, 91-101, 103, 105, 136-37, 152, 157-60, 286
    and death, 170-74, 182-86, 193
    definition of, 195
    "demythologizing history," 131-32, 172
    and divorce, 196-97

doctrinal differences in, 193
and ecological crisis, 71-2, 96-
    98
and eternal life, 119, 169-77
ethnicity of, 216, 220-21, 223,
    296-97
and Exodus, 133-36, 149
and Genesis, 92-100, 103, 105,
    158-60, 273, 285
and human personality, 189-99
and judgment, 171, 187
and land, 162-66
and linear (temporal) concept of
    history, 73-82, 100, 111-
    12, 117-38, 152, 154, 161,
    162, 209, 283-87
and new theology, 210, 225,
    227-38, 242-44
and resurrection, 182-85
and salvation, 193, 195
and science, 106-9
sects of, 71, 214-16, 221
and social involvement, 215-16,
    223-24, 285-86
and support of Indian move-
    ment, 58, 65
tax exemption, 223-24
Church, Frank, 10
Civil rights movement, and
    church, 60-63, 71, 132
collapse of, 64
Indian movement paralleled
    with, 46-49
Indian participation in, 59-62
and social gospel, 68
Cochiti Pueblo, 266
Code of Iowa, 33
Collier, Dr. Donald, 34
Collingwood, R. G., 105
Colville Reservation, 65
Common Cause, 72
Cornwall (Ontario) Bridge con-
    frontation, 11, 12, 21
Cornwall-Northern New York
    Bridge Company, 12

Cottier, Allen, 15
Counterculture, 62-63
Cox, Rev. Harvey, 62, 69, 96,
    102, 132, 133-34, 136, 201,
    202, 237, 244, 299
Crain, Rev. Mike, 228, 229
Cram, 206
Crazy Horse, 256
Creation, Christian view of, 91-
    101, 103, 105, 136-37, 152,
    157-160, 286
    Indian view of, 91-92, 95-96,
        99, 101-4, 113, 138, 150,
        154, 157, 161, 167
    scientific view of, 106, 148
    Velikovsky's view of, 139-150
    See also Genesis
Creek alliance, 114
Crow, 166
Cullmann, Oscar, 182-83, 184,
    185
Curley, 166-67
Custer Died for Your Sins, 44

Dalton, Daniel, 31
Darrow, Clarence, 159-60
Death, Christian attitude toward,
    169-74, 182-87, 193
    Indian attitude toward, 167,
        174-78, 180-81, 183-87
Death and Rebirth of the Senecas,
    The, 51
"Death of God" movement, 132
Death song, 179, 180
Deganiwidah, 113, 201
Delaware, 113, 205
Demonism, 243, 270
Department of Agriculture, 8, 24
Descartes, 106
Dine, see Navajo
Divination, 265
Dodd, C. H., 131-32
Don Juan, 52

Donner Foundation, 45
Doubleday publishers, 144
Druidism, 165, 295
DRUMS, 21
Dubos, Dr. René, 97
Dupré, Louis, 135-36
Duwamish, 115

Earth in Upheaval, 144
Eastman, Dr. Charles, 99
Ecology, 63-64, 71-72, 96-98
Eikerenkoetter, Rev. Frederick J.
    II, 240
Einhorn, Arthur, 30
Eisenhower, Dwight D., 61, 62
Enuma Elish, 158-159, 160
Erdoes, Richard, 52
Evangelism, *see* Fundamentalism
Evans, Dan, 29
Excavation, of Indian burial sites,
    29, 30-31, 32, 33-34, 66
Exodus, 133-36, 138, 149, 152-53
    Velikovsky's theory about, 139-
    42, 149, 151
Explo '72, 233-34

Fairservis, Walter, 124, 125
Farb, Peter, 43-44, 53
Federal government, 3, 7-11, 14,
    15, 21, 23-25, 26, 28, 29, 35-
    36, 86, 259, 266
Field Museum of Natural History
    (Illinois), 34
Fire, John, *see* Lame Deer
Fishing rights controversy, 25, 26,
    27, 29, 49
Five Civilized Tribes of Okla-
    homa, 181
Fonda, Jane, 19
Ford Foundation, 45
Foretelling, 265
Fort Laramie Treaty, 15
Fort Lawton, 18-19

Frank's Landing fishing rights
    controversy, 25, 26, 27, 29,
    49
Fuller, Buckminster, 78
Fundamentalism, 68, 71, 79, 86,
    87, 170, 195, 226, 239, 240,
    241
Future Shock, 69, 73, 78

Gallup (N.M.) Ceremonial, 12,
    13
Gallup Indian Center, 13
Gardner, John, 72
Gaster, Theodore, 134, 136
Genesis, 92, 100, 101, 103, 105,
    158-60, 273, 285
    See also Creation, Velikovsky
Geronimo, 41
Ghost Dance, 66, 191, 250
Gemmill, Mickey, 20
Gnadenhutten Massacre, 205
"God Is Dead" theology, 132
Goldwater, Barry, 10
Gordon, Cyrus, 126-27
Gordon, Nebraska incident, 35-36
Gortner, Marjoe, 240
Gorton, Slade, 14
*Gospel of the Red Man: An In-
    dian Bible, The*, 207
Graham, Dr. Billy, 68, 199, 234-
    35, 236, 240, 242, 243
Great Mystery, 203
Great Pyramid of Cheops, 125
Great Spirit, 93, 96, 104, 115
Greening of America, The, 69
Gregory, Dick, 29
Griffin, Robert, 10
Guest, Rev. John, 237

Haas, Nico, 239
Handsome Lake, 51
Harris, Fred, 10
Hayes, Ira, 5

Healing ceremony, 253, 263-64, 265, 297-98
Hebrew religion, 117, 118, 120, 124, 130, 135-36, 141-43, 151, 158-59, 162, 163, 189-91, 210-11, 212, 217-18, 222, 262
Heidegger, Martin, 131
Heim, Karl, 107
Heine, Heinrich, 164
Henry, Carl F. H., 241
Hesperus Peak, 267
Hetrick, Barbara, 45
Hiawatha, 41
"Historical Roots of Our Ecological Crisis, The," 96
Hollenwerger, Walter, 243
Holyland, U.S.A., 230-31
Hopi, 27, 42, 67, 103, 116, 154-58, 253, 258, 266, 279, 292
House Made of Dawn, 40
House Subcommittee on Indian Affairs, 6
Hubbard, Linda, 13
Huerfano Mountain, 267

I *Have Spoken,* 44, 55
Idea of Nature, The, 108
Immortality of the Soul or Resurrection of the Dead?, 182
Indian Claims Commission, 9, 43, 266, 282
Indian Heritage of America, The, 43
Indian Reorganization Act, 43, 219, 252
Indian studies program, 261-62
Indian tribal religion, and afterlife, 181-83
  and American culture, 247-71
  ban of, 251
  books about, 50-53
  and brotherhood of life, 103
  calendar stick, use of, 113
  and communalism, 107-8, 201, 202, 204, 216-20
  and conception of deity, 92, 200
  and conception of history, 111-117
  and creation, 91-92, 95-96, 99, 101-4, 113, 138, 150, 154, 157, 161, 167
  culture heroes of, 113
  and death, 167, 174-78, 180-87
  and divination, 265
  and dream interpretation, 203
  and foretelling, 265
  Ghost Dance of, 191, 250
  and healing ceremonies, 253, 263-65, 297-98
  and human personality, 189, 200-8
  and Indian Reorganization Act, 219, 252
  individual dimension to, 202-4
  and land, 7-11, 15-22, 67, 71, 75, 81, 138, 156, 161-63, 166, 175-76, 247, 266-67, 270, 293
  and language bonds, 222
  and naming ceremonies, 202, 203, 217, 253
  nonphilosophical quality of, 298
  revival of, 62, 66, 248-49, 253, 254-61
  and rock painting, 152-53
  and salvation, 200-1
  and science, 106-9
  and spatial conception of time, 88-89, 102, 150, 154-55, 161-62
  survival of, 249, 252, 268-71, 290
  threats to, 222-23
  and unity of nature, 101, 103-5, 108
  and vision quests, 203, 259, 270
  and winter counts, 112
  and world ages idea, 115-16
  See also specific tribes

Indians of Chicago, 21, 24
Indians of Minnesota, 30-32
Inquisition, 123
Inter-District Council, 257
Interior Department, 4, 8
Intertribal ecumenical council, 263
Iowa graveyard incident, 32, 33, 66
Iroquois, 12, 19, 20, 34, 51, 113, 116, 181, 203
Iroquois League, 113, 114
Ishi in Two Worlds, 42
Israel: Its Life and Culture, 134-35

Jackson, Henry, 10
James the Just, 118
Jay Treaty, 11, 12
Jeans, James, 108
Jesus, 93, 100, 101, 117, 118, 119, 120, 136, 169, 170, 183-84, 185, 189-92, 195, 196, 211, 213, 226, 241, 242, 295
Jesus movement, 67, 210, 226-27
Johnson, Lyndon B., 8
Jones, LeRoi, 47
Joseph, Chief, 35, 41, 49, 54, 175, 205, 251
Joseph, Young Chief, 175
Josephy, Alvin, 43, 44, 50, 53
Journey to Ixtlan, 53
Judo and Karate for Christ Camp, 228
Jung, Carl, 164-65, 166

Kachinas, 266
Kahn-Tineta Horn, 11, 12
Kant, 106
Kierkegaard, 67, 68
King, Dr. Martin Luther, 46, 47, 51, 60, 62-63
Kiowa, 180, 217

Klamath, 217
Krishura, 156
Kristofferson, Kris, 234

Lahota, 181
Lame Deer, John (Fire), 51-52, 185
Lame Deer, Seeker of Visions, 51-52
Land, importance of to Christians, 163-66, 295-96, 298, 300-1
importance of to Indians, 7-11, 15-22, 67, 70, 75, 81, 138, 161-63, 166, 175-76, 247, 266, 267, 270, 293
Landowner's Association, 257
Las Casa, Fr., 277
Lawrence, D. H., 176
League of the Iroquois, 20, 22
Leakey, Louis, 123
Leary, Timothy, 62
Levitan, Sar, 45
Lewis County Historical Society, 29
Linear time (conception of religious reality), 73, 74, 76, 79-85, 152, 154, 162
creation and, 91, 100, 137-38, 162
as view of history, 111-12, 117-38, 154, 161, 209
Literature, about and by Indians, anthologies, 44-45, 53-54, 55
government reports, 45
histories, 41, 42, 43, 44, 53
novels, 40, 53
regarding religion, 50, 51, 52
works by Indians, 41-42
Little Big Man, 40
Little Wound, 256
Liturgy of the Earth, 97-98
Logan, 218
Lummi, 252
Luther, Martin, 163, 238

McIntyre, Carl, 244
MacKenzie, Dick, 15
McKusick, Marshall, 32, 33
McLuhan, Marshall, 78
McLuhan, T. C., 44-45
Macmillan Company, 144
*Man's Rise to Civilization As
    Shown by the Indians of
    North America from Prime-
    val Times to the Coming of the
    Industrial State,* 43
Mandan, 161
Marjoe, 240
Marshall, Chief Justice John, 249
Maxey, Rev. Cecil, 238-39
May, Rollo, 186
Means, Russell, 36
Media, Indians and, 17, 41-42,
    45, 50, 55
Medicine Creek Treaty, 115, 176
Memoirs of Chief Red Fox, The,
    44
Menominees, 21
Menzel, Donald, 146, 147
Metcalf, Lee, 10
Metea, 174-75
Miami Indians, 34
Michener, James, 69
Mingo, 218
Mini-movement(s), 78-79, 86
Minnesota Historical Society, 31
Mohawk, 11, 12, 30, 253-54
Momaday, N. Scott, 40
Monotheism, 79, 80, 292
Morgan, Michael, 37
Mormonism, 208, 219, 223
Mount Adams, 267
Mount Rushmore, 22
Mount Shasta, 21
Mount Taylor, 266

NAACP Legal Defense and Edu-
    cation Fund, 60
Naming ceremony, 202, 203, 217,
    253

Nation of Strangers, A, 69, 73
National Council of Churches, 21
National Indian Youth Council,
    42, 43
Native American Church, 250
Navajo, 12, 13, 28, 42, 138, 161,
    217, 253, 255, 258, 267
Neibuhr, Reinhold, 234
"New frontier" theology, 227-28
New Indians, The, 42, 44
"New Property, The," 69
New Testament, 129, 131, 203,
    229, 230
Newcomb, Tom, 207
Nez Percé, 35, 54, 175, 205
Niehardt, John, 35, 51
Nietzsche, 67, 68
Nisquallies, 25
Nixon Agonistes, 69
Nixon, Richard M., 9, 10, 38, 68,
    202, 235-36, 267
Nordwall, Adam, 15
Northwest Coast Indians, 103
Northwest Ordinance, 279
Nuremburg trials, 61

Oak Creek Canyon, 267
Oakes, Richard, 20, 37, 38
Oglala Sioux, 22, 256, 257
Oglala Sioux Civil Rights Associ-
    ation, 256
Ogden, Rev. Richard, 231
Old Tassel, 205-6
Old Testament, 82, 117-18, 120,
    121, 122, 129, 130, 134, 142,
    149, 150, 162, 203, 210
Omaha, 186
Onondaga, 20
Other Dimension, The, 135
Oursler, Fulton, 149

Pacific Gas and Electric Co., 20
Pacific Northwest Indians, 83, 253

Pacific "Trust Territories," 280-81
Packard, Vance, 69, 73
Papago, 113
Pawnee, 117, 161
Paxton Herald, 33
Payne-Gaposchikin, Cecilia, 146-47
Peabody Coal Company, 42, 266
Pedersen, Johannes, 134-35, 136
Pensée, 147
Pentacostal movement, 243
Percy, Sen. Charles, 10
Peterson, Les, 31
Philadelphia Inquirer, 33
Physics and Philosophy, 108
Pima, 113
Pine Ridge Reservation, 258
Pipestone Quarry, 267
Pitkin, Stan, 26, 27
Pitt River Indians, 18, 20, 21
Plains Indians, 103, 252
Plato, 106, 121, 183
Potawatomi, 174
Powell, Peter, 51
Protestant Reformation, 120, 163-64, 172, 197, 213, 216
Pueblo, 7-9, 10, 161, 248, 253, 266
Puyallups, 25

Quality of Life, A, 69
Quinault, 14, 15

Rain dance, 106, *see also* Hopi
Rauschenbusche, Walter, 68
Ray, Robert, 33
Rebel, The, 70
Red Cloud, 204, 256
Red Fox, Chief, 220
Red Jacket, 54, 206
Red Lake Chippewa Indian Reservation, 28, 78

Red Man's Religion, 50-51
Reich, Charles, 69
Religion and Philosophy in Germany, 164
Reservation(s), Indian 17, 27, 28, 31-32, 218, 222, 251-54, 258
Revelation, 80-81
Rice, Sgt. Ernest, 5, 185
Roberts, Oral, 232-33, 240, 264
Robertson, Robert, 6
Roosevelt, Theodore, 7-8
Rosebud Sioux Reservation, 258
Running Moccasins, 32, 33

Sacred Pipe, The, 51
St. Augustine, 93, 121
St. Benedict, 97
St. Francis, 97
St. John, 92, 190, 191, 192
St. Paul, 100, 117, 118, 191-92, 196, 211, 286
St. Regis Mohawk Reservation, 19, 253-54
St. Thomas Aquinas, 121
Sakokwenonk, 30
San Francisco Indian Center, 16
San Francisco Peaks, 266
San Juan Pueblo, 266
Sand Creek Massacre, 250
Santa Clara Pueblo, 266
Satanic cults, 87
Satank, 180
Schneider, Kent, 237
Scopes trial, 99
Seattle, Chief, 54, 115, 176, 184
Secular City, The, 69, 133, 201, 237, 299
Seeliger, Rev. Wesley, 227
Seneca, 206, 268-69
Senate Interior Committee, 8-10
Separate Reality, A, 53
Sepulveda, Juan de, 277, 290
Seton, Ernest Thompson, 207
Seven Arrows, 52, 67

Sheep Mountain demonstration, 22
Shooter, 102
Shrine of Our Lady of Guadalupe Hildalgo, 165
Sioux, 15, 16, 17, 18, 22, 35, 50, 51, 56, 73, 99, 102, 112, 114, 181, 201, 252
Sitting Bull, 41, 204-5, 251
Smith, Ira F. III, 33
Smohalla, 201
Social gospel, 68, 86
Socrates, 183
Son of Old Man Hat, The, 42
Sorkin, Alan, 45
Spatial time (conception of religious reality), 76, 77, 78, 79, 81-89, 159-60
and creation, 91, 137-138, 150, 159-60, 161-62
Spellman, Cardinal, 123
Standing Bear, Chief Luther, 73, 105, 256
Stanley Island, 19
Staubach, Roger, 233, 235
Stay Away, Joe, 40
Steiner, Stan, 42-43, 44
Stoney Indians, 104
Storm, Hyemeyohsts, 52, 67
Street, Rev. Noel, 229-30
Stride Toward Freedom, 47
Student Academic Freedom Forum, 147
Sun Chief, 271
Sun Chief, 42
Supernova, 152-53
Susquehannock, 33, 34
Sweet Medicine, 113-14, 201
Sweet Medicine, 51, 52
Systematic Theology, 94, 137

Taneks aya, see Biloxi
Taos Pueblo, 7, 8, 9, 10, 259
Teachings of Don Juan, The, 53

Tecumseh, 251
Temporal conception of religious reality, see Linear time
Territorial Imperative, The, 74
Thayer, Bishop, 232
The Prophet, 251
"Theology of the Earth, A," 97
Tillich, Paul, 93, 94, 95, 137
Toffler, Alvin, 69, 73, 78
Topka, 155
Tortured Americans, The, 44
Touch the Earth, 44-45, 49, 55
Toynbee, Arnold, 186
Tracy, June, 13
Trail of Broken Treaties, 3-7, 37, 45
Treaties, 7, 11, 12, 15, 19, 23-24, 54, 95, 115, 176, 257
Tribal elections, 260-61
Tribal membership, 255, 258
Tribal religion, see Indian tribal religion
Trudeau government, 279, 282
Tuscaroras, 21-22
Tutankhamen, 173
Twenty Points platform, 37, 38

Udall, Stewart, 44
Underhill, Ruth, 50-51
Unjust Society, The, 44

Van Allen, James, 147
Velikovsky, Immanuel, 139-151
Vice President's National Council of Indian Opportunity, 6
Vietnam War, 19, 63, 64, 199-202, 235, 287
Vision Quest, 203, 259, 270
Vitoria, Francisco de, 276

Wakan Tanka, 102
Walking Buffalo, 104

Walla Walla, Treaty of, 95
Wallace, Anthony F. C., 51
Walum Olum, 113
War Bonnet, Matthew, 34
Washington Post, 5-6
Washoe, 217
Waters, Frank, 116
West Branch Project, 33
"When Our Grandfathers Had Guns," 13
When the Legends Die, 40
White Bear, 116
White Buffalo Calf Woman, 114
White, Lynn Jr., 96, 97
Whitehead, Alfred North, 106, 109
Wilkerson, Don, 234
Williams, William Carlos, 66, 176
Wills, Gary, 69, 243
Wilson, Edmund, 254
Winnebago, 5, 34, 185

Winter count, 112
Worcester, Rev. Samuel, 249
Worcester v. Georgia, 249
World In Collision, 139, 142, 144, 146, 148-149
Wotan, 166, 292
Wounded Knee incident, 38, 66, 256-58
Wovoka, 20

Yahweh, 292
Yakima, 54, 267
Yaqui, 52
Yehochanan bone, 239
Yellow Thunder, Raymond, 35, 49
Young Chief, 95, 96

Zuni, 13, 28